friction 5

friction 5

best gay erotic fiction

edited by jesse grant
and austin foxxe

alyson books
los angeles | new york

MANUFACTURED IN THE UNITED STATES OF AMERICA.

THIS TRADE PAPERBACK ORIGINAL IS PUBLISHED BY ALYSON PUBLICATIONS,
P.O. BOX 4371, LOS ANGELES, CALIFORNIA 90078-4371.
DISTRIBUTION IN THE UNITED KINGDOM BY
TURNAROUND PUBLISHER SERVICES LTD.,
UNIT 3 OLYMPIA TRADING ESTATE, COBURG ROAD, WOOD GREEN,
LONDON N22 6TZ ENGLAND.

FIRST EDITION: FEBRUARY 2002

04 05 06 a 10 9 8 7 6 5 4 3

ISBN 1-55583-715-8

LIBRARY OF CONGRESS CATALOGING-IN-PUBLICATION DATA

FRICTION, VOLUME 5 : BEST GAY EROTIC FICTION / EDITED BY JESSE GRANT AND AUSTIN FOXXE.—1ST ED.

ISBN 1-55583-715-8

1. GAY MEN—FICTION. 2. GAY MEN'S WRITINGS, AMERICAN. 3. EROTIC STORIES, AMERICAN. I. TITLE: FRICTION FIVE. II. GRANT, JESSE. III. FOXXE, AUSTIN.

PS648.H57 F755 2002

813'.01083538'086642090511—DC21 2001053412

COVER PHOTOGRAPHY BY JOHNATHAN BLACK.

Contents

Preface

Welcome to the fifth volume in the Friction: Best Gay Erotic Fiction series. My esteemed co-editor Austin Foxxe and I are especially proud of this year's tome. This is the third year we've worked together on this series, and we both feel we've put together our best collection yet. We have included work from more authors and more sources than in any previous volume, and thus we have more interesting and varied stories than ever before. Whatever your interest, we've got it—hustlers, vampires, bathhouses, '70s retro, exhibitionism, huge cocks, virgins, daddies, romance, science fiction, and even cross-dressing sadomasochists. Never fear, though, the quality of the prose is as high as ever. And the erotic content? Well, we don't subtitle this series Best Gay Erotic Fiction for nothing.

Austin and I would like to thank Terri Fabris for her editorial assistance. Without her hard work, this book would never have made it to press.

Enjoy!

Jesse Grant
Los Angeles
December 2001

For the Asking

by David Wayne

People are always asking me how I met Travis, and I always tell them that we met here at The Pub, which is true enough. If they want more details...well, I generally make them up fresh every time. That's why there are so many conflicting stories about Travis and me. I always loved a mystery. I've discovered that I love *being* a mystery even more.

But you say that Jamie told you to ask me. Well, that's something else entirely. That means I'm going to tell you the true story of Travis and me and the night we might, and I swear, Scout's honor, that it's the real true story.

And maybe, by the time I'm done, you'll understand why I'm telling it to you.

• • •

I first met Travis right here, on the very spot where you and I are standing now. It was a Thursday night—The Pub is always cruisiest on Thursdays for God knows what reason. The place was packed from bar to backroom with men, but Travis caught my attention the instant he pushed through the door. He just didn't fit in. Hell, he didn't even make the effort to fit in. If anything, Travis's appearance was a concerted effort to hide just how handsome he was. In a room full of stretch Lycra, he was dressed in a pair of work-stained Levi's and a worn leather jacket. Beneath the stubble on his face, though, his jaw was hard and square; his T-shirt, timeworn and damp with sweat, clung to a torso that was finely muscled. I remember all of these details in retrospect, but at the time they were eclipsed by one thing: his eyes. Piercing, playful, and squinted just slightly, Travis's eyes surveyed the room; I was acutely embarrassed when his gaze locked onto mine as if he had sensed my stare. I became even more embarrassed when he began to wade toward me. He walked through the crowd like he was haunting the place. People shivered and stepped away as he passed, but no one turned to see what had disturbed them.

At last he reached me. His eyes scanned me up and down, then he turned and pressed his firm belly against the bar railing.

Jamie was the bartender that night, like he is every Thursday night. I knew Jamie in the usual ways that gay guys get to know each other. He was the ex of an ex, for one thing. Furthermore, I'd sucked him off once in the sauna of one of the local bathhouses. I was pretty sure, though, that Jamie didn't remember that little incident. The point is that the bar was a din of chattering voices and drumbeats, and Jamie was having trouble keeping up with the orders. He appraised Travis's threadbare appearance and filed him in the "light tipper" category before turning his attention to the other clamoring customers.

I found myself shouting, "Jamie, two beers."

Jamie looked at me, looked at Travis, then raised a disapproving eyebrow; but he dropped a pair of wet brown bottles in front of us and scooped up the bills I'd laid out.

"One of these for me?" Travis gave me a half smile.

"If you want," I answered.

Travis stared at me for an uncomfortably long time.

"Yeah, I want." He took a swig from the beer I'd bought. I watched his Adam's apple bob as he swallowed, and I felt something kindle in my groin. Those flames were fanned when Travis shrugged out of his jacket, revealing a broad chest and beautifully muscled arms.

"My name's Jack," I said, sticking out a hand in greeting.

Travis took it, his hand warm and firm in my grasp.

"I'm Travis. It's a pleasure." He released my hand, letting his fingertips graze my palm. He looked me in the eye as he did this, his eyes kindling with thinly veiled amusement.

I was at a loss. I hate that awkward moment when you meet someone in a bar and it's not clear whether or not you're going to fuck, so you have to find something to talk about.

"So, what do you do?" I hazarded lamely.

"What do you mean?"

"You know, your job."

He snorted into his beer. "Am I going to have to fill out a credit report too?"

His lips curled in amusement, signaling that he was enjoying my disorientation.

"Just curious I guess," I finally managed.

He was silent for a moment as he stared out into the crowd. "I hate pissing contests. No offense, but you don't care about my work. Fact is..." He turned to look at my face. "Fact is, I'd be disappointed if that was all you wanted."

His left hand slid down his side, his thumb catching in the belt loop, leaving his fingers curled next to the none-too-subtle bulge in his jeans. He watched me staring at his crotch, and then I felt his eyes slide down my body, giving me a similar appraisal. He gave a friendly laugh.

"Look," he said. "I know what you want; you know what you want. Why don't you just ask?"

His face was blank, his expression very matter-of-fact. I felt my stomach churn. I felt something twitch a bit further south too. He stretched casually, his T-shirt slithering up his torso to reveal his abdomen and the recess of his navel.

Maybe you'll find it difficult to believe how hard it was to say what I wanted. In my mind, I could see him naked. I could hear the rumble of his throat as passion lowered his voice to a growl. I could smell the musk of him. I could taste the sweat of him. The desire burgeoned within me, but the words couldn't get past the watchdog of my tongue.

He downed the last swallow of his beer and waggled the empty bottle. "Thanks for the beer."

He started to slip on his jacket, and I knew with absolute certainty that he would leave—and that he wasn't going to make this any easier.

"Last chance," he said. "Just ask. What do you really want to do?"

"I...I want to sleep with you."

He smiled, a look of victory in his eyes.

"Well, I'm hoping that 'sleep' is a euphemism…but close enough. Come on." He took my hand and guided me through the dancing throng. As we passed through the door, his hand slipped from my grip and moved to the small of my back, shepherding me through the densely packed vehicles—a Gordian knot of steel and fiberglass that wouldn't be untangled until closing time.

"There's no way you're going to get your car out of here," I said uselessly.

He gave me a wolfish grin. "Who says I have a car?"

And with that, he pulled me into the darkness of the alley behind the club. Moonlight spilled into the narrow space between the buildings like a waterfall into a grotto. The light glinted off the cases of empty bottles, and I could smell the stink of stale beer. As we slipped into the shadows, my hands trailed along the wall, which pulsed beneath my fingers to the occult rhythm of the drum and bass seeping through the mortar.

The alley dead-ended, and we found ourselves in the darkened alcove of a disused back door. Travis leaned his back against the wall and pulled me into his grip. In the darkness, our lips met. Travis's arms encircled me, and I succumbed to his embrace as our tongues danced. The kiss seemed eternal, but eventually, painfully, it came to an end. I opened my eyes to meet Travis's stare.

"There's one condition," he said.

"A condition for what?"

"Sleeping with me."

I was no longer thinking about sleep, but I played along.

"What's the condition?"

"You can sleep with me tonight, but first you have to fuck me as hard as you can."

"What, right here?" I said incredulously.

"Why wait?"

His hands were already pulling at my belt. It cinched tighter about my waist, then went loose. As his hands unfastened the top button of my jeans, he leaned into me, pushing me against the wall. One hand crept into my jeans and tugged playfully at the hair growing from my groin.

"No underwear?" he teased. "Naughty, naughty boy."

I heard my zipper descend as his hand slipped deeper into my pants. Like a curious dog, my cock rose up to sniff the stranger's hand. He grasped it firmly, noting its heft, then pulled it out through the open V of my fly. He squeezed, and I swelled in his palm. With my stiffening cock as a leash, he pulled me toward him. Our lips met, and his free hand grasped the back of my head, pulling our faces tighter. Our kiss was frenzied, and all the while he jerked roughly at my exposed prick until it stood out from my body like an embedded knife. I clutched his hips and thrust my groin against his, feeling something stiffen in reply within the denim enclosure of his jeans. I sucked his tongue into my mouth, chewing on it and bathing it with my own saliva. Without breaking the coupling of our lips, my hands slid around his waist to rest at the top button of his jeans. He wasn't wearing a belt, and his fly seemed to burst open of its own accord. I pushed his jeans down his flanks, and was amused to hear the clatter of change as his pants pooled around his ankles. My fingers traced across his abdomen, dipping downward to find the root of his cock. I pushed at the base and found it as stiff and firm as my own. Our fingers brushed as we brought our cocks together within the confines of our two palms.

I broke our kiss, moving along his jaw line to the tender flesh beneath and behind his ears. I bit gently, and he moaned, crushing against me. He spread his legs, and I nudged my cock between his thighs. I drove forward, my prick forging through the coarse hair that forested behind his balls. The sensation of his rough hair against my cock's tender head was excruciating and exhilarating. The fingers of both my hands worked their way into his crack, and my right index finger found what I was searching for. His hole gaped open, and with just the sweat of our bodies, the tip of my finger slipped inside him. He gasped, and I pushed deeper in reply. I strained forward with my hips, hoping to let my cock join my fingertip in the warmth of his asshole, but my dick's reach stopped agonizingly short. Travis's knees buckled slightly, but even that wasn't enough. There was a whisper in my ear, and it took a moment's concentration to recognize it as Travis's guttural chant of "fuck me, fuck me, fuck me..."

I pushed him away with my free hand, keeping my finger tucked into the opening of his chute. Wordlessly, I pushed on his shoulder, signaling him to turn around. He pivoted on his heel, but the tangle of his pants snared him. He tripped forward, catching himself with his hands on the wall opposite me, and let out a started yelp. I drove my finger deeper inside him, and he yelped again, his muscles tightening. I pulled back slightly, and he relaxed, then eased himself down onto my finger. I hunched my hips forward and let my cock burrow between his cheeks to crowd my busy fingers. He sensed the pressure and pushed backwards against me. I thrust my hips, nosing my dick in deeper and deeper into his crack. I was leaking lube, and with a few strokes he was wet.

He turned his face, and in the moonlight he was unmasked. The guarded irony had slipped away, and all that remained was desire. I didn't have to ask if he was ready. Pulling my finger out, I positioned the head of my prick at his opening. I thrust forward, and his knees buckled as I stabbed into him. There was a moment of eerie calm, as we adjusted to each other's bodies. We were frozen at the brink of ecstasy. And then, clutching one another, we fell into it.

I won't say that my first time with Travis was indescribable—just that description doesn't do it justice. I'm sure you know what it's like to fuck a man, and I'm sure you know that even though the mechanics are roughly the same every time, every time it's different.

God, was this different.

I didn't fuck Travis so much as ride him. He moved as if electrified. I grasped his writhing hips and plunged into him again and again, battering against him as if he stood between me and ecstasy; my cock was a battering ram and his body the unyielding door. The alcove was cramped, and the sounds we made were echoed and amplified. My ears were filled with the moist slapping of our bodies and the guttural sounds that had supplanted language. I felt something exploding behind my balls, and I pressed my face into his back, wishing that I'd gotten his jacket and shirt off so that I could taste his flesh. All sensation was eclipsed as I felt myself ejaculating inside him. I accented each spurt with a savage twist of my hips, and found that I was still thrusting long after I was spent, as if I'd forgotten how to do anything but fuck. At last my body stilled, and I slipped out of him, my cock deliciously raw. As I took in gulps of air, my spent passion turned to tenderness. My hands circled his waist, and I kissed his neck.

"I kept my end of the deal," I whispered.

"Mmm-hmm..." was his only reply.

I backed away, breathless, and leaned against the opposite wall of the doorway. Travis was still spread-eagled against the wall, his back heaving. In the monochrome moonlight, posed against the decaying brickwork he looked, for all the world, like a Bill Costa photograph.

As I reached to pull up my trousers, he turned toward me. The first thing that caught the moonlight was the rigid shaft of his cock, so engorged it actually jerked with each beat of his heart. The second thing that caught the light was his face...and that wicked, wicked smile.

Travis is fast—everybody knows that. You can tell by his feline, feral bearing. But unless you've actually seen him move, you just can't appreciate it.

He was on me before I could let out even a squeak of surprise, and we fell in a tumble into the open air of the alley. I tried to say something—*anything,* but his lips silenced mine. His body was heavy on top of me, and I could feel the heat and insistent pressure of his cock between our bodies. At first all I could think was, *This jacket is calfskin,* and then I just didn't care anymore.

My eyes closed, and I just let go.

Just as suddenly as he had leaped on me, he was gone. I opened my eyes in bewilderment, lifting myself onto my elbows. Something yanked my pants down around my ankles, then pushed my knees up to my chest. Instantly Travis was on top of me again, backlit by the moonlight, which was dim compared to the demonic light flashing in his eyes. I kicked feebly, my legs trapped by both his weight and the tangle of my pants. Something poked at the opening to my ass. I thought it was a finger until the sheer girth of it became apparent. I panicked, tightening against it. Travis's face dropped down to mine, and something in his kiss told me: "Trust me."

Again, I let go.

Travis's hands were braced on my shoulders as his cock slowly worked its way into me. I was hungry to have him inside me. I writhed to accommodate him, but pinned as I was, there was nothing I could do to speed the process. His cock crept into me with the stealth of an assassin, and I was powerless beneath its advance. At last I gave up movement and lay still. It seemed like an eternity, but at last I felt the solid brace of his pelvis against my backside and knew that he had reached his limit. I felt his cock flex inside me, and I reveled in the fullness of it.

Just as slowly as it had entered, Travis's cock began to retreat, leaving a void as it withdrew. I would have begged him to fill me, but I'd forgotten language as such. I simply moaned in distress. When he actually popped out of me, I gave out a cry. Travis laughed low in his throat, then kissed me. His tongue drove itself into my mouth, and just as suddenly, his cock drove itself back into my body. Soon he had worked out a rhythm, his tongue and cock collaborating to fuck me at both ends. I felt an uncomfortable pinch in my groin and realized that my stiffening prick was trapped pointing downward. I reached between our bodies and pulled it free. Still wet with semen, it slipped easily between our bodies. I managed to get in a few strokes before Travis pinned my arms over my head.

I think Travis could have continued until dawn at that excruciating pace, but as if cued from some external source, he began to increase the tempo of his thrusts. Unable to move my limbs, I focused my movements on my tongue and lips. I was intoxicated by the slide of his tongue as it mirrored the slide of his cock through my ass. With each thrust, the rough texture of his belly sent a thrill through my cock. Travis broke the kiss, gasping for breath, but the intensity of his thrusting into my body didn't abate. My mouth uncovered, I began to cry, to howl. Travis was silent, but I could feel the barely audible rumble of a growl in his chest.

I looked up, and the stars were eyes looking down on us, and I knew that Travis and I, at that moment, were the center of the universe—that everything was watching us. The epiphany pushed me over the edge, and the orgasm hit me like a tidal wave. Travis cried out, and he thrust deeper than he'd been before. I felt my bowels fill with the warmth and wetness of him. He hovered above me, trembling, and didn't move or speak until his softening cock was expelled from my body.

I opened my eyes to look at him, and found myself frozen in fear instead. Above us, there were no stars—only eyes and leering faces. Five, 10, 15 men encircled us. Travis sensed my tension and looked around us. He said nothing, simply extracted himself from my embrace and stood up. He offered me his hand, still keeping a wary eye on the onlookers. I accepted his help, and pulled myself to my feet, feeling foolish with my pants around my ankles, and thinking that I didn't want to die like this.

One of the faces stepped forward, and there was a familiarity to him that I didn't immediately recognize. He looked different in the night air, away from the strobe lights and smoke machines. It wasn't until he spoke that I recognized him.

"Um...can I be next?"

My God, I thought. *It's Jamie.*

• • •

So that's how I met Travis, and that's how me and Travis's little organization got started. Weekly meetings are held every Thursday behind the pub. No trouble with the cops because we've got two cops in the club. No trouble with the bar because...well, because we've got Jamie.

Jamie liked you enough to tell you to talk to me. I can see Jamie made a good choice, and I can see by the look in your eye what your answer is going to be, but I have to ask you the question anyway, because it's club rules. Yeah, I can tell by looking at you just what you want, but it doesn't mean anything if you don't say it yourself.

So here's your chance. Just ask: What do you really want to do?

Nasty

by Mel Smith

I looked up, and he was staring at me from across the walkway. He was one of those smoldering straight boys whose blatant contempt for queers undoubtedly harbors a need to have his ass plowed until the cows come home.

His eyes never left me. The sneer never left his face. He wanted to hurt me.

Well, he was about to learn that this queer wouldn't sit and wait to be bashed. "What the fuck are you staring at?" I said.

"I'm staring at you." The voice matched the look.

As much as I hated to admit it, he was hot. Thick brown hair, a couple of days' worth of beard, black eyes that ripped through flesh, a body as sleek and powerful as a Harley Davidson, and a mouth that would look incredible with a cock crammed down it.

I hated him. I hated his repressed, hypocritical, breeding ass. I wanted to pound that ass with my cock, then pound his face with my fists. Or vice versa. Either way, the asshole needed to know that not all queers are easy targets.

I sat up straight on the bench. I knew my 6 feet 2 inches of iron-pumped muscle would be intimidating, even to a shithead like him. "You want a piece of me?"

He moved toward me very slowly. He had no fear. This was going to be nasty.

I stood when he was about three feet away. I only topped him by about an inch. Up close, he was even hotter.

He put his face in mine. It dripped with loathing.

My hands balled into fists.

"Yeah, I want a piece of you." I could almost taste his hate. "My ass eats cock for breakfast and I'm wonderin' if you're man enough to feed it."

OK. Now that is *not* what I expected him to say.

He caught me so off-guard that I almost flinched, but I held it together and grabbed a handful of that thick, brown hair. I yanked his head back.

He snarled.

"I already stuffed five sluts like you this morning, and it ain't even 10 o'clock yet."

He licked his lips. I'd never seen anyone do it nastier.

I pulled his head back farther. "You want to do it here, pig, or does the little girl need some privacy?"

He dropped to his knees in the park in broad daylight and started chewing on my denim-covered cock. He sounded exactly like a fucking dog, panting and growling as he soaked my crotch with slobber. I pushed his head roughly against my straining rod. He chewed even harder.

I pulled him to his feet by his hair. I grabbed his crotch and squeezed.

He snarled again, his eyes shooting sparks at me.

His dick felt like a fucking bazooka. It took everything I had not to let him see me sweat. There was nothing I liked better than to tear up a big-dicked bottom. The bigger they are, the harder they come.

"You're coming home with me, fuck boy, and when I'm done with your ass, it won't be able to eat for a week."

"You better hope that's true, because it gets awful ugly when it's hungry."

"Boy, you couldn't get much uglier."

The corner of his mouth curled up. He knew I was lying, but I couldn't let him get the upper hand.

I yanked his hair and squeezed his cock harder. He flinched, and the sparks became rockets.

"I want to see what I'm getting before I waste my fucking time on a whore like you," I said.

Without a second's hesitation, he undid his fly and pulled down his pants. He wasn't wearing any underwear and nine inches of uncut meat sprang free, wedging itself between my legs.

I was going to fucking lose it before we even left the park.

I took hold of that meat, and it throbbed in my hand like some living being. I lifted it and pushed it back against his stomach. I hefted his nuts with my other hand and tried not to let him see me giving thanks. They were huge and heavy, dangling like a bull's. I could see his loads of spunk hosing down my carpet as I fucked the shit out of him.

"I want to see the rest."

He turned away from me and bent over. I took the opportunity to catch my breath.

I lost it again as soon as I looked.

His ass was a fucking trampoline, tight and bouncy. If I slapped it with my cock, my cock would slap me right back. The cheeks were solid, meaty mounds that could be used like handles to steer while plowing.

I took a hold of those cheeks and dug my fingers into the flesh. My thumbs spread them wide, and I said a silent prayer.

My prayer was answered.

A tasty, tight hole puckered and unpuckered at my thumb tips. It wasn't begging me to fuck it, it was daring me to.

I slapped his ass hard.

He yelped, then spit into the ground. Still bent over, he looked back and up at me. "Think you can fill it up?"

"Fill it? Asshole, I'm going to fucking burst it."

He stood and pulled up his pants. He left the top three buttons undone. A ripe mushroom poked straight up, peeking out of his foreskin.

This is the one, I thought. I'd finally found a bottom nasty enough to survive my abusive monster. I was sure of it. This one wasn't going to be tamed.

Those eyes of his challenged me, while he slipped his finger and thumb inside his foreskin and teased the mushroom until honey oozed out of the slit.

My tongue almost came out, it looked so fucking tasty. But I stopped it just in time.

"I want to see what you got too, before I waste the trip."

I put one hand around his throat and slapped his cock-teasing hand away with the other. I yanked his foreskin out as far as it would stretch. The mushroom bloomed inside.

"I don't fucking show you anything unless I want to. Is that understood?"

He smiled, but the cockiness had slipped a bit. A chink in the armor. I yanked harder on his skin. "Is that understood?"

"Yes, sir." It was still a snarl. Not even a hint of submissiveness.

God, he was perfect.

I took my key ring out of my pocket. It was big and loaded with keys. I pulled out his pants and slid the ring down onto his cock. I buttoned up his fly and could picture the keys digging into his balls. The tip of his mushroom was still visible over the waistband, dripping precome like a leaky faucet.

I walked to my car, and he followed. I got my extra car key out, and I made him ride in the backseat. "You touch yourself, and I'm booting your slutty little ass out of this car."

"Afraid you can't keep your hands off of me?"

He was pushing it. "When we get to my place, it will be more than my hands I'll have on you." I started the car. "Open your mouth again and I'm climbing back there and shutting it for you."

There was silence.

I looked in the rearview mirror. He was staring at me, the smuggest grin I'd ever seen plastered on his face.

He held my stare for a couple of beats more, then he slid down in his seat. His knees opened wide, and his fingers spread across his thighs. His T-shirt was bunched up, and I could see fluid from his cock filling up his belly button. The outline of my keys was visible through his jeans.

While he watched me watching him, he started pulling and arranging the seat belts. I thought, at first, that I had flustered him so much that he wasn't able to put his belt on correctly. Then I saw what he had managed to do.

His crotch was tied in a harness created by the seat belts. I could only imagine the kind of pressure it and my keys were placing on his stiff boner.

He licked his lips again, in that slow, tantalizing, shit-eating way he'd done before. Then he began to rock rhythmically, strangling his basket with every move forward. His head lay back, and a low growl vibrated from his throat. The bastard was masturbating.

I had to give him credit. He wasn't touching himself.

I looked at the road and fought the need to squirm in my seat.

Could this be love?

We reached my house, and he followed me in. When I turned around, he was on his knees, pulling at my fly.

I slapped his hands away. "I didn't give you permission to do that."

He looked up at me through long, dark lashes, his eyes still smoldering.

"Stand."

He stood.

"Take off everything except my key ring."

He did it slowly, his eyes rarely leaving mine. My keys jangled with his every move.

He was giving me time to look. He knew a man would have to be dead not to like what he was seeing. His skin glowed like highly polished wood. His nipples were exactly the way I liked them—familiar with abuse but still young and tender. They stood at attention, their shiny gold hoops twitching with every beat of his heart. His abs were carved into his flesh. I could've done my laundry on them. His thighs were powerful without bulging, and his arms and legs were highlighted by the blackest hair I'd ever seen, giving his skin an even higher gloss.

I looked and I liked—God, did I like—but I wouldn't give him the satisfaction of showing it.

When he was done, he started to put his boots back on.

"I said, 'Just my key ring.'"

He stopped and looked at me, missing half a beat. Then he smiled, and rose to his full six feet plus.

I liked my bottoms completely bare. It made them look more vulnerable. But as my eyes traveled over him one more time, I realized it only made this one look more incredible, like some natural beast, raw and wild.

I led him by my keys to a straight-backed chair sitting against the living room wall. A small table with a drawer stood a few feet away from it.

"Sit and put your hands behind you."

He obeyed.

"I don't want to see your hands in front. I don't want you to touch me. Is that understood?"

He gave me that look up through his lashes again. God, he was a tease. A nasty, slutty, fucking tease.

"Yes, sir."

I stood back, about a foot in front of him. I opened my fly and set the monster free. It thrust forward like a lance and hit him in the face.

His eyes grew huge, and the smirk disappeared.

I thought, for a moment, that I'd lost him; that it was fear I saw in his eyes.

Then those smoldering eyes burst into flames, and he whispered, "Chow time."

I watched my precome inch down his cheek. "Does just your ass eat cock, or does your face get hungry too?"

The smug smile was back. "It's just all one long chute to me."

The image of my snake sliding down his throat and poking out his asshole made my legs shake. There was no way to hide it.

His smile grew bigger.

I was going to have to make him pay for that.

His hands were behind his back, gripping the rungs of the chair. I grabbed a handful of his hair with one hand and my cock with the other. His mouth opened wide, and I shoved my way in with one long stroke.

He retched hard once, and phlegm oozed out around my meat. His hands came forward, then stopped, and gripped the seat of his chair.

I felt the back of his throat convulsing against my cock. His knuckles were white, and the fire in his eyes shimmered with moisture.

I was about to back off, when I felt his throat open up and my cock slide forward some more. His hands released the chair and returned to their place behind his back. The smirk was gone from his lips, of course, but now I saw it in his eyes. They twinkled at me.

I couldn't help but smile back.

As his lips disappeared into the hairy darkness of my crotch, I realized how right I had been. His mouth did look incredible with a cock crammed down it.

I held his hair and his ears, and I fed him a feast. I fucked his face hard, slamming it with my body, over and over. The corners of his mouth started to tear, and a trickle of blood came out of one of his nostrils. His hands, for the most part, stayed behind, occasionally getting knocked loose by my ramming.

I looked into his eyes, sweat blurring my vision, and I saw them glaze over. Then, unbelievably, he winked at me.

I almost lost it before reaching the main course.

I pulled out quickly and shoved his head in his lap. I closed my eyes and took some deep breaths, trying to keep it under control.

Still holding his head down, my legs started to quiver. His labored breathing and twitching hands, still valiantly held behind his back, were pushing me over the edge. I wasn't going to make it.

Then his body suddenly relaxed under my touch, and I wondered, *Had he surrendered, or had he gotten a second wind?*

Not knowing gave me the strength that I needed, and I knew I was going to be able to dole out the punishment he so dearly deserved.

I yanked him off the chair, and he landed face first on the carpet. My key ring went flying. He was on his knees, his ass sticking straight up in the air like the anxious little whore's hole it was. With effort, he tucked his arms under his head, covering his face.

Still, I didn't know if he'd given in, or if he was just waiting for more.

I grabbed the chair and threw it across the room. I opened the drawer and took out a tube. I shoved the end in his ass and filled his hole with lube. The empty container followed the chair.

I rolled two condoms onto my cock; I'd had too many tear on me from the strain.

I looked down on his body, feeling pumped and voracious. Then everything came to a stop. His ass suddenly looked too vulnerable, too perfect. It was plump and full and pink with sweat. He couldn't control the tiny shivers that shook it.

No matter how much he had asked for it, did anything so perfect really deserve such brutal treatment?

As if he could read my hesitation, his voice rose up to me.

"Don't worry. Guys with monster dicks like yours often suffer from performance anxiety."

That was all I needed.

I drove my jackhammer straight down into him. He howled like a dog, and I pulled all the way out just so I could plunge it right back in again. My body slammed him into the floor with every ram of my cock.

He soon began making animal noises. All kinds of animal noises—pig grunts, dog whimpers, rabbit screams. Have you ever heard a rabbit scream? It makes your skin crawl.

Still, I wouldn't let up. His hands were clawing at the carpet, but he couldn't get a grip. His knees gave out, and he started to fall to the side, but I held him by the hips and kept him in place.

Every time I thought I would come, I'd picture that smug smirk or hear one of those cocky statements, and I'd find the strength to hold on for a few more thrusts.

Suddenly, his body began to jerk, and I heard those loads of spunk splattering onto my carpet. He let loose with several screaming sobs, his hands still searching for a hold. I pulled him up onto his knees as I dropped onto mine. I held him tight as I continued to pound his ass, watching in amazement as rope after rope of come rocketed into the air.

Then I heard him gagging, and I wondered if maybe he was right—that it was one long chute and my cock had reached up into his throat.

With that, my balls could take it no more. I pulled out, and he fell forward. I ripped off the condoms, and he rolled onto his back. I stood and held onto my hose, draining every ounce of fluid from my body onto his stomach, chest, and face.

I bucked with the power of an orgasm, the likes of which I had never felt. I had devolved into something less than human, grunting and shouting and shaking as if possessed.

When I had squeezed the last remaining drop onto his twitching body, my brain started to function again.

The fog lifted, and I looked down on him. He seemed barely conscious.

I knelt beside him and realized, with regret, that I had ruined another one. Like all the others, when he came round he would either run for the door, frightened and damaged, or he would become an obsessive puppy dog, shadowing me like I was his master.

Neither was the reaction I wanted.

His face had dried blood and rug burns on it, and it was sprayed with come. Looking at him, almost comatose, he no longer looked hot and nasty. He only looked, quite simply, beautiful. I realized with a shock that beneath the sneer and the growth of beard, he couldn't have been much older than 20.

How could I ever have believed that he truly understood what he had been asking for?

I did my best to mask the concern in my voice. "Well, slut, did you get your fill?"

The eyes opened, and embers flew out at me. His voice was weak, but the sneer was still there. "I guess this can last me until dinner-time."

I smiled. It was definitely love.

Damn, this was going to be nasty.

Pig

by Phillip Mackenzie Jr.

When I get home from the gym, Alex is in the kitchen, looking like he's just rolled out of bed. It's 10 P.M.

"Hey, man," I say as I drop my bag and head for the refrigerator for water.

He grunts something at me and turns away. I hear him shuffling back down the hall.

Not that I expect anything else. Whatever I say or do is always met with the same slightly quizzical stare.

"As always," I say aloud, "good to see you. Nice chatting with you. But I know you're busy, so don't let me keep you."

Alex has a way of making me feel not just inconsequential but slightly ridiculous. He looks at me as if I'm a laboratory chimpanzee, as if he's amazed that words come out of my mouth despite my being a lesser life form.

At first I mistook his behavior for poor social skills, until one day when I asked him if he'd been shy when he was a kid too. With little more than a look, he insinuated that he could talk to me but simply didn't find it worth the effort.

Believe me, I've tried. I talked about my job—until he made it clear that what I did was a drain on society. I talked about music—until he accused me of contributing to the downfall of culture. I tried to talk about books, but that seemed to cause him physical pain.

Sighing heavily, I drop myself onto the kitchen chair and kick my shoes off.

• • •

I hate having a roommate. The second bedroom made a great office—and a great place to store all the crap that wouldn't fit anywhere else, like the bike I barely rode anymore, the extra stereo I'd refused in a fit of immature vindictiveness to let my ex take when we split up, and the weight bench that served as a place to put the boxes of books my brother dumped on me when he moved to Montana with his girlfriend two years ago.

But I really needed that membership at Crunch, and the trip to Florence was too good to pass up. And don't get me started on the rigorous demands of appropriate attire and hair as well as the combined introduction of the new Macs and DVD. Well, all of it put my credit card through a too-vigorous workout. Which was all OK, until the record company folded one morning, and after three weeks I was forced to take a job as a personal assistant to a B-list producer who inevitably took it out on me when no one returned his calls—which no one ever did.

Which explains my roommate, Alex. An assistant professor of anthropology, he is actually poorer than I am, but that doesn't stop him from assuming an air of superiority, which is now primarily manifested through a steadfast refusal to interact with me—or even to engage in rudimentary conversation.

I have a fairly realistic estimation of myself and a very good idea of my place on the food chain, but I also know I'm not stupid, can be fairly witty, and can embark on a superficial discourse on current events, which is pretty much all that is asked of you in L.A.

And when I finally realized I needed a roommate, I imagined something along the lines of *Three's Company*: a set of fun-loving misfortunates sitting cross-legged on each other's beds, bemoaning our love lives, and cooking up pasta primavera in our little kitchen. Instead, I got Apartment Zero.

It's amazing how exhausting this is. And frustrating. Is it any wonder then, given the beating my ego takes on a daily basis—combined with the double whammy of the drought in my dating life and spike in my libido—that I've begun spending more time and money than I should in computer chat rooms?

Fuck it, though. The thing is, in there I can be anything I want. I'm not some beaten-down, beaten-up walking advertisement for early-21st-century ennui. I'm an out-of-control, uninhibited, radical, streetwalking, turn-me-upside-down-and-fuck-me-sideways alley cat of a sex monkey.

I can walk through the door, strip out of my clothes, and slide my ass down over the thick hard shaft of some straight frat boy sitting alone in his room and let him ride my tight hole until he shoots his sticky load into my guts, and then I can get up and walk away while he's dribbling into his pubes. I love that. Who cares if it's actually some fat middle-aged Judy Garland queen tickling his pecker with one hand and the keyboard with the other. Who the hell knows what he's fantasizing about either?

Not that I'm hard on the eyes in the real world. Despite my current financial restraints, I've never given up my gym membership, which has succeeded in not only relieving the stress of my current state of affairs but also resulted in a physique that demands display in a Dolce and Gabbana black silk tank top. When I face the full-length mirror on the bathroom door, my abdominal muscles are visible without flexing, even when I stand 20 feet away at the end of the hallway.

Yes, I'm bragging. I've earned the right. At least I'm not like Alex, still waiting for that gamine starving-artist look to come into vogue.

I feel my dick starting to uncoil inside my jock, and I slip a hand inside my shorts to encourage it, when I realize Alex might make another foray into the kitchen and find me sitting here playing with myself, giving him one more thing to feel superior about.

That's another thing about having a roommate. If you can't walk around naked, you sure as hell can't jerk off in the kitchen.

Alex's door is directly across from mine, so I always have to make sure mine is closed firmly if I'm going to get it on with myself. I hear it click when I close it, but I give it an extra nudge just to be sure. Then I walk over and turn on my computer.

As I'm slipping my shirt over my head, I hear that I have mail.

My mother: Read later. My ex: Discard now. Frank: Well, let's see what he has to say.

"I have tix to Jeff Stryker in *Doing Hard Time.* Tonight, 8 P.M. Wanna go?"

I'm glad I didn't check my E-mail until now. What's with these porn stars doing theater? We want to see your dick or your ass or both. We want to watch you come. In close-up. That's it. Period. We don't want you to do anything else. Ever. And we sure don't want to hear you talk. Got it? Good.

I plop my ass down on the chair and head straight into Man2Man. First, I check out the supposedly live guys. One guy is fingering his asshole, but the digitization makes it look like he's breaking his finger. Another guy has just come and is starting to go limp. Damn, missed the show. But looking at his still-oozing slit restarts my cock, so I head for a chat room.

Darkman is there, and so is AssCrazy. They always are.

"Hey, Toybox." (That's me—OK, I know, but I was under pressure when I came up with it.)

"Hey, guys. Anything up?"

"Me," says AssCrazy. "I just got back from that Jeff Stryker show."

"Jesus, she is so tired," says Darkman.

"Maybe, but that pole makes my loins ache," AssCrazy responds.

Hung4U pipes in: "I saw Ryan Idol in *Making Porn,* and I'd take him over Stryker any day."

I am wondering again if AssCrazy was really Frank, when Rdy4Bear logs on and almost immediately heads for a private room with Darkman.

Hung4U and AssCrazy are still debating the finer points of porn-star appendages when someone new logs in: NickName. That's actually kind of funny.

The instant message pops up on my screen: "Hi."

"Hi," I shoot back.

"Toybox, huh?"

"Yeah, Nick, Toybox. What of it?" OK, so I'm a little crabby still.

"It isn't any lamer than the other ones," NickName says, seemingly trying to tone things down.

"Thanks."

"Wanna get outta here?" he asks.

"Sure," I say. I like the direct approach. It cuts through the bullshit, acknowledges why we are all here, and saves time. We click to a private room.

"Take off your clothes," he says.

I slip my shorts down to my ankles and slide a finger along the edge of my jock, feeling the sweaty dampness of my curly cock thatch. I'm wondering what this one is into, as I massage my crotch. I'm cool with being ordered around in here.

"Tell me," he says.

"My shirt is off. I'm rubbing my hands over my chest. I just worked out, so I'm a little sweaty."

"Smell your pits," he insists.

I turn my head and sniff. It's a little gamy but not bad.

"Tell me."

I'm a little thrown. What am I supposed to say now? "I stink," I type back tentatively.

"You fucking pig."

My terminal almost snarls, and my dick twitches hard. Oh, yeah. Oh, yeah, baby. This is gonna be hot. "I am. I am a pig. I'm a filthy fucking pig," I type back hurriedly.

"Show me your little pig pecker."

I slip my jock down around my thighs, and my dick rises up, pulsing from its nest of brown curls. I slide my hand down under my balls, squeezing them, rolling them around inside the sac.

"DON'T TOUCH IT!" his words scream back at me.

"I'm sorry."

"You don't do anything unless I tell you to."

"OK," I start to type and then erase it and type, "Yes, sir."

"DON'T CALL ME 'SIR,'" he screams back.

Shit. Maybe I should have typed "Yes, Daddy." Crap. Who is this guy anyway? Peppermint Patty? Fuck it. It's Saturday night, and of course I don't have a date, so if it was going to be a little daddy-boy scene, I could get into that.

It's certainly different. I hadn't done that scene yet. I don't really think it's something I'd get into out in the real world, but in here, like I said, you can be anything you want for 20 minutes.

"Get down on your knees," he tells me.

I assume this is figurative, but just in case, I push the chair back and kneel down.

"I'm on my knees," I let him know

"Do you want my cock?"

"Yes, please," I type, praying it's the right thing to say.

"Beg for it," comes his response.

All right. This is a little much. But OK, my dick is bouncing happily away down there, so what the hell: "Please show me your cock. I need your cock. I really need it. Please give it to me."

"I don't think so."

What the *fuck* is going on here? I reach down and palm the head of my dick, slicking it with ooze. Screw this guy. I'll touch myself if I wanted to. I start typing again: "Please. I really want to see your big cock. I want to touch it. I want to suck it."

"Can you suck it good?"

"Yeah. I can make it feel real good," I tell him.

"Can you take it all the way down? Can I fuck your tonsils?"

"Yeah. Oh, yeah, I can take it. Let me show you," I play along.

"Are you gonna make it hard enough to fuck your little toybox?"

"Yeah, it's gonna be so hard. It's gonna rip right into my hot, tight ass."

"OK. You can touch it," he allows me.

Finally! Jesus Christ.

I run my hand down my dick in a long, slow shuddering stroke and then slip my fingers down under my balls, which are tightened up around the base of my shaft. My middle finger finds the tight knot of my asshole, and I start rubbing in tiny circles.

"I'm taking it out now," I type one-handed. "I'm unzipping your pants and slipping my hand inside. Oh, God, it feels so good."

"TAKE YOUR FUCKING HAND OFF YOUR PITIFUL LITTLE PRICK RIGHT NOW!"

My dick bounces, and I actually gasp as I jerk my hand away. Fucker. What a dick. But I had to admit, this little game had its hot side. I'm harder than I could remember being in a long time. Hmm. Maybe there is something to this, after all.

"I'm sorry," I type back lamely.

"If you want my cock, you give it the attention it deserves. Do you understand me, pig?"

"Yes."

"That means both hands. Now open your mouth."

I actually do this! What am I thinking?

"I'm just gonna give you the head because you didn't listen," he teases.

But his efforts are working. I feel it. The slick rubbery head of a monster shaft rubbing my lips and leaving them slick with precome. I can smell the heated funk and taste the salty tang of cock. The head of my dick is purple with frustration, weeping golden liquid, begging for attention.

"Your mouth is sweet, little pig."

My fingers are no longer on the keyboard. They're buried in wiry curls of hair, full of wrinkled ball flesh; my mouth stretched by cock, my tongue aching sweetly from pressure and friction as he pumps my face.

I reach up to type: "God! God! God! Yeah, fuck my face! Fuck it! Fuck my throat!"

"OH, YEAH!" the words hit my screen—and at the same moment I hear it. I mean really *hear* it. From across the hall.

What the hell? I'm thinking. "Alex?" I type and then erase it.

My heart is pounding in my throat, and my dick rapidly deflates.

"Take that cock. You cock pig," flashes across my screen.

Oh, sure. Snotty, rimless-glasses-wearing, intellectually pretentious Alex as Überdaddy? Right.

No way. I settle back down on my knees and start typing again, my cock swelling as I fall back into the mood. I give him what I hope will thrill him more: "Yeah, it feels so good. You taste so good. God, I love your cock!"

"Stand up," he says.

I stand, my cock jutting out and dripping on my keyboard. I swipe the sticky drop with my finger and put it my mouth.

"Bend over," comes his next order.

I lean forward placing both hands on my desk.

"Ask me to eat your ass."

With one hand I begin typing: "Please. Please eat out my tight hole. Stick your tongue up my asshole. Make it nice and wet."

"Oh, your ass tastes sweet. Nice and sweaty." At least I get a compliment from him.

He has me back in that mode. "Oh, God, yeah," I say, "tongue my hole. Jesus, you're so good. God!" I am feeling it again, the sandpaper roughness of a man's face between my cheeks, the rasp of a tongue against my puckered crack, the nip of teeth, the blast of hot breath. Fuck, this guy is hot! Goddamn, he's hot!

"You think you can take this big cock up that tight little hole?"

"Yeah. Fuck, yeah," I assure him.

"You want me to plant a big load right up there, don't you?"

Oh, Christ. I almost come. My untouched prong jerks, and my balls spasm, ready to spew their contents all over my screen. I grit my teeth and clamp a hand around the base of my shaft to keep from shooting, and then jerk it away guiltily. I get back to the keyboard: "Yes, I want your load. I want to feel your hot come inside me."

I feel hard thighs against the back of my legs, hands pulling my ass cheeks apart, a thick finger sliding into me—and then another. I feel a long, hot, thick pole of flesh against my back and low-hanging hairy balls against the smooth flesh of my butt.

"I'm ready. Fuck me now, please," I type jerkily.

"I'll fuck you when I'm good and ready, pig," he says, clearly not willing to relinquish his control.

"I'm sorry," I type almost wearily. Jesus H. Christ—this could get old.

"Don't you tell me when to fuck you. I oughta leave your ass right here for that."

"Please don't. Please, don't leave. I just love your cock so much, I got carried away," I work to give him a plea.

"I was gonna be gentle because you were a good little pig, but now I think I'm gonna rip you apart."

"Please. Yes! Fuck your little pig as hard as you want."

"Yeah, your little pig hole feels nice and tight."

I'm past caring. Call me a pig, swear at me, treat me lower than whale spit on the bottom of the ocean. I don't care at this point. Just give me a cock up my ass.

"TAKE THAT COCK!" he screams at me as I feel a huge mass of male muscle breach my chute and slam into my guts like a red-hot poker.

"YEAH!" I scream back

"FUCK!" he howls.

And again...I *hear* it. From across the hall.

I fly backward from my computer, my dick swinging crazily as I leap at the door. Cracking it open, all I can see is a light coming from under Alex's door. I tiptoe across the hall, and press my ear to the door. I hear the clicking of keystrokes, that's all.

As I scurry into my room, I pause, ready to click the door shut. Heart pounding crazily, I slowly swing it back open. My unhandled rod is jumping and jerking, and sweat trickles down between my pecs.

It is Alex. Alex who fucked my throat and slapped his balls against my chin. Alex's shaggy bush I had buried my nose in. Alex's tongue that had wormed up inside me, setting me on fire and making me beg for the monster cock he crammed into me a few seconds later.

"You love my big dick, don't you, dick pig?" he had typed during my frenzied foray across the hall.

"Oh, yeah, your cock feels so good. God, fuck me harder!" I type back frantically, pulling my desk and chair away from the wall so I can sit in full view of the door.

What if he opens the door? It's Alex. Weird, dark, cynical, mean Alex. Skinny, punky, freaky Alex.

Who would have thought it? I try to imagine Alex's thin lips saying the words "dick pig." My hard-on throbs, leaks, and jumps untouched. My balls are like rocks. My ass is aching, imagining those lips against my quaking hole.

And his cock, thick and slick with my juices, burying itself deep inside me, then sliding out to the crown before slamming back into me, turning every inch of my chute into raw nerve endings. Alex's cock. Alex's cock?

"You like me pounding your tight pig pussy?" his words flash at me.

Yeah. I love it. Alex. God damn it. Not Alex. Fuck, why did it have to be Alex? I hate that fucker for doing this to me, but...Jesus...just keep doing it.

"I fucking love it!" I scream out loud. And keep screaming, "Yeah, fuck me harder, Alex! Fuck me harder!"

The screen stays blank. Then footsteps in Alex's room. I turn toward the door legs spread, dick standing straight and proud, my hands dangling by my sides.

His door flies open. The first thing I notice is the tattoo. A snake stretches from his cock over his chest and coils around his left pec, its mouth open over his nipple. Its sinuous body accents his own lithe muscularity. Long, flat planes of muscle stretch over his chest and stomach, sinewy cables over his arms and legs. A patch of dark hair nests between his tits, narrows to a thin, dark line over his belly before spreading out again into a dense patch of black curls between his legs. Following this trail, my eyes are riveted on the pole of flesh pointed almost straight up, curving slightly to the right at the head. His hand grasps it along with his heavy, hairy balls, pointing them directly at me. Without saying a word, he turns back to his computer, his hard ass flexing as he walks.

With his eyes locked on mine, one hand gripping his cock, slowly massaging it, his other hand types, "Show me your asshole."

Silently, I lift my legs and spread them, scooting down in my chair until I feel the cool air of the room against my throbbing pucker.

Alex types more: "Stick your finger in."

I put my index finger in my mouth and suck it slowly. A thin strand of saliva stretches and breaks as I lower it between my legs and rub it against my fuck hole, slipping a tiny bit in, and then with a quick twitch I push it all the way in.

I can't believe I'm doing this. That I want to do this. That I'm looking at Alex, pale and hard, staring at me with those reflectionless dark eyes, his hand stroking himself as he watches me finger-fucking myself.

"You want me to fuck you?" he asks aloud.

Not trusting my voice, I type, "Please!"

He spits into his palm and slicks it over the length of his twitching cock. "I'm fucking you," he says as if he were telling me the weather.

Dry-mouthed, I watch his hand travel the length of his dick, pulling the skin tight as he drives toward his bush. My finger matches his slow rhythm. Adding a second finger as he picks up speed, I drive into my hot center, finding the hard knob of my prostate.

He spits again, pounding at his prick as his balls pull up, jerking inside their sac.

"You like my thick cock, pig?" he asks conversationally.

"Jesus, Alex." I gasp. I want him inside me. To fuck me for two days and then shoot gallons of Alex spunk all over me. I want to swallow his cock and massage it with my throat until he fills me with come.

"Are you my little fuck pig?" his voice hitches slightly.

"Yes." I breathe, transfixed on the blur of his hand on his swelling muscle. Its purple head looks primed and ready to blow.

I drive another finger into my hole, and my body spasms as if hit by 10,000 volts of electricity.

"You gonna take my hot load?" his eyes bore into me, impaling me.

"Fuck. Oh, fuck, Alex, I'm gonna come. Oh, God, Alex, please let me come."

His hand stops, and his toes curls. Then his legs shoot out, and every muscle in his lean body pops as his cock fires a white stream that hits him in the throat.

I'm frozen. My fingers are pressed tight against the throbbing knob at my center, as jet after jet of sperm flies from the flaming crown of his shaft, abstractly painting his abdomen; as his body jerks and a sound like grinding machinery fights out of his clenched teeth. I imagine it shooting into me, burning my guts, filling me until I overflow and it pours out of me.

I lose it. I can't stop to save my life. My ass ring clamps down on my fingers, the velvety muscles inside clench, and the room disappears in blackness. The first blast never hits my body at all, but I feel it coursing up the length of my cock, ripping the hole open and flying into space. My balls seize and release, and a flood of come pours out of my cock, burning my skin and bringing a scream from my throat that I had never heard before.

I come back into my body, shivering and trembling, the funk of jism in my nostrils, the cooling slickness of it covering me from nuts to neck.

Alex rises from his chair, his own load running in rivulets into his dark bush, and walks toward me. He stops, and the corner of his mouth jerks upward in a half smile.

"Pig," he says, and then with one foot kicks the door shut.

Str8 Guyz
by Dominic Santi

I was starting to wonder if I'd been watching too many pornies. Sure, my JO sessions were great. Seeing all those naked dicks really turned me on. I was getting worried, though. At 22, I still hadn't figured things out. I mean, I liked having sex with girls. But I shot buckets watching guys get fucked. I imagined it was me—a buff, blond, and maybe a little bi-curious football player—throwing my legs in the air and getting my ass plowed. Since I'd never been with another guy, I didn't know if I really wanted what I thought I wanted. But I loved watching and jerking off. I'd rented every pornie the local vid store carried.

"You realize these are, um, all different?" the slender redheaded clerk had asked politely the first time he scanned a mixed basket of het, gay, bi, and "all-anal orgies" for me.

"I'm versatile," I mumbled, blushing as I grabbed my bag and hurried out the door. After a few weeks, though, Stan and I got to know each other pretty well. He was openly gay, and he got off on recommending all the hottest new vids to me. I kind of practiced cruising with him, making eye contact, trying to scope out his crotch without looking away or blushing too much, despite how cute he was.

Stan was the one who'd put the flyer for the local gay chat line in my bag, along with a couple of het vids and the new all-male flick, *Silver Foxes.* I was trying to hide the boner I'd gotten from looking at the cover. Hunky older guys turned me on something fierce.

"One of my online buddies worked on this video, dude. He's the film editor for Studline Video—a real daddy type in his 40s."

Stan stared pointedly at my crotch as he handed me my change. "I told him I knew somebody who was going to love *Silver Foxes,* a straight boy who rented every kind of smut video and had a real thing for older guys. That's you, Michael, my friend."

"Oh, man," I blushed, moving my hard-on even closer to the counter. "Why did you tell him that?" I wanted to grab my stuff and run, but I needed to wait until my dick settled down, so that I wouldn't embarrass myself going past the old ladies perusing the G-rated section.

"Studclippr thought it was way kinky, dude. He said he'd like to meet you." Stan smiled innocently as he passed me my vids. "We'll be online around 11 tonight. Address is with your receipt—if you're not, um, too busy with these."

My face flaming, I clutched the bag in front of my crotch and rushed out the door. To make a long story short, the video got me so turned on that I went to the chat room. Stan made the introductions. Studclippr and I really hit it off online, and later when I called him on the phone. I came twice before I finally blurted that I wanted him to really fag me out.

Studclippr laughed until he almost choked. He promised to turn me into "a perfect little pussy boy." Since I was so nervous about actually doing it, though, we agreed to wait until Saturday night to get together so that his boyfriend would be out with some buddies and we'd be alone.

Studclippr—Don, actually—lived a couple of towns over. When I got to his house, I was surprised that he looked just the way he'd described himself in his profile: a trim, muscular 6 foot 4, with quiet hazel eyes and thick, black, silver-streaked hair—on his head *and* peeking out of the front of his half-open cotton shirt. I'd thought everybody lied in their profiles. I mean, there's no way my cock is 10 inches! But Don was a real hunk. My dick started twitching the minute I saw him.

Even his house reflected his style. It was relaxed and comfortable, with bookcases lining the walls and a large overstuffed leather couch facing a huge oak entertainment center. The electronic equipment filling the shelves was awesome. It had all the latest bells and whistles. LEDs blinked everywhere, and a killer sound system was playing cool techno tunes, just like in the soundtracks to my favorite pornies. The whole room reminded me of a kick-ass movie set.

I was getting really nervous, though. My hand shook a little as I took the bourbon Don offered me. I sipped slowly, trying to calm my jitters, concentrating on the familiar, reassuring burn in my throat. We sat on the couch, me perched stiffly on the edge of the cushion, Don casually resting his arm on the back as I fidgeted next to him. Finally, he set his drink on the coffee table and said, "Do you want to talk for a while, first?"

"Um, about what?" I asked, rubbing a sweaty hand on my jeans.

"Never mind," he laughed softly. He lifted the glass from my fingers and put it down next to his. Then he leaned over, took my chin in his hand, and lowered his face to mine. And he kissed me.

Oh, wow! I hadn't thought about kissing—I mean, with a guy. People don't kiss much in the pornies; they go straight to the fucking. But Don pulled down on my lower jaw, poked his tongue between my lips, and my gut flip-flopped all the way down to my dick. Man, did he know how to kiss! It wasn't like anything I'd ever done with a chick. Don's mouth was strong and greedy, like he was hungry to taste me. And his tongue was so hot! I felt like I was melting against him. Without thinking, I kissed him back, exploring the inside of his mouth. I jumped when he started sucking on my tongue. The rhythmic tugs vibrated all the way down to my nads.

"Wow, dude," I whispered, suddenly wondering if his mouth would feel that hot on my cock.

"It's OK to hug me, Michael," he said. Surprised that he called me by my name, I just realized he'd wrapped his long arms loosely around me while we'd been kissing. I fumbled against him, pressing my hands to the smooth, firm flesh of his back. His kisses were driving me nuts. My dick was stretching out into my jeans, bending almost painfully. Finally, I had to resituate myself.

Don grabbed my hand and shook his head. "Let me."

I closed my eyes as he carefully manipulated the thick denim, straightening my dick out so it could stretch up along my belly. I'd never had another man touch me like that. Don's fingers moved so easily, like he really knew how to handle a cock. And it was going to make me shoot.

"Oh, shit!" I gasped, my whole body stiffening. Don's hand immediately fell away. I panted against him, holding him tight as I climbed back from the edge.

"Take it easy, sport," he laughed. "We've got plenty of time. I'm certain that handsome 10-incher of yours will shoot more than that once tonight."

I tried to unobtrusively hide my face in his shoulder. "Um, it's not really 10 inches. I, uh, embellished a bit for my profile."

"Really?" he laughed. "I never would have guessed."

My face blushed hot against him as I inhaled the rich, warm man-sweat scent of his shirt. "I figured nobody would be interested if I said I'm only six inches."

"Anything more than a mouthful is a waste," he said. This time, he rubbed my thigh as his lips descended on mine. It was a long time before I could think clearly again. God, I could get addicted to kissing like that. The next thing I knew, his tongue was trailing down my neck, swirling over my Adam's apple, gliding over my chest. I hadn't even felt him unbuttoning my shirt before it was already off and he was licking my bare skin. I jumped when he swiped his tongue over my nipples.

"Wow, dude," I moaned, pulling his head closer. "That feels good."

"You'll be sore tomorrow," he laughed, his breath cool on my damp skin, "but it will still feel good. Think of me when your shirt moves against your skin."

Before I could answer, Don pushed me down on the couch and started really chewing my tits. I winced and squirmed as he teethed, my cock twitching at every sharp nip. Pretty soon, my whole chest tingled, and I was so tender and turned on, I could hardly stand it. I pushed him away and yanked his shirt open, flattening my hands against the furry, muscular wall of his chest.

Don's nipples stood out like stiff pink buttons. He sighed contentedly as I pinched one firm point and gently twisted it.

"They sure are sensitive," I whispered.

Don's laughter rumbled under my fingers. "Yours will get that way too—with practice." He leaned over and started tonguing the bulge in my crotch, and I almost stopped breathing. His breath was hot and wet, even through the heavy denim. I was still panting when he sat back, tugged my jeans open, and slowly pulled them down. My cock popped up immediately, waving wildly in the air, the head completely bared as Don worked my shoes and socks and pants off.

"Very pretty," he said, smiling as he stood and stripped. "I like uncut dicks."

I was too busy staring at him to answer. Don's tool wasn't monster-sized, not by porno standards, but it had to be at least eight inches—dark red, thick, and heavily veined. I swallowed hard, suddenly uncertain about where I wanted that sword of flesh to go.

"Um, you're really big," I said nervously.

Don threw back his head and laughed. "Don't worry, sport. When the time comes, everything will fit where it's supposed to." He knelt on the floor next to the couch and slid his long, strong fingers purposefully up my thighs, massaging deep into my tense muscles. As I relaxed, he carefully lifted my scrotum into his hand and rubbed my balls between his fingers.

"Very nice," he said, his firm, pink tongue swirling slowly over my nuts. The hair on my ball sac was wet with his spit as he sucked first one, then the other sensitive orb into his mouth and washed them with his tongue. "These feel primed to shoot."

I moaned as he probed the base of my shaft and slowly licked up. Don looked like he was eating an ice-cream cone, tasting me, peppering me with soft little kisses. I shook when he delicately probed the tender slit in the head of my cock. I was so hard I thought my dick was going to break. With no warning, Don opened his soft, warm lips and slid them all the way down my shaft, sucking me over the heat of his tongue and into his hot, tight, wet throat.

I yelled as I exploded. Don pulled off just in time, my come spraying his face as I bucked and spurted beneath him. Fuck, oh *fuck,* that felt good!

Don rubbed his cock against my thigh as he wiped the creamy white ropes into his hand and lifted his spermy fingers to my open lips.

"Lick," he ordered.

Still panting like a fiend, I sucked his dripping fingers clean with the fervor of the possessed. My come was sweet and slippery, and I loved the way it slid down my throat.

"You have a very talented tongue, Michael. Your mouth is going to make my dick very happy."

I groaned, my face heating with embarrassment and overpowering lust as Don rose up over me, gliding over my still-twitching meat. He carefully straddled my chest, his huge cock now resting lightly against my cheek.

"Get acquainted. Take your time, I'm not going to move. Just watch your teeth. If you do something I don't like, I'll tell you."

I felt shy. I felt kind of embarrassed. And I wanted to touch that big red cock and those low-hanging furry balls more than anything I'd ever wanted in my life. I ran my hands over him, exploring, moving his velvety soft dickskin over the pulsating flesh beneath. I tugged softly on his wrinkled sac, rubbing his heavy balls between my fingers.

"Feels nice, Michael," Don moaned. "Taste them if you want to."

Blushing, I slid down and opened my mouth. I licked the crinkly hair into whorls, inhaling his thick, musky, all-male scent. Don's balls were too big to fit in my mouth, so I grabbed his hips and bathed his sack until his breathing got faster and he was wiggling above me. Then I slowly worked my way up, tasting the slightly salty skin of his rock-hard shaft, tracing the path of the full blue veins that traversed his heated red flesh. I'd wanted to suck a man's dick for so very, very long. Don jumped when I tickled my tongue into the V of his glans.

"Keep going," he panted. "Kiss it. Let it know you want to be friends." He shivered as I wrapped my hand around his shaft and slid the skin back and forth. "Fuck, yeah."

I wanted to be good friends with Don's cock. I opened my mouth wide and sucked the velvety soft head in, slowly and tenderly, just the way he'd pulled me into his hot, wet mouth.

Don's whole body tensed.

"Stop!" he gasped, grabbing my head. "And stop sucking!"

I froze, holding myself perfectly still as he pulled himself free.

"Damn, boy," he panted. "I can't remember the last time one dick kiss brought me that close to coming."

"Thanks," I blushed, inordinately pleased with myself and my newfound cocksucking skills. I liked what I was doing. I loved the feel of his heavy cock on my tongue and the masculine taste and smell of his skin. When he told me it was OK, I cupped his ass and pulled him back into my mouth, letting the saliva run down my chin as I slurped and sucked and played to my heart's content with his wonderful human man-toy. Even making myself gag felt good in a weird sort of way. I kept teasing the back of my throat with his dick, a little bit, then more and more, seeing how much I could take, relishing the way Don groaned and his cock got even stiffer each time I gagged and my throat clenched around him.

I whimpered in frustration when he pulled back. His chest heaved as he moved down between my legs.

"You learn quick," he laughed shakily. He pulled my legs up, grabbing the pillow out from under my head and stuffing it under my butt. Then he reached under the table and pulled out a huge bottle of lube and a pile of rubbers. "Now it's my turn to play. You comfortable?"

"Yeah," I said nervously.

Don's eyes twinkled as he winked at me. "I'm going to stretch your hole open now." He shook his head as I shivered at his words. "Don't worry, it's not going to hurt. In fact, it's going to feel really good. When you want more, just grab your legs and pull them back toward your shoulders so you can open your ass up better for me."

I nodded, skeptically certain that I wouldn't be doing that. I jumped as the lube squirted into his hand, jerked again as his cool, slicked fingers brushed into my crack. In spite of myself, I moaned, instinctively pushing my ass towards him as he started massaging my asshole.

Don's fingers played my ass like a musical instrument, rubbing and stretching, loosening my sphincter until it fluttered against his fingertips. He looked me right in the eye, his grinning face framed by my upthrust cock and tight balls, and slid one finger slowly into my hole. I cried out, lifting my hips towards him, greedy for his touch, as he teased in and out, gradually pressing deeper, a second, then a third finger joining the first. When his other hand joined in, a lone digit pulling me firmly open in the other direction, I closed my eyes, grabbed my legs up tight to my shoulders, and spread my ass as wide as I could.

Don finger fucked me senseless, stretching me loose and open for his cock. I wallowed in the sensations flooding my asshole, writhing and panting as my dick oozed each time he massaged my prostate. I didn't open my eyes until his hands left me.

Don was sliding a rubber over his huge, hard, deep-red pole, slathering the latex with lube. He looked me straight in the eye as he squirted out another handful and pressed it up into my butt. I clamped down hard against his fingers.

Don shook his head at me. "Don't tighten, Michael. That will only make it hurt, and I'm going to fuck you now."

I nodded sheepishly. I wanted it. My asshole twitched with craving for him, but I was still embarrassingly afraid. Fortunately, Don seemed to pick up on that.

"Don't worry," he smiled. "I'll go slowly. There's no rush. Relax and let your body adjust to the feel of a good fuck. It's going to stretch and it's going to burn, and if you tighten up, it's going to hurt like hell." I shuddered as the head of his dick pressed against my asshole. "But no matter what, then it's going to feel great."

I gasped as Don's dick started in and my hole reluctantly stretched to accommodate him. His face was a tight grimace as one strong arm braced over me and the other directed his cock into my suddenly clenched sphincter.

"Damn, you're tight. Pull your legs back farther, and don't fight me, boy. Your ass lips are kissing my dick—they want to be fucked. Listen to them!"

I tried, concentrating on the feelings in my asshole, gasping at the stretch and the burn as Don slid in a tiny bit more. He wasn't pressing fast, but he wasn't backing off either. I lifted my head high and saw just the tip of Don's dick poking inside the ring of my hole. My guts clenched at the sight. Fuck, that looked hot! It was my favorite penetration scene, the one I so rarely saw in the pornies, when the top first slid in and the bottom gasped and opened for him. My asshole spasmed, reaching out. In that second, the head of Don's dick popped all the way in.

And the pain hit. I yelled, my eyes watering as my sphincter tightened around him like a rubber band and squeezed.

"Easy." Don's voice was soft and soothing as he leaned over and kissed me. He backed out slowly. Just as fast, he was right back in. It hurt, but not as much. My asshole couldn't clench quite as hard around him. He stroked in and out again and again. It took me a minute to realize he was going deeper each time.

The pain was more like a low burn now, stretching me open to take the iron hard shaft impaling me. Suddenly, my ass lips gave way, like they'd finally decided to quit fighting me. I watched in wonder as my stretching, burning asshole quivered one last time and Don's glistening red shaft slid all the way into my ass.

It was the hottest fuck shot I'd ever seen in my life. Even better, it was my butt hole being stretched full with a warm, living dick. I groaned as Don started fucking me—I mean, really deep-fucking me. My eyes fed each sensitized stroke and my asshole's hungry grasping kisses to my brain and cock, until I felt like I had to pee and my piss slit oozed man juice each time Don's shaft slid in deep. I jerked my precome-slicked foreskin over the head of my dick, the added sensation echoing down to my ass lips and back up again as I twitched in ecstasy.

"That's it, boy," Don gasped as he ground into me. "Beat off while I fuck you. It'll be a helluva come." He laughed as I wrapped my hand around my dick and pulled up hard, my fluttering asshole sucking him in deep. "Damn, you have a sweet pussy. You've opened up right nice for an uptight little straight boy."

I didn't care what I was. I wanted to be fucked, hard and long and rough. And Don was moving too slowly.

"Faster," I gasped. "Please." I groaned out loud as Don rabbit-punched into me a half-dozen times. My hand flew over my dick. I arched my ass up to him, opening myself as wide as I could. "Fuck me," I panted, loving the way the words rolled over my tongue, pleading for what my hungry asshole needed. "Fuck me, fuck me, fuck me, fuck me! Please!"

Don's laughter filled my ears as my body drew in on itself. The climax was starting deep in my guts, where his strong, thick cock was pounding the orgasm out of my joyspot. My balls crawled up my throbbing dick as Don's steel-hard shaft slid over my hypersensitive sphincter. My ass lips kissed him uncontrollably, begging for his touch.

Don shouted and ground into me, the fuck sensation surging through my prostate as I passed the point of no return and my ass clamped down tightly around him. I yelled as my dick spurted into my furiously pumping hands, and my whole body convulsed, my hot juice splatting onto my chest and into my open mouth and next to my ear. I thought I'd died and gone to heaven.

I could only watch, gasping like a landed fish, as Don pulled out, threw off the rubber, and shot his wad onto my belly. His grunts of satisfaction echoed in my ears as his dick emptied itself in thick pools of white cream covering my body. Don leaned over and rubbed his body over mine, my oversensitized dick jerking as he smeared our joined jizz together between us and collapsed on top of me.

He didn't move for a long time. I had no complaints. Don was taking most of his weight on his arms, and I was totally blissed out, my suddenly very tender—but very happy—little boy pussy winking and purring beneath me. I laughed as I realized I was no longer "bi-curious." I wanted to get fucked again—soon!

"What's so funny?" Don smiled, raising up over me, and planted a kiss on my lips.

"Me," I grinned, hugging him to me hard. "Thanks for making my first time great."

"My pleasure," he said.

"I had a mighty-fine time myself." I moaned, totally satisfied, as he sat up and our sticky cocks pulled apart.

While I was getting dressed, Don walked over to the entertainment center and rummaged around with the electronics. When I looked up again, he tossed a videotape into my hands.

"Only copy in the world, pal: *Straight Boy Vid Kid Loses His Virginity to the Studline Editor*. But if you ever want to check out the business, bring your demo here back to me, and I'll arrange some introductions. You're a natural."

I was too stunned to know what to say. Don gave me a quick hug on my way out the door. I hugged him back ferociously, wincing as my shirt moved over my sore and super-tender nipples. Then I was laughing again.

I laughed all the way home. I couldn't wait to watch the video. I knew it would always be the hottest thing I'd ever see. Maybe I'd break down and show it to Stan. Shoot, maybe I'd even show it to some of Stan's buddies. And maybe, just maybe, I'd take it back to Don, and let him show it to *his* friends.

A Night at El Gallo

by Bob Vickery

I wake up with a start, staring up at the inside of the packing crate I've been using as a makeshift coffin. It's something Bela Lugosi wouldn't be caught dead in; I think it once contained fluorescent tubes. But, hey, you use what's available.

I crawl out, a little groggy, shaking my head. Vaslo is sitting at the table by the window, reading an American newspaper. He's wearing Bermuda shorts and a shirt with green parrots on it. "Good evening," he says with his old-world formality.

I just grunt something as I climb to my feet and look at his outfit. "What'd you do, mug a Hawaiian tourist?"

Vaslo smiles his ironic smile. He's gained a few pounds of muscle since my escape from Van Helsing and our flight to Mexico a year ago, and it suits him. During the day, while I sleep in my box, he works out in the beat-up little gym down the street, pumping iron with the *chicos.* "I just thought I'd wear something a little tropical tonight," he says. He leans back in his chair and stretches. I note how his biceps bunch up, how the light accents his finely molded face and gleams on his slicked-back, jet-black hair. He looks at me and grins. "Are you ready for breakfast?"

"You have to ask?"

Vaslo removes his aloha shirt, then stands up, unzips his shorts, and lets them drop to the floor. Naked, he walks across the room toward me, slowly, letting me drink in the beauty of his muscular body. I sit on the floor, my back to the wall, waiting, my heart beating hard. His thick, spongy dick sways from side to side with every step he takes. He stands over me, hands on hips. I slide my hands up his thighs, across his hard belly and the furry mounds of his pecs, and I squeeze his nipples—not gently. Vaslo's grin loses some of its friendliness, and his dark eyes take on a wolfish gleam. His dick slowly lengthens and hardens. My belly growls with hunger; I feel ravenous, but I go slow, drawing out the moment. I bury my face in the fleshy folds of Vaslo's balls and breathe in their pungent scent. I think of the creamy sperm teeming inside this meaty, red pouch, and saliva pools in my mouth. Vaslo runs his fingers through my hair, and I part my lips. His balls spill into my mouth. I roll my tongue over them, sucking the loose sac, as Vaslo rubs his dick against my face. "Are you hungry, Joe?" he murmurs. "Would you like to feed?"

I say nothing, but simply look up at him, my mouth open, like a baby bird waiting for the fat worm of Vaslo's cock. He slides it between my lips, and I savor the feel of the tube of flesh filling my mouth, the push of the cock head against the back of my throat. My eyes stare into Vaslo's, and I probe into his mind, searching for the pleasure center. I find it and give a little mental twist. Vaslo sighs loudly, and his body shudders under my touch. It's a special gift that vampires of my sort—the sperm eaters—have, a kind of telepathy that can send waves of pleasure into the minds of the men who feed us. Vaslo begins pumping his hips now, slowly at first, then with a quickening tempo. I fuck his brain like he fucks my mouth, pushing a throb of pleasure into him with each thrust of his cock. Soon Vaslo becomes drunk with pleasure, his eyes wide and crazed, his breath broken into sharp gasps. I play him like a virtuoso plays his instrument, taking him to the brink of orgasm, pulling him back again at the last moment, only to take him even closer to the edge. Finally, I decide it's time, and at the next thrust of his dick, I give a sharp, hard mental jab to his brain that triggers his orgasm. Vaslo cries out, and his cock pulses in my mouth as I flood his brain with pleasure. The hot sperm squirts across my tongue, and now I join Vaslo in his ecstasy, drinking thirstily, tasting the sweet, salty flavor of his load. Vaslo whips his head up, and his body squirms in my arms. I continue to suck on his cock, draining the last few precious drops like a baby sucking on his mother's tit. Strength pours into my body. I take his dick out of my mouth and look up at Vaslo. Grinning, I say, "Damn! Nice and spicy!"

Vaslo grins back. "I wanted to give you something with an extra kick. I've been eating jalapeños all day."

We collect ourselves and sit at the table awhile as Vaslo drinks shots of tequila. He tells me how his day went. Music floats in through the open window from the cantina across the street, occasionally punctuated by laughter and shouting. After a few minutes of this, I discretely clear my throat. "We better get going," I say. Sperm-eating vampires need several feedings before their hunger is curbed. Vaslo knows this, and he accepts it without jealousy—as long as I always start with him.

Vaslo takes a sip of tequila, looking at me over the rim of his glass. "I heard of a place today, from some of the *chicos* at the gym. It sounded...promising." He refuses to tell me more. "Let it be a surprise," he says, sidestepping any questions, "a special treat for dessert."

We start off the evening at the botanical gardens. Vaslo waits by the kiosk next to the entrance as I walk down the narrow path among the giant ferns and palms. The men who cruise here know me well, know the body-wrenching orgasms I can give them, and they vie eagerly for my attention. I pick one from the crowd whom I haven't tried before: a muscular day laborer with a broad peasant's face. In a matter of minutes I'm kneeling in front of him, and his thick, curved dick fills my mouth like a kielbasa sausage. My fingers grip his smooth, hard ass cheeks as he plows my face with his cock. I probe into his mind, find his pleasure center, and push hard. "Santa Maria," he gasps as his warm, thick load, tasting of *frijoles* and beer, floods into my mouth.

Vaslo and I cruise the city, occasionally pausing while I drain the load from some young man we chance upon in an alley or along the waterfront or sitting in an open window on some deserted street. Sometimes Vaslo joins in, kneeling beside me, taking turns sucking the offered cock just to keep me company. Other times he stands to the side, watching, or waits farther down the street until I'm done. A little after midnight, Vaslo takes me by the elbow and hails a cab. "Now for something special," he says.

He leans forward and murmurs an address in the cabbie's ear. I lean back in the seat, watching the city speed by. After a long stretch of darkness, we come upon a square that blazes with light. We pay the cabbie and climb out.

We're in some kind of honky-tonk stretch of cantinas and strip joints. Vaslo looks around until he spots a pale blue cement building sporting a neon sign that blinks the words "El Gallo."

"There it is," he says. Loud music pours from the open door. He walks inside, and after a couple of beats I follow him.

The place is a single room, hazy with cigarette smoke, with a small stage in the front. A skinny boy with a dick like a garden hose dances slowly, pumping his hips to the rhythm of the rock guitar that is playing over the sound system. Men fill the room, sitting at the tables that ring the stage, shouting to each other over the music and mostly ignoring the dancer. We take a table by the stage.

A server comes up, and Vaslo orders a beer for himself. He glances at his watch. "It's almost 1 A.M.," he says. "Time for the headliner." I glance at the boy on the stage. In spite of the size of his dick, I don't find him attractive, and I let my mind wander, looking idly around the room. It's a diverse crowd: locals, a few soldiers, some gringo tourists. One table is surrounded by a group of young sailors wearing the uniform of the German navy. After a few minutes, the music stops, and the dancer walks off the stage.

I can feel a change in the room, a certain kind of charged attention. The men crowded at the tables have stopped talking and their eyes are trained on the stage. "And now, gentlemen..." a voice says in Spanish over the loudspeaker, "please welcome Miguel." A song starts playing, something slow and bluesy. The lights go out, and then a spot is trained on the stage. A man is standing there, dressed simply in a loose-fitting white shirt and dark chinos with snaps that run along the length of each leg. He has a powerful body, with broad shoulders and a tight, muscled torso that tapers down to narrow hips. The light makes his crisp black curls gleam, accentuating the features of his face: the wide, sensual mouth, the strong nose, the dark, deep-set eyes. Swaying his body, Miguel slowly unbuttons his shirt and then shrugs it off. He bends down and undoes the snaps along his legs, and with a quick tug yanks his pants off and lets them drop. He stands there on the stage, naked except for his socks, his muscled body slick with a light sheen of sweat, his hard dick sticking out. I stir in my seat, leaning forward to get a better view. Vaslo smiles, but says nothing.

The music stops suddenly, and the house lights go up. Miguel stands there, shoulders back, hands half-curled into fists, his cock jutting straight out. His eyes slowly scan the audience.

"This is where it gets interesting," Vaslo leans forward and whispers. "According to my friends, every night he picks a volunteer from the audience and fucks him on the stage in front of everyone." His grin widens. "It's considered an honor to be the one selected."

Miguel's eyes move from man to man. For a brief moment they lock with mine. He holds my gaze and raises one eyebrow. I smile and shake my head. He glances at Vaslo and then back at me again. I shake my head a second time. Miguel finally picks one of the German sailors, a young blond man no more than 19 or 20, with the face of a choirboy. The sailor shakes his head, blushing furiously, but his buddies won't hear of it. Laughing, they pull him out of his chair and push him toward Miguel. Smiling, Miguel takes him by the hand and leads him onto the stage while the audience shouts and claps their approval.

Madonna's "Erotica" starts playing. Miguel kisses the blond sailor lightly, playfully, as he pulls the boy's uniform off. Soon they are both standing naked on the stage. The sailor's body is lean and pale under the harsh glow of the spot. His cock juts out, candy-pink and fully hard, topped by blond pubic fuzz. Miguel wraps his hand around both their dicks and strokes them slowly. He turns and grins at the audience, who applaud again. The blond sailor smiles shyly, blushing and embarrassed, but clearly enjoying the exhibitionistic thrill of it all. I find the perverse innocence of this scene wildly erotic.

Miguel bends down and pulls a condom packet and a small bottle of lube from his sock. He tears the package open and slowly rolls the condom down the shaft of his dick. He squirts a heavy dollop of lube onto his hand and smears it into the ass crack of the blond sailor, who leans forward, hands on knees, to give Miguel easier access. Miguel positions himself behind the boy and slides his hard dick up and down the length of the sailor's crack. The sailor's body squirms under Miguel's hands, and he pushes his hips against Miguel's crotch. Miguel grins broadly, his white teeth flashing in his dark face. Dick in hand, he pokes his cock head against the sailor's asshole and then enters him slowly, inch by inch. The blond boy groans loudly, and his buddies shout out words of encouragement. When Miguel's dick is buried to the hilt in the sailor's ass, he stops and holds that position, as if presenting a tableau for the audience: the two men joined together, Miguel's dark, muscular body—a sharp contrast with the pale skin of the German.

Miguel begins pumping his hips, slowly at first, drawing his dick out almost to the head and then plunging it back into the sailor's ass. His tempo gradually quickens, and it doesn't take long before he's giving the sailor a serious ass pounding, his dick thrusting hard up the boy's ass, his balls slapping against the boy's pink flesh. My table is right next to the stage, and I can take in every detail: the slide of Miguel's dick in and out of the sailor's asshole, the furious strokes the sailor gives his own cock, the slapping sound of flesh on flesh, the sharp, pungent smell of sweat and sex. The sailor is bent over, his face inches from mine, his eyes squeezed shut. Suddenly, he opens his eyes, and his gaze meets mine. I stroke his face, and then without thinking lean forward, seize his head in both my hands, and kiss him. The sailor's lips meet mine eagerly, and his tongue thrusts into my mouth just as Miguel's dick thrusts up his ass. I reach over and twist his nipples, and the sailor cries out, his voice muffled by my mouth on his. Miguel croons to him in Spanish, his eyes feverish, sweat pouring down his face, his body gleaming with it. Madonna's voice rises high and clear through the room, engulfing us as the sailor's tongue plays with mine, and Miguel continues the serious business of giving this boy the ass pounding he so obviously wants. I break away and stare into the boy's eyes, probing his mind. When I find his pleasure center, I give a push.

The sailor's body trembles under my hands, and he gives a long, trailing groan. "Are you going to shoot?" I ask him. He nods. "Then give your load to me!" I say fiercely. The boy nods a second time and stands up. I climb out of my chair and onto the stage, and slide my lips down his cock just as the first squirt of come throbs out. The sailor cries out as I suck thirstily, his sweet, young load flooding into my mouth, intoxicating me. His body spasms convulsively, wrenched by the orgasm and the pounding Miguel is still giving him.

Miguel pulls out and walks to the edge of the stage. He whips off the condom and shoots his load out into the audience, laughing. I open my mouth and catch a few stray drops, like coins being tossed from a Mardi Gras float.

Vaslo and I don't leave the club until after 4 in the morning. By the time our taxi deposits us at our doorstep, the eastern sky has lightened to pale gray. We race up the steps. I have just enough time to crawl inside my box. I give Vaslo a quick kiss. "Thank you, my friend," I murmur. "It was a special night." Vaslo smiles back. His smile is the last thing I see before I pull the box lid over me and sink into dreamless sleep.

Heads and Tails
by M. Christian

"Suck it," he told me, and so I did. Willingly, eagerly. I opened my mouth, pushed out my lips and took his swollen cock head in. It would have been nice to say it was a sweet candy cane, but let's be realistic. It tasted like hard cock. A good hard cock, but a cock nonetheless: salt, the bitter bite of precome, the shit tinge you always get down there, the musky reek of hormones, of excitement.

A good taste, a damned fine taste. A cock taste—and I tried to get every inch of it, and him, down my throat. I've sucked my share, some even bigger than this great beast filling my mouth, but for me—then, there—it was the only cock in the world.

I sucked him as he moaned. I was not the first, definitely not the last, to play the skin flute—a bad metaphor in its original antique context, but a favorite with my twist: yes, lips around. Yes, I was sucking and not blowing. But I really *was* playing him, applying my lips and making lovely music escape from him.

And what beautiful tunes I was making him perform: moans, groans, sighs, hisses—the entire scales of pleasure. I couldn't do my own singing, of course, with his instrument tickling the back of my throat, but I did hum and moan a bit in accompaniment.

Then it was time to stop—slowly, I opened my jaws even wider and let his hard cock slide free, the thick head popping up from my throat, glancing off my teeth, past the roughness, playfulness of my flickering tongue and then out. Shimmering, gleaming with a dribble of precome and lots of my spit, he came free, tapping against my nose with his strength, the iron of his shaft.

"Time to toss it, boy," he said, grinning wide and wonderfully mean.

• • •

Dancing in the light, twirling around and around, a sparkling bit of silver in the twilight room. Fast, so fast, he reached out and caught it—snatching the coin before he even fell past my eyes. A slap against his burly forearms. A peak under his hand, seeing the side—but showing me nothing but a wicked grin. "Tails."

I returned the smile, wiping my mouth free of my come-sucking drool. Keeping my eyes on his, relishing the hunger in his gray irises, I reached over and gently took up the bottle of baby oil.

Then I wasn't facing him—but rather a white wall, a small expanse of eggshell. I knew, soon enough, that I'd be memorizing, registering every crack, every deformation. I would never be able to look at that small spot of wall without thinking of what would come next.

Ass high, I offered myself to him—no, I gave him my asshole. He had the rest of me, or could have as much as me as he wanted, but I knew all he wanted right then was my asshole. I'd heard the compliments, so I showed my hole to him with pride—"a pink delicacy," "a fuckable rosebud," "such a pretty fuck-hole," and so much more.

His hand on my ass—hot, rough, strong. Just, at first, holding me, gripping one of my cheeks. Preparatory, a way he shakes hands with the ass he's going to fuck. Then a gentle pressure around that "wondrous asshole"—a slow, steady pressure around my "delicate hole"—and I know that he's in me. A finger, at first, but still he's within me. It feel good—a gentle invasion. Good, but not great—and so I growl, feral and hungry, demanding something greater, more powerful, more feral.

And he delivers. Up the gradient of sensation—passing the tickling entry of that finger and beyond...beyond even my own fingers, my own toys. He is not just big, he is not just huge. He is beyond all of that—and all of that is now beyond the lips of my asshole, deep within me.

And so he fucks me. God, yes, he fucks me—in and out, a fucking, two-stroke engine of cock and legs, balls slapping against my ass. I can feel his hot invasion, his piston-stroke hammering deep inside me. I don't do it often, but I do it then—hot tears rolling down my cheeks, burning me. But they are not sadness leaking. No, they are tears of wonderful pain, wonderful suffering. It's a good kind of hurt, the sexy hurt of being fucked good and hard.

Then it's over, but not with the usual curtain call. No, this time it doesn't conclude with his hot come in the hot recesses of me. No, he pulls free long before that, long before the come boils free of his great big hairy balls.

• • •

Again, the shimmering ascent of the coin—a twirling dance in the dim light of my bedroom. For the first time I notice the denomination and feel a delightful wave of shame that I'm worth only five cents.

He doesn't show me the side the coin lands on, after he slaps it silly on his arm. Instead, he rolls back onto his wonderfully tight ass, showing me his rock-hard cock—and such a cock it is. I know where it's been, my asshole still throbbing from its absence, but that doesn't take away my hunger for it.

An echo, a touch of déjà vu: "Suck it."

So I do, taking his thick cock into my hungry mouth. It didn't taste like shit—but then I wasn't in a position to really tell, or care. All that mattered was my mouth was around his cock, his head down my throat, his hairy balls tickling my chin. All was right in the world: I was sucking on my lord's cock.

I was somewhere else, lost in the sensation of his thick shaft sliding in and out of my mouth, fucking my tonsils, screwing my throat. I was lost, hovering beyond it all, in a place of pure lust and driving, hammering love. Distantly, I was aware my cock was throbbing, hard, and that my feverish hand was jamming up and down along it. It felt good—that was sure—but his cock down my throat felt even better.

Then, Jesus, he came—my Master, my Lover. He came. At first I thought it was just part of my sucking, the twitching that flowed up and down his throbbing cock, but then he started to fill my throat, up into my mouth—his hot, salty jizz, his steaming come. I swallowed and swallowed and swallowed some more, sucking his sticky come down my throat as I massaged him, squeezed his shaft with my mouth.

Sometime during this I came too—jetting onto the sheets, my own orgasm quaking my knees, pulling myself free of his gleaming cock, to fall, panting, onto the sheets.

After a point, we slept, curled up in my tiny bed—a warm embrace of spent bodies—with just the tiny cool spot of a coin, pressed against my chest, to remind me of why were we sleeping.

Virgin in the Bathhouse
by Grant Mather

I had just moved to Seattle, where I was going to start my second year at university. I had heard about a place I was dying to try out, a notorious bathhouse in the city. Fairly shy and just 19, I was still cherry as far as gay sex went. I had fooled around with a few girls, but found it not to my liking. I knew deep down inside what I liked, and going to a bathhouse, I hoped, would provide what my shyness had prevented me from experiencing thus far.

I had my mind blown, not to mention my young, aching cock. And much more. It was a wild night, one I couldn't possibly ever forget. It began as I was buzzed inside a locked door, a towel and condoms handed to me along with my room key. I had no idea what to expect, other than what I had read in a gay travel guide. There was supposed to be a sauna, showers, steam room, video room, and guys, guys, guys.

There was a maze of cubicles, and on my way through the dimly lit hallways to find my room, I passed by an open doorway and spotted my first bare ass. I stopped dead in my tracks and gawked. On a small mattress sprawled a guy totally naked, on his belly with his legs spread, providing a perfect view of his butt. I didn't even see his face. All I could focus on was that naked ass, spread out and seemingly available. It was round and sexy and wide open. My cock sprang to instant attention, and I nearly dropped everything and leaped into the small room to cop a feel of that ass.

I managed to tear myself away and find my own room a few doors down. I was fumbling for the key when at least four different guys sauntered past wearing nothing but towels. I supposed that was the dress code for the bathhouse. I shut the door while I undressed in the small cubicle, which had nothing but a locker and a small single bed with a sheet and pillow on it. I could barely turn around in the small floor space. I stripped, my cock stiff and throbbing. I wrapped the towel around my hips and attempted to hide my big boner, then had to laugh. What was I there for? Sex. A hard cock wasn't likely to be a taboo there.

Techno music reverberated through the narrow halls as I left my room and tentatively set off to explore. I only made it about a dozen yards. I passed one open doorway where someone was leaning back under the room's garish light while whacking off and staring out at me. My eyes zeroed in on his huge, spit-slick meat before I hurried off, bumping into an almost naked guy, feeling his hot skin against mine briefly before we both moved in opposite directions. The next doorway that was open did me in. I peered inside to see another guy on his belly, naked. He was looking back at me, and he smiled, which surprised me. I managed a shaky grin back.

"Like what you see, cutie?" He whispered huskily.

I hesitated a second or two, but the sight of a hard, big ass spread out in front of me, obviously being offered up for the taking, reeled me in like a hook at the end of a fishing line. I didn't quite manage to say anything as I moved into the room beside him, but with shaky hands, I reached right out and clutched the beautiful butt in front of me.

"Shut the door," he said. He seemed much more relaxed than I was. I obeyed, still keeping one of my hands on that ass, not quite believing I was actually feeling a hot butt. I turned back to him and put both hands on his ass cheeks, mesmerized by the hefty feel of them. He had his light dimmed, and once I got used to the illumination, I noticed his skin was deep brown; he was probably Latino. My hands were nervous as I ran them over the hard butt mounds, exploring and squeezing and loving every second of it. I pulled apart his hairless brown cheeks and caught sight of his asshole, my eyes going wide. The wrinkled pucker twitched, and he raised his ass to meet my hands, spreading his thighs wider.

"Go ahead, feel it," he whispered.

I was staring down at that hole when he suggested I touch it. My hands moved of their own accord. My fingers grazed the brown button, the silky lips pouting and then parting. One fingertip poked at it, and then suddenly slid inside like a knife into butter. It was lubed! My finger dove in past the second knuckle—warm, palpating flesh caressing it. I had my finger up a butt hole for the first time. I felt faint; the air was sweltering due to the saunas and all. I just couldn't quite believe I was there with my finger up a greased butt hole, and with a stranger I had never met.

A part of me thought I should ask his name, but then I suddenly felt my towel being pulled off and a hand gripping my stiff cock. "Oh, man, yeah..." I stuttered out as that hand stroked me slowly.

I looked over, and the guy was grinning up at me, his head and upper body half-turned towards me. He was good-looking, and was definitely Latino with short dark hair and bowed lips. His hand was rubbing up and down my suddenly exposed cock appreciatively.

"Nice meat, nice body, you're quite the cute little stud," he crooned while playing with my hard boner. I was thrusting into his hand and shoving my finger as deep up his greased hole as I could. I had never been hotter, and my legs were shaking so bad I wasn't sure I could continue standing.

He was quick, grabbing a condom from the small shelf beside the bed and ripping it open, then wrapping my stiff bone immediately after. I had no time to contemplate his intentions before his head moved and he swooped down to envelop my cock in his wet, burning mouth. I shrieked, and nearly fell on top of him. He grabbed my hips with one hand and my balls with the other and held me inside his sucking mouth. The twirling tongue and vacuuming cheeks were miraculous. My finger was busy jamming in and out of his squishy butt hole, and my hands were groping his hard butt while I was huffing like a madman.

It took all of about two minutes for me to blow my wad. I grunted and fell on top of him, come filling the condom over my meat as he sucked me to heaven.

"Thanks, pal. See you around," I heard as my rod slipped from that warm cavern and the guy beneath me rolled over. My finger reluctantly slid out of his hot ass-furnace, and I stood up to gaze down at him. I had no idea of bathhouse etiquette, but I could figure out that he was dismissing me. I gave him a shaky grin before grabbing my towel and departing.

I found the showers through the maze of rooms and stood under steaming water contemplating my recent sexual encounter, my first blow job and first ass-groping. There were another few men in the showers, checking me out with either furtive or bold glances. A couple had hard cocks and were stroking them, right there in the open. I was already getting horny again.

I left the shower and moved off down another hallway. There were doors open, and men in various positions under bright or dimmed lights. Every time I saw a bare ass or a hard cock I got hotter and more excited. Somehow I found myself in a darkened room at the end of a hallway. At one end a large television screen dominated the wall. My eyes grew accustomed to the light, and I noticed there were rows of wooden benches along the opposite wall. There were about five guys seated or standing in the room. I looked up to see a trio of blacks on the screen going at it. Huge, black cocks went up tight, black assholes. I heard moans, and at first thought they were from the porn flick, then realized they were coming from two of the guys standing against one wall. A tall blond had his hands against the wall, and a shorter blond was behind him. They were fucking! Right there in the open!

I had never seen anything like it. I had watched a few porn films, and of course looked through gay magazines, but this was the actual thing. Both guys were young and looked in fairly good shape, their muscles tensed as the one behind thrust his hips forward into the butt of the other. They were moaning, and sighing, in rhythm to a steady pumping from the one behind. I could smell sweaty sex.

I stood and watched like a lusty voyeur, which I was. The two got wilder and wilder, the one behind banging the other with deeper and harder strokes. One of the men seated got up and joined them, groping both of them all over with his hands while they fucked themselves to loud, grunting orgasms. I observed from the doorway breathlessly until it was over.

I stumbled from the room and back down hallways where it seemed almost every door was open and there were naked men and hard rods and wide-spread cans. I couldn't get my own sexual encounter out of my mind, that guy spread out there with his butt up and waiting for someone to come in his room and play with it. And the two guys fucking like rabbits in the video room. I suddenly knew what I really wanted, wanted more than anything else.

I found my own room and staggered to my bed. I left the door open and the light on. I lay on the bed on my stomach with my head turned so I could watch the doorway. I spread my legs, discarding my towel. I was completely naked. I could hardly believe I was doing it! But it felt so sexy, so hot to be lying there like that, not knowing what was going to happen next, or with whom. My normal shyness made the situation even more exciting. It was something I could not have imagined myself doing before that moment.

A couple guys passed my room, glancing in. One halted, his eyes fastened on my naked ass. I felt so vulnerable, my cock got harder and stiffer under my belly, and I unconsciously rolled my hips as I rubbed my meat into the mattress beneath me. That must have been the signal the watcher was waiting for. He barged in, closing the door behind him.

I was nervous, this sudden stranger closed in with me, no words spoken. He was bigger than me, over six feet tall, and very muscular. Handsome too. He had dark eyes and thick brown hair in a mop cut above his ears. Those eyes met mine, piercing and penetrating. I could see the lust there, and then he licked his lips, and I knew he was hot for me. That thought was enough for me. I opened my thighs like a slut and nodded my head, my throat too constricted to speak. I was offering myself, blatantly, naked on my belly with my legs spread. Nothing I had ever experienced before had been so thrilling.

He didn't smile, but he let out a big sigh and dropped his towel to the floor. I saw a huge boner twitching at his waist, and imagined it going up my butt, which is what I wanted more than anything right then.

"Fuck me with that thing!" I heard my own strangled plea. I was shocked at myself, but the heat of the place—all the naked men, the smell of sweat and sex that seemed to pervade the atmosphere—was unleashing my deepest desires, forcing my inhibitions to disappear like mist.

"You got it. I could fuck such a sweet ass forever," he said, his voice deep to match the breadth of his brawny chest. I stared at his cock, so big and hard that my thighs trembled and I licked my lips. He was already rolling a condom over it while I watched with fascinated eyes.

"Got any lube?" He asked.

Lube? Then I recalled that the night attendant had given me a small tube of the stuff when I entered. I fumbled on the tiny shelf and found it, offering it to him with trembling hands. He grinned, and I returned a weak one of my own.

"I got a big one. Can you take it?" he asked, rubbing glistening lube up and down the stiff prong. I stared at it, not answering at once. I wanted it, but I had a cherry butt hole, and I imagined it might hurt like hell to have something that large up me. The thought of pain did not deter me, though. I was much too aroused.

"I've never been fucked, but I can take it," I murmured, slightly embarrassed.

He laughed, although he was still rubbing up and down with his lube-coated fingers. "I'll take it easy. How about I finger your asshole first?"

I nodded my head and spread my thighs wider. He was staring down at my ass, and the greedy look in his eyes had me even more worked up. He reached out with one big hand and grabbed me. As soon as that big paw seized my butt cheek so firmly and confidently, my shivering abruptly subsided. I felt as if I was all at once melting, as if I was becoming a passive, willing hole for the taking. His fingers slid right into my crack, feeling around, searching and finding my pulsing butt hole. I sighed as he rubbed the outer edges of the sensitive button with that lubed fingertip. I sighed deeper and laid my face down on the pillow as that finger slid inside me.

It was so strange, I went completely limp, which was probably why that finger glided so easily up me. I felt like a small, hard snake was teasing my guts. I threw my thighs wider and sank into the mattress, moaning loudly as if I was already being fucked.

He frigged me in and out with that finger, then added another. That I definitely felt as my butt lips were expanded and my fuck-tunnel was massaged from the inside. I lay there and took it with slobbering moans. I felt him climbing up on top of me. The heavy, warm weight of his thighs went between mine, parting them farther. I allowed it, and lifted my ass to meet the hard pole that poked into my crack. His fingers were still slithering in and out of my asshole, stretching it deliciously, causing my guts to ache and my balls to tighten. I hoped his cock would feel as good.

The fingers slid out. I felt the blunt head of his cock pressing at my greased ass entrance. I wanted it so bad, I just pushed back and impaled myself on it. A huge knob entered me, stretching me so far apart I wondered if I was going to tear in two. It hurt for only a nanosecond, then it was sheer bliss. I was getting filled with big, hard cock! I felt as if I was stuffed full, as if that cock head was as big as a baseball bat.

"I'm in, I'm going deeper—oh, man, what a sweet fucking tight hole!" He groaned above me, his breathing rapid. His body was heavy over mine.

I loved the weight; I loved the feel of his big hands as they gripped my waist and he held me still so he could shove his cock deeper. "Oh yeah, yeah, bury your cock!" I grunted, wiggling my butt in an effort to get more of him in me. I was enflamed; I wanted to be pounded and rammed and stuffed with cock.

He obliged, slowly at first, feeding me his huge meat an inch at a time, then withdrawing, then going deeper. I squirmed and wiggled my butt, stretching my asshole open through my gyrations, loosening it so I could take more and more. I had dreamed of this moment, not quite knowing what to expect. It was much more than I had hoped for. The heat of his body over mine, the way he moaned, the feel of his stiff thing inside me, the mashing of my prostate and the tender squishing of my cock underneath us all combined into a rapture I wanted to last forever.

He began to fuck me full force after a few minutes of teasing. I lay there and took it eagerly, his big body drilling down into mine while I squealed and even laughed. I was practically hysterical. His sweat dripped all over my back and neck, and then he lay right over me and held me and pounded his hips into my willing butt.

I was coming. Jizz was drooling out between my belly and the mattress. My asshole was twitching around his driving meat.

"I'm shooting in your ass!" I heard through the fog of my draining orgasm.

I had been fucked. I lay there exhausted as he crawled off me. He looked down at me and smiled. I looked back at him and didn't say a word. He reached out and gently caressed my naked, just-fucked butt.

"You got a beautiful ass. How about a second round later?"

I blinked and stared up at him. He wanted more?

"My name is Dylan." He was still smiling.

"Mine is Grant. Come back later. I'll be waiting," I replied finally, his hand still stroking my butt.

He left me there. The night was young, I realized. And he was going to fuck me again later. I grinned and lay back to think it all over. It was the best night of my life.

The Sordid Life

by Jay Starre

I waved goodbye to the other lawyers and secretaries as I entered the elevator on Friday night, and without a second thought my coworkers returned my pleasant, bland smile.

One hour later I was facing my wall-length mirror in the bedroom and offering that identical smile to my reflection. Off came the tie, the dress shirt, the perfect navy-blue suit slacks. I faced myself in my underwear. Underneath that suit had lurked my gym-buffed body. I had worked out like a fiend that morning at 6 A.M. in the office gym in preparation for that night. I flexed my biceps, and my smile broadened, hinting at the wickedness concealed behind my soft grey eyes. I stripped naked, stroking my cock into a stiff boner, licking my lips and winking at myself. I laughed out loud as I dressed—no underwear, a pair of skin-tight jeans with rips in the knees—and as I turned to stare at my reflection, I made a couple of rips in the right places to offer a glimpse of my pale-white butt cheeks. A stained green T-shirt, taut across my large pecs and bulging biceps, a pair of dark work boots with heavy black soles, and then the final touch, a dark baseball cap placed backward.

The transformation was complete. Even my neatly trimmed goatee suddenly seemed to have become scruffy as I leered at myself and stuck my tongue out to take a sensuous swipe across my pursed lips. I was ready.

Another half-hour and I was at the Torpedo. At 8 o'clock the place was deserted, the doorman appraising me with a wink and a thorough cruise of my well-revealed body. I didn't mind that no one was there; I knew what lay ahead, a sordid night of sucking and fucking if I had my way. The anticipation itself was arousing, and my cock was rock-hard beneath my jeans just upon entering the nightclub. I went upstairs to one of the numerous bars, one that was out of the way and sure to be deserted.

"What'll it be, stud?" the young tender smirked, winking and leaning over the bar to stare up into my eyes. *"Fuck me"* was written all over the cute little blond.

I leered back, already in character as I suddenly leaped over the counter and dropped to my knees in front of the startled bartender. "What the hell! What if someone comes in…? Oh shit!" He groaned as I ripped open his fly and fished out his cock, slurping it up into my hot mouth and tongue-bathing it furiously.

The music pounded around us as I knelt on the floor and sucked cock like a depraved slut. The poor barkeep was caught between his lust and his fear as he moaned and thrusted an instantly erect tool deep into my willing mouth. I sucked him all the way in, feeling his meat throb and pulse around my throat and tongue. I vacuum-sucked, ticking his balls at the same time. He humped my face and swore while looking around frantically for the approach of any customers. He was lucky: No one arrived before he suddenly let out a yelp, and I knew he was about to come. I pulled his twitching cock out of my mouth the instant before he erupted. I shoved it back into his pants and held it there while he shook all over and come filled his underwear.

"Thanks, I'll have a beer." I laughed, rising and grinning in his face. I wiped my mouth and then, while he stared at me with a stunned look, planted a sloppy kiss on his pretty lips.

"It's on the house," he said, managing a shaky smile after I had clambered back over the counter. A pair of flamboyant queens arrived just then, and I left with a wink and a grin.

That was a good start to a sleazy night, but the taste of that hard pipe in my mouth was definitely getting me hot for more action. I wandered the various rooms—the place was huge with three floors—and checked out the few brave souls who had arrived early. I caught the eye of one older guy sitting alone in the corner, a tough guy by his leather look: dark vest and gleaming aviator cap. I nodded, nursing my beer bottle like it was a stiff pecker and then heading for the nearby bathroom. He followed.

I went into a stall and turned to face the half-open door. Leather-guy was there. He came inside and we stared into each other's eyes. He was in his late 30s, grizzled beard, big body, dark eyes, handsome. I groped my crotch, then slowly unzipped, pulling out my swollen meat.

"Suck me," I said. He laughed, but I merely leaned back against the wall, straddling the toilet and pumped my cock up into a drooling spear. The big thing was too tempting, and he went for it. He was leaning over and slurping on it before I said another word. I gripped his shoulders, wide and strong beneath his T-shirt, and held him against my waist.

He suckled me like a calf at the teat. Wet lips and a vibrating tongue went up and down my shaft and nuzzled at my balls. I leaned back and closed my eyes, letting him pull down my pants and grope my butt while he sucked me with his big lips and busy tongue. Spittle dribbled around my nuts and down my thighs. My pants were around my knees and he was digging at my butt crack as he gurgled noisily around my stiff meat. I heard someone come in the can, but I ignored whoever it was. Straddling the toilet, hearing someone using the urinal, and gripping Mister Leather's broad shoulders as he slurped and licked my cock brought me to the brink quickly enough. When I knew I was about to blow, I yanked my meat out and lifted him up, shoving my erupting cock up under his T-shirt and sliming his stomach. I filled his shirt with come. "No need to thank me," I said.

He was grinning as I disengaged finally and pulled up my pants. He was a good sport.

That had the ache in my balls alleviated for a bit at least. It had taken longer in the bathroom than I had thought, and the place was beginning to fill up. On the main floor there was already a crowd on the dance floor, most of them without shirts and writhing to the beat of techno-pop. I joined them, sliding into the center of the male mass of flesh, pulling off my own shirt and discarding it against a wall on the floor. It took only a few minutes of gyrating to the music to work up a sweat, especially as others joined the crowd and we inevitably began to jostle one another in the confined space.

I bumped up against a young dude, who turned and grinned at me with beer-hazed eyes. Those eyes traveled up and down my naked chest appreciatively, and settled on my bulging crotch. He winked at me and turned around, managing to bump his butt into my hips as he continued dancing.

He hadn't recognized me, but I knew him at once. He was a junior lawyer in the firm, new since the spring. There was no way he would have thought the sleazy, shirtless, baseball-capped stud he was leering at would also be a lawyer at the firm. I had to laugh, then decided to have some fun. I realized the young pup was dancing alone, just as I was. His back was turned to me, but his butt was grinding in circles and he had his face half-turned so he could see me out of the corner of his eyes.

I moved in and began to dance right behind him. When he writhed backward, I humped forward, "accidentally" slamming into his butt with my crotch. He moved closer. I gripped his sweaty, naked shoulders and began to dance with him, grinding my crotch into his tight little ass. He leaned back against my neck and closed his eyes, writhing against me in a haze of beer and music and sweat.

My cock wasn't quite ready for action yet, but it swelled enough to give my little lawyer friend a thrill. With him leaning back into me and grinding his ass as if he was getting fucked right there on the dance floor in front of all those other guys, I decided he was ripe for a lewder scene. I turned him around and held him against me as we continued dancing. I dropped one hand to his crotch and found a stiff bone beneath his jeans. His mouth moved in the semblance of a deep moan, which I couldn't hear over the blaring music. I gripped his cock and began to massage it through the material of his pants. He shuddered and wiggled against me, squeezing my tits with both hands and humping the air as I stroked him harder and harder while the music reached its pounding crescendo.

I felt his cock pulsing in orgasm right through his pants, and then the material getting wet with spume. He was shuddering against me, almost collapsing. I held him up just long enough for his orgasm to subside, then with a light kiss on the lips, I abandoned him to the 50 other naked men oblivious to it all.

I'd had my fun, but now I was definitely getting horny again. When the young dude had shot his load, my own cock had fully stiffened. All the hot men I was shoving my way through only intensified my lust. I worked my way upstairs, passing men who gawked at my naked chest and pressed into me, staring into my eyes, winking, smelling like excited animals in heat. A darkened corridor, the only light coming from a dim bulb in the ceiling: The openings on each end were filled with groping men, some half-naked like me, others with their pants down and their cocks out, stroking or sucking or even fucking.

Then I felt a body pressing into me from behind. I turned, staring at a vaguely familiar face in the dimness. It was dancing boy; the young lawyer had followed me. *All right,* I thought.

I leaned over and whispered in his ear, swiping at it with my tongue at the same time. "I'm gonna fuck you. Bend over."

He managed to whisper back, "Got a condom?" before I turned him in my arms and pulled him back against my crotch.

"And lube," I answered. Then I was undoing his pants and pulling them down. Others surrounded us, lost in their own diversions; others passed by, staring as I shoved Young Law's pants and underwear down with one hand and slid the other into his sweaty ass crack. I found his asshole right away, slick and welcoming. I fingered it while I played with his cock, still sticky with come but rising right back up. I kissed his neck as I took a condom from my pocket and wrapped my cock with it. I pinched open a tube of lube and squirted the whole thing up into his crack, then rubbed it in with my fingers, all around his quivering butt hole and then down to his balls and then up between his thighs and over his stiffening joint. He was leaning back into me exactly like when we had been dancing before, putty in my hands. I bent him over, poked my hard cock against his slippery slot and began to work it in. The small opening fluttered and spasmed, then gaped open to allow my fat cock head inside. The convulsing ass lips massaged my meat as I slowly impaled his butt.

I fucked him like that, with his pants around his ankles, his hands on his own knees, and his cute ass wiggling around my shoving pecker. The music from the dance floors was muffled in the darkened corridor, but the steamy sighs and groans of men engaged in impromptu sex acts filled the void. I was grunting along with the rest as I savaged the butt in front of me. I drilled and shoved and pounded. The slick orifice responded willingly, wrapping around every thrust of my cock with eager lust. Young Law met my every poke with an appreciative wiggle of his cute butt.

There was a guy directly in front of us. Tall, muscle-bound to the extreme. He was staring at me, clutching his crotch. His tank top stretched impossibly over the hugest pair of tits I'd ever seen on a guy. I fucked my bent-over partner with pounding rhythm as the stranger moved closer, then suddenly he was pulling out his own whanger, a huge beast with a dripping plum head. He took Young Law's face in his hands and wiped his mouth with that monster cock. Young Law opened up his sweet lips and tickled the giant head with his tongue. Then Muscle Dude was bending forward and kissing me. He sucked my tongue into his wet mouth, almost ripping it out. He gripped my head with one hand, Young Law's with the other.

Between us, the hapless young lawyer was impaled from both ends. I could feel his butt hole quivering with wild excitement as he took two cocks. I got tongued by Muscle Dude, his tight grip on my neck hotter than hell.

Then I shot. I hadn't realized I was that close, the whole experience so much on the edge the orgasm occurred without any warning. But Muscle Dude knew what was happening. With his grip still firmly on my neck, he was turning our bodies, pulling me down on the floor against the wall while I was still spurting inside the condom wrapping my cock. Somehow I was on my back, with Young Law on top of me, slobbering over my neck and chest. Then my thighs were raised, my pants pulled off over my boots.

I could see Muscle Dude above us, with my pants in his hands and a smirk on his face. I knew what was coming. I wanted it, I wanted to be butt-fucked there on the floor while Young Law watched. Muscle Dude scooted up between my thighs. He shoved them back against my chest, with Young Law between us, still kissing my neck and chin. I was smothered with male flesh, then I felt slippery fingers at my bared asshole. Lube coated the outer rim as I sighed and opened up to Muscle Dude's explorations. I groped down between my thighs and found his mammoth meat. He had put a condom over the thing, extra large no doubt. That was enough for me. I lay back and shut my eyes and waited.

Enormous flesh pressed against my butt hole. "Take it up the ass just like I did." I heard a lewd whisper in my ear. Young Law was crouched between us, his arms wrapped around my back, his mouth in my ear.

I just opened up to the big thing. I was ready, mentally, to be fucked. I wanted to be on the floor in the hallway with naked men all around, getting it up the ass. The lubed head popped inside me, and I gritted my teeth and felt the rest of the monster tube penetrating me. I lifted my butt and shoved back. The stuffed feeling was incredible—I wanted it inside me, the bigger the better. My asshole expanded, caressing the invader like a hungry mouth. I squirmed my butt around, the weight of Young Law on my belly and hips like a human blanket. I reached down and felt Young Law's splayed hip—there was a beefy paw there. I felt fingers probing: Muscle Dude was tickling Young Law's squishy butt hole with three blunt digits while he fed me his huge beef-stick.

We lay entangled and moaning on the floor, squirming like one beast. I felt that giant salami up into my lungs as he slowly fucked me full-stroke. Young Law shot his load all over my chest as those big fingers stretched him wide. He lay there like a limp rag doll while we fucked with him between us. Muscle Dude had stamina, and I found myself erect again. My cock rubbed up into the sticky, slick belly of Young Law as my prostate quivered around the banging Muscle Dude offered it.

I floated off into fuck paradise, nothing else in the world mattering. A big cock up my butt, warm male flesh surrounding me, the stench of sweat and body odor rank in my nostrils. Just before I came again, Young Law himself got hard once more and fed me his cock while I gurgled and groaned until I spewed a second load inside the condom wrapping my boner.

Muscle Dude pulled out and whacked off over us, ripping off his condom and spraying us both with gooey strands of spume. He left us there.

I couldn't find my pants, and my shirt was long lost. I thought of sneaking home naked through the back streets of the city and got hard again. But I found my pants so that final sordid experience was denied me.

With a sore butt and a satiated cock, I stumbled home. I looked at myself in the mirror, half-naked, sweaty, come-stained. I ended the night on my hands and knees with a big dildo shoved up my butt in front of the mirror, reliving the best fuck of my life. I sprayed my own thighs with come and fell asleep on the floor, the dildo still up my ass.

At work on Monday I had just left a meeting with the partners when I bumped into him: Young Law.

"Excuse me, Mister Blane," he said, gazing up into my eyes. There was a moment of disbelief as he suddenly recognized me.

I smiled, my tidy suit, neatly combed hair, horn-rimmed glasses the perfect disguise. His eyes screwed up for another instant, as if he thought he'd made a mistake.

Then I grinned. I leaned over and whispered confidentially in his ear. "Gone dancing lately?" With no one watching, I casually reached out and gripped his crotch, right through his perfectly creased slacks.

He was still gasping as I strolled nonchalantly down the hallway.

Ah, the sordid life! It made all the rest worthwhile.

On a Night Like This

by Thom Wolf

"European guys are so fucking hot!" I said, casting my eyes around the crowded bar.

"Why do you sound so surprised?" Neil asked.

"I guess I'd never really thought about it before."

It was 6:30 on a Friday night, and the bars of Canal Street were packed. The gay men of Manchester were out in force, looking immaculate in their tight uniforms of sleeveless T-shirts (which they called "vests") and designer jeans. There was a reason why the bars were so busy—the same reason that had brought me halfway across the world to England.

I was on a pilgrimage to see my idol. The guys back home had looked at me incredulously when I told them where I was going and who exactly I was going to see.

In the States very few people have heard of Kylie Minogue. If they remember her at all, it's for a cover version of "The Locomotion" in the late 1980s: a kitsch one-hit wonder. In Europe and Australia Kylie Minogue is a megastar, second only to Madonna in terms of chart success and way out ahead of Janet and Mariah. I have followed her career from the start, building up a collection of (expensive) imports. When Kylie announced her "On a Night Like This" European and Australian tour, I knew that I might never get another chance to see her perform.

There was a bonus to my trip that I had not foreseen. Kylie has a massive fan base of adoring gay men. After having been in the United Kingdom for just over a week, I had already seen her in concert twice in Glasgow; this was my second night in Manchester, and I had been laid 10 times so far.

If my broad accent was a turn-on for the British guys, then their regional tones were equally effective for me. I only had to walk into a bar, order a drink, and pretty soon someone would come over and talk to me. It worked every time.

Neil—27, great-looking, great body, incredible blue eyes—was a fellow Kylie fan I had met on the Internet. We hooked up for the first time yesterday afternoon and were fucking each other within a couple of hours. Not bad going. Neil had a tight little body and an even tighter little ass. I planned to spend the rest of my time in Manchester getting to know him intimately, though not exclusively. There were far too many attractions on the U.K. scene for that.

Neil's boyfriend, Mason, was joining us for the concert; we were meeting up with him in a pub. Neil assured me that Mason was cool with him fucking around and that we were sure to hit it off. I hoped so. My tongue almost hung out of my mouth when I got my first glimpse of Neil's lover. For some reason I was expecting another Neil-style twink. But Mason was 6 feet 4 inches of dark-skinned, brawny perfection. He was older than Neil by a good 10 years, and his coppery eyes shone with the wisdom of a man who had fucked hundreds of guys.

Neil left us talking while he went to the bar for a final round of pre-show drinks. Mason was polite and witty, there was great warmth in his voice and his brown face crinkled with handsome lines when he smiled. But the courtesy and politeness we afforded each other was sham. When Mason spoke he addressed himself to the bulge in my jeans. Likewise I directed my answers to his colossal chest, barely contained in the tight cotton of his "I Love Kylie" vest. Before the night was over I knew that we would fuck.

Neil came back with our drinks. I caught the excitement in his eyes as he sensed the chemistry between his lover and me. He handed me a bottle of beer.

"So when do you go back to the States?" Mason asked.

"The end of next week. I'm flying back after the first of the London shows."

"You must be a real fan to come all this way for a series of concerts," he said.

"My friends think I'm insane," I said. "But they don't know what they're missing. Not just Kylie but this whole country. It's amazing." I had fallen in love with England in my short time there. Especially Manchester, which was of special interest to me as the location for the original series of *Queer As Folk.* Canal Street was just that: an entire street of gay bars running along the side of a city canal. I was staying at the Princess Hotel, which was only a couple of minutes walk from the scene—handy for dragging cute guys back to my bed.

We finished our beers and set off for the concert. The venue was a 15-minute walk away from the bars. I had discovered the previous night that it was just as quick to walk there as to ride in a taxi through the busy city streets. I was reminded of a Pride march as the streets were thronged with hundreds of gay guys all heading in the same direction for their appointment with a diva.

Although I had already seen the show more than once, I was still excited. Neil walked between Mason and me with his arms around our waists. What a perfect night this was going to be. I wouldn't have to worry about any postconcert comedown tonight. Not when I could look forward to getting naked with these guys.

We got to the venue and pushed our way down to the front, eventually securing a spot about 10 feet from the stage—my closest position yet on the tour. The place filled up quickly, as over 4,000 fans filed in. We soon found ourselves hemmed in on all sides. Mason, the tallest of our group, stood behind us, creating a little more room.

We stood patiently through the support act, waiting for the main show to begin. My nerves were jangling. The screams were deafening, as the lights went down and the pop goddess made her entrance, descending from the roof on a giant glittering anchor and then transported around the stage by a shipload of muscle-bound boys dressed in sailor suits. She dazzled the entire crowd as she belted out her trademark disco tunes in an exhausting show.

I felt a bond with every person in the audience as we all came together in the euphoric name of disco. When Kylie sang "Your Disco Needs You," she touched the soul of every gay man present.

Halfway through the show I became aware of something happening behind me. Mason's hands circled my waist, and I felt his hard cock press insistently against my ass. High on the music, I pushed my buttocks back against him but didn't take my eyes away from the action on the stage. Mason rubbed his bulge persistently against my butt, swaying gently to the music. I could feel he was big.

I began to grow hard myself.

His hands moved around my body, drawing me against his chest. He brushed his fingers over the flat of my stomach, tweaked my nipples through my vest. He discovered my nipple ring and twisted it. His breath was hot on the back of my neck. I rubbed my ass against his bulge.

His mouth moved near my ear. "Don't move," he said. "I'm going to fuck you."

I thought he was joking, until his fingers began to unfasten my jeans. He popped open the buttons on my fly, waiting to see if I would protest before sliding his hand inside. I groaned as fingers closed around my cock, squeezing through my pants. He rubbed the hard shaft. I could feel myself leaking into the cotton.

I waited breathlessly, my eyes glued to the stage, while Mason stuffed his hand down the front of my pants, his fingers finding my naked cock. He wrapped his hand around it and jerked slowly.

"You horny bastard," he hissed in my ear. I started humping his hand. In no time at all, his palm was sticky with precome. He stroked my dick from the shiny head to the thick root, all the while grinding his hips against my ass.

The crowd seemed to close in around us. I felt light-headed. *I shouldn't allow him to do this,* I told myself unconvincingly. But now that he had started, there was no way I was going to stop him. I was his.

He tugged my jeans and underpants down over my waist, baring my ass. He started squeezing my butt. His fingers burrowed into the crack, jabbing my hole. He wriggled inside. I gasped. Fuck, I was tight! My ass hadn't been explored in over two weeks. All the British guys I had met so far had been willing bottoms. My own hole was out of practice.

Mason didn't waste any time. He sucked his fingers and shoved a couple into me. He squirmed around inside, prying open the tight walls. I pushed back against him, forcing my hole to open up and receive him. I was hot, ready for him. The heat of 4,000 bodies pressing in around me roused my passion. I wanted his cock in my ass. Right here in this crowded concert hall I wanted to be fucked.

Mason pulled out his fingers. I felt him unzip himself and then his long hard meat against my bare ass. On stage Kylie Minogue sang about getting physical, oblivious to the two guys in her audience who were about to fuck.

Mason wrapped his left arm around my waist and held me tight against his stomach. His left hand guided his cock into my crack, positioning the wet head against my hole. I waited while he manipulated his shaft to the right angle. My heart was thumping harder than music. Slowly, gently, he pressed into me. I worked my ass, opening, pushing, allowing him inside. He gradually moved in deeper as his arms squeezed me tighter.

I was breathless. It felt so good, standing there surrounded by thousands of guys, perspiring, my hero singing on stage, a huge cock inside me. It was better than any dream come true.

Mason pushed till all of his cock was inside me, then he pulled almost completely out, then went back in. I moved my ass with him, rocking, grinding. sucking him deeper. It was a defining moment in my life: watching Kylie perform live while I had a big cock quivering in my ass. No other fan would be able to cherish a moment like this.

I gripped my cock, working it slowly, not wanting to draw attention to us. Mason was giving it to me in short, sharp jabs. He was close. He kissed my neck. Held my body tighter. I felt his cock stiffen and then the flood in my ass as he unloaded his balls.

I came in powerful spurts, shooting my white load over the ass of the guy in front of me. I watched my jizz dribble down the back of his black jeans. He was oblivious. Even Neil who was standing beside me, captivated by the performer on stage, was unmindful of the performance that had taken place right next to him.

Mason remained inside me for a while before slowly withdrawing from my sloppy hole. Nobody seemed to notice us as I hitched my jeans back over my freshly fucked ass. Mason held onto me for the remainder of the concert.

I had lost my senses. I couldn't speak or even think straight. I sang along to the songs and savored the wetness in my ass. It was the best comedown from orgasm I had ever experienced.

After the show we headed back to Canal Street. I was desperately in need of a drink. At the bar of Via Fosse, Neil and Mason began to kiss me. They both whispered in my ear all the things that we were going to do to each other when we got back to my hotel.

It seemed that on a night like this everything was going to be perfect. Just like the concert, I was in no hurry for it to end.

Gay Pride Day in East Jesus, Minnesota

by Simon Sheppard

When Richie got back to his hometown, that Midwesternly boring place he and his friends had nicknamed "East Jesus," not much had changed, but then why should it have? Going off to college wasn't like dying, and even your death wouldn't really change your hometown, he figured. It'd just mean you'd make a lot fewer trips to the Burger King out on Lucille Road, even when they had that 99-cent special on Whoppers.

He had come back, with mixed emotions, to spend the summer at his parents' house. East Jesus was one of those picture-book-pretty farm towns that hid, Richie knew, a not-so-beautiful heart. The fact that Richie's family was Japanese-American, one of the few families of Asian descent ever to settle there, hadn't helped. There were the usual to-be-expected taunts, of course, but as stupid as they were, they still hurt. Maybe even worse were the nods to liberalism, like when his sixth-grade teacher had asked him to explain Chinese New Year to the class. He'd done his best—Richie almost always did his best—but when he got home and told his parents about it, they were livid. "What's next?" his father thundered. "Confucius' Birthday?" It had taken Richie a few more years to figure out just why they'd been so mad.

So when he figured the *other* thing out—became aware that his slanted eyes and ocher skin weren't the only things that set him apart— he'd kept his attraction to other boys a secret, deep and dark. It wasn't till he'd gone off to college two states away that Richie Yoshida had let the little beastie out to play.

Even then, it hadn't been easy. He desperately wanted so many guys, including, distressingly, his to-all-appearances-straight-as-anything roommate. Richie always, it seemed, had a hard-on; he just didn't know what to do with it. Sure, there was a gay students' alliance on campus, but he'd been too chickenshit to join. One night he'd circled around the hallway for at least 10 minutes, passing the meeting room's closed door six or seven times before glumly giving up. He was, he figured, pretty much a hopeless case.

Then he discovered the men's room in the visual arts building. There was the hole drilled into the wall between two stalls. There were the hard-on drawings and requests for sex scrawled everywhere; they got painted over regularly, only to reappear within a few days, miraculous as stigmata. And there was the Skechers-clad foot that made its way past the partition into his stall. The foot tapped as if by accident, but it was pretty clearly no accident. Richie bent over to steal a glimpse into the neighboring toilet, and there, bent over, was a good-looking blond boy, his face alarmingly pink from the blood rushing to his upside-down head.

"Slide under the stall," the blond boy whispered.

"But..."

"Slide under."

"How? I won't fit."

"Christ." An exasperated whisper. "Just your legs and crotch, OK?"

Richie's dick was already hard as an uncircumcised rock. He managed, sitting back on his heels, to get it on the other side of the stained partition, where the blond boy took it expertly into his nice wet mouth. It didn't take long for Richie to come, and to his surprise (Richie had tasted his own come once and found it unpleasantly gamy), the blond boy swallowed every drop of it down.

Richie began to spend almost all his afternoons hanging out at the visual arts building. The blond boy, it turned out, was a regular, as were several other young men. He gave them nicknames: Curved Dick, Football Player, Too Much Cologne. Eventually, he ran into the blond boy outside the confines of the men's room. Richie would have ignored him, but the blond boy struck up a conversation, and his easygoing manner and wide smile put Richie at ease. They went to a movie together, then to bed—the first time Richie had ever had real full-fledged lying-down sex with anybody. It was a revelation.

By the end of his freshman year, Richie Yoshida had joined the gay students' alliance and come out to his close friends. He'd even told his roommate, who'd said, "That's cool," but started turning off the light before he stripped down for bed.

Then came finals, the end of the school year, and the trip back home to East Jesus—and, he figured, to several lonely months of jerking off in the downstairs powder room, with its basket of scented soaps and its unintentionally camp wallpaper of pink poodles and Eiffel Towers. He'd have to keep secrets; he still couldn't get up the courage to come out to his mom and dad. But he had a decent summer job at his father's plumbing supply store, and he needed the money.

He'd been home for a few weeks when in late June he spotted Bob Kondyra. Richie was with his mother at the supermarket. "Can I help you out with your bags?" said a sort-of-familiar voice, and when he looked, it was Bob Kondyra, wearing a supermarket uniform.

Kondyra (everyone called him by his last name) had been—well, you could call him a "greaser." All through school he'd sported an unfashionable pompadour. His attitude had been even worse than his grades. But Kondyra had been, maybe as a result of being held back once or twice, the first boy in Richie's class to reach puberty. Back then, every trip to the gym locker room had been an occasion for wonderment. Kondyra's body had hair where the other boys just had dreams, and his dick had been startlingly big.

Kondyra was the envy of the prepubescent; despite his evident social liabilities, he seemed to have no problems finding girlfriends, and if some of the girls had bad reputations, well, so did Bob Kondyra.

"Richie?" said Kondyra.

"Yeah," Richie said, "I'm back here for the summer. Mom, you remember Bob Kondyra?"

"Sure thing. Hi, Bob." His mother smiled, though every word she'd ever heard about him had been bad. Richie hadn't told her about Kondyra's dick, though, which throughout high school had remained prodigiously larger than average, filling Richie with barely suppressed desire whenever the boys hit the showers after gym.

"We should get together, Richie," said Kondyra. "Catch up."

"Sure thing," said Richie, though he was more than a bit surprised. When Kondyra had taken notice of him in school at all, it was, Richie recalled, with scarcely concealed contempt.

He might have forgotten about the whole thing if it hadn't been for that dream the next night. Richie rarely remembered his dreams, and when he did, they almost never had much to do with real life. But there it was: a dream about a motorcycle, a mysterious road that went nowhere, and Bob Kondyra. And Kondyra's dick. When Richie woke up he'd puddled the sheets with come.

So he went back to the supermarket the next day and made it a point to run into Bob Kondyra. Bob, it turned out, had the next day off, a Sunday, and Richie would be welcome to come over and talk about old times.

After Sunday dinner, Richie borrowed his mother's Ford without telling her where he was going. He smuggled out a half-bottle of Scotch as he left the house.

Kondyra's place was pretty much what he expected, down to the Pamela Anderson poster on the wall. Things started out awkwardly enough, but fortunately Kondyra had left the TV on when Richie arrived; sitcom noise papered over the silences. Generous applications of Scotch, though, soon made things almost relaxed.

"I always figured you didn't like me, Richie."

"That's not true." A convenient semi-lie.

"I figured you thought I was stupid."

Silence.

"You got a girlfriend, Richie?"

"Nope, not now." Richie took another burning swallow of liquor.

"You ever had a girlfriend, Richie?"

What was he getting at? Should Richie tell the truth or not?

"What do you mean?" Richie's head was swimming.

"I mean," and Kondyra fixed him with a semi-drunken stare, "that you always wanted—"

"Wanted?"

"To *suck my dick.*"

There was really nothing to say.

"You can suck it if you want."

It had to be a trick. On TV, Richie suddenly noticed, John Ritter and Suzanne Somers had gotten into a spat. *"Chrissy!"*

"You can suck it." Kondyra's hand was kneading his crotch.

"Um..." said Richie, and then couldn't think of any more to say.

Kondyra unzipped his fly and pulled out his penis. It was, if not quite as large as Richie had remembered, still a sizable piece of meat, and it was getting harder by the second.

Richie took another swig of booze and dropped to his knees. There, just inches from his face, was the thing itself—Bob Kondyra's notorious dick.

"All you guys want to suck it," Kondyra slurred. "You want to suck it even more than the chicks do."

Clearly, more had been going on in high school than Richie had suspected. *Which guys?* he wanted to ask. *Which guys wanted to suck it?* But he couldn't, because by that time his mouth was full of Kondyra's swelling cock. It was just a tad ripe, and it stretched his jaws, but it was otherwise thoroughly satisfactory.

"Oh, yeah," Kondyra mumbled, "feels good."

The *Three's Company* rerun had given way to the evening news. The supposed president was saying something about bringing religious faith back into public life. Richie sucked harder. There was a commercial for antacid. Kondyra reached for the Scotch bottle and gulped down another swig.

"...In cities from New York to San Francisco," the TV announcer was saying, "homosexuals by the tens of thousands celebrated the anniversary of a riot at a Greenwich Village gay bar, a turning point in the movement for homosexual rights." And some guy started gushing about what a wonderful day it was and how he'd come all the way from Oregon to San Francisco just to march in the big parade.

"Look at them," slurred Kondyra. "Look at them fucking faggots."

Richie could have taken his mouth off Kondyra's dick, could have just stood up and gotten the hell out of there. But he didn't. He sucked harder, accelerated the pace, until Bob Kondyra half-rose from the chair and shot a big load down Richie's near-gagging throat.

Richie stood up, wiping his mouth on his sleeve and, grabbing the Scotch bottle, said levelly, "Next time, ask another fucking faggot to suck you off, OK?"

He walked unsteadily to the door, let himself out, and got into his mom's Ford. He was, he knew, a long way from the land of rainbow flags, rainbow bumper stickers, rainbow necklaces and rings, from Dykes on Bikes and gay marching bands. Driving cautiously, he headed back to the house he grew up in. The place he grew up in. East Jesus, Minnesota.

Courtside
by R.J. March

Clay Newton decided to go queer, I guess, the second time he was in my parents' hot tub. It was the smoothest transition from hetero to homo that I'd ever been a party to—not that I've been invited to many of those parties. One day he was shelling out a couple hundred bucks to pay for the Kleiven girl's abortion—yeah, it really was his—and the next he was sitting in the hot tub with me, his foot between my legs, trying to work his big toe up my ass, munching on Taco Bell and wondering out loud how my little chin beard would feel against his newly razored balls. This from a boy as dedicated to pussy—to my knowledge, anyway—as Rocco Sifredi, and with a dick to match—not that I'd seen it before then. Even that night in the hot tub, our second, we were both wearing shorts. Still, Clay's jams were tight enough across the crotch to disclose the thick wad there, a covered terrain I was all too familiar with.

I didn't know him for shit, to tell you the truth—I mean, not in the classic sense. I was watching my parents' new condo as they traveled across the USA in their trailer. I was between jobs, between apartments, and between boyfriends. Clay lived next door with his parents and was just out of college, with a bullshit degree in business. He was as ambitious as I was that summer. The only straining I did was over some Internet porn. I'd thought about trying to hook up with someone online, but it seemed like too much trouble. Besides, there was Clay next door.

One day I was jacking off to some Internet pics of guys in Speedos when I heard the dribble of a basketball next door, followed by the rattling vibrating hum of the backboard taking another shot. I traded the porn for a few stolen moments at the front window, watching Clay Newton work up a sweat in his driveway, shirt discarded, shorts sagging to reveal the waistband (and then some) of his Structure briefs.

It wasn't just that he was built, that his shoulders were nearly three feet from deltoid to deltoid, that his pecs were tipped with wide brown nipples surrounded by rings of dark hairs. It wasn't just that his fine rippled gut dipped down, separating his bared hipbones, or that his calves were as thick as Sunday hams. And it wasn't just that his green eyes, overshadowed by the sweep of dark bangs, glanced my way as I pulled on my spit-soaked hard-on. No: It was the thick bobble in his shorts; the jumping, banging baggage there that he fumbled with again and again, constantly poking, pulling, tugging, scratching, readjusting. I ruined my mother's curtains that day—and many others, watching him miss easy layups, dribbling back to the end of the drive with one hand, the other dug deep into the bunched crotch of his shorts.

One day the ball glanced off the backboard and bounced into my parents' yard. I hadn't really noticed, trying hard to avoid making another mess on my mother's sheers, cuffing my dick closer and closer to a glutinous end, having watched my neighbor huff and sweat and grope himself the past half-hour. I opened my eyes for one more inspirational glance, ready to put down another basketball fan's load, when I noticed his driveway was empty. Just then, Clay stood up, holding his ball, catching me window-side with dick in hand. I dropped to my knees, not knowing what else to do, quickly trying to figure what he might or might not have seen from his vantage point, given the height of the window sill. He'd probably seen everything, at least at quick glance, I decided, as come dripped out of my sorry cock dejectedly.

"My ball," I heard him say through the window. I tried to nod solemnly. He smiled as I let the sheers fall closed. Then I crawled out of sight behind the sofa, wounded with mortification.

• • •

I didn't have to do anything around the house except make sure I sent out the checks for the household bills on time, which were all written, dated and stamped for me—a piece of cake. There were boys who mowed the lawns. These lawn boys, they looked younger than 18, but the one who did my parents' yard, who eyed me up as I sprawled on a hammock (spread-legged and spilling out of my shorts, no less), swore he was 21—same as me, and he went for his driver's license to prove it. I'd already given him a beer and a shot—a clear shot of my crotch—and he found something else to fumble for in his pocket, namely a hefty semi. A fountain of hair rose up from his ripstop shorts; they were slung low on his hips, exposing the top half of his boxers. His shirt hung like an off-centered tail from his back pocket. He hadn't told me his name yet.

He eyed the house suspiciously, as though I had some hidden surveillance center or a surprise birthday party secreted inside. He emptied the beer with a couple of loud swigs. I watched his lips come off the bottle. He burped softly and lifted the brim of his palm-greased baseball hat. His eyes were Hershey brown, and the stubble on the side of his head was transparent.

"You want another?" I asked, and he looked at the house then turned, glancing over his shoulder. The idle mower sat in the middle of clipped green. He was done for the day; he knew it, I knew it. He handed me the empty, nodding.

• • •

His cock hung like a tree branch from his groin, wood-stiff, drippy. He studied my mother's Lladro collection, my father's hand-carved duck decoys, and the collection of pictures of me from kindergarten through high school, through 13 different hairstyles.

"Black eye," he says, looking at sixth grade. So far, he'd been monosyllabic, and I hadn't minded much, enjoying a man of few words and a dick like a billy club. He asked which way to the toilet when we first entered the house, and came back with his dick hard and poking out his fly, not bothering or needing to explain. He looked down at his thick, bobbing pole, and I fell back on my father's recliner.

"You like it?" he asked. I shrugged. What wasn't to like?

"It's big, right?" he asked, and I gave him my best "sort of" nod.

"Damn straight," he said, and he slapped it around, sending droplets of pre-jizz flying. I imagined my mother coming home and walking around the living room, asking my father, "Where in heaven's name did all this *semen* come from, Walter?"

"You think so?" I asked, and he smirked. His glance dropped to the front of my shorts.

"Is that big?" he said, and I shrugged again.

"Size is relative," I told him, and he snorted.

"Well, meet my motherfuckin' cousin," he said, stepping forward. I sat up, leaning toward him, wanting to get closer. Pink and thick and heavy-headed, his cock swayed in front of me, and the want I felt for him made me dizzy. I made a grab for him, getting his warm tube in my grip, and I pulled him to me, pulling out crystalline pearls that formed in the slot of his piss hole.

His shaft was harder than any other part of him—bones aren't as hard. His expression was grim, and he covered his chest with folded arms. I made his grass-stained shorts fall to the floor, admiring the inventive plaid of his boxers. I heard him breathe through his nose, short bursts that usually signal something strenuous—resolve or something, I thought, picturing a diver on the board, about to attempt a triple whatever, so I was not expecting the huge gush that sprayed my face and the arm of the recliner.

"Christ," I said, and he said, "Sorry, bud."

"There's more, though," he added, and he took my hand off his cock and started jerking himself off. He stared hard at the tented front of my shorts, wet with white dots that weren't mine. His balls banged against his fist, and his cock made a slapping noise against his palm.

"Let me see it," he grimaced, the words tight and lip-bound. I hauled out my cock. It's a stubby, blunt thing with a head reminiscent of a portobello mushroom cap. His lower lip shined; the pink tip of his tongue flickered just inside. He slapped his cock around like a wad of pizza dough. He stepped out of the shackles of his fallen shorts and climbed aboard the USS *Recliner* with me, straddling my middle. His cock lay between my tits appreciatively, lolling about in the cleavage I'd built with bench presses and inclined-flye workouts. He left a buttery trail there, fisting himself again.

I wanted him to lean back so that he might feel the press of my dick against the cleavage of his ass cheeks. I wiggled a finger behind his balls, and he moaned and let me wiggle my way inside him. He steadied himself by placing one hand by my head, and I stared into the mossy cave of his underarm, smelling him. His asshole was tight and as discretionary as a New York bouncer; he let me in a little at a time, joint by joint, until I could press on the inner doorbell, the hardened knob of his prostate, gaining full access, total entry.

"Awww, Stuart," I heard him say.

"Hmm?" I asked. "What's that? Stuart?"

The boy blushed down to his chest, his cheeks looking like they'd been struck. "Me," he said sheepishly. "I'm Stuart." I smiled and pushed into him. His eyes closed, and he put his face close to mine. I could smell his quickening breaths. He whispered something again, "Stuart," and humped my finger. My cock filled his ass crack, riding along his tailbone. His ruddy dick, surrounded by a dark bush, was slippery; it rutted my belly as his buzzed scalp rasped my cheek.

I opened him up and played my dick against his fingered hole, testing. He bumped his puckered lips against the fat head, making noises that sounded welcoming. I got inside a little at a time, making him gasp and squeeze his eyes shut. He took what he could as he could, slowly working his hole down the length of my shaft until he was satisfied with his intake. He grunted, though, when I took my first tentative thrust, which was as gentle as I could manage. "You ain't the first," he said, because I was probably looking a little cocky.

"The second, though," I told him. "And the first had a tiny prick."

His mouth hung open. "You're like a palm reader."

His ass had an exceptionally firm grip, a real he-man handshake, and was furnace-hot. *We might not have to do anything more than this,* I thought, holding the boy who had curled up against my chest, his lips at my neck, his fingers in my ear. I felt every rippling shudder his insides made, playing my dick like a slide trombone.

I held him by the ass, keeping him far enough away to allow for some thrusting. I eased out and then back in, and then out again, and he was perfectly still, his tongue darting out of his mouth and onto my throat.

"Is this OK?" I asked, and he nodded. He played with my tit and I heard him say he liked it fine. I went into him a little more insistently.

"Yeah," he said, tilting his head back. His eyes were still closed. I fucked him harder, and he said "Yeah" with each thrust. I made each one deeper and more forceful, trying to make him say no, to say stop, but he kept on saying "Yeah," and then I couldn't stop myself. I slammed into him, making loud grunts that grew louder the closer I got to coming.

"Not yet," he whispered. "Not yet, not yet." And he started fisting himself with short tight strokes, trying to catch up with me. I opened my mouth, and he stuck his fingers in there, and I squirted off into him. I looked down to see his cock gush, come flying out of him in thick white ribbons between us, draping my chin, my chest, my gut.

• • •

"And then he licked me clean," I told Clay.

"Get the fuck out," Clay said loudly. "His own splooge? That's fucking sick!"

I stared, incredulous. *Could it be that he's never eaten his own jizz?* I thought. Impossible. I wasn't having it.

"Fuck you, Newton. You've eaten your own and you know it."

He looked at me, shock all over his face.

"That is fucking gross," he said simply. "It's like picking your nose and eating it."

I shrugged my shoulders. "Yeah? So?"

He shifted in the tub, reconfiguring his long legs. His toes popped out of the water to my left. He draped his arms along the fiberglass edge behind him. He changed the subject.

"So, you're a basketball fan too?" he said with an arrogant grin.

I dipped into the water, letting it rush across my lips. "I like to watch," I said after a moment of silence.

"You sure do," he said, shifting his body a bit, his huge calf bumping me. "Don't mind watching myself. I wouldn't mind watching you and your lawn jockey doing a little one-on-one."

"Wouldn't you?" I said. I propped myself over his feet, pressing my wrist against his ankle. He toed my forearm. "And just what do you hope to gain from such a spectacle, Mr. Newton?"

"Well, Mr. Flanagan," he said, smiling goofily, "a little insight. A little insight."

"Take off your shorts, Clay, and I'll give you some insight."

I watched him finish off another taco, getting shredded lettuce in the frothing water. "All in good time, Wade," he said, his mouth still full.

• • •

Not long after that night, there was a knock on my door. I figured it was Clay and was surprised to find the grass-cutter, Stuart, on my doorstep.

"I think I left my lawn mower here, sir," he said, liquored up and giggly. He had his hands shoved into the pockets of his oversize jeans. His shirt was too big, too, and did not reveal any of the sweet contours I'd had opportunity to familiarize myself with the week before.

"You left something, but it wasn't a lawn mower," I told him, and he grinned lopsidedly. I opened the screen door, and he stumbled through, falling against me; I could smell the whiskey and cigarette smoke from his evening out. Catching him, I felt the muscles of his arms, the tightness of him. He bumped my chest with his forehead, butting me, and I held onto him, closing the door.

His shirt fell to the floor; he was more nimble-fingered than I would have expected. His ribbed tank top glowed against his tanned skin. "Gotta beer?" he said, swaying. He played with himself through the front of his jeans.

"Later," I said.

I stripped him down to his hard-on in the middle of my parents' living room. His cock was beautiful, jutting from a thick chestnut bush. I went to my knees and started to suck him. He grabbed my head roughly—perhaps lustfully, but probably more to steady himself, and before I tasted even a drop of precome he asked if he could "sit this one out." He fell onto the couch, his head rolling back; his dick stood thick and tall. He lifted his head, squinting at me. "Well?" he said. "Get going."

I got between his legs, my hands on his smooth thighs, and put my mouth on the fat pink head of his crotch monument. I licked into the split and tasted the first seepage, working up a good amount by squeezing his shaft like a near-empty tube of toothpaste.

"Aw, Stuart," he said. I agreed.

"Shtuarr," I gulped.

He used his hips to derrick my mouth with his fat cock. I chugged on him, holding on to his waist, after positioning his bare feet on my thighs. He played with my hair and said sweet things I couldn't hear. I had him at the back of my throat and kept him there, holding him still, trying to swallow his fat dick head.

"Well, Jee-zus!" he whispered, leaning forward to watch. When I pulled myself off him, my spit hung between us like a thick rope, and he patted the side of my face lightly and said, "Boy, you got that right!"

Standing, I got myself out of my shorts and gave him my dick to contemplate a while. He sucked me roughly and without any finesse, holding my shaft like a Ball Park frank. It felt great nonetheless, and I put my hands on my hips and enjoyed his handiwork. He gobbled and snorted and huffed all over my crotch until, just when I thought he was getting *really* good, he leaned back and said, "Well, let's get to some fucking!"

He pulled me onto the couch with him and turned me over, getting me butt-up across his lap. He licked a finger and poked it between my ass cheeks. He found my hole easily, and found my hole easily. I was only too happy to be the recipient of his big, fat cock. I squirmed and put up a good fight, all the while working my dick across his muscular thighs. He got hold of me and maneuvered me into a sitting position, squatting over his oozing pole. I sat on him, his cock filling me like none had before. I gasped like a virgin, and he laughed behind me.

"I hear that all the time," he said, all proud of himself. At that point, I was glad to be facing away from him, not wanting my grimace to give him any satisfaction. I slipped down his shaft slowly, careful now not to show any signs of discomfort. When I felt his pubes on my stretched-out ass lips, I took a deep and well-deserved breath. *Mother*-FUCKER, *he's a wide one,* I was thinking. He reached around me on both sides and played with my tits and put his mouth on my back, licking between my shoulder blades. He pumped his big prick up into me, invading my innards. *My spleen!* I thought, or whatever you call that thing he was poking. I managed to pivot myself on the staff of his cock so that I was facing him. Now he could chew on my nipples and I could more or less control what he did and didn't hit up inside me.

"Aww, Stuart," he said, looking me in the eye. His tongue played between his lips. He grabbed my ass cheeks and brought me down on him hard, and my dick bounced off his muscled gut. He spat on it, on us, and made a slick slide for me. I was slipping between the two of us as he gripped my ass again and fucked me hard.

"You're big, you're fucking big," I said, putting my face near his, wanting to kiss him. He looked away.

"Someone's watching," he said, his face stony and still.

"Probably my fucking neighbor," I said. "He's cool."

"Yeah? Cool," Stuart said as he continued to slide up into me, although he was becoming a little more showy, getting me face-down on the couch, our asses to the window, fucking me with broad, ball-slapping thrusts. One hand behind his back, he pumped me hard, his hips smacking against the flesh of my behind again and again. I squeezed down hard on his prick, my own about to burst, and he sucked in his breath.

"Man!" he spit and yanked himself out of me, leaving my hole gaping. I felt him shoot all over my back. I scrambled then, getting on my knees, not wanting to get any more come on my mother's sofa. I turned fast and tossed off a nut all over Stuart's face, just able to make out the shadowy figure behind the sheers: Clay Newton hanging courtside, watching the whole dirty scene.

• • •

"Man," he said, dipping low in the hot tub. "You two were fucking hot. That's all I got to say." His feet floated between my spread legs, and his dick bobbed between his own. It was charming, all pink and fat and sturdy-looking—an excellent piece and quite a bit larger than I'd given him credit for. He found my soft spot with his big toe, and I swallowed some tub water. He laughed at my spitting, and I heard him say over the roar of water that he was seriously considering switching teams—"For a little while," he said. "You know, experimental and everything. Hey! I shaved my nuts, did you notice?" He lifted his torso up out of the water, and I leaned close to inspect, my balls draping his feet.

He grabbed a taco from the bag behind his head. "You hungry?" he asked.

I couldn't answer; my mouth was already full.

Kinky Wet Khakis

by Lance Rush

Back in the day when you needed a favor, you'd go to Rex. He ran things in our neighborhood. He walked around with a kind of sleazy importance, and he co-owned a small porn theater. It was a cum-shot across the street from where I lived. On the outside, it was like any other porn house. I figured it catered to horny trench coat types who'd drop a load before heading back to the wife.

One summer when I needed a job, I turned to Rex. At 6 foot 2 and 195 streetwise pounds, I pretty much knew the score. I'd seen my share of trash, jerk-offs, and gutter-fucks, so Rex let me work the ticket booth. I never expected to see so much gay action in a straight joint. But that was the summer I stopped believing in labels. Man! The wild and raunchy shit I witnessed in that place would fill a year's subscription to the best stroke mag!

Young guys, street cats, and pretty hustlers prowled the aisles, cruising for horny trade. Sometimes they'd sit a few seats from a manic masturbator, waiting for a sign of interest, then they'd chip in and give him a hand. Sometimes in the john, straight cock collided with a gay dude's lips. In a place like that, a hard cock didn't give a shit about gender. A horny dick just wants to get off.

Then there were those rattling stalls. So many times I'd banged on doors after counting four sets of feet, sniffing the reek of ass. I'd bang to the jangle of belt buckles and zippers quickly zipping.

Once, behind the screen, I heard this commotion. I walked back there and aimed my flashlight. Two older guys were all over this young stud, licking him from both ends, getting crazy with it. The sight of them stiffened my cock. Hell, I wanted to join in, but shit, I was a trusted employee—albeit an employee with a raging prick.

After being around that scene, I realized something: No matter how rough or rugged, if a man gets hard or horny enough, that straight label vanishes quicker than it takes to whip out his drooling dick.

The following is my own dick-drooling story: It was raining heavy cocks and balls that night, when this tall black man dashed through the door. His Members Only jacket was wringing wet, his khakis soaked so thin and wet, I didn't have to strain to see the print of his dick. And man, what a schlong it was! Damn thing hung down his wet leg in a long, casual bulge. Dude had the kind of dick that made guys like me stare and lick our lips.

Sometimes I'd see a patron and wonder about his trip, guess what he was into. But this dude, I knew, had come to watch pussy getting fucked. From his looks, you'd bet he'd rather fight to the death than switch ball teams. He must've been the tallest man I'd seen that night—easily 6 foot 5 or 6 foot 6. He was lanky, butch-handsome, with dark copper skin, a bushy mustachio, and a fearsome unibrow.

"What's showing?" he asked. His voice was deep, but not unfriendly.

I had no idea. Men in those places didn't give a shit about the titles, only the fuck scenes. "Something hot, I'm sure," I said as he handed me a ball of wet singles. Yes. It was all there, which told me he'd been inside this joint before.

"You say it's hot, huh?" he said with a sly wink, squeezing his cock. It seemed like either a straight man's gesture, a tease, or a blatant come-on. I couldn't figure which. But I'd swear his khaki-clad pipe had gotten longer and plumper as he stood there, and it really got to me.

I wanted to say, "Not half as hot as you!" before he proceeded through the door, past a red light bulb and into the waiting dark. I imagined him casting a long hot shadow against that sliver slip of light as he took a seat in a row scattered with men, faces straight ahead, their cocks stirring.

Patrons came—literally and figuratively—then left. I'd glance at them drifting past the ticket booth, not one as hot as him. Was he still inside watching that fuck flick and writhing in his seat? Was he beating that dick, moaning, groaning, about to shoot his load? I couldn't stop thinking about how he'd tried to start a conversation, how he gripped his long shrouded prick as he looked at me. Usually, I would read or do crosswords to ease the boredom. But that night, I just sat there playing with my dick.

Every hour or so, I had to check the place, make my rounds, quash any illegal activity. Yet secretly I was always hoping to find some. That night, the time to check things had come. The darkened seedy den was beginning to thin, but the smell of raunch and the high odor of cock remained. Just past the door, some randy fucker was on his knees, going down in a feeding frenzy.

"Yeah! Oh, shit. Suck! Get it all down. Mmm! Suck that big dick!" one man demanded in a whisper.

"Hey, dudes. Not here! All right! Take it someplace else!" I warned.

Neither one moved.

I shined my light on them. First, to the one on his knees, then higher, and…it was him! That long, cool black brother getting sucked hard and loud by one of those late-night hustlers! I let the light linger on his beauty. This man's pipe was absolutely Titanic! The proud owner pulled his schlong away. Then in a show of big dick defiance, he shook it at me. Dude had enough dick to feed a multitude of cocksuckers. Last thing I needed or wanted was to tussle with him. In fact, job or not, I wanted to push the sucker to the grimy floor, latch on to that schlong, and chow the fuck down! The two of them finally disengaged. But the vision remained as I sat in my booth, stroking my rod to the edge of shooting, thinking of that long hard dick.

Closing time was 2 A.M. At the end of another long and sticky night, only the janitor and I remained on the floor. Rex was upstairs, probably getting his dick blown while counting his mounting dough. I figured I'd checked the place pretty thoroughly. But as I went into the john, there he was again: that hot black brother in the wet khakis! Rex would've pitched a bitch! Not I. Dude was standing over the sink, dousing his face with water, looking even better, wetter and hotter than he had before. His shoulders were very broad, and his height excited me. Strange how cool he seemed, as if he were expecting me. His dark eyes met mine in the mirror.

"Yo, man, you gotta leave. We're closed now," I said, though I was kind of glad to see him.

He didn't say a word; just stared back at me, water running down that handsome brown mug. He looked a little isolated standing there, and more than a little intimidating. Was he gonna kick my ass?

"Fuckin' killjoy! You know, you stopped me from bustin' a nut tonight, man!" he said angrily.

"Sorry. I had to stop you guys. I could lose my job letting that shit go on," I said in defense.

"Yeah? So why did you hold that light so long on my dick?" he asked in a challenging voice, suddenly turning and stroking that long, sleek column inside his khakis. Oh, damn! He busted *me*. Still I couldn't help gawking at his big damp package.

"Bet you wanna see it again, don't you?" he taunted. "Don't you, cocksucker?"

Hell! I was already seeing plenty. I saw a wet spot where its club head poked through, and that spot was starting to widen. I could see *it* needed relief.

"I paid my money to get off in this place. But because of you, tryin' to be somebody's cop, I didn't bust my fuckin nut, did I? Shit! You better give me a refund…or something," he said.

And with that, out it came with a mighty thrust! The Great Black Bar Speared Up! Shit! That freakish fucker had to be 11 inches long! It was starting to lift from its anchoring nuts. I watched the horny throb of it, thickening, poking up and at me. Man! That hot shaft loomed straighter than a fucking arrow as it wavered long and hard from the zipper of those khakis.

"What you got going on in those jeans, huh? Is that a little boner, I see?" he teased.

Sure it was, but there was nothing "little" about it. My rod's normally seven inches, erect. But sometimes, in the presence of big honking dick, the fucker surprises even me. That night, it grew and mounted and raged into a fat, steel-hard 8-, maybe 8½-inch tube, just from looking at him. He boldly strode up to me and rubbed it real slowly. I thought my pole would burst into steam.

For some reason, he thought it important to tell me he was straight, as if my dick or I even gave a shit at that point. So a straight man was rubbing my joint? A hand was a hand, and I liked his hand. Mmm...The way it probed me, knowing where to touch, how smooth, how rough...

"Probably seen more pussy than you'll ever see dick. That's a fact. Nothin' queer about me. Got four kids and another one on the way," he bragged.

It was a strange moment to tell me this, but long hard cocks always do have lousy timing.

The crest of his rod poked my thigh as he unzipped me, hauled out my prize. I was proud of it, growing all bone-erect and shiny with early jizz. He smiled with his eyes, sure by then that I dug him, really liked him in a big way.

Just as I reached out and grabbed a hot handful of long dark meat, the man pulled back. Grabbing a shock of my hair, he led me down to that huge, pulsating log, that big oozing crown.

"Go on. Suck it! Show me how bad you want this big straight motherfuckin' dick," he said.

Its leaking eye gaped at me. A dark ripe plum called out to my lips. Flicking my hot tongue inside its wide piss hole, made the whole wedge jump, shiver with excitement. My lips enclosed it tightly. Its fucking pulse was fast. I slurped pumping veins and knots. The knob was so hot, it throbbed like a jackhammer on my tongue. I went down that pipe as far as I could, before I reached that choking point! I belched it back. He pumped it slow and slick through my compromised lips. His hips motioned, almost sensual, as his balls dragged my throat. Mmm. He placed my hands to his smooth, boulder-hard cheeks, and I licked his pole with growing lust.

Mmm, yes! Big man, big dick. Long, hot and pulsating dick. Such a sweet motherfucker!

But then came those signs letting me know he was close to exploding. Those long, sleek thighs began to tremble as his big nut bag slapped violently to my chin. He wasn't sensual then. No. He fucked my mouth, plowed my jaw, battered my throat with that imposing bar. The size of his suckmeat made me clumsy. Suddenly I was spitting goo, sputtering and moaning like his cock-crazed fool. It took some doing, but I pried my lips from his juicy, vividly hard meat.

"Yeah. Go on! Shoot it! Shoot it! Shoot that big fuckin wad, man!" I encouraged.

"Naw. Hell, no! Not until I fuck that ass!" he said, shaking his long, shiny slab at me.

He dropped those khakis, ripped off his shirt. Muscle and long, bobbing dick was all there was to see. He was lean and taut, his tight killer globes were the moist color of good Valentine's chocolate. I wanted a bite of his Hershey's Kisses nipples. I wanted to lick the building sweat from his balls. But did I want that giant dong wrecking my ass? Oh, hell yes! I was transfixed by the thing. It looked hard and capable of inflicting serious ass-splitting pain.

He drew me close, and palmed my butt like a basketball, which I'm sure he played, judging by the long glossy planes and sinews of his body.

"Gonna let me fuck this tight piece of ass, huh? Sure you will. You like a big dick up there," he said assuredly, smacking my ass, real hard. Then he drew back and walloped it again. It stung!

"Get that ass up on the sink, and let me at it!" he demanded. His take-charge attitude decided things for me. I watched him shimmy a safe along his throbbing plank. He jabbed three rough fingers up my ass and sent them deep! Then, pulling away, he spat on them and lodged even deeper. I swooned from the sweet raunch of it, wanting the real thing.

So did he. He aimed that pole straight through my bunghole as I teetered on the sink, legs akimbo.

"Owww! Aww-awww! Shit! Shit! SHIT!" I cried. My inner cheeks flexed, but I wasn't ready for that impact. It was a whole different dick up my ass. It felt longer, more brutish than it had in my mouth. The hard thud of his knob kept slicing a rough path through me. The long, vein-jagged shank hit hard, spanking me repeatedly.

As my ass floated over the basin, I looked down and saw a churning knot in my aching belly. Shit! Was that his cock? Had the fucker reached that far!

The pain of his dick racked me from tits to toes as he tossed my legs across his shoulders. He took a breath, then plowed my ass with deep long-dicking strokes. That agony of his prong was melting away. In its place, a sweet-burning ache of lust made me delirious for his next thrust.

"You like that, don't you?" Beat your dick for me! That's it. Beat it red and hard!"

As he forged and lunged that cock deeper through my chute, I wondered how often he fucked men. Was it only in dark theaters, when he needed to bust a nut? Was he mad at the wife? He must've been, he banged like a man mad at someone. He fucked hard and jarring, making me pitch, making me spasm from every fucking inch.

He struck my butt with heavy hands. My ass registered his plowing plank and smacking balls as he threw his all to me. Beneath his gust, I beat off swiftly. By then, I was an 8-inch tower of boiling cum ready to shoot. All at once, he pulled out, discarding the rubber, and he exploded. His fucking load was astounding!

Great bursts of vaulting jism spewed in spurts, smearing me, the sink, the floor, the mirror at my back. Shit! What a fucking trajectory! Man, just watching that fucker lurch and spray did it for me. I came in a gasping, shaking fit of mayhem, splooge flying, hot cream slopping both our dicks."Ah! Shit! Damn! Think I must've shot about a pint tonight" he huffed, tucking that big black straight beauty away. Looking around that wrecked john, raunched out in dripping blades of cum, I believed him.

It took a moment before I could move, let alone pull clothes back on my distressed body. Then, we sneaked around back. I slyly let him out the locked movie house, hoping Rex had shut off the video monitors that recorded the wild night's cumin's and goin's, and I watched the tall silhouette of the man who'd fucked me raw, as he dashed into the rainy night, his khakis growing wetter—like my dick.

Long Road Home

by Sean Wolfe

I stepped onto the bus with less than my usual enthusiasm. In fact, the long string of four-letter words that rambled through my head surprised even me. A couple of them must have slipped through my tight lips, because the driver gave me a stern look of disapproval as I handed him my ticket. "Oh, well, fuck him," I muttered as I readjusted my backpack across my shoulders and fought my way down the narrow aisle. It wasn't his car that had broken down two days ago. Nor was it his stubborn sister who had insisted on having him sing at her wedding. He hadn't flunked an algebra test because he had to make last-minute travel arrangements and couldn't study, nor had the $150 he'd been saving for a new stereo been sacrificed for a bus ticket. "So fuck him," I said to myself as I looked back timidly to make sure he hadn't heard my tirade of profanity.

The bus was less than a third full, and there were only two stops between Wichita and Amarillo. As the bus pulled away from the stop and maneuvered its way back onto the highway, I scanned the empty seats to find which would be the best. I stumbled past a group of eight elderly women occupying the front seats and cackling like a bunch of hens. Obviously, I wanted to be as far away from them as possible, but not so far away that I was sitting next to the stinky bathroom in the back. So I hiked my backpack into the overhead bin about two thirds of the way back and sat in a relatively empty section of the bus.

Despite a crying baby and a few excited young kids in the very back of the bus, I was able stretch out and fall asleep relatively easily. The low humming of the diesel engine and swaying motion of the big bus helped me stay asleep until it ground noisily to a stop a few hours later.

I woke up and rubbed my sleepy eyes just as the Brady Bunch in the back of the bus shuffled noisily past my seat and off the bus. I was thankful to have them off. I realized that I now had the entire back of the bus to myself and breathed a sigh of relief as I stretched and looked out the window. The sun was just setting on the horizon, and I figured I had a good chance of sleeping the rest of the way to Amarillo…just as soon as I emptied my bladder.

Walking to the bathroom in the back of the bus, I wasn't surprised that I had a semi hard-on. *Pervert,* I thought as I realized that I was aroused by the not-so-small amount of pain due to the pressure in my gut. I walked into the bathroom, shut and locked the door, and pulled my swollen cock out of my jeans and aimed it at the toilet. Just as the steady stream of piss began to pour into the basin, the bus jerked into reverse and began backing up. I wrapped my left fist loosely around my dick and tried to keep the flow somewhere near the bullseye, and reached out with my right hand to steady myself against the wall.

A small mirror mounted on the wall was positioned just right so that I saw my own cock in the reflection. Though almost finished peeing, my dick was still fat and tingled in my hand, and I toyed with the idea of staying in the bathroom and beating off. Then I heard a faint male voice yell from outside and suddenly the bus halted to a stop, knocking me off balance and ridding my mind of anything other than getting back to the safety of my seat and back to sleep.

I stuffed my cock back into my jeans and buttoned them up, then washed my hands in the tiny sink. Walking back to my seat, I was glad to see that the entire back of the bus was still empty. Besides the eight old ladies up front, there were only three other people on the bus, all seated near the front. Maybe I'd move a few seats farther back away from the cackling hens up front, I thought as I got closer to my seat.

Or maybe not. As I sat down and leaned my head against the pillow propped against the window, I noticed a young guy directly across the aisle from me. He was stretched across two seats, reclining in exactly the same position I was in. Obviously, it was his voice I'd heard yelling for the bus to stop while I contemplated beating off in the bathroom just a moment ago.

He was about my age, maybe a couple of years older. His long, muscular legs hung over the side of the seat into the aisle. He was wearing an Oklahoma Sooners sweatshirt, and it looked comfortable on his massive chest. A matching Sooners baseball cap was perched atop his short blond hair; and even in the semi-dark of the bus I could make out the faint stubble on his chin and upper lip. I was envious. Even though I was a sophomore at Wichita State University, I still could not grow much facial hair. This guy was probably a senior at U. Oklahoma, I reasoned, as I continued admiring him.

His eyes were already closed, but I imagined them as bright blue. The arms crisscrossed against his chest were hairy and thickly muscled, a fact I could confirm because the sleeves of his sweatshirt were pushed up almost to the elbow. He had broad shoulders and a thick chest, and as my eyes wandered lustfully down his torso, I saw that his waist was fairly small: a stark contrast with the rest of him.

The bus pulled back onto the highway and accelerated to its cruising speed as I arranged my pillow and leaned my head against the window so that I had full view of my new friend. My eyes found their way to his crotch, and I took a deep breath as the massive bulge there commanded my attention. One of his legs was leaning against the back of the seats in front of him, while the other stretched across the empty seat next to him and into the aisle between us. I had a perfect view of his crotch, and it didn't take long at all before I felt my dick stir in my jeans as I stared.

The road was a little bumpy and jerked the bus around clumsily as we left the city limits of Liberal, Kansas. The motion caused my dick to stiffen even harder in my jeans, and I watched the guy across from me with barely confined lust as he slept. As we crossed the Oklahoma Panhandle border, I noticed the bulge in his jeans growing even bigger. I swallowed hard as he tilted his head more comfortably on his pillow. With his eyes still closed, he reached down and shifted the dick in his jeans so that the round bulge quickly became a long, thick line stretching down the inside of his thigh.

I forced my eyes shut and tried to rid myself of all thoughts of this hunk so that I could sleep, but it was useless. My own dick was throbbing so hard it hurt, so I dipped my hand into the waist of my jeans to rearrange myself. Just then the bus hit a pothole in the road, and the bus jerked heavily. My eyes opened sleepily, and I looked across the aisle at the new guy. The corners of his mouth were turned up just slightly into a grin.

I was horrified as I realized my hand was buried deep inside my jeans, groping my cock, and that he was watching me. My heart dropped into my stomach as I fumbled to pull my hand out of the front of my Levi's.

Mr. Oklahoma Sooner leaned forward, reached up, and turned on the little spotlight used for reading when the bus was dark, as it was now, and leaned back onto his pillow against the window. I could see his smile better now, and twin dimples graced his cheeks in the almost completely dark bus. He licked his lips sexily and raised one eyebrow at me as I freed my hand from its confines. I was right...his eyes were bright blue, and they sparkled at me tauntingly.

If I hadn't already lain down, I would have fallen from shaky knees just looking into his beautiful face. I felt myself blushing, but Sooner was completely cool and collected as he moved his gaze from my eyes to his own crotch. It was obvious he meant for me to follow, and I did so almost involuntarily.

When my eyes reached his midsection, I saw his hands squeezing and tracing his hard-on teasingly. A lump formed in my throat as I stared at the fat mound pressing against his leg. He moved one hand from his bulge to the top of his jeans and unbuttoned them slowly. In one quick move he unzipped the blue jeans and reached inside to pull his fat cock out into plain view.

The overhead light was positioned perfectly so that I saw his cock in all its beauty. The skin was very light and stretched tight around one of the fattest shafts I'd ever seen...or even imagined. His hand, though large, barely fit around it. A huge, throbbing vein pulsed along its underside, and several smaller, but still significant blue veins branched off from the main one and wrapped around the dick.

I looked away quickly to make sure none of the remaining passengers were watching us. We were safe; the old women were engaged in a card game, the remaining three passengers were all sleeping several rows in front of us, and the driver had closed the tinted glass door separating his sanctuary from the main coach.

So I quickly looked back. In the few seconds that I had looked away, Sooner had pulled his jeans halfway down his thighs. I gasped as I saw his huge dick completely free. Now I could see that not only was his cock rock hard and mammoth in size, but his balls were also enormous and hung low between his spread legs.

My eyes darted back and forth from Sooner's face to his cock, unsure which sight was more beautiful. His eyes never left mine, however, even as he gripped his big dick in one hand and stroked it slowly. He jerked himself for several minutes, then moved his hand away from his cock as he closed his eyes and leaned farther back into his pillow. I could tell he had gotten himself close, and my thought was confirmed as I stole another quick look down at his dick. A large, clear drop of precome oozed out of the slit in the big head, wiggled there for a moment, then slid slowly down all 9 or 10 fat inches of throbbing muscle until it disappeared under his balls.

He gestured with a little jerk of his head for me to come over and join him. Looking at the front of the bus once more, and sure I was not being watched, I crawled quickly across the aisle. Sooner spread his legs as wide as he could to give me room, and I squeezed myself between his massive legs, completely out of the aisle and view of anyone who might look back. My face was inches from his cock at this point, and I smelled his clean, musky scent wafting into my nostrils.

"Lick it," Sooner whispered huskily.

I did. Starting at his heavy balls, I stuck out my tongue and lapped at whatever remained of his trail of precome. His balls twitched as I licked them, and I was only able to pull one at a time into my hungry mouth. I could taste the mixture of soap, sweat, and precome that glistened his skin, and a shiver worked its way through my body.

Reluctantly, I moved from his balls and began licking my way up his rod. His veins pulsed lightly against my tongue as I slowly worked my way up the fat pole. When I reached the top, my mouth opened wide, and I wrapped my lips around his thick head. A low moan escaped his throat, and I felt one large strong hand grip the back of my head and push me deeper onto him. His cock filled my mouth easily, and my tongue licked as much as it could of the big pole inside my closed mouth as I continued swallowing.

"Yeah, man," he said when I had half of his dick stuffed in my hungry mouth.

It was at that point that I realized I couldn't breathe and panicked. I stifled a gag as quietly as possible and breathed deeply through my nose, which automatically caused the back of my throat to open wider. Sooner seized the moment, and thrust my head harder into his crotch. His large cock head pushed its way past where my tonsils had been about 10 years ago, and my eyes widened as I felt the fat length of his entire pole spreading my throat muscles apart. He didn't stop pushing the back of my head until my lips touched the base of his cock, where it met his ball sac.

I never knew I was such a gifted cocksucker until I felt him fucking my mouth with greater and greater intensity. If anyone had told me I'd be able to deep throat such a big dick I would have laughed at them; but here I was, swallowing it whole and even trying to get more. I don't know how long I sucked his huge dick, but I could have gone on like that for hours. Sooner had other ideas though. As I licked and lapped and swallowed his cock, he reached down and unbuttoned my jeans, sliding them carefully down my legs until they were around my ankles.

"You want it, don't you, kid?" he sneered sexily.

"Mmm-hmm," I answered through a mouthful of cock.

"Stand up and turn around."

I was reluctant to let go of his cock from my mouth, but he lifted me with strong arms and turned me around so that my chin rested on the head of the seat in front of us and my exposed ass was inches from his face.

Sooner put a gentle hand on each of my ass cheeks and played with them lovingly as his mouth worked my hole. I felt his soft lips kiss my ass cheeks gently, and slowly work their way closer to my quivering hole. I cursed myself for not being able to control myself, but when his hot lips surrounded the tiny circle and sucked on it gently as his tongue slid all around it and then slowly and strongly snaked its way inside, I moaned deeply and forgot everything else.

As he kissed my twitching hole, I lost my breath and shot a load of come all over the back of the seat in front of me. This made my ass spasm even more around Sooner's tongue, and he laughed quietly even as he slid the last inch of his hot tongue inside me and tenderly bit my ass.

I thought we were finished, and was about to pull up my pants and head back to my seat, but Sooner pushed my hands away and shifted in his seat so that one strong leg was planted on either side of me.

"Come here, man. Sit on me," he said.

There was really no choice on my part; he held me by the waist and steadily moved my body so that I was sitting in his lap. I felt his huge cock head press against my ass and took a deep breath as he pulled me down onto him. His hot, throbbing pole felt like it was three feet long as it forced my ass muscles to spread and twitch around it. He didn't let go of my waist until I was completely impaled on his fat cock.

Then he moved his hands away from me completely and began fucking me slowly and deeply. I moaned a little too loudly as his hot fat cock speared my ass and made bright, sparkly lights float in front of my eyes. I felt his breath and his lips hot on the back of my neck and ears, and squeezed my ass even tighter to let him know how much I liked it. He moaned deeply, then bit my ear softly and whispered, "Turn around. I want to kiss you."

It was not the easiest request in the world, but I was determined to do it. I lifted my knees up to my chest, which forced every fat inch of his dick deeper into me, and slowly turned around on the hard rod until I was facing him. When I looked at his beautiful face, his eyes were closed and he was biting his bottom lip. His low moan confirmed he was enjoying it as much as I was.

He opened his eyes and smiled at me, and I thought I would melt then and there. "Kiss me," he instructed, and I did. His lips were soft and full and sweet. His hot tongue slid sensually into my mouth at the exact moment his huge dick slid out of my ass, making sure my body was never empty at any one time. Then, as the big cock slid slowly back into my hole, he withdrew his tongue from my mouth and nibbled my lips lovingly.

We fucked like this for 15 or 20 minutes. I could tell he was getting close, so when he reached down to stroke my cock, I didn't stop him. Just the feel of his strong warm fist wrapped around my dick was all it took. I blasted a load even larger than the first one a few minutes earlier. Hot, steamy cum shot out of my dick and landed all over my T-shirt, and all over the front of Sooner too.

When the first spurt of my load hit his chin, he leaned his head back and smiled. At the same time I felt his cock in my ass grow incredibly thicker and pulse in long throbbing bursts. The tip of his cock head was deep inside me, and I felt the warmth of the latex as it filled with his come and pressed against my prostate.

When both of us were exhausted, we slumped against each other for a minute or two. Suddenly, the driver announced that we were approaching Dalhart, Texas, our last stop before Amarillo.

"This is my stop, man," Sooner said, and gave me a quick kiss as he lifted me off his shrinking dick.

A couple of people up front began moving as well, and that got me up and moving. I quickly pulled up my pants and shuffled clumsily back over to my seat. Sooner carefully removed the condom from his deflated cock, twisted the end of it into a knot, and tossed it across the aisle to me with a wink. The long rubber chute was half-filled, and the come inside was still warm. I smiled as he finished fastening his Levi's and pulled his gym bag from the overhead bin. He walked to the front of the bus without a glance back, and was on the street almost before it had come to a full and complete stop.

I carefully packed the used condom in my backpack, not sure why I'd ever use it—or what I would ever use it for—but wanting to keep it anyway. The trip from Dalhart to Amarillo was only about an hour, and I slumped back into my pillow and prepared to grab a well-deserved nap before reaching the Big A and facing my family. My ass tingled the last leg of the trip, and my throat and jaw were very sore, but it didn't take long at all before I'd chalked this trip as one of my all-time favorites.

Sliding Home
by Mac O'Neill

"Hey, man, you want a beer?" Greg West asked, glancing vaguely toward the living room where Pete Palmer was sitting.

"Sure." Pete nervously rubbed the palm of his right hand with the thumb of his left hand. He was sweating profusely, although Greg had the windows open and the ceiling fan was rotating above him with a dull, incessant whir, like a misplaced propeller blade.

Greg had already stripped off his sweaty jeans and sneakers, and was naked except for a worn institutional-white jockstrap. He groped distractedly at the white meshed fabric at his crotch, then, bending slightly at the waist, peered into the white light of the refrigerator. A moment later, Pete heard the unmistakable fizz-pop of aluminum cans being snapped open.

The first time it happened, Pete had felt like he'd physically left his body and was merely watching off to the side, like some impassive observer. He couldn't even admit to himself that his mind could entertain such wanton, unnameable desires. Yet there they were, vandalizing his mind; festering beneath the surface like a bad wound, aching and throbbing, refusing to heal. He seemed to be in a state of perpetual arousal. His balls ached, but even worse, his heart appeared to beat only when Greg was around.

Then it happened one evening, as though he had willed it upon himself; the Rubicon was crossed. They were driving back from a softball game in Orlando, when Greg pulled down a dark country road to find a place to piss. The night was hot and muggy—a typical Florida evening, when the air is so sticky and palpable that breathing is like trying to inhale damp cotton candy.

Greg found a long gravel road leading along the Gulf of Mexico and pulled the pickup alongside a towering growth of sea grape. Pete got out and walked around to the driver's side of the pickup. He stretched luxuriantly, looking absently toward a small cay in the gulf. Greg got out and casually unbuttoned his jeans. His groin was covered in obscene tufts of wild dark hair, like animal fur. Pete took a hearty chug from the bottle of beer in his hand, which was now lukewarm, and stared at the dense overgrowth spilling out of Greg's open fly. The light from a pale full moon splashed across the calm, glassy gulf.

Reaching into the fly of his jeans, Greg did a kind of semi-squat and pulled out his penis. It was fleshy, heavily veined and massively wrinkled, with more than an inch of puckered cowl hanging past the helmet-shaped cock head. Easing the foreskin back with his thumb, Greg let loose a long, steady stream of warm piss. Pete glanced obliquely, if only momentarily, at the translucent yellow stream. It sounded amatory, like summer rain splattering against hot pavement.

Greg watched passively as Pete watched him relieve himself. Then, with a slight, almost imperceptible movement, the stream of warm piss flowing from his cock splashed against the sand at Pete's shoes. "Hey!" Pete protested, jumping backward. His eyes shifted toward Greg's, which were impenetrable in the dark night.

Pete knew he should have objected, but every ounce of logic and reason had deserted him months ago. He wanted this man more than he had ever wanted a piece of pussy. He wanted his hairiness, the bold, blatant masculinity that reached out and took whatever it wanted without question. He closed his eyes, surrendering his virility to one more masculine than himself.

"Sorry, man," Greg half-grinned. With his cock still dangling out the fly of his jeans, Greg pulled the sweaty T-shirt he was wearing up over his head, throwing it into the back of the pickup. His chest was sculpted, massive, matted with tufts of dark hair; as he turned slightly sideways, the bulging flesh of his immense pectorals protruded above his hard, flat belly like a set of masculine teats. Testosterone and sweat seemed to ooze from every pore of his half-naked body and mingle with the salty night air, like the scent of some overpowering feral aroma. He didn't utter a syllable, yet seemed acutely aware of precisely what he wanted—and that Pete would give it to him. Greg gripped his cock; the fleshy appendage filled his fist. He shook his dick to arousal, until it grew in girth and length. Before Pete realized what was happening, he could feel his fingertips stroking the thicket of wiry black pubic hair that stretched above Greg's sweaty crotch to the perimeter of his upper thighs, forming a dark, wide triangle. He buried his face into the dense fur and inhaled the pungent, musky scent of sex and male sweat.

Expressionless, yet with a tacit air of arrogance about him that absorbed and aroused Pete, Greg stared at his friend on his knees before him in the sand. He lifted the swollen meat of his cock to Pete's mouth, then leaned back against the hood of the truck. Pete would do the rest, and Greg would watch and savor the moist, warm touch of his friend's mouth milking his sex.

Pete pulled the soft, fleshy meat from his mouth and admired it for a moment before nibbling and toying with the extended, velvet-textured foreskin. He pulled back the soft, jagged cowl and took the expansive knob of Greg's cock head, which seemed too meaty and voluminous for him to properly service, into his mouth. He sucked hard, awkwardly at first, feeling the peach-shaped knob dilate and press against the back of his throat. He pulled it from his mouth and licked the underside of the enlarged shaft. Quietly, Greg reached down, grabbed his meaty cock in his fist and inserted it in Pete's mouth; he felt his nuts hitch and graze Pete's chin. He moaned so deep and low in his throat that the sound, both sensuous and solicitous, aroused Pete's nipples.

Pete felt his own cock rise in his jeans, hard and hot against the moist flesh of his inner thigh. He liked being subservient to this ex-Marine, and when he felt Greg's massive hands firmly clutch his head, he moaned spontaneously, his come squirting uncontrollably inside his jeans along the hard flesh of his upper thigh.

Greg reached down and cupped Pete's chin in his broad, rough hand. His cock, corpulent and ridged obscenely with thick, extended veins, pulsated with sexual ardor. He pumped Pete's moist mouth with his own distinctive rhythm: fast and hard, then slow and easy, feeling his supple, enlarged cock head sliding easily down Pete's throat, as if each had intentionally been made to fit the other. Greg moaned, clasping Pete's head firmly in his hands, the long stray hairs sprouting from his nuts flush against Pete's chin, like a beard. He drove the meat of his shaft deeper into Pete's throat and, without preamble, a profuse ejaculate of warm semen gushed from the meaty center of his cock head in quick, furious squirts. Pete swallowed hard, but the come kept flowing, filling his mouth until it dribbled down his chin, dripping to his chest like salty raindrops.

Greg stood gasping for a few minutes, then, slowly recapturing his breath, he patted Pete impassively on the cheek as though he were petting a favorite pet. He rubbed his hand across his belly and stretched his massive arms into the air. Speechless, Pete watched as Greg nonchalantly stuffed his cock back into his jeans and climbed into the cab of the pickup, as though nothing as intimate as man-to-man cocksucking had taken place. He and Greg never spoke of it afterward.

Now, here he was again, uncertain if anything was going to take place, fooling himself into thinking that he didn't care. Pete had come to the gradual realization that with Greg, man-to-man sex happened spontaneously; no gushing or wooing or prolonged foreplay, just fortuitous and circuitous events that led to the satisfaction of Greg's sexual appetence. Pete had become a willing pawn and an ardent player due to his own search for sexual fulfillment. He now lusted after Greg West in the same manner he had first lusted after Julie Palmer. But this was different, more hard-edged and desperate—unquestionably masculine.

Greg turned to Pete, his fingertips deep in the dense hair at the center of his chest; he scratched his left nipple abstractly. "Hey, buddy, I'm going to jump in the shower. How 'bout you?"

Pete nodded casually, camouflaging his vehement lust. "Sounds good," he replied, agonizing briefly over the slight, almost perceptible tremor in his voice.

In the bathroom, Pete stripped off his clothes and watched Greg's naked body out of the corner of his eye, struggling to keep his semi-hard cock from becoming fully erect.

When the water was just the right temperature, Greg glanced over his shoulder, his eyes gravitating briefly to the dark triangle of pubic hair above the pendulous prominence of Pete's exposed dick. He smiled condescendingly, scratched the full sac of his drooping nuts, and climbed into the shower, arrogant and positive that Pete would follow.

"Hey, get my back for me, man," Greg said nonchalantly, handing Pete a bar of soap. Then, with that same unnerving, patronizing smirk added: "And keep your cock away from my ass, understand?"

For a brief millisecond, the expression on Pete's face resembled that of a panicked animal, trapped in the ominous sight of a hunter's loaded gun. He hated himself for the boyish, love struck way he sought the approval of such a glaringly masculine man.

After Pete had soaped Greg's muscular, V-shaped back, Greg rinsed off and grabbed the soap from Pete's hand. "Turn around and I'll do you."

Pete swallowed hard and leaned into the shower, bracing his extended arms and hands against the tiled wall, his back to Greg. He closed his eyes and felt his dick stiffen. He sighed as Greg's soapy hands roamed freely over the corded muscle of his exposed back; water collected in his pubic hair and dripped from the smooth curve of his cock head to his toes.

Then, abruptly, Pete gasped; Greg's hand had moved from his back to the cheeks of his ass. He closed his eyes and swallowed hard as Greg's hand moved between his thighs, under his dangling cock and balls. A sudsy hand slipped between his cheeks, and with a slight pressure, rubbed provocatively, slowly, against his sphincter. Under the splashing water, Pete could hear Greg's breathing growing heavier, like his own, fraught with tension and undeclared appetite. His cock grew so hard that it hurt.

Behind Pete, Greg lathered his cock and probed Pete's asshole with a soapy finger—first one, then another, stretching and lubricating the tight muscle until it accepted a third. "You're pretty tight," Greg said in a deep, feverish tone, more to himself than to the man he was about to fuck.

Pete gasped aloud and arched his back. He wanted it, wanted whatever Greg was about to give him. He was so flushed and unnerved, burning with such an intense, prurient desire, that he didn't hear himself moan, or realize that he had pushed the cheeks of his white ass into Greg's body.

With one hand, Greg gripped Pete's shoulder firmly, then poised his swollen cock head at Pete's puckered rim. "Oh, yeah," he moaned as he thrust his hips forward. Pete's virgin ass was tight, like a fist gripping his cock.

Pete groaned and gasped for breath, air coming to his lungs in short bursts. He flinched hard at the unsuspected pleasure of being penetrated by his leatherneck friend. His ass had swallowed Greg whole; no pain, just intense, immediate gratification like he had never before experienced. He forced his ass back, into the moist, wiry nest of Greg's pubic hair. He could feel Greg's muscular body press into his bare, wet back, and Greg's hot, steamy breath against his ear.

Greg brought his hand down and gripped Pete's wet ass hard, making a bright red impression. He thrust his cock forward with the full force of his body weight and watched the distended, heavily veined shaft of his dick disappear into the tight grip of Pete's moist insides. He bludgeoned him hard, ramming his dick so fiercely against him that the thick vein in Pete's neck stood out as he bucked and groaned. He wanted to ride Pete, give him a good, long Marine fucking like he'd never had before, but the tightness of Pete's ass muscles condensed around Greg's swollen cock head with such a smooth sucking sensation that he could barely control his climax. He slammed his naked body into Pete's backside with ferocious abandon, plowing him again and again, straining to get every inch of his hard cock inside him.

Pete reached behind himself and clasped a hand around the back of Greg's thick neck, bucking and gasping each time Greg's cock slammed into the firm white cheeks of his aching ass. Finally, when Pete was unable to take another inch, Greg withdrew his cock. Rinsing himself, he stepped out of the shower, grabbed a towel, and began drying off, leaving Pete embarrassingly erect and unsatisfied. Greg threw Pete a towel and told him to follow him to the bedroom.

Pete watched with awe as Greg's naked body turned and left the bathroom. There was something stimulating about watching this man's exposed body—the curves of hard muscle, the elongated flesh bouncing lightly beneath the dark bush of pubic hair. He studied him so intently that it was as if he'd never seen a man walk upright before.

"I want to watch you finish me off," Greg said in that casual manner he had about himself as Pete entered the bedroom. He was sitting on the edge of the bed, his hand buried in the pubic hair at his groin, his cock dangling provocatively over his suspended balls.

Pete knelt between Greg's thighs. He could feel the heat of Greg's intense stare upon him, watching, waiting. He closed his fist around Greg's pendulous cock and felt its girth. Greg reached down and brushed his fingers lightly against the stubble of Pete's cheek. Then he grabbed Pete's head and pulled him in close, whispering, "You want it, don't you, buddy? You've wanted it all along, right?"

Pete nodded, aroused by the tacit understanding that had developed between them. He knew what he was doing now. He took Greg's engorged cock head in his mouth and looked directly into Greg's eyes. Greg groaned from the pleasure, his eyes locked on Pete's. He reached down and brushed a finger against one of Pete's nipples, then leaned in close to his ear. "You're *my* cocksucker, huh?"

Pete nodded again, steadily milking Greg's cock. He worked his mouth down to the wild pubic hair around Greg's dick, feeling it brush against his nostrils. He cupped Greg's dangling nuts in his palm and squeezed until Greg winced and moaned "Oh, baby" deep in his throat, so intimately that a shiver ran up Pete's spine.

Pete slid his tongue over Greg's swollen cock head, milking the Marine's engorged sex until he felt Greg's muscles tense and the familiar, pleasing sensation of warm semen filling his mouth. He swallowed hard, sucking every last pearl of come from his partner's cock. Greg writhed and moaned at the intensity of his ejaculation, at the violent sensitivity centered in the tender flesh of his swollen cock head.

Pete stood, his cock hard and distended, oozing with precome. He stepped forward and guided his cock to Greg's mouth for the first time. Clasping Greg's head in his hands, Pete pumped his cock down Greg's throat. Greg clutched the cheeks of Pete's firm white ass in his palms and squeezed hard, forcing Pete's substantial cock deep into his mouth. Pete was so aroused, it took him all of a minute to come, and he suddenly found his voice. "Swallow it, Greg," he muttered, his eyes fluttering, clamping shut as he felt the rise of come surge from his cock into Greg's masculine mouth. Greg reached up and clutched at Pete's supple brown nipples, pinching and twisting them hard between his fingers.

Pete withdrew his cock and rubbed it across Greg's face. He leaned down and lightly punched the hairy ripples of Greg's stomach muscles. Love pats, he would come to call them.

Ripped Rasslers

by Bearmuffin

I was super-ripped for the Mr. Olympia 2000 title. But I lost to Muhammad Belizar, a hot 24-year-old Ethiopian sporting 36-inch arms and a 15-inch cock.

I was disappointed, but those were the breaks. After I had congratulated Muhammad with a friendly squeeze on his humpy butt, I went to the locker room to dress. I had just slipped on my jeans when Mr. Grant handed me a business card.

Grant worked for Don Wildfire, the biggest wrestling promoter in the business. If you played your cards right, Don would shoot you to the top.

"I'm always looking out for new talent," Grant said with a friendly grin. His eyes were running up and down my body. He licked his lips. "I know Mr. Wildfire could use a fine specimen like you."

"I'll think about it," I said. I finished dressing and drove back home.

I pondered Grant's offer. What the fuck? Lots of bodybuilders had gone into wrestling. Some had made big bucks. I figured I'd had my last shot at Mr. Olympia. So I called Grant. "Tell Wildfire I'll see him."

Grant was pleased. "You won't be sorry," he said. Then he gave me an address and hung up.

The next day I drove to a warehouse located in a seedy part of town. But I didn't worry about that. With my 6-foot-5 frame, 30-inch biceps, and tree-trunk thighs, nobody was going to fuck with me.

I looked straight into the security camera as I rang the buzzer. Seconds later, the door opened. I climbed a long flight of stairs until I reached the loft on the top floor.

In the center was a huge wrestling ring where a pair of jock-strapped studs were grappling on the sweaty canvas. After I had taken in the astonishing sight of those two bronzed, muscular dudes glistening with sweat, I turned to see a big blond naked dude sitting on a rim chair.

It was Wildfire. He was in his late 40s and in great shape with thick muscles and a hairy chest. He wore a huge black cowboy hat and black cowboy boots. And he was smoking a black cigar. He stroked his firm thick cock while a muscle-bound wrestler lay beneath him. The dude grunted like a pig as he sucked hard on Wildfire's sweaty asshole.

Wildfire ignored me for a few moments while he jacked off eagerly, keeping his big blue eyes on the two wrestlers. Then he glanced at me. He broke out in a huge grin. His eyes flew to my bulging crotch.

"Glad ya could make it, son," he drawled in a thick Texas accent.

I noticed his cock jerk up. A thick strand of pre-cum oozed from his piss slit. It trickled down over his vein-etched cock. Wildfire licked his lips.

"Why don't you get comfortable?"

I quickly stripped to my jock and faced him, arms akimbo.

Wildfire's jaw dropped. "Whoa! Fuckin' hot bod! Grant sure as hell wasn't exaggerating when he described ya! His cock was bobbing up and down with excitement. His toothy grin had become a lecherous sneer. "How's about posing for me?"

I was always turned on by posing. Regardless of whom I was posing for, my bulge would get bigger and more defined as I posed. "Sure," I replied.

As I went through my standard posing routine, Wildfire ogled me. His thick lips were twisted in a lustful snarl. "Ohmygod, ohmygod," he kept on moaning, jacking himself off into a real frenzy. For a moment I thought he was about to topple from the rim chair and shoot his wad.

I capped off my routine with a little trick I'd learned from Muhammad. I bent over, grabbed my ankles, and spread my legs. With my cheeks split wide open, Wildfire had a bird's-eye view of my asshole.

"Ah, Fuck! Ah, Holy Fuck!" Wildfire screamed as he shot a thick boiling cumload that landed right on my butt hole. Then he barked, "C'mon stud. Let me lick my cum off your fuckin' hot butt."

I pushed my ass against his eager face. I felt his thick, fat, sandpaper-rough tongue glide over my haunches. Then he stuck his snake-like licker right into my hole.

He began lightly circling my anus with his tongue tip. That really drove me crazy making my cock bolt straight into the air. I grabbed my crank and began fisting it. Wildfire was a champion rimmer. I was only to happy to let the fucker eat my hole until I popped my rocks.

But Wildfire had no intention of letting me cum. Not just yet. He slapped my butt and pushed me away. "Plenty of time for that later," he snorted. "I wanna see you wrestle!" He shot a look at the two studs who were still wrestling.

"Carlos!" he barked. "C'mere!"

Carlos dropped his opponent on the mat. When he saw me, he broke out in a lewd smile. He jumped out of the ring and sprinted over to us.

Wildfire's greedy eyes ran all over Carlos's gorgeous Colombian bod. He was 6 foot 4 with barn-house shoulders, corded biceps, shelf-like pecs, and the dick of death. The head was fat and wide. Ready to tear a hole right through his jockstrap.

Wildfire jerked a thumb toward me. "You're going to wrestle him," he said to Carlos.

Carlos grinned. "You're the boss." Then Carlos gave me the once over. His sexy green eyes glittered with lust. He grabbed his throbbing basket and winked at me. "Let's wrestle!"

The dude he'd been wrestling hopped out of the ring and kneeled in front of Wildfire. He began sucking his cock. The other wrestler continued to rim him. Wildfire lit up another stogie, leaned back, and shouted, "Start rasslin'!"

Carlos and I hopped into the ring. Carlos was a horny motherfucker. I knew he wanted to take me down so he could plow me with his Colombian buttwhanger. As much as the thought of getting totally reamed by that bronzed beauty might have appealed to me, nobody was going to fuck me. No, sir. I was a total top.

Carlos kept grabbing my cock and squeezing it. I whacked his butt a few times. Each time I did it, Carlos whimpered and moaned like a little boy. I figured he wouldn't mind me fucking his ass. I just hoped it would be as tight as it was hot. I like a dude's glute muscles to grip my cock and milk my cum out for all its worth!

I didn't know any wrestling holds apart from what I'd seen on TV. But it wasn't hard to get Carlos on his back. Within seconds I'd tossed Carlos on his face. His ass was wriggling in the air. So I stuck a finger inside it. His butt hole rumbled like a volcano ready to erupt.

"Ay, sí papi," he moaned like a big pussy. *"Chingame, papi, chingame bien!"*

Wildfire bolted up. "He wants you to fuck him, son!" he said with a hoarse chuckle.

Wildfire pushed the cocksucking wrestler away from his thick, upright cock. He snorted like a bull, obviously aroused by the scene. He tossed me a tube of lube, which I caught with one hand.

"Fuck him!" Wildfire frothed at the mouth. His eyes rolled up wildly. "Fuck that big Brazilian *puto*!"

Before you could say "butt-fuck," I had squeezed a glop of lube on Carlos's anxiously twitching pucker. I placed the head of my cock flush against his anal ring. Then I rubbed my cock head all along it. The friction made Carlos pant and squirm all the more.

"Please, *papi,* please fuck me!"

"Fuck him, goddamn it!" Wildfire roared as he plopped back on the rim chair. He grabbed the cocksucking wrestler by the hair and plunged his cock down his throat.

I slam-dunked my cock right inside Carlos's ass. Carlos was medium tight, so my cock was able to snap right past his tight anal ring. Smoothly it glided down until the root of my cock struck his fat balls.

"Ay...ay...ay..." Carlos whimpered.

He reached down between his legs and began whacking off. I started to slowly hump him. Carlos was a real hot piece of ass. His butt muscles sucked around my pumping cock like a greedy mouth. I felt like leaving my cock inside his hole and letting him massage it with his talented sphincter, but I knew Wildfire expected a good show, so I gave it to him. I pumped away slowly at first, gradually building up a steady rhythm until you could hear my balls slapping against hot sweaty butt.

"¡Dios mío!" Carlos gasped.

Meanwhile, Wildfire was bellowing at us to get it on. "Fuck him, fuck him, fuck him, fuck him!" Wildfire screamed while he yanked on his tits. He was still being serviced by his two wrestling slaves, one eating his ass and the other sucking his cock.

I plowed full steam ahead. I was whipping my head back and forth. Hot sizzling sweat flew off my hair.

"Give him the works!" Wildfire bellowed.

I boldly grabbed Carlos' firm waist for support as I fucked the holy shit out of his steaming Colombian ass.

"*Ay, ay!* I'm cumming, amigo! *I'm cumming!*"

Carlos suddenly slammed back against me as he shot his wad on the canvas. His ass muscles gripped my cock so hard I thought it'd snap right off. I was ready to cum inside Carlos but Don had something else in mind. He leaped from the rim chair and howled. "No, no, no! Give it to me. Shoot your load *at me*!"

Wildfire rushed to the ring. I yanked my cock from Carlos's butt and aimed it right at Wildfire. He grabbed the ropes and opened his mouth. I fired a huge fuckin' cumshot at him. It flew right over his head.

"Oh, God, no, fuck no!" Wildfire screamed in agony. Luckily, the second cumshot hit him square in the kisser.

"Argh!"

Wildfire's tongue flew out from between his sweaty lips. He ate my cum like a greedy cum-pig. He grabbed his crank, jacked it a few times, and out splooged his hot stinking load. I splattered him with a third, fourth, and fifth cumshot. I shot all my cum until Wildfire was drenched in hot steaming jism.

Wildfire ordered the two slaves to lick my cum from his body. Then he turned to me. "Goddamn, son. You're hired! Carlos will show the ropes, won't ya, boy?"

Carlos looked up. He had a shit-eating grin on his thick, sensuous lips. "We're going to be good friends, amigo!" He reached up to squeeze my cock.

"Yeah," I said. "Real good!"

Fantasy Cavern
by Aaron Hawkings

I was only 20, and still a virgin that winter of '75, and I was on vacation. It was one of those serenely beautiful mornings you can find off the Hawaiian Islands, and our boat had cruised to a quiet cove and dropped anchor. The promise of the light breeze was not for a storm, but for a respite from the heat.

Most of the passengers had taken to the decks to sunbathe and cast their fishing rods in lazy anticipation of a quiet day. I was restless—the endless blue of the horizon was calling to me. I felt like a swim, and there was the mystery of the cove and the nearby tropical forest beckoning.

The Hawaiian pilot assured me it was safe, and winked at me with a broad bright smile. "There is a cave along the shore. You can swim there and be alone. It is very, very fantastic."

I smiled back and turned to the water to dive in. It was cool and refreshing. I swam with determined strokes, since I was a powerful swimmer and quite used to the ocean. As my arms sliced through the salty blue sea, I kept my eyes on the tropical jungle ahead. I spotted the open darkness of the cave the pilot had mentioned.

Why had he winked and grinned like that? He certainly was a handsome devil. His dark skin was without blemish, a creamy chocolate that was consistent across virtually hairless limbs. He was quite a hunk, with a big body. His muscles were huge, and his powerful butt was practically a wonder of nature. His honey-colored eyes sparkled when he smiled. His short dark hair was a skullcap of curls atop a round and pleasant face. His lips were full and wet.

I realized I had a growing erection as I was thinking of him. I smiled as water slid across my body, allowing my tight swim trunks to pleasantly stretch over my hard cock. I was horny and more than a little bored.

I found the mouth of the cave. Water lapped at the rocky walls and entrance. I halted and peered inside. I realized I could stand—the water was only thigh deep—so I rose and walked forward into the dimness.

It was truly fantastic. Somewhere above there was an opening, and light streamed down to illuminate the chamber. The water was transparent and glowing with reflected light. I felt as if I was entering a magical, sacred place.

I floated in the shallow water and stared upward at the light raining down on me. I closed my eyes and allowed the gentle rocking of the waves to soothe me. There was very little sound, only the splashing of the waves echoing in the small cavern.

I sighed and opened my eyes to survey my surroundings. There was a floor above the water where smooth stone glowed in the eerie light. I climbed up on it and lay outstretched on my back. I spread my arms and legs and laughed out loud. It felt good to be alone and quiet in this mystical place. The cool air was countered by the warmth of the sun's filtered light from above which shone directly down on the stone I lay upon.

I closed my eyes and let my mind wander. The Hawaiian pilot floated into my thoughts. My cock got hard, and I reached down to skin off my trunks. I was completely naked on the stone floor, the bare flesh of my butt sliding sensually against the slick smoothness of the stone. I took my cock in my hand and began to caress it slowly.

The pilot's name was Joseph: not very Hawaiian. But the rest of him was. Imagining his perfectly formed ass had my hand moving faster over my dick. He didn't wear a shirt most of the time. His pecs were muscled slabs, with dark large nipples that stood out. His belly was very smooth and hard. I fantasized about his dick and balls, probably creamy brown and thick and fat. I imagined rolling his balls in my hands while I poked at his hard butt with my tongue.

I raised my legs and gasped for breath. My hands were flying over my dick. My gasps were loud in the quiet of the cavern, echoing above me. I was about to come, when I felt water dripping down over my heaving chest. My eyes flew open to see Joseph, the object of my fantasy, kneeling over me, his wet body the source of the cool drips.

"What the fuck—" I stuttered, but his hand went over my mouth, and two of his fingers slid inside it.

I sucked savagely on those stubby Hawaiian digits as I attempted with all my willpower to hold back from shooting a load of jizz all over my own belly. I stared up with wide, startled eyes into the grinning face hovering over me.

Joseph was naked. His big body was sleek and wet like some kind of dark and huge sea otter. I glanced down to see an impossibly fat cock poking out from beneath his belly. It was as hard as mine.

"Yes, I've been thinking of you. Would you like some of my native loving? Want some Hawaiian ass and cock?" He murmured. His deep voice rose up and bounced off the dripping rocky walls of the cavern, like some kind of obscene whisper of the gods.

I couldn't answer, not with those large fingers exploring my mouth. I imagined how wide my eyes must have bulged as Joseph rose up and straddled me. He was sitting down over my throbbing cock.

I felt wet flesh envelop my cock. His butt crack clamped around the rapidly twitching rod. I rose up with my hips, thrusting between the smooth globes of Hawaiian butt. I moaned, hearing the animal echo of my own lust.

"Fuck my Hawaiian ass, white boy," he whispered. The vulgar echo floated above us.

I needed no encouragement. I was squirming beneath his substantial weight, shoving my cock into the slippery crack between his butt cheeks. He was chuckling as he gazed down at me beneath him. Then I felt his butt hole with the head of my cock. I began to press into that spot with wild lust. I was an animal, a sea creature without a brain, only a cock and an open mouth full of two large fingers.

My cock entered the heat of his insides, hot anal lips parting and swallowing it with welcoming ease. He did not groan, his deep chuckle unchanged. He was enjoying it. He rode my long, stiff rod like a rolling wave, undulating up and down effortlessly. His brown body was darker in the exotic light. He seemed a part of me as my hips rose up to meet his rolling body in a synchronized dance. This was the stuff of all my fantasies, unrealized until now, of course. In reality I was virgin, cherry. In my dreams I had fucked innumerable hot asses and sucked hard cock after hard cock. But this was real, or at least I thought it was.

I didn't care if it was real or not, as I sucked on Joseph's dark fingers and my cock exploded up his slippery asshole. He knew I was coming. His hole pulsed and fluttered around my spewing poker. His voice encouraged me, outrageously sexual commands that struck some deep chord in my psyche.

I felt him slide around me. My cock slithered from his warm hole. His large, muscular body held me, his fingers came out of my mouth, and I groaned helplessly. He held me as his hands explored, pinching my nipples teasingly, then almost painfully. Those big hands lifted my legs and caressed my ass crack, poking and prodding at my wet asshole. He moved me so that the lower part of my body was floating in the water while his mouth descended to smother me with a deep kiss. His tongue went far inside me while his fingers split my asshole apart and entered with the ocean water swirling around them. My balls floated in and out of the water as he lifted my hips up with his digging hands. My cock was washed clean and remained ramrod hard, exactly as it would if this were a fantasy. Don't we all have giant hard cocks in our dreams? Mine felt huge and potent right then with his fingers twisting deep up my butt and his tongue slithering inside my gaping mouth.

His kiss went on and on. His fingers were inside my asshole while I floated half in water and half on land. There was no essence of human thought left to me, only the sexual sea animal I had become. He did not speak with his mouth over mine. The lapping of the waves rocked us both.

Then he lifted me again and set me down on my belly, crouching over me with his immense presence. I had not uttered a single word beyond my first protest. He lay over me, careful not to crush me. But I was captured anyway, unable to move away as his fat cock began to probe at my vulnerable asshole. The large knob head pressed into me, stretching my already well-fingered anal opening. The pain was ephemeral; it disappeared even as a deep ache and throb replaced it. I was buried under his dark flesh.

He fucked me, whispering in my ear, tickling it with his long thick tongue, sucking on it and grunting with the effort of his body to impale me fully. He went deeper inside my guts, his fat cock a solid ram that opened me up. I felt as if I was dissolving, becoming an appendage of the native lust above and surrounding me.

I had never surrendered like this before, even in my fantasies. Now I was experiencing the real thing, although it was so magical and dreamlike, it may as well have been another fantasy. My inhibitions were nonexistent, just as they would be in a dream. I knew then that I would do whatever he wanted, and that I would love every moment of it.

My asshole was an open cave for his thrusting member. My fuck hole had no limits—there was only insistent, undeniable need centered in that part of my anatomy. One arm stretched out to float in the water while I was fucked. It was brutal on one level, sublime on another. He spoke with vulgar urging in my ear, and pounded into my ass with his monster cock. He seemed in control, but I believed he was as much a victim of the mystical cavern as I was.

He did not come inside my ass. Instead, he rolled off me with gasping grunts and slid back into the water. While he cooled off, I lay immobile, staring at him in the glittering light. I had no will to either escape or to go forward.

He rose back out of the water, a brown giant of muscular flesh. He was smiling again, softly with pools of gentleness in his eyes. He cradled me in his lap, set my face over his throbbing cock, and let it slip into my mouth. I sucked on it, tasting the salt water and the dripping come that leaked from the knob head. He caressed my wet hair with his hands, held my mouth over his cock and crooned in singsong Hawaiian. My fevered imagination believed his unintelligible words were as vulgar as those he had uttered in English. My cock was still hard where it lay on my belly. I reached down and took it in my hand while I sucked on the big meat between my lips.

It was like a cow's huge teat, or a fat piece of salami, or a hot length of hard wood all wrapped up in one. I slobbered and moaned, my breathing coming faster as I whipped at my cock with one hand. He reached down and gripped that flying hand with iron firmness. My cock throbbed in our combined grip, his throbbed inside my sucking mouth. Then he was coming. Warm salty sperm flooded my mouth and throat; I swallowed and swallowed. His firm hand would not allow me to jerk my own cock, which was pulsing and throbbing with unreleased desire. I tasted his come, like ocean spray.

He carried me into the water, dragging me under the waves. I stared up at the light as it filtered through the translucent water, a vision of heaven. He pulled me out of the sea and back onto our stone bed.

He lay back and lifted up one of his brawny legs, displaying his balls, dick, and winking butt hole. That hole was hairless, brown and sea-washed clean. He stared in my eyes, commanding me with his soft gaze. I knelt down and buried my face between his legs. I tongued his balls, his crack and then the silky entrance to his insides. I kissed his anal hole, and it fluttered open and welcomed me.

He urged me on with his hand on the back of my head. I serviced his butt hole just as I had serviced his dick—willingly, lovingly, with burning desire. The salt of his body mixed with and became part of the salt of the sea. I tasted ocean and sweat and man. Through it all, there was not a moment when I questioned what I was doing; it was all hot, it was all sexually mystical, it was the stuff of dreams.

This time I could play with my cock unimpeded by his iron grip. He had that saved for my head, pressing it into his ass crack as he moaned and chanted in Hawaiian. His voice rose up to hit the ceiling and bounce back to break over us like the waves beside us. I knew in some corner of my mind that I was causing that wave of sensual song with my tongue in his asshole, and it stimulated me to greater heights of desire. My cock felt like an electric eel in my hand, burning and swelling until it finally erupted in an unstoppable geyser of hurtling sperm.

My Hawaiian lover coated my head with another load at almost the same moment. His shout echoed and reverberated, rocking us both as we sprayed come like sea beasts. My lips tasted his salty ass before I rose up and collapsed over his heaving body.

We embraced as I lay on him. He kissed me again. Then he slipped away into the water and was gone. I stretched back on the stone in the cool quiet for another endless span of time. Until I drifted off into a dream-filled sleep.

I awoke sometime in the afternoon. I gazed at the dripping walls one more time before entering the water and swimming back out into the brilliantly blue afternoon. I half-expected the boat to be gone. It wasn't.

Joseph welcomed me, while the other passengers ignored me. His grin said it all. He winked again and turned away. I watched his rounded butt cheeks rise and fall as he ascended to the wheel of the boat.

The engines revved, and we roared away from the secluded spot. I felt human again, the clear skies and open water dispelling the sexual funk that had overtaken me earlier. But there at the helm, the wind blowing through his short dark curls, stood Joseph.

When he turned and graced me with that special grin, I realized it wasn't over yet. I grinned back. I laughed out loud, waving my arms above my head to feel the wind and salt spray. The day was so fine. Even if it had been a dream, a fantasy, deep in my heart I now knew what I wanted, and that I would take it if I could.

Joseph was still grinning. My dick rose up stiff in my swimsuit.

Patience Is a Virtue
by Kevin Johnson

I think it's a universal rule that all gay boys have a crush on their best friend. It's certainly true of Carl and me. When Joanne introduced us, I was dumbstruck—he was fucking beautiful! Taller than me (not difficult, I'm only 5 foot 6), with blond hair, a square-jawed face, and a great body. I had no doubt he was straight, because Joanne was the kind of girl who settled that question pretty quickly. Joanne, Carl, and I always hung out together, and Carl had no problem with me being gay. We'd go out on our own if Jo wasn't free. He'd even flirt with me a little bit, but I knew it didn't mean anything.

Gradually, I started to realize how much I really liked Carl. A dozen times I drifted away while looking at him, at the biceps that stretched his sleeves, or the rounded butt cheeks that filled his jeans. I imagined him stripping, offering his body to me to do with whatever I wanted, letting me touch him and lick his dick until it was stiff and dribbling on my face...and then I'd realize we were in the middle of a conversation. I'd stutter and blush and try to hide the bulge in my pants.

He was perfectly comfortable around me—he didn't even mind sharing a bed if he stayed over. I never got any sleep on these occasions. My head was swimming with lust, and I had to fight every urge to grab my raging dick and beat it. He was due to stay over one time when my parents were away. Carl arranged to have a crate of beer, and about eight of us came. Carl had invited four of his buddies, and I invited J.P., a guy I had played around with once, and Paul, a straight friend. We sat and drank and talked, the guys telling how far they had gotten with various girls. While I wasn't interested in the gory details about sex with females, the others seemed to be fascinated to meet a real-life homosexual and couldn't stop asking me questions.

"How much have you actually done, Kevin?" Carl's cute friend Jason asked me. "I mean with another guy."

"Actually, not that much. There was this one guy I met. We just had oral sex, and I enjoyed it."

"How about you, Carl? How far have you gotten with Jo?"

"I...haven't done anything with Jo," Carl responded. "It just never felt like the right moment. I shouldn't tell you this...but I think I'm gonna dump her." Everyone was amazed. Jo was not the kind of girl who got dumped. "In fact," he continued, "I think I have feelings for someone else. Don't ask me who, 'cause I can't say anything yet. And don't any of you dare tell Jo before I do."

We promised not to say a word. The guys asked more questions—how I knew I was gay, how early I had realized it, and if I've never thought about girls at all—but there was one question I didn't expect.

"Don't you worry about how big your dick is?" Paul instantly went red in the face, embarrassed he'd brought up the subject. "Every guy looks at other guys' dicks, just to compare. In the showers, or whatever. Don't look at me like that, you guys. You know we all do it." Reluctantly, they all agreed. "Straight guys worry about it, and we don't ever get near another guy's dick.

But you gay guys can actually compare another guy's dick while it's, like, in action. What if you're not up to scratch?"

"I...think I'd be OK," I responded, "as long as the other guy's not too small, anyway. I guess I'll get used to other guys being smaller than me, 'cause I tell you, I got a pretty big dick."

Carl's friend Dan laughed. "How can you have a big dick, little guy? You're only three feet tall."

"I bet I got a bigger dick than you, fat boy," I taunted. "I bet you can't even see yours past your fat belly."

"Who says you got a bigger dick? How much you wanna bet?"

"I got a ruler over there on my desk, and I can prove my dick is bigger than yours."

"Well," Carl said, "I guess there's only one way to solve this. Kevin, go get your ruler. Let's see for real who's got the bigger dick!"

I went and picked up my 12-inch plastic ruler. I was already throwing a bone just from all this talk of dicks. Carl took the ruler and held it out. "Come on, Dan, you first. It was your idea, after all."

"You can't be serious…" Dan stammered.

"You started it, so you can't back out now," Carl snorted.

"I'll only do it if the rest of you do it," he muttered. "I don't wanna be the only one standing here with my dick out."

"Come on, boys," Jason said, "let's show Dan how it's done!" After a few glances around the circle, Dan's noodley little dick made its first appearance. I knew I had won my bet right there, but now that we were at this stage, I was going to make sure I enjoyed it.

Dan pulled at his little pud, trying to get some life into it. The rest of us had no problems. I had been hard long before. J.P. was staring at the other guys, but I only had eyes for Carl. From the time his dick first flopped out, it took maybe three seconds until he was standing tall and proud. Dear God, it was beautiful. As it arced up over his muscular stomach, I realized it was even bigger than mine!

Since Dan still wasn't hard, Jason took the ruler first. "I got seven inches, boys," he announced before passing the ruler on to J.P., who eagerly took it and held it against his raging stiff dick. "Six inches," he said in a panting whisper. Paul measured in at just under seven inches. It was my turn next, my chance to prove that a little guy could still carry a dick to be reckoned with. I held the ruler next to my stiff shaft. "Eight inches." Carl flashed a big smile right at me. It almost made me shoot my load right there.

Dan had worked up as much of a hard-on as he was gonna get, so he took the ruler and quickly held it to his cock. "Five inches," he muttered, pulling his already softening dick back into his pants. The other two measured at seven inches and six inches, and then my ruler made its way to its final destination.

"Looks like I beat you, Kevin," he smiled, "although you put up some stiff competition." I didn't even notice my dick sticking out while I watched Carl. There was no doubt his dick was easily the biggest in the room, but he took a perverse pleasure out of making us wait, saying, "Patience is a virtue, boys." Carl counted. "Six, seven, eight…my God, nine…" Carl looked up and smiled slowly.

"Nine and a half inches. You got a big dick, Kevin, but you get second place."

The excitement of seeing Carl's beautiful cock finally pushed me over the edge. I urgently fumbled with my painfully hard dick, only just managing to get it back into my shorts before it began pulsing and jerking as I shot off a massive load. I prayed that the other guys didn't notice. Carl glanced at me with a look that could only have meant he knew what was happening. It was a really intense look, as if to say "I know, Kevin, I know. And thanks."

I was horrified; I could never look Carl in the face again. I sat in shock, barely noticing when the guys drifted out, making their way home. I guess after everybody had shown their dicks, there was nowhere else for the party to go. They caught cabs or walked if they didn't live far. Eventually, only Carl and me were left. I had never felt so uncomfortable in my life. Carl was on the couch, with his legs spread, drinking a beer. He looked up at me and smiled.

"Finally," he breathed, "I have you all to myself."

"What's that supposed to mean?" I asked, completely confused.

"It means I'm glad the other guys left, 'cause all that talk of sex, and seeing your big hard cock at last, made me so horny I just wanted to grab you and fuck you right here on the couch."

"But..." I could hardly speak.

"I'm gonna dump Jo. I was never into her. I have feelings for someone else. I told you that."

"Who?"

He got up from his seat and came over to me. With a gentleness that belied his power and strength, he touched my face. "You, silly."

He lifted me with his strong hands until our bodies were so close, I could feel the heat of his skin. He slowly brought his lips to mine. Just a touch at first, the kiss blossomed into a passionate battle. I lifted his shirt and felt the hot, firm flesh underneath. Carl did the same, his hands roaming over my naked chest, stroking the smooth skin.

"You're so beautiful..." I panted.

"I think you're beautiful too, Kevin," he whispered. "I've been wanting to do this since the moment I met you."

Carl knelt down, chuckling as he felt the dampness in my pants.

Undoing them, he stroked me through my sticky underwear, then stretched out his tongue, and an electric tingle shot through my body. He pulled down my shorts, and my stiff dick sprang out. He smiled, stretched his lips wide, and slipped them over the end. He didn't stop until the head of my dick slipped into the hot, wet tightness of his throat. My breath caught, my legs went weak, and I nearly fell over. I never imagined anything could feel so good. It wasn't long before I shot another load, and he swallowed every drop. My dick didn't go soft for a second.

He stood up and led me over to the couch, urgently wrestling his dick out into the warm air. I pounced on it, licking it from head to base, going absolutely crazy over every beautiful inch. Carl threw his head back with a hiss of pleasure. He shed his jeans and pulled a small foil packet out of his pocket. Giving my dick a few more affectionate licks, he slowly rolled the condom down over it. I never imagined Carl would willingly take another man's dick up his ass, but that's exactly what he was getting ready to do.

He stood over me on the couch and squatted down. I felt the tight ring of muscle easing itself onto my shaft, and Carl moaned. I asked if it was hurting him, and he shook his head and forced himself farther down. As he settled into position, I realized that I could still reach his huge erection with my mouth. Carl began to lift and lower himself on my shaft, sending more incredible sensations through my body, while I sucked greedily at his dick. Then he stopped, lifted off, and got down on all fours, looking at me with glazed eyes.

"Come on, Kevin," he pleaded. "Fuck me like you really mean it."

I got behind him, pointing my shaft down toward his glistening asshole, and gently slipped back inside. He urged me on, to go faster and harder, to really give it to him. I couldn't help but do as he said. I drove my dick into him with an energy I never knew I had.

"I'm gonna come again…" I gasped. The spasms shook my body, and my dick swelled up inside Carl's ass, blasting out shot after shot. I collapsed helplessly onto Carl's muscular back. I couldn't believe it—my dick was still hard after three of the strongest orgasms I had ever felt. I was so exhausted, there was no way I could do any more. But again, Carl had other ideas.

He gently laid me down flat on the couch, then covered me with his own beautiful body, kissing me passionately. The feeling of his giant penis, aching for attention between us, started to bring me around again. He hitched my calves up in the air, and I felt cool breath against my asshole. When he flicked at it with his tongue, I almost cried with pleasure.

Carl stretched another condom over his incredible dick and covered it with lube. "Don't worry, baby," he said, "I won't hurt you. I'll take it slow. You'll love it, I promise." I believed him with all my heart, because his tongue had relaxed me so much, but more than that, because Carl had called me his baby. I was hopelessly in love. He slowly teased my hole with the tip of his dick, nudging and pressing until I was practically begging him to put it in. I felt the thick head slip through the ring of muscle. My head fell back, my mind went blank, and my eyes glazed over with a fog of pleasure. He was right; I did love it. No pain as I had feared, only exquisite pleasure.

Carl gradually slipped one inch after another into my body, and I rose higher into heaven with every one. Finally, he started to pull himself back out, grazing past my prostate, sending waves of ecstasy through me. His pace grew faster and faster, until he was slamming his enormous dick into my virgin ass. Only a few minutes later, Carl let out a howl, and his entire body tensed up. The sight of all that muscle straining over my body made my own dick puff up, and I shot yet another huge wad of cream all over my chest without having even touched myself. I felt Carl's big dick spasming in my ass, and it seemed to go on forever. Minutes later, Carl slowly dragged his massive shaft out of my ass. He fell on top of me with a big goofy grin, his sweaty chest slipping against my come-covered one. We both began to calm down, stealing quick kisses in between gasping breaths.

"How do you feel?" he asked me gently. "Did you like it?"

"Oh man, it felt wonderful!" I told him. "It was the most amazing experience of my life." Then, before I could stop myself, I blurted out, "I love you!" Carl breathed a sigh of relief.

"Kevin, I love you too. I want to be with you forever." He kissed me again, fastening our lips and tongues together like Super Glue. I was so excited by everything, I came again as we lay together, the sperm spreading its warmth across our stomachs. "My God, boy, what the hell are you made of?" Carl exclaimed in amazement. "Do you realize you've come five times tonight?"

"It's just what you do to me. I can't help it. I've been patiently waiting for something like this for so long. Like you said, patience is a virtue."

"Well, everything comes to he who waits, baby. You don't have to be patient anymore."

Full Nelson

by Greg Herren

The ring room was well-lit, the walls lined with mirrors and posters of men in wrestling gear. Mark was putting a tape into his camcorder. He whistled. "Looking good, Ross."

"Thanks." Ross wasn't my real name. Not that making wrestling videos under the name Ross Matthews would fool anyone. "What do you know about this kid?"

Mark shrugged. "Not much. He's a looker, though."

I'd been making videos for several years. I sat down on the floor and started stretching. I hated losing. I also hated wrestling guys I knew nothing about. My stomach started churning a bit. I always get nervous before taping a match. There's always that first time, that first loss. There were several guys on the video circuit who would love to see me get beaten on tape.

My opponent walked into the light. He was a beauty, with short, curly dark hair. Mid 20s—27 at most. About six feet tall. All muscle. His shoulders were broad, his waist narrow. Purple square-cut trunks emphasized the shape of his thick, hard legs. He smiled at Mark, then climbed through the ropes and started stretching. I watched him. His ass was round, hard as a rock.

OK, I told myself, *forget he's beautiful. He's gonna want to be the first guy to beat you on tape, make a name for himself by whipping Ross Matthews.*

I climbed through the ropes. He grinned at me. I didn't smile back. He walked over with his right hand out.

"Gino Matarese," he said. I stared at his hand. His smile faded. "OK, then."

I said nothing.

"OK, guys." Mark said. "Roll tape."

The bell rang.

Gino smiled at me and struck a pose. "You want some of this?" His muscles looked carved out of granite. Veins bulged.

Cocky shit. I pulled a double biceps. "Come on, boy."

We started circling. He feinted forward a couple of times. I stepped back. We locked up, pushing at each other.

Damn, he's strong, I thought. He was muscling me back into a corner. *Keep your head, watch for an opening.* I felt the corner pads against my back. I spread my legs apart for balance. He dropped my arms and drove his right knee into my abs.

I hadn't seen it coming and wasn't ready for it. All my breath was driven out. I started to double over. He kept the knee coming up—once, twice, three times. *Goddamn!* I tried to get some air. He grabbed my head and neatly flipped me over his shoulder. I landed on my back in the center of the ring. Disoriented, I shook my head, trying to clear it just as he dropped a knee into my abs. He grabbed my right arm in an arm bar and cranked. I rose up onto my side with a yell. He shoved his right knee into my neck. *Fuck!*

"Come on, old man, give it up," he grunted. I slapped at him with my free arm. The pain was blinding. He eased up a little. I sucked in some air just as he applied his grip again. Tighter. "Give it up."

"No fucking way," I choked out through gritted teeth. He pulled again. A jolt of pain wracked my body. An involuntary shout escaped my mouth. Jesus. He lightened the pressure and I took in some deep breaths. I braced myself for him to put the pressure back on and thought quickly, *How can I get out of this?*

"FU-U-UCK!"

"Come on, old man," he taunted me. "Give up. I'll break it."

"No way," I gasped. I got my knees under me. There. I pressed up with my free arm and my legs. I was aware of his legs on either side of my head. I looped my free arm around the closest leg.

"FUCK, FUCK, FUCK!"

He laughed.

And let go.

My right arm dropped down to the mat. The shoulder and upper muscles of the arm were throbbing. I gulped in air, tested the arm.

His legs tightened around my head. He dropped to the left and my head, trapped between his legs, turned my entire body to that side. A jolt of pain shot through my neck. He tightened his legs.

"No way!" I yelled. I grabbed hold of his thighs with my arms. That was futile. His legs were too strong for me to pry them apart. He let up, then tightened again. Blood was pounding in my head. My neck was screaming with agony. He cranked it on again. Hard. Red dots appeared in my vision.

"OK, OK, OK!" I slapped at his leg. "I give, I give!"

He let go and rose to his feet.

I raised up on all fours and twisted my head from side to side. My neck was stiffening up. My arm was aching. I gulped in air. *Keep away from his scissors!*

"Get up, old man. You want some more of me?"

I looked up. He had struck a double biceps. He was smiling, taunting me, striking more poses, showing off his muscles. Then I noticed his dick was hard, longish and thick inside those purple trunks that clung like skin. He ran his hands over his chest and stomach, stopping just above the top of his trunks.

I stood up slowly, shaking my head to clear the cobwebs. "You're gonna pay for that, boy."

"Oh, I'm scared." He laughed.

OK, boy, I thought. We started circling again. We locked up. This time I powered *him* back into the corner. I stepped back, letting go, raising my arms. A clean break, not like the shit he pulled. He smiled as I backed off, then he came forward. His left leg rose so fast I didn't see it coming. The next thing I knew, his foot had been driven hard into my stomach, my air was gone, and the force of the kick was driving me backward. I fell onto my back, my head swimming from the sudden shock of the blow. I felt his fingers grabbing my trunks. He yanked my suit off, exposing my cock and balls, and threw it in my face. He backed off. Through the roaring in my head, I could hear his laughter. *I will not lose to this prick. I will not lose.*

He was still laughing.

I saw red.

I got to my feet. He was standing a few feet from me, grinning. I wanted to wipe that grin off his fucking face. I drop-kicked him square in the chest. He saw it coming, but too late for him to do anything. He fell backwards into the ropes, which propelled him forward. I drove my right fist into his stomach. He crumpled over the blow and fell to the mat. I reached down and grabbed hold of his trunks and yanked. His ass was so beautiful that I paused for a second to admire it. There was a slight line of white running along just above those perfectly hard, round, tanned cheeks that dropped down into the crack. I straddled his back, yanked his head back, and shoved the trunks in his face.

"Thought you could humiliate me, did you, punk?" I taunted, rubbing his sweaty trunks all over his face. I sat back further on his back, dropped the trunks, and used both hands to yank his head back. I shoved my legs under his arms and settled in. The camel clutch is a guaranteed submission. The pressure goes into the lower back. A flexible guy can hold out for a while, but not long.

Let's see how limber you are, Gino. I pulled back.

He screamed.

"Come on, boy," I said. "How does this feel?"

He was gasping for breath, which exploded out of him in moans.

"Not so tough now, are you?"

"Fuck you!"

"I can sit here all fucking day." His back muscles were straining, his arms useless. I let go of his chin with one hand and slapped his ass. It was hard.

I felt my cock stiffening.

I cranked back some more.

"I GIVE, I GIVE, I GIVE, I GIVE!" Gino screamed.

"I give, *sir,*" I said quietly.

"I GIVE, SIR! I GIVE, SIR!"

I slammed his head down onto the mat. I stood up and kicked him in the side. He rolled onto his back, moaning. His dick was still rock-hard. He grabbed his back with both hands and rolled onto his stomach. He came up onto his knees, arching his back up.

I nudged him with my foot. "Get up, boy."

He stayed there.

I dropped a knee into the small of his back. He screamed. I grabbed a fistful of hair and dragged him to his feet. I punched his gut with my free hand. He doubled over. I straightened him up and slugged him again. I let go of his hair and spun him around, slipping my arms through his and locking my hands behind his head. I shoved down, pulling him back against me. My cock slipped into the crack of his ass.

Damn, it felt good there.

I cranked down on his head. He screamed again. I walked him over to the corner and started pounding his head into the padded ring buckle. He was slightly bent forward, and his hard ass was pressing against me.

My cock got harder.

I pulled him back and, using the nelson, drove him down to the mat. I was now on top of him, rubbing his face into the mat. I let go and rolled him over onto his back. I sat on his chest and started slapping his face.

"Come on, tough guy."

I leaned forward and allowed my cock to brush against his lips. Sweat was rolling down his face. His eyes had the hunted look in them. I've seen that look before.

He knew he was beaten.

I stood up, pulling him up by his hair. I yanked his left arm up, wrapping my right leg over his left, and yanked him over to the side—abdominal stretch.

He screamed.

I drove my free elbow into his side.

"OK, OK, I give, I give!"

"I give, *sir.*"

"I GIVE, SIR! I GIVE, SIR! You FUCKER!"

"Now, that wasn't very nice," I said as I drove my elbow into his side again.

"Please! PLEASE! PLEASE!" His voice broke.

Good enough.

I let go. He crumpled down to the mat.

I looked at him, spread out there on his back. Beaten. Beautiful. Sweating.

I climbed through the ropes and grabbed a bottle of lube and a condom. I stood over him as I slipped the condom on my cock, which was now aching. I poured some lube over it.

I got down on my knees and pushed his legs apart.

He looked up at me. "Hey, what are you…?"

I slipped between his legs, stroking my dick. I shot some lube onto his thick dick and rubbed it. He closed his eyes and dropped his head back. With my other hand I found his asshole, and slowly started massaging it. A low moan escaped from him. He brought his hands up to his nipples and started pinching them gently.

I smiled.

I put the head of my dick up against his asshole, and started slowly moving my hips back and forth. Not enough pressure to force my way in, just enough for him to feel it, want it. I took one of his nipples in my mouth, teasing it, swirling my tongue over it, nipping it slightly with my teeth. He began moaning and lifting his hips up.

I slipped the head of my cock inside and stopped.

His eyes shot open. He inhaled sharply.

I just sat there, still, waiting to feel his muscles down there relax and allow the intrusion. I gently started moving my hips from side to side, feeling it loosen just a little, and began nibbling on his nipple again. He gripped his own cock and started stroking it slowly.

I eased my cock in a little further.

"Oh, yeah," he moaned, barely above a whisper.

I started making a circular movement with my hips, feeling the resistance inside starting to give a little bit.

In a little deeper.

His entire body was relaxing now.

A little deeper.

He brought his legs up and over my shoulders.

He wanted it. Bad.

I drove in fast, not getting all the way in, since he wasn't ready for the surprise of the sudden onslaught of my cock. His eyes popped open. He gasped. I stopped, not moving, letting his body adjust to it.

"Oh God, oh God, oh God, oh God…" He locked his eyes on mine. "Fuck me," he groaned. "Fuck me hard."

I didn't move.

"Please."

I slowly began pulling back from him, my cock withdrawing in a slow steady motion. His eyes closed again. When the head was all that was left inside, I plunged in fast and hard. This time I got all the way in. I flexed my ass, trying to force everything in that I could.

"Oh, my GOD!" he screamed. I started moving my hips again in a circular movement. And then I started to fuck. Sliding my arms under his back, I clamped my hands on his shoulders and pulled him down securely on my cock, locking him in place. Then I came up on my knees a little, spread them apart for leverage, and started pumping my cock up his ass hard and fast. This guy wanted a piece of Ross Matthews? Well, he was gonna get it—all that he bargained for and more.

I fucked him good and hard for a solid two or three minutes, ramming my hard cock deep up his chute. I would have loved to fuck his hot punk ass for hours, but I was so heated up from the match that I knew I wouldn't last long. Neither would he. He was panting and moaning. Sweat was running down his face. His body was trembling. His hand was jerking his cock. I knew it was time to bring it to a climax. I pushed up with my feet, bringing his ass up off the mat, and leaned forward, driving my cock into his asshole to the hilt.

He came with a scream of pure ecstasy.

His body trembled and convulsed as his cock erupted. One shot landed in his hair, a couple on his face. His cock kept shooting. On his chest, his abs. He was trembling, convulsing, gasping with each shot that came out of him. When he was finished, I slid my cock out of him.

I straddled his chest and slipped my condom off. I lubed up my bare cock and started stroking. His eyes were half-closed and glazed-looking, but he brought his hands up and started pinching my nipples. I looked down at his beautiful pecs, glistening with his sweat and his come, and shot my own load into his face, his hair and on his pecs.

I stood. He grabbed his trunks and wiped his face. We looked at each other.

He stood and put his arms around me. Our lips met in a sweet, tender kiss. My hands went around and cupped his beautiful ass while our chests came together, our mingled come slightly lubricating them.

He pulled his head back. "I want a rematch."

"Anytime, kid." I smiled at him.

I looked over at Mark, the cameraman. His shorts were down around his ankles, and a drop of semen hung in a string from his dick, but the camera was still running. "Did you get all that?"

"Oh, yeah."

I grabbed Gino's hand. "Come on, kid, let's get cleaned up."

Body Parts

by Alan Mills

My last memory was a slight prick and a warm, sweeping light. Then I'm here, waking slowly to a red flash and another red flash, blurry and difficult to discern. And I feel it, the fluid all around me, clear and syrupy, invading me through my nostrils and my mouth, filling me even down into my lungs. I realize quickly where I am, what I am, and I panic and start kicking and punching, fighting sluggishly against the Plexiglas door that holds me in. Each blow is a pointless struggle until I finally maneuver my legs upward and press my bare feet against the smooth surface, pushing outward with my naked back against the metal cylinder I'm in until the seals give way and the door bursts open, and my small world explodes into a different one.

Naked and awkward, I pour out of my container with the flood, sliding clumsily around the slick, narrow floor until I finally get a hold of the cell across from mine. Leaning against it, I stand for what is in actuality the first time in my life, even though I have memories of walking and running, so many memories, some so vivid it's as if they happened only yesterday.

With several violent coughs I force the salty, sweet liquid from my throat, vomiting until I take my first real and painful breath of natural air. Horrified and confused, I look up into the face of the girl inside her tube. Through the synthetic fluid, her skin looks blue, but she's young, and as I step back carefully on the cold, wet floor, I see my own reflection in her glass, and I'm young too, nearly 19, exactly as I was when my parents brought me in.

Glancing around the room, I count the cylinders. There are 10.

And at one end of this hermetically sealed vault is a door. I suddenly remember all of this, remember how I walked into a room like this before, remarking on how there should be 12 units per vault, like eggs in a carton, but understanding the efficiency of 10 when it would come down to accounting. And I remember the size of this complex and the relatively small staff. It could take some time for anyone to notice what has happened, I decide, and so I try the door, but its steel lever doesn't budge.

With nothing else to do, I look around, growing surer of my steps as I look into each cylinder, one after the other. Two of the cylinders are empty, but all of the occupants are young, which seems to make sense. When I reach the sixth one, I notice an arm has been removed, and it shocks me for a moment until I see who's sleeping in the next chamber down. In awe, I reach out to touch the Plexiglas, tracing my fingers over the refracted image inside. I smile at the brown bangs floating gently past his dreaming eyes, the subtle rising of his smooth chest, his tight stomach and small waist. His perfection makes me proud, and I sit on the floor across from him, amazed, and after only minutes of silent pondering, I stand and start examining the mechanism that keeps him in.

Of course it is designed to be simple: The appropriate button is green and marked RELEASE. I push it: The fluid drains, the door opens, and the exact reflection of myself falls into my arms while coughing liquid from his lungs. "Where am I?" he asks as I pull him from his cell.

"You know."

Wiping the embryonic fluid from his eyes, he glares straight at me. "Why did you wake me?"

"Something went wrong, and I revived by accident. It will be a while before a tech comes, and I wanted someone to talk to. I guess I got lonely."

I back away from him, a bit ashamed, and I can see that he's about to yell at me, but then he doesn't. He just goes quiet for a moment, looks around the small vault, and says, "Of course you were lonely. I probably would have done the same thing."

I smile, and he laughs, and then we laugh, sitting down opposite one another on the wet floor to wait for the inevitable together. As we each get comfortable, we end up positioning ourselves in almost the exact same way: feet on floor, knees up, thighs open, with hands covering crotches. However, with the vault being so narrow and the floor being so slick, our feet slowly slip toward each other until our toes touch. At first we both resist it, but ultimately our feet end up bracing each other until finally we both give in, pressing our toes together and laughing playfully whenever we wiggle them.

For some reason, we don't say anything. We just sit there, staring, each an exact replica of the other with slick fluid glistening all across our skin. Eventually, we slide our feet closer, deeper into the other's space, rubbing calves or gently touching the insides of each other's thighs. Our breathing gets heavier, and I feel my cock—swollen, hard, and heavy—pushing up against my hands. I see his, too, his hands not completely covering the entirety of its mass.

"Why did you really wake me?" he asks, touching my nuts with his toes. I feel fear as he moves his hands and lets me see his cock at its hardest.

"I don't know," I say, moving my own hands while his big toe moves up the underbelly of my own erection.

"You were curious, weren't you? You saw me and wondered what it would be like."

"OK," I admit, "I did. So what?"

He pulls his foot away and stands over me, stroking his still-wet cock above my face. I raise myself to my knees and stare at it: my own cock like I've never seen it before. "You know," I say, "I'm not into guys, but..."

"I know," he says. "This is different. It's also narcissistic. But who cares? Just shut up and put this cock—your cock—into my mouth."

And I do as he says, letting the sweet, salty taste of it slip over my tongue. I close my mouth over it, sucking the embryonic fluid off it, as it pumps down my throat until all I'm left with is the taste of clean flesh and the more truly salty taste of his precome.

"Oh, man," he moans as I work harder on getting him off, taking his cock so deep down my throat I can feel his wet pubes on my nose. Suddenly he shouts, "No! Stop!" as he pulls his cock from my lips. He gets on his knees in front of me and takes my cock into his hand before stroking it softly. "You almost made me come," he explains, "and I'm just as curious as you are." With that, he puts his hands on the floor and lowers his mouth to my own aching cock.

I suck in a deep breath as my crown slips past his lips. His mouth feels moist and soft, and I stroke his damp hair, gently angling his head so I can watch my tingling cock pump deeper into my own young and handsome face.

The heat of my skin rising, his own scent just as familiar, I run my hands up and down his slick back. Smooth, young, and flawless, his body, my body, is that of an angel. Eventually, one hand makes its way to his firm, strong ass, and as I reach into the cleft to find the spot I know is there, I feel him pulling away from my cock. Innately understanding just how much I can get away with and how much I can't, I grip the base of my cock and rub the head on his tongue, while I gently massage the tight opening at his nether end.

Slowly relaxing and becoming more trusting, he goes back down on my cock and reaches one hand between my thighs to rub my own sensitive opening more roughly. Already slick with the fluid we both have been living in, his asshole softens and pulses open under my touch. Slowly slipping a finger in, I make him gasp and pull off my cock just before I myself get too excited.

Recovering quickly, my reflection flips himself onto his back and licks upward into my ass. I moan loudly, looking around at the sleeping faces watching us, before I lower myself and suck his cock into my mouth.

We go on like that for quite a while, touching and licking and probing every inch of each other in a desperate quest to discover more about ourselves. In the process, I touch parts of myself I'd never taken notice of before and see parts of my body I've never been able to get close to, tasting and dipping into sweet, pure, virginal aspects of myself in a way no single lonely human being ever could.

Eventually, I go for the ultimate experience. I push my boundaries and straddle my copy, rubbing what could easily be considered my own cock against the hot, moist opening to my inner self. Afraid and excited, I look down at myself while I slick up the familiar ridges of his cock with the sterile fluid all around and over us. "You're safe, right?" I ask jokingly.

He laughs, pumping his eager cock upward in an attempt to claim my ass. "I've never even eaten or breathed air up to this point, let alone had sex."

"I remember eating," I say, calming myself for a moment.

"That's not the same. Those memories aren't really yours."

I stare down at him, knowing that we are both saddened by that truth. "Then kiss me," I say.

"Why?" he asks with a grin. "I thought you weren't into guys."

"No. He's not into guys. He has a girlfriend...or a wife by now. All I've ever had is the past few hours with you—what amounts to my whole life. So, kiss me, because despite what either of us remember, neither of us has ever even been kissed."

Suddenly, my other self sits halfway up, holds me firmly and sucks my lower lip between his teeth before licking my lips and thrusting his warm tongue into my mouth to move passionately against its duplicate. My own arms wrap around his neck as I receive his kiss and return his fervor, as his solid cock opens me up and slips deep inside my body.

At first I cry out, feeling impaled, struggling to free myself, but he doesn't let me, taking my protests into his mouth and breathing them back into my lungs. But as I relax, the pain subsides. It still hurts as he thrusts upward, but the pain becomes more bearable, and then enjoyable. Soon I'm riding him, feeling the full length and girth of my own cock deep inside me, spreading me open in an intimate way that only my own cock could provide.

I keep riding him, bouncing my ass down onto his cock, while he holds my wet erection, letting it pump between his fingers and his palm. I feel him thrusting up into me, his ass flexing against the floor between my calves, his outer thighs tensing against my feet. Getting closer himself, he tightens his grip on my cock. "No," I whisper as the sensations become too great. "I...I want to fuck you too."

"Don't worry," he pants. "You can fuck me later. Right now, I just want to push this hot load out of both of us."

With that, he thrusts up into me harder, pulling me down roughly by my cock. In moments, I explode, sending thick bullets of come over his chest to his beautiful face and wide-open mouth. At the same time, I imagine his cock shooting an identical load into my ass, so pent up and powerful that I can almost feel it in my throat, even as I feel its warmth dripping down his embedded shaft.

I slump down on top of him, and he holds me, both of us sweaty and sticky from the slowly drying liquid that coats our skin. I roll over next to him and watch him wipe the come from his face, only to lick it from his fingers. I move closer and get a taste for myself. He laughs, saying, "We taste good, don't we?"

I grin and rested my head on his chest, enjoying the proximity of another human being, enjoying the soft beating of another's human heart.

It's less than half an hour later when the seals of our vault release and the bulky metal door opens outward. Dressed in white coveralls, the tech on the other side stands there shocked for a moment as we quickly stand to receive him. He steps in and looks around, immediately walking up to my cell and taking notes on his computer pad.

"It woke me accidentally," I say. "I think it's damaged."

The tech looks back and says evenly, "I can see that." Then he looks at my partner. "But how were you revived?"

"I let him out," I say quickly.

"Oh, you did," the tech says gently. "Well, let's put you back in your chamber—and let's put you in one of those over there."

"What if we don't want to go back?" my partner asks.

The tech barely reacts. "Your original is the one who put you here. You do want him to be healthy and even totally young again whenever he needs to be."

"But this wasn't my idea. It was my dad's," I point out.

"No," says the tech. "*His* dad's. It was his dad's. Don't get confused about that. It will only make this more difficult for you."

"He's right," says my other self. "We're here for a reason." Without another word, my matching self steps into his own cylinder and lets the tech seal him in.

After punching a few buttons, the tech gently guides me into a chamber at the other corner of the vault. "Can't I be in one near him?" I ask.

"There's no point to that."

I step back into the new cylinder feeling frightened and desperate. "Our owner's father commissioned five of us. At least tell me if we're the only two left or if there are others in vaults outside this one."

The tech stops to think for a moment before shutting the door. "Client information is privileged, and you aren't the client, remember?" Then he shuts the door, leaving me feeling like I've been locked in a coffin. I punch and kick the Plexiglas, but the tech just leans his weight against it as he hits the right buttons. Without further warning, fluid starts dripping down the curved walls to pool around my feet.

I look over to my partner's corner, but I can't get a clear view of what's happening to him. The warm, thick liquid reaches my knees. It's already deep enough to appear light blue. "Tell me," I shout, "how many are left? How long have I been here? How long before he needs me? How long before he needs *him*?"

But the tech doesn't answer. As the fluid splashes around my chest, I try to calm myself, repeating over and over, "This is my purpose. This is my purpose." But it doesn't quite work. Fighting for consciousness all the way, fighting for the memory of what I had just shared, I strain upward, holding my chin above the salty, sweet-smelling liquid. From up here, I can just see him, sleeping quietly in his blue, liquid-filled tube. The tech steps back and watches me. I press my lips to the roof of my cylinder, struggling for that last inch of real, precious air, trying to stay calm, trying remind myself, "This is my purpose. This is my purpose. This is why I'm here."

From Nada to Mañana

by JackFritscher.com

Nicaragua. Shit! Managua, a nightmare. Hanging upside down by my boots lashed to the fan in the center of the room, I spin in slow circles, bombed. My blood, my sweat run down from my feet to my face. Inside my camouflage boxer shorts, my thick dick, bigger than my daddy's, hangs down past my navel. Prime uncut American meat. Choice Kansas cornfed. I feel my foreskin peep open around the blood-thickening head of my cock, descending hard. It's Jack Daniel's making me turn around and around, tripping me out, on who I am, who I was, where I was, and where I'm headed. My hand reaching on my dick feels better than good and brings me floating down from the circling fan to the bed.

I'm getting this sick feeling. The kind you feel when you know you're living on the edge. The kind that only feels right when your jaw aches from one punch too many in the good-time bar of the Hotel Managua. The only pain that feels better is the ache in your own knuckles from breaking some other poor fucker's jaw. Weird shit, man. A barroom brawl gives me a hard-on. But that's another story.

I wrap my bruised fist around my dick, strip the foreskin back, and slowly piston it like a steam train starting up back in the hills with swarthy young Sandinistas riding shotgun on the cattle guard. Grinding noise and puffing smoke. Soot from the 'stacks blowing back into the cattle car packed with boxes of rifles, half from the USSR and half from the good old USA. Nicaragua's like Abbott and Costello: Who's on first? You think I care? I pledge allegiance to cash, although I confess a weakness for American dollars. I may be a merc, but born in the USA, a traitor I'm not.

My dick in my hand feels as smooth and sweet as the tough young soldier who, no more than a snot-nosed 18, lay back two nights ago in an empty boxcar on a slow-rolling train and smiled his *"Sí, Señor"* smile when I stood over him, kicking his combat boots apart, spreading his legs, kneeling down between his thighs, reaching under the bands of cartridges X-ing his torso, unbuttoning his shirt, rubbing my callused hands over his hard chest, diving in on his nipples, pinioning his muscular arms back with his shirt, licking his sweaty armpits, tonguing down his tight belly to the cinched equator of his belt. His juicy young Latin body was all promise of big dick.

"Americanos," he said, "you all want the same thing."

"The same thing you want."

"Asshole!" He said it and smirked.

"Dick." I corrected him.

"Asshole wanting dick." He spelled out what he meant.

"Red-white-and-blue cocksucker," I said.

He shrugged his shoulders and moved both his young hands to the pistol in his belt. Sex and death and the whole damned thing. But his palms passed over his pistol, and he smoothed his hands down over his camo crotch. "How much, you say?" he asked. He laughed when he saw I thought he meant to sell his dick for trade. "No," he said. "How much you bet me my dick is bigger than yours? My dick shoots more than yours. Eh? *Hombre a hombre.* Twenty-five bucks maybe? Fifty? A hundred?"

"No way, José," I said. "Fifty." I sized him up. He was a handsome fucker. No more than a kid. I figured, like the rest of them, he'd been soldiering for six years, since he turned 12, and he had grown fast from boy to man before the murmuring dark of his first night in camp was broken by his first penetrated grunt of pain turning to unexpected pleasure before sunup. Every country—I know, because I've seen plenty—trains their young recruits the same, the same being that the older soldiers doing what I was trying to do to this young Latin stud to kill a long train ride from nada to mañana, and us still more than a 150 clicks from Managua, Nicaragua—"such a heavenly place," as the Tin Pan Alley lyrics go: "You ask a señorita for a sweet embrace." Shee-it! Fuck the señorita. Or better, don't fuck her. Fuck her brother.

"Put up." He grinned. He stuck 50 bucks American on his Russian pack. His white teeth flashed between his perfect brown lips crowned with his black moustache. He was an arrogant young bastard who followed the handsome Daniel Ortega, the way our revolutionary foot soldiers followed Washington. He smiled when I stuck 50 bucks next to his crisp cash. The rattling boxcar vibrated around us as it pulled through the hot, humid jungle night.

"You want to measure it," he asked, "soft or hard?"

"First soft. Then hard." I rubbed my fingers over my own covered cock. He rubbed himself the same. His tongue moved slowly, tip first, from between his lips, exactly the way the tip of a hardening cock slides out between the tight lips of foreskin. He slick-wet his berry-ripe lips. My heart leaped to my throat the same in sex as in combat. My cock tucked and rolled. I moved from between his legs and knelt on the outside of his left thigh.

Bold, he popped the buttons on his fly, raised his butt, and stripped his hips and thighs down naked. His huge uncut cock lay atop the furrow between his hairy legs. A good 12-incher. Maybe more. Maybe a lot more. The jungle night was tossed by deep shadows under the tropical moon. He grinned at me. "You can beat my meat?" he asked. His voice swaggered. Back in the States, he probably had cousins—illegals—hustling 42nd Street. If they were hung like him, they'd be rich in no time flat. His soft olive-skinned cock stretched long as a snaking hose. My fingers tipped along the incredible length of his dick that was as soft as velvet. The tight curlicues of his dark pubic hair forested its base and his big studnuts.

"Are there any more at home like you?" I asked.

He grunted. "This is Latin America, Señor. There are always more at home like me. That is the point." He gently but firmly pushed my hand away. "Are there anymore," he asked, "at home like you?" He spit past the open target of my face into the darkness. In the light of the full moon spilling into the open door of the slow-moving railcar, his smile was part contempt, part joke, and all young lust. "Now," he said, "you show me your big North American prick." For the first time he called me his nickname for me: "Señor El Norte, show me your big white dick."

"You talk big."

"I am big." He tightened his naked groin muscles and flexed every veined inch of his exposed cock.

Whether I was hung bigger or smaller, I had won the bet by getting him stripped part-naked. Very sexy. Fifty bucks had peeled his dick from his uniform. I stripped my rod free, flopping it out, kneeling next to his left thigh. His eyes widened. He grabbed my cock at its root and stared at it as if he had never seen big blond *Estados Unidos* dick up close. He liked it. I liked it. Jeez! Stuck fuck in the middle of nowhere, rattling like two BBs in a boxcar, probably going nowhere fast, we were a fair match, dick to dick. Different, but we had a couple of beauties. We both knew it. We both recognized it. His lip of dark olive foreskin was maybe an inch longer than mine; but soft, inch for soft inch, our bet was a meatman's draw; but hard, he'd win, I could tell, by a mile. I took his dick in my hand while he held on to mine.

"Even stephen," I said.

"OK," he said.

"There's only one way to win this fucking 50 bucks," I said. If there's anything I find worth studying, it's a man with a big soft cock. But if there's anything I want, it's making a man's big soft cock stand up stiff and hard. "This time, kid, I'll bet you another $50 that you're bigger hard than I am."

"That's no bet, El Norte."

"But it's a sure thing to get me what I want."

He laughed, spit in his hand, and stroked my stiffening rod, until my dick stood rock-hard pointing straight in his face. My hand worked his meat, mauling him up to full attention.

Anybody standing along the tracks that night could have seen in the door of the train rumbling by in the hot Nicaraguan moonlight the single-frame shot of two soldiers hand-pulling each other's meat, stripped, their uniforms dropped around their knees, slapping and rubbing chests and bellies, tongues wrapping, sucking spit, blowing air down throats, rebreathing, sucking the air back out, twisting nipples, making hard-assed love in an almost empty cattle car on a half-deserted troop supply train.

War is a hard time in a harsh place, and nothing soft passed between us in our rough wrestle toward cumming. We panted and grappled like soldiers. Our dicks bobbed and weaved. I pulled him to his feet and jammed our bellies together, grinding meat into meat, sportfucking, challenging for the kill, hands pulling the other's dick, gun barrels jousting, ramming cock heads and long shafts between sweaty thighs, fucking slick dick between hot legs, balls bouncing, big dicks slamming, ready to burst, rocking with the roll of the train.

He put his hands on my buzz-cut head. He had big arms. He tried to force me down to my knees to suck his cock. I grappled with him, wanting to ram my dick down his young throat, but he was too strong. I let him be too strong. He resisted me. I let him resist me. The next roll of the train slammed us against the wood wall. I stumbled on my pants tangled around my combat boots, stumbled because I wanted to stumble, because every time, fucking with young soldiers, I lose the upper hand, I feel I've won.

I'm the kind of hunter who eats what he stalks.

He forced me to my knees. The full glory of his huge cock manifested itself over my face. My mouth opened, and he drove himself in, head and shaft and crotch hair, balls banging my chin. I took him the way I'd wanted him, all the way in, sucking him in deep, swallowing him in deeper, holding his huge cock, his teenage daddy-cock that who knew had made, and would make, how many babies, sucking his salty seed-taste deep inside me till I could hear, above the rumble of the train, the roar in his throat that charged his slam-driving fuck of my face with his big cock.

Each lunge brought him closer to cumming. My left hand held his *toro* balls tight against my chin. My right hand slapped my own cock to the edge. Spit ran from my lips, dripped on my chest, wet my cock. He grabbed my ears in his hands and, holding my head dog-steady, almost pulled his 12 hard inches from my mouth. I sucked hard on his grenade-head not to let him escape, but escape was not what he wanted.

He wanted surrender.

He started a slow drive into my mouth, inch by inch, sliding the full length of his massive rebel meat down my throat, still holding my ears, then driving the final inch down my throat, cutting my breathing, me trying to gasp around the eight-inch circumference of his dick, feeling his explosion coming, like far-off cannon fire, advancing, igniting, cumming, blowing off, exploding deep in my throat, concussions of his seed spewing hot shrapnel molten-deep in my throat, gushing out around his cock, flooding my cheeks, his cum shooting out of my nose, blowing out of my snotlocker, my own cock cumming under the passion of his relentless face-fucking. I wanted what I got, and I got what I wanted.

When he pulled his weapon from the deep holster of my throat, I slumped forward on my knees and wrapped my arms around his strong young thighs.

"You win," I said. "I know when I'm beat."

"Your president too," he said, "should know that about us."

All the world's a smart-ass.

The fucking palm trees in the moonlight passed by the open boxcar door, and I thought the trees were moving and we were standing still.

So here I am, cha-cha-cha, crashed in this crummy hotel room with a throat still sore from two days ago, and a memory I'll never forget of Carlos, or Paco, or Esteban, or whatever his name was unless his name was Jack Daniel's which is a name, sweet Jesus, I never forget, because I am Señor El Norte. I know, because a young Sandinista with brown eyes, a salt-lick taste, and a 12-inch dick told me so. But he's gone. Maybe dead by now. That's too romantic. He's not dead. Tonight he's cribbing in somewhere, probably with some pretty Chiquita banana, maybe not drinking as hard as me, but then he's too young to have much to forget. He's not 34, crapped out in a room with an honest-to-Christ flashing neon sign outside the window, listening to the monsoon rainstorm batter the glass.

El Norte has got to get his ass out of Nicaragua!

A man can be out too long, especially when he's between assignments. He forgets who he is and which side he's on. I've been paid cash money by at least three different flags to tackle the same covert mission. I use that money well, which is how I started drinking sometime the night before last at the only male whorehouse in greater Managua, a famous place—if you ask the right people—no sex maniac ought to miss. I've been a regular for maybe a year.

Luis de Aguilar, the owner, invited me to a game and a gamble that keeps me coming back. He knows I'm hung big, and he knows I like size, so he prides himself on scouting the biggest cocks he can to beat my meat. Luis de Aguilar knows I'll pay up to $100 an inch for better-than-ordinary, nicely attached young dick. One of my "Size Nights" at Luis de Aguilar's can cause inflation to ripple through the Nicaraguan economy. But, hey, I'm goddamned El Norte. I get paid big. I spend big. I suck big. Bigger is always better, and maybe because I'm blond, Latin meat looks all the sweeter: brown shafts, cocoa foreskins, olive-ripe dick heads. Cha-cha-cha.

That's how I know I better split. There's plenty of mercenary work, but fuck it: I've been out so long, all I want to do is play. Suddenly, this summer, I'm turning into that fucking Sebastian Venable, and I remember how dark young Latin men did lunch with him. But that hardly stopped me that last night at Luis de Aguilar's, when Jack Daniel's and Sebastian and I went out into the heart of darkness for one last time, straight to the neon flash of La Cantina de Luis.

When a country's at war, anything goes. In the back off his main bar, Luis de Aguilar had converted a storeroom into a pari-mutuel betting operation, sort of like on horses, where those who bet on the winners divide the bets or stakes, minus a percentage for the management. Luis de Aguilar was no more a fool than the dozen or so CIA operatives and other U.S. and Russian military advisers positioned around the small smoky room and watching the action—except the bets here weren't on horses but on the horse-size cocks of the contestants. Take me to any hot little room in any war-torn little country on a Saturday night in a makeshift bar where men forget to be reminded about women, and I'll introduce you to half the Pentagon.

Luis de Aguilar's gambling show was in Round 3 when I arrived. I liked it. I saw three young studs: two Nicaraguans and one blond Swede—a merc with big tattooed arms. Hold this picture! They were standing buck naked, butts twitching, with their dicks wrapped hidden in soft brown chamois rolls, laid out like bagged sausage on a crotch-high wood counter. The Swede was jittery. He kept both hands busy dialing the nipples on his big hairy pecs where the number 2 had been painted with black gun grease. The shorter Nicaraguan, a black-bearded Bull, naked next to him, put his fingers in his teeth and whistled for Luis de Aguilar. "The gringo plays with his tits," he said. "He cheats."

"Fuck you, *Numero Uno,*" the Swede said, swiping his big paw at the number painted on the short man's pecs and belly.

The crowd called out for more. The contest was for size of cock; but sometimes size of mouth was a good kick-ass kickoff. The crowd of bettors was able to see no more than each contestant's body. The three players stood naked except for the tight wrap of chamois-skin leather around their cocks. The bettors, lunging with money, cigars, and whiskey, handicapped their bets based on general body size. They gauged particularly the size of fingers and noses and feet, three sure signs of cockiness. Nearly everyone bet on who had the largest dick, but some hedged their stake, betting on who had the smallest, which, considering Luis de Aguilar's back-office auditions, wasn't that small, since a man auditioning less than eight inches would never be invited to strip down, chamois-wrap his dick, flop it out on the table, and stand naked, working the crowd, trying to get the bettors to go for him, because, win or lose, he got a sweet percentage of the total bet on him. What a contest! Three naked men trying to convince a crowd of national soldiers and international paramilitaries to bet big cash on the size of their big cocks.

I sucked off Jack Daniel's again. My own cock stirred at the temptation to enter Luis de Aguilar's inchworm contest just one time before I split Nicaragua. What man doesn't fantasize he could win a cock showdown? As the bottle splashed down from my face, I recognized the third contestant, the second Nicaraguan, not the short Bull who had complained about the Swede's tits, but the taller, juicier one, the hairier one, the one I hadn't realized was so hairy—two nights before—on the supply train when all I wanted was to deep-case his big foot-long throat-sausage. The fucker had won my 50 bucks. What did I care? I'd swung long and hard on his massive meat that he—"With great pleasure, Señor"—had crammed as far back down my throat as he possibly could. He hadn't killed me with it, but I suspected men lay dead, dying happy, smiles on their faces, with their throats torn open, where he had face-fucked before.

"*¡Hola!* Luis de Aguilar!" I shouted. "Two hundred bucks on Number 3. What's his name?

"El Capitán," Luis de Aguilar shouted. He was a tout fast with nicknames.

El Capitán, oh yeah, recognized me, he did, and grinned. He pointed at his wrapped cock resting on the table, then shook his fist, warning me not to reveal the long secret of his one-eyed pants-snake. God! It thrilled me to think of the nerve some young studs have—like they're God's fucking gift to man, which they are—to strip down and laid their dicks out on tables for strange men's inspections and bets, because they're confident they're sporting the biggest dick around. Who first tells them that, and at what age?

The three young men stood 1-2-3, *uno-dos-tres,* shoulder to shoulder with the Swede sandwiched like white meat in the middle. Soldiering had hardened their tough young bodies, but in their faces, especially in the face of the 18-year-old El Cap, a sweet trace of boyhood's sunset glowed. Their muscular bodies sweated under the bright spotlight of the gaming table. The shorter Nicaraguan stood his ground like the Bull he was. The Swede was the kind of perfect military blond who always shows up whenever anyone throws a war, a crusade, or a barroom brawl. El Cap, lean as a Latin boxer, was the mean fighting machine that keeps a hungry guerrilla army going past all endurance.

Blue smoke from fine Havana cigars, gifts from cousin Fidel, wafted through the bright light. The crowd, most in jungle camo uniforms still sweaty and bloody, armed to a man, loud with booze, eager with lust, cheered as the last bets were placed. Outside, machine guns fired off in the night. Hardly anyone bet the short, swarthy Bull had the biggest dick. Most went for the tattooed blond merc, swayed by his attitude and the size of his powerful Swedish body, but the smart money quietly bet on El Cap. I'd sucked him in the dark and had no real idea how much bigger than big he might really be hung. I wanted to know. I wanted his long gun of a prick down my throat again.

Luis de Aguilar fired his pistol into the ceiling. Plaster dust fell. A basso whore upstairs screamed drag-soprano. The crowd cheered. Not a man in the room would have bet he himself would see tomorrow. The three naked men, with their dicks bagged and laid out along three yellow school rulers nailed to the table, concentrated, thinking those thoughts a man thinks when he wants to, hands off, make his cock hard. The Swede's chamois bag inched forward first. The short Bull grunted, and his bagged dick edged past the Swede's. El Cap, running his own dirty movie on the inside screen of his closed eyes, ignored their contest like a runner pacing the leaders till they run themselves down.

The race was on. The Swede's dick was approaching eight inches. At eight inches on the yellow ruler, Luis de Aguilar's move was to unwrap the dick from the chamois bag, but the naked, hardening dick had to stay untouched by hands, inching along the edge of the yellow ruler, until it hit 10, when the contestant could finally take his meat in one hand to palm-drive it up past 11 inches, to 12, 13—however far it would harden.

The house record was painted in red on the green table: 14 inches of bone-hard cock, set by a Texas cowboy who'd driven his red Ford pickup into Managua one night, so three-days-drunk he never knew he had crossed the border out of Texas into Mexico and kept heading south on unmarked back roads, finally ending up in Managua, Nicaragua. Cha-cha-cha! That's the great seduction about Central America: A man can drive there.

The bearded Bull was in a sweat; his big cock ached for a hand job, a blow job; he had the meat, but he needed the pull. The Swede hit eight on the yellow ruler, and Luis de Aguilar stripped his big, fat blond cock free of the chamois. His dick was a beauty: thick blond porcelain veined with blue traceries, tipped with a big nipple of uncut foreskin. The crowd applauded. Even those who hadn't bet on the Swede had to cheer the sheer beauty of his manhood rolling, stretching, lengthening toward nine inches, then past nine, untouched, toward 10.

The Bull wasn't doing bad for himself. A dozen mestizo soldiers from his ragtag outfit spurred him on, yelling to him like they personally knew how big his cock was, shouting obscenities to him to make it bigger, reminding him what a big face-fucker he sported between his hairy thunder-thighs. The squat Bull bared all three of his gold-rimmed white teeth in his black-bearded face and strained.

His chamois-roll slid past eight inches. Luis de Aguilar stripped his bull cock bare, careful to accidentally touch it, careful to accidentally stroke it, entrepreneuring the man's hard-on, figuring to make the contest more interesting for the house at La Cantina de Luis. The Bull roared as Luis de Aguilar, who was also known as Lois de Aguilar, stroked his cock.

The crowd cheered. A beer bottle flew overhead and smashed against the wall. The Bull's dick thickened and inched past nine, straining on the yellow ruler for the 10 he knew he was hung with, the 10 inches and maybe more, depending on how excited he was, like this moment with the crowd cheering his size, aching to beat the gringo blond, worrying about the too-quiet kid next to him with his dick wrapped in chamois and laid alongside the yellow ruler like a secret arms shipment about to be exposed on the table.

The Bull's dick hit 10 inches. Luis de Aguilar blew his whistle. Bull grabbed his dick, stroking it carefully, watching the Swede's dick inch toward 10 and hit the magic number. Again Luis de Aguilar blew his whistle. The Swede took his own dick in hand. Shoulder to shoulder, the two soldiers beat their meat, slamming their rods down side by side, blond against olive, along the yellow rulers. The Bull was pulling 11, and the Swede was right behind.

"El Capitán!" I shouted. "Number 3!"

El Cap grinned at me and spit, the way he liked to spit, past the two soldiers masturbating next to him. He flexed his powerful butt and blasted his wrapped cock straight past eight to nine inches on his yellow ruler. Luis de Aguilar blew his whistle. The crowd roared. Men started clapping. "Take it off! Take it off!" Luis de Aguilar unrolled the chamois from El Cap's cock. A cheer rose up. Untouched, El Cap's dick writhed and rolled, stretching hard past the 10-, 11-, and 12-inch marks. He was stud with a bullet. The wet eye of his advancing cock head, peeping through its big dark foreskin, was set on 13. The Bull and the Swede paused in amazement. "Oh shit!" the Swede said.

"¡Dios Mío!" The Bull should never have looked at the size of El Cap's cock. His own lust for sucking big dick undid him. He shuddered, spasmed, tried not to, but couldn't help cumming, turning, shooting his hot load slop across El Cap's thick pipeline

still heading untouched past 13 on the yellow. The Bull fell back. His own 10-inch boner, eight inches around the base, stuck straight out from his bull-body, dripping sperm like the animal cock it was. He raised his thick arms in salute. The crowd cheered. Sweat that I wanted to drink ran from the inside of his big biceps down into the twin thickets of his dripping hairy armpits. The Bull may not have been the biggest stud, but he was big and he was stud. A general, an adviser from the Potomac, waved at him two $100 bills, which easily matched his winnings from Luis de Aguilar's "Inches Derby," and made him the general's conquest for the night.

The Swede, buck naked against the snazzy color of his tattooed arms, stood alone next to El Cap, who had yet to touch his inchward cock. The Swede spit in his hand and stroked his own rod, working his blond beauty for every last micro-inch he could add to his hard-on. He stripped his foreskin back, pressed his thighs into the table, tweaked his hard nipples, slapped his dick down the length of the yellow ruler, and watched the head hit square on 13. The crowd cheered. The Swede grinned "Yeah, yeah," but he knew it was all he had in him. If there is a hell, it must be having the good luck/bad luck of a 13-inch cock that's still not big enough.

The Swede had no alternative. I'd have done the same thing. He nodded to Luis de Aguilar who blew his whistle. He spit in his hand, looked straight into El Cap's eyes, got his go-ahead, and did the honors. He touched, actually touched, El Cap's untouched cock topping 13 on the ruler. He lifted the cock up, his face amazed at the cock's gorged volume-weight, teasing the cock's tip with his fingers, stroking the cock's silo-length, feeling the cock's throbbing growth, then finally—El Cap's cock size so overwhelming—falling to his knees in front of El Cap, opening his mouth, his brilliant blond moustache catching the light, his own big meat bouncing with lust, wanting the young rebel soldier's cock rammed down his throat, begging for his head to be drilled.

The crowd went wild.

El Cap turned to me. I held up $300, which was only a fifth of what I was going to win from my bet on his cock. He winked. Three hundred was OK. He held up one finger to signal me his intent. Then he dropped his big balls into the blond's waiting mouth. His olive dick showed to huge advantage measured up across the grid of the square-jawed blond face that looked like the map of Sweden. Men whistled. The blond crossed his eyes, adoring at close range the monster cock.

Finally, El Cap pulled his hairy nuts dripping saliva from the Swede's bulging cheeks. The blond's own meat was ready to blow in his hand. El Cap's dick loomed over him. His mouth opened, and to the slow stomping of feet that grew louder and faster, El Cap drove his drill-rig cock inch by inch past the blond's moustache and lips and tongue and deep down his throat where he rooted in and held his position, with at least four more inches to go, as he heard the crowd shouting *Ole!* and watched the Swede's eyes, which were crossed again—the Nordic blond face impaled on the huge Latin dick. El Cap waited for the Swede to give the nod for the final thrust and, when the nod of surrender did not come willingly from the blond, took the final choking slide down his throat—so final, so good, so victorious, the vanquished Swede shot his load between El Cap's naked calves, and the house came tumbling down.

El Cap pulled his dick slowly out of the gasping blond merc's throat. Luis de Aguilar ran to him with a tape measure, sure he had a new house record, but El Cap gently pushed Luis away and said, "Not now." He meant "not ever." He had no intention of becoming a man measured by his cock.

Yeah. Sure. Cha-cha-cha. Later that night, and for several weeks thereafter as I hung around Managua, with several side jobs crossing into Honduras and dodging Contras, I was privy to every fucking inch of the private parts of my own El Capitán, and my lips, now that they've been stitched back together, are sealed.

All I'm saying is that against El Cap, measure for measure, that famous-hung drunk cowboy who'd driven his 14 inches in from Texas one night to Luis de Aguilar's "Inches Derby" probably ain't much to write home about, which is something me and Jack Daniel's have got to do one of these first mañanas before El Norte finally hauls his ass out of where he don't belong.

Exhibit 114a

by M. Christian

As we walked through the Chinese ceramics collection, I could tell he seriously wanted to suck my cock. Then we turned right, our steps echoing through the transplanted funereal grandeur of Egypt, and I felt his admiring eyes on my ass. I didn't wear my tightest jeans for nothing.

"There's a funny story about that," he said, walking beside me and indicating a gigantic suit of armor that looked like the carapace of some tremendous four-legged beetle.

I didn't say anything. Funny story or not, I didn't bat my long blond lashes at him or shake my perfect butt just to look at brass and silver codpieces. I felt like telling him so just to get him to get on with it, but I could only push the bitchy taste treat so far. I wanted him hungry, not frustrated, so I stopped in front of the gleaming man and let him stand way too close to me. "This turned up in Europe about, oh, 10 years ago—part of the collection of this eccentric Italian nobleman," he was explaining. "Great example of high-medieval armor. Everything was there, pretty much intact, which is quite extraordinary—everything but the shin guards. Now, the piece is incredible, even without the guards, so when the museum had a chance to acquire it, there wasn't a lot of kicking and moaning from the trustees—"

"That's incredible!—I mean, that they wouldn't kick up a fuss," I said, shining my lovely eyes at his shy and furtive ones.

"Uh, yes," he said, risking a sweet smile. "It really is a remarkable find, so it didn't take a lot of arm wrestling. But like I said, the shin guards weren't there. Sometimes we'll...you know...fabricate some, just to able to show what the complete item would have looked like, you know."

"But isn't that dishonest?" I said with a grandiose gasp of naïveté. Anyone else would have glowered with sarcasm. But Professor Robert Garret, senior curator of the New York Metropolitan Museum of Anthropology and Natural History, just let a fragile smile flash cross his face. He wanted me so bad.

"Ah, Matthew, you'd be surprised by the amount of heartfelt chicanery that goes on behind these columns. Anyway, as I said before, this fellow has a good story. So we made the shin guards. And there he was, a lovely example of medieval armor wearing fake shin guards, when someone stumbled on an unusual package in the basement."

"Let me guess," I said, snaking a hand around his waist, pulling him slightly toward me. "The other piece of the armor!"

"Yes!" he said, frisky, playfully punching me in the shoulder. "Missing, separated for Lord knows how long, and they were right here in the basement. Incredible!"

I couldn't have cared less, but I grinned sweetly again at him, trying my darnedest to radiate sugary sensuality. It worked, I guess, because that's where we kissed for the first time—under the gleaming masculinity of some dead king.

• • •

He turned out to be a good kisser: just the right amount of so-soft lips, gingerly, then a passionately pushing tongue. That surprised me. Nice. Not what I wanted, of course, but still a nice surprise, and a lot better than I'd expected. I'd expected his kisses to be clumsy, sloppy, or sopping wet. I mean, when I started doing my research, I'd expected him to be a balding dwarf with halitosis. Instead, I found the curator to be older, yet strong, with a kind of classical elegance to his graying temples.

And he wasn't just a senior curator—discoverer last year, senior curator this year. I have to admit that my prejudice hadn't been very logical. If he'd been pudgy and reeking of mothballs, he hardly could have searched around the base of Olympus Mons and come up with…well, come up with the artifact that had changed everything.

Some didn't believe his discovery; that's fine. Maybe their minds were too small to take it all in, what it all meant. But I knew when I first heard about it. Knew instantly what it meant, how it changed all of us, all of mankind; and I knew then and there that I had to see it for myself, had to see it with my own eyes. Thus, here I was in New York with Robert Garret—the very man who had dug in the rusty Martian soil, the man who had found the artifact.

"That's what makes it all worthwhile, you know," Garret said, taking a break from our kiss to look philosophically at my face. Before I could say or do anything, he reached up and played with a lock of my hair, making me feel like a precious boy in front of his thoughtful father.

Not a mood I was trying to create, so I bent down again and touched my lips to his. *Yes, a very good kisser.* My cock strained in my jeans, begging for a touch. Still, despite the throbbing urgency of my dick, I broke the heavily breathing kiss we'd been sharing to look back up at the armor—thoughtfully, I hoped. "It's all so incredible. All this—so old and so rare," I said, taking his arm and leading him back toward the Artesian wing.

"It's more than rare, Matthew, it's history. It's not a time line, not a story," he said, stopping suddenly in front of a Zulu shield. "It's real, covered with dust from the African plains, touched with blood from God knows how many battles. That's what makes it incredible. To hold something like this in your hands and know for an instant what this great king must have felt—the weight of it, the reality of it. It's a thrill." But the way he turned and looked at me told me that it would also be an incalculable thrill to feel my rock-hard cock slip between his tight ass cheeks.

I tugged again, and he followed. Down past stuffed Eskimos, a hall of crucified butterflies, a sliver of moon rock, and a model of an iron molecule with ions the size of basketballs.

Hand in mine, he seemed to delight in being the child for once, being pulled along among the exhibits with energetic glee. While I admit that the thought of getting those ugly pants off him and tasting the sweet come from the head of his cock did excite me, I was much more thrilled with getting him back toward the restoration and examination rooms.

We stopped again, back where the museum hid its more educational and less flashy exhibits. Next to a diorama of dusty-fleshed mannequins of aborigines bowing up a fire, we kissed again. This time, however, I dropped my hand down to the front of his brown slacks and flicked my fingers across the obvious tent. In the middle of our kiss, lips and tongues sliding together, I smiled. The tent was no pup and even might have qualified as circus-size. Not breaking the oral dance, I wrapped my hand around his rigid dick and carefully, slowly, stroked him until it was he who broke our hot kiss for a deep, long moan.

"Hey, Professor," I said, feigning even more innocence, "did you hear about that thing they found on Mars?"

Ah, that smile: Even through a fog of thumping testosterone, his professional pride beamed like the sun. "I think I know what you mean. In fact, I'm the one who found it."

"No!" I said, intentionally stepping away from his surprisingly strong hands that had been squeezing my ass. "You're kidding!"

"Nope, that was me, all right. I was doing survey work out of Burroughs's Base, trying to confirm a crazy theory of mine that some of the water channels we'd been observing in the deep sedimentary layers were just a bit too regular to have been cut by polar runoff. I really didn't know what I'd found. At first it was just a weird irregularity on the deep-scanning radar. But when I dug it up and saw what it was, well, you can imagine how I felt."

"So it's really...alien?"

"Well, that hasn't been completely confirmed yet. The problem is that since no one's ever seen anything like it, we don't know if it's really artificial or just the product of a highly unusual series of geological actions."

I wanted to hear this, but I also wanted to keep it moving; I put my hand on his cheek. He suddenly turned his head and kissed the palm of my hand. My tent jumped up even harder. "But what do you think?"

"Me? I really don't know. I'd like to think that it's an artifact—and it's looking damned good that it just might be—but I don't want to let my, um, passions get the better of me. In this business, it's always best to wait until you have all the evidence you can get before making a hypothesis." He held my hand against his face, stroking his cheek with my palm.

He did have a lovely face, actually: kind but strong. Unusual for someone whose business card said "curator," but then I reminded myself that he'd been picked for the Martian research pool, so he couldn't be a complete microscope jockey. In a sudden flash I envisioned him, lean and powerful, jogging around the exercise wheel of one of the big Martian ships, shadow-boxing and gleaming with well-earned sweat. Still part of that flash, I wanted to lick the salt from his nipples and from the firm valley of his crack at that magical spot where spine vanished into the fold of his ass.

"An alien thing…oh, Robby, I'd love to see it," I said, leaning close so he could feel my chest against his own.

"Well, I really can't, uh…" he said, suddenly stern, tenure and status causing its own flash behind his eyes.

"Please, Robby, pretty please?" Then I kissed him, and as we kissed I pushed my hard cock against his crotch, knowing, as our dicks dueled in our pants, what his answer would be.

• • •

His access card got us through an almost invisible back door and down a stark hallway into a maze of workrooms and labs. Finally, we came to a glass box in the middle of a huge room full of calmly humming machinery.

After so long, I finally saw it with my own eyes.

"There it is. What do you think?" he said, standing with his back to the box, the box on the simple steel table, the box containing that lump of red sandstone. He smiled at me, knowing all too well what I was looking at, gleefully keeping his eyes on my face for the blast of awe he knew would be coming.

I didn't disappoint. How could it not be a made thing? It was squat, ugly, like a heavy onion, but with a well-weathered, curving loop descending from the narrow top to the fat base and, 45 degrees around the side, the twin stumps of where a similar loop—another handle?—had been. It didn't look natural, and it sure didn't look human.

I stared for a long minute, until I realized he might be getting nervous. "But it's so ugly," I managed to croak out, thinking anything but. In my mind I was there, on the ruddy surface of that other world, holding it in my hands. I wore clothing that moved like water, like heavy smoke; my mind was complex and wonderful, like lightning, like a glacier.

He laughed, turning to look at it with me. "It is, isn't it? But if it is manufactured, well, it could be the most important thing in the history of mankind."

I felt the thin winds of Mars on my translucent skin, my imagination embellishing the horizon with the smooth undulations of organic homes, the stabbing spires of tremendously high towers like the spines on the back of some deep water creature.

I felt his hands on my back, tracing the knobs of my spine in a lazy figure eight. Then they wrapped around me, rubbing his fingers lightly across my hard nipples. "But, you know, even if it doesn't turn out to be anything but a weird rock, it's still incredible."

No, it was what it looked like. It was something from…something from another world, another people. It was a rusty, dusty lump of sandstone that meant, just by existing, that we were not alone.

I sniffled with sudden tears, turning quickly to kiss him again. His hands eagerly found my cock this time, and I sensed a furious, hungry kind of energy about him. It was as if standing next to that glass box and its very special contents somehow were fueling his essence. I understood and felt it also burning deep in me. My mind was lost on the windswept plains of Mars, but my cock was also screaming for his mouth, his tight asshole.

Suddenly, he was kneeling on the black-tiled floor, pushing his face against my crotch. Knowing what was coming, I rested my hand on the top of his head, distantly hoping that he'd manage to get my cock out easily.

He did. For someone who had done so much and now worked among the halls of the dead, he was actually pretty adept at (a) getting my cock free of my (now severely tight) jeans, and (b) sucking me. Good, oh yes, damned good. Like his kisses, he used just the right amount of lips and tongue, but now he could also use a lot more of what he'd been blessed with: the ridges at the top of his mouth, the sudden cool shock of his teeth, the deep socket of his throat. I let him suck me until I couldn't stand it anymore. I pushed him away playfully but firmly, and turned to press my palms against the cool glass of the box.

It was there he fucked me—cock sliding in and out of my hungry asshole, his balls tickling my tight cheeks, the head of his dick tapping delightfully against my swollen prostate.

He fucked me hard and passionately, slapping thighs against my ass. He fucked me thoroughly, each inch of his big dick going in and out, in and out. He fucked me with everything he had; distantly, I heard his shoes squeak on the floor as he dug in for more and more traction.

As he fucked me, I jerked off, stroking my cock with my sweaty palms. When he came, after what seemed to be hours, I came too, splashing my creamy jism onto the crystal glass in front of me. He was good—very good—but as he fucked me, as he came gallons into my ass, I wasn't thinking about him or his dick or his lips. Not once.

My face against the glass, I stared at the object he'd dug up out of the Martian soil. My wonder and amazement filled my mind as his cock filled my ass; and while his cock was great, it was the wonder that I'd really come to see.

• • •

Seeing him out into the cold New York night, I couldn't help but grin. Matthew was just what I needed: young, passionate (absolutely), and with just the right amount of blind enthusiasm for the otherworldly. When I first sat down in that pressurized tent at the base of Olympus Mons and put together that ugly lump of Martian sand, and then walked back to the base with just the right blend of amazement and skepticism, I was really hoping for someone like Matthew to come along. I am totally amazed that it has taken this long for one of his kind to be so drawn to the otherworldly that they'd be willing to indulge in sexual rituals to get close to it—even if "the artifact" is a clumsy fake.

Data acquired. Now I look forward to going home. Still, it is humans like Matthew that will make me miss this quaint little world—and its passionate, if naive, inhabitants.

Who Walks in Moonlight

by Barry Alexander

Keosauqua clung to the tangle of roots a strangling fig had woven around the giant banyan tree and tested the air. The scents were heavier than in the canopy: rotting fruit, animal musk, and a darker scent he thought came from the ground itself. A monkey had passed recently, and the sour reek of its urine was overpowering.

Sweat trickled down his chest and under the piece of tapa cloth hanging from his hips. He reached under the cloth and rubbed the sweat into the thick hair curling above his shaft. His shaft thickened and hung heavily between his legs. He couldn't resist stroking himself a few times before he let the cloth drop back. The beads on his karait rattled, reminding him why he was here. He adjusted the empty pouch on his hip and sighed.

He had only three days to find the lair of a jaguar and return with the proof of his right to be a Massema. Though he had seen 18 drys, Keosauqua would not be considered a complete man until he returned with one of the snakes that bedded with jaguars. A body snake did not hunt. It curled beside a large sleeping body and waited for the scorpions and spiders that were drawn to the animal's body heat. With his own body snake to watch his sleep, he could leave his parents' branch and begin his own. He supposed it would be Taleeta who would share his branch. As well her as another. His friends bickered over which girls were the most beautiful, but to Keosauqua they were much the same.

Keosauqua looked down at the green darkness and hesitated. Few sunspears pierced the shadowed gloom. The ground looked solid enough, and he knew of strange creatures who lived at the bottom of the world, but he thumped it with his spear before he could bring himself to set foot on its strange surface. His callused feet, used to curving around branches, found little support on the smooth, damp surface. He teetered badly until he learned to flatten his arches. Keosauqua found it strange to walk using only his feet. His hands felt awkward with nothing to do but hold his spear.

Keosauqua padded softly through a forest that seemed strangely empty. He saw no animals, though sometimes he heard rustlings. The calls of birds and the rasping of insects seemed remote. For the first time in his life, he felt alone. Far above, in the wind-tossed canopy, boys and girls played as they had yesterday, chasing each other in the hot sun. Below the laughing children, women gathered fruit for the evening meal, while the men hunted for birds, lizards, or a green-furred sloth.

Keosauqua searched all day, but found no sign of jaguars. When the shadows changed from green to black, Keosauqua climbed into a tree for the night. He settled against the trunk and waited for sleep. The clamor of birds and animals swelled into the nightly chorus. Over the squeals and whistles and laughs boomed the cries of howler monkeys. The sounds shrilled to an unbearable pitch, then stopped. For a few moments, there was silence. Then the night creatures woke and wove their own songs into the silence. Bats fell onto ripe fruit, chittering and quarreling over their finds. And somewhere below, jaguars opened their saffron eyes and began the hunt.

Morning came, and the dawn chorus was as loud as the evening song. Harpies shook their wings as they took to the bright morning air, and fleeing monkeys plummeted through the branches like ripe fruit. Mid afternoon, Keosauqua discovered a clearing. He looked up with shock at a sky as blue as a man bitten by a click beetle. The sun poured hot and golden over a dance of azure butterflies. Birds darted through a shower of sunspears. The hot sun made him feel sleepy. He stretched out on the moss-furred bark of a fallen tree, closing his eyes against the brightness of the sun. The breeze played softly over his bare skin.

When he opened his eyes, he stiffened with fear at what he saw. Above him a thousand cold eyes glittered. The eyes above stared fixedly at him, never blinking. Keosauqua was afraid to move and attract the attention of whatever guarded this place with such vigilance.

He moved his hand a finger's width. Nothing happened. Slowly, slowly, he slid off the tree. When he was safely concealed at the edge of the clearing, he felt compelled to look back. As he watched, the glowing face of Moravial, the pale lord of death, rose above the trees, his cold white arms slowly reaching into the clearing. Keosauqua closed his eyes and waited for those clinging arms to bind him fast with a touch colder than death. He heard steps and opened his eyes cautiously.

Across the clearing, heedless of the deadly light, a tall man strode. Keosauqua wanted to call out a warning but could not. Surely the man would die or go mad, but the deadly glow did not harm him. He walked as boldly on earth as a god, but the old ones had always said that the gods were fairer than a man could bear. This was clearly a man, but he was like no man Keosauqua had ever seen. His broad, handsome face was marred with a scar high on his cheek, where a Massema man would carry the blue spiral. The point of his spear caught the light and glittered in a strange way. And he did not wear a karait. Keosauqua touched the empty pouch hanging on his own hip. A man was never careless with his karait; too much of his being was woven into it. The measure of his life and his kills hung in that tassel of carved bone and wood beads.

Keosauqua was shaking when the stranger walked from the clearing and passed into the dark. What could it mean, a man who walked the night earth? He puzzled on it long that night, but found no answers. Perhaps it had only been a vision, a walking dream the forest conjured in the moonlight, not a man.

The next morning, he put away the visions of the night, as a man must. There was still a lair to find and an empty bag to fill. Late in the day, he finally spotted the signs he was seeking. The scent grew stronger as he followed the spoor: hot, musky—jaguar. He got as close as he dared, then climbed into the trees and silently followed the scent until he was above the lair. The jaguars snarled and stirred restlessly when they caught his scent, but he was so high in the canopy they could not see him. When he did not move or make a sound, they quickly settled down.

As evening came, the jaguars woke. They sniffed and snarled under the tree for a while, then left to hunt. Keosauqua waited until he judged them far away, then descended quickly and silently. He found a deep hollow hidden under the giant roots of a banyan. He could not see what might be in their lair, but he leaned his spear against the trunk and cautiously crawled inside.

As he probed the hollow, he could almost feel the jaguars' hot breath on his neck and their claws raking his back. Something brushed against his hand, and he grabbed it. A snake bit him. The bite was painful but not dangerous. He caught the snake just behind the head. He backed quickly from the lair, uncoiled the snake from his wrist, and dropped it into his karait. He recovered his spear and was just about to swing himself into a tree when he heard a sound behind him. He spun around, holding his spear ready. He saw a flash of gold and black, as a jaguar flung itself on his outstretched spear. The spear snapped under the cat's weight, and the cat fell to the side, its talons raking long furrows in Keosauqua's arm. He grabbed a liana and scrambled up the tree. But the spear only slowed the cat; it was up in a moment. Fast as Keosauqua climbed, he knew the jaguar was faster. Then his wounded arm gave, and he fell.

In desperation he drew his belt knife. He watched hopelessly as the cat backed slowly down the tree. Its ears flattened and its tail swished angrily. The broken shaft of the spear protruded from its shoulder, and blood glistened on its dappled hide. Muscles bunched under its sleek pelt, and it launched.

Suddenly, a spear split the air by his head and buried its shining point deep in the jaguar's breast. In mid leap, the cat crashed to the ground. Keosauqua turned and saw the stranger who had walked unharmed through moonspears. Keosauqua caught his breath at the beauty of the man. Only a beaded necklace and a leather loin pouch hid the perfection of his smooth bronze skin. His slender body was tautly muscled, as sleek and supple as the jaguar's. His silky black hair was cut short in a fringe across his broad forehead. He was larger than Keosauqua, older, and stood proudly clutching his spears. Eyes unblinking, he matched Keosauqua look for look. Keosauqua couldn't look away, compelled by the intensity of the man's deep brown eyes. There was something about him that set Keosauqua's pulse racing.

As the stranger crossed the clearing, his eyes locked with Keosauqua's. The man stopped, his bare chest inches away. Heat radiated from his body. Keosauqua trembled as the man placed a hand on his chest. Warm fingers traced the lines of Keosauqua's chest. The man smiled as his fingers brushed against one of Keosauqua's nipples. He caught it between his fingers and squeezed. A line of fire leaped through Keosauqua's body. His shaft stiffened in delight.

Keosauqua stood paralyzed under the touch. No man had ever touched him this way. His body ached with sudden need. He shouldn't be permitting this, but it might be dangerous to offend the stranger. Besides, he didn't think he could move away as the slender fingers continued their intimate exploration of his body.

Abruptly, the man stopped. Keosauqua tried to speak to him, but the man only made strange chattering sounds. The man pointed to the jaguar and to the forest, but his gestures made no more sense than his voice.

He turned from Keosauqua and walked to the dead jaguar. Putting his foot on its haunch, he yanked his spear free. He thrust the spear into the ground beside the cat's head. Squatting on his heels, he dressed the beast, packing the choicest bits in a bundle made from the great cat's pelt.

The man made more of the strange sounds and gestures, then walked away. Without meaning to, Keosauqua found himself following. The man walked swiftly along a trail Keosauqua could not see, so instead he watched the smooth play of muscles in the man's hind parts as he strode steadily through the forest surrounding him.

They came to a small clearing. Keosauqua watched as the man built a fire and speared pieces of meat onto sharpened branches. Soon the smell of roasting flesh started a gnawing in his belly. The fire spat as the fat dripped and greedily licked the chunks of meat with many fiery tongues.

The man pulled one of the branches from the fire and handed it to Keosauqua. Eagerly, he pulled the meat from the cooking stick, tossing it from hand to hand as it burned his fingers. The stranger grinned, watching him. The meat was charred black on the outside, red and juicy inside. Grease ran down Keosauqua's face, and he caught it with his fingers and licked them too. He thought he had never tasted anything so delicious. He tried to thank the man, who could only give him a puzzled smile.

The man showed no sign of leaving the clearing for the safety of the trees. Keosauqua felt a strange reluctance to leave as well. He kept thinking of the way the man had touched him. To distract himself, he opened his karait and took the small snake gently from the bag. She opened her lidless eyes and spat at him. He uncurled her with his fingers and laughed as she hissed and stubbornly rolled back into a tight coil. Maha, he would call her—little one. The man looked up at his laugh with a strange expression in his dark eyes.

Keosauqua flushed as the man's eyes traveled slowly down his body. He put the snake back in his karait as the stranger stood up and walked over to stand above him. Keosauqua's eyes scanned slowly up his legs. The leather pouch between the man's legs hung heavily, and a rich, musky scent filled Keosauqua's nostrils. He breathed deeply, becoming aroused by the exciting aroma. His shaft hardened in quick jerks, lifting the tapa cloth at his waist. A new hunger stirred him. Unable to resist his desire, he reached up with trembling hands to untie the thong confining the intriguing bulge in front of him. The pouch dropped free, and Keosauqua was awed by the size of the manspear pointed at him. Thick veins twined around the mahogany shaft. A thin pucker of skin gaped open, revealing the deep pink head. A drop of moisture dripped from the opening and pattered to the ground below.

Keosauqua closed his fingers around the rigid shaft, marveling at the warm silky skin. Another drop of moisture quivered at the tip. Without thinking, he leaned forward and caught it on his tongue. The taste was intriguing. He pushed his tongue inside the opening and lapped for more. Above him, the man groaned and pushed Keosauqua's head closer.

Keosauqua licked greedily inside the opening and nibbled at the velvety skin. He pulled the skin back and swirled his tongue over the bulbous head. His hands explored the man's body as his mouth explored the stranger's manhood. He filled his hands with the man's fat, furry balls as his tongue traced the thick veins along his shaft.

The man pressed him closer, the head of his cock smearing juices over Keosauqua's lips. Keosauqua opened his mouth, and the thick shaft pushed inside, resting heavily on his tongue. It was hard and hot, and Keosauqua wanted all of it. He didn't understand the hunger that drove him; he only knew he had to have more. He pushed forward, sucking hard as he tried to take all of the manspear into his mouth. His lips stretched around the heated flesh filling his mouth. The man thrust hard, driving his shaft against the back of Keosauqua's throat. For a moment, Keosauqua held his breath. His nose was pressed deep into the dark hair curling above the shaft. When the man pulled back, Keosauqua inhaled deeply, then drove himself forward. The man's legs trembled as Keosauqua fell into a rhythm, his head rising up and down. Keosauqua sucked harder, eager to taste the manseed he knew the stranger was getting close to spilling.

The man pushed Keosauqua's head away and drew him to his feet. He quickly removed the cloth about Keosauqua's hips and his karait. He pulled Keosauqua into his arms and kissed him eagerly. Keosauqua sucked greedily at the tongue exploring his mouth. It was moist and sweet, like some exotic fruit. The man's hands stroked his shoulders, then moved down to cup the hard mounds of his hind parts. Keosauqua ground himself against the man, pushing his throbbing shaft against the man's. It felt so good to be this close to another man, bare chest against firm bare chest, bare thighs against strong bare thighs.

They were both gasping when they broke the kiss. The stranger led Keosauqua over to a fallen tree, thick with moss, and pushed him back against it. Keosauqua lay back, thighs spread open, his shaft hard against his belly. The man leaned over him; his warm tongue lapped Keosauqua's nipples, teasing them into hard little nubs and sucking them. Keosauqua thought he had never felt anything so delicious. Then the man nipped one of the nipples, and the intense pleasure made Keosauqua's cock drizzle juices all over his stomach. Keosauqua trembled in anticipation as the man moved lower, tonguing his stomach and licking up the sticky fluid coating his belly. The man flicked his tongue lightly at Keosauqua's navel, then sucked gently at the little nub. Keosauqua groaned with pleasure. His hands paused in their exploration of the sleek contours of the stranger's body to stroke through his silky hair and push his head lower.

The man made him wait for it. Keosauqua moaned in frustration as the man's tongue fluttered over the insides of his thighs. The man wrapped his lips around one of Keosauqua's balls, sucking and washing it with his tongue. He nuzzled Keosauqua's cock, rolling the heavy shaft against his face and gently tugging the wiry hairs with his lips.

"Take it," Keosauqua pleaded.

As if he understood, the stranger licked the fat tube, then closed his lips over the glistening red cap. Keosauqua sighed with relief as he swallowed half the shaft. The man sucked strongly, driving Keosauqua right to the edge.

The man pulled off and positioned Keosauqua's body until he was resting completely on top of the broad trunk. The moss was cool and soft against his skin. The man climbed onto the tree also and knelt over Keosauqua and caressed his firm body with fingers and mouth. Twisting with pleasure, Keosauqua writhed beneath him. He pulled the man down, his lips eagerly seeking the warmth of the man's mouth. They kissed passionately, cock throbbing hard against cock as they embraced.

Keosauqua locked his hands around the hard mounds of the man's buttocks and hunched his hips upward, pressing their inflamed cocks more tightly together. The man rocked forward, driving his shaft along Keosauqua's. They were both dripping so much fluid that the man's cock slipped easily over Keosauqua's. The pressure of their bodies created a tight, warm tunnel, which they plowed again and again as they coupled, mouths and bodies locked together, passionate cries echoing through the clearing. They came swiftly, rutting against their bellies.

Sweat streamed off their bodies. They lay panting against each other as the heat from the fire washed over them. The man sat up and smiled down at him. Keosauqua couldn't help smiling back; he was so beautiful. The man peeled a thick pad of wet moss from the tree and cleaned the mingled sweat and manseed from their bodies. The man kissed Keosauqua and murmured something he could not understand, but it didn't matter. He understood the touch of the man's fingers on his body well enough. The second time was even more wonderful.

For the first time in his life, Keosauqua stretched on the bare ground to sleep, as calmly as if he were in his own tree. He curled against the man's body, legs twining together. In the morning the man was gone, and only the scattered ashes of a cold fire proved that he had ever been there. Keosauqua could not search for the man; it was time for him to return to his people.

When dark came again, he took Maha out and settled her at his side. A chance moonspear caught her cold eyes, and they glittered. He did not move from the light, as once he would have. Instead, his eyes followed the light, and he thought of the stranger.

"He is moon-touched," they would say, if he told his story.

He must make himself forget. Perhaps it had only been a vision. In the morning he would put those visions behind him. But tonight...tonight his thoughts were full of moonspears and star-eyes...and a man who walked by moonlight.

Chain Male

by Scott D. Pomfret

A cluster of gargoyles guards the door to the club. They are dressed all in black. They have leather holsters to carry their bellies. They are beefy and bald, and their eyes glitter. They check IDs and take no shit and wear muscle shirts that say OBEY ME.

Behind a velvet rope, we wait in line outside the club like a line of suppliants at the castle walls. After they accept the price of admission, the club is revealed. It is a revelry, one of a dozen carnivals that litter the night, like a medieval fair on a wide plain beneath a walled city, open to wanderers, crusaders, and errant knights. The club woos the lonely traveler with electronic spectacle and siren promises and raw flesh. It is softness after the hard road.

But that false sense of chivalry is a deceit. Bandits without honor wait inside. Pockets of men stand in clusters like tents, keeping their secrets—though for a price they'll display the wonders they have looted from far-off worlds.

Languid men droop into place on the long sofas, but I never lose my guard. I wander among the pretty patrons, sampling the merchandise. I never give up my name, as if it is a secret that has the power to undo me in the hands of the person to whom I reveal it.

The bar is a wizard's lair, where the skinny black boy in a Hawaiian-print shirt takes drink orders and remembers them forever. He mixes weird potions and watches out for the bandits who drop unintended roofies in unattended cups. The old dragons who do not dance shovel crumpled dollars on the bar and ogle the younger crowd and demand more grog and breathe fire and remember when they used to turn heads. Their clawed hands find my back pocket as I lean over the bar to order another drink.

The virgin comes into the club much later than I did. He is perhaps 19, maybe 20. He has been lurking outside, gathering courage, waiting for the moment of elevation from squire to knight, waiting for the time to be right. I watch him in the mirror over the bar. As he passes the gauntlet of drinkers and dancers, he acts as if he does not have to choose. His strides are long.

The dance floor seethes like a witch's cauldron. It is a frothing, lawless place, where the flesh parades under a confetti of flashing light. Princesses in spectacular drag flutter softly. At the margin, timid boys like pretty maidens fan themselves against the heat.

The virgin slows, stops, turns infinitely slowly, as if he is being sirened. He understands instinctively that this is his destiny. He turns his sweet ass to me, and he stares. He maintains a careful habit of rocking from heel to toe. He has never seen men coupled in dance; he has never watched a man kiss another man. He thinks, *Is this allowed? Should I be here?*

He concludes, *I am safe.*

Fanlike, nervous gestures emanate from his hands and spread all over his body, seeking loose ends. He produces a couple of glow sticks. He has obviously been saving them up for tonight. He breaks them with a quick, short violence that is erotic, and out of the violence fire grows in his hands, flutters, breathes, expands, flutters some more. The fire becomes two quick butterflies mating around his head. And then the music takes control, nets and captures them, and trains the boy's movement to its own ends.

His ramrod posture dissolves into liquid. The movement draws me to the rail that skirts the dance floor. I take a place next to the predators, who survey the fresh meat from the raised dais, the highest point, the castle's turret. Their rapacious gazes are boiling oil poured down on the dancers below.

A pouting, shirtless boy with perfect pecs flits his eyes at me. They cross me, hold me; the disco ball turns in his pupils, and then they go dead. A gargoyle passes close to check the marked hands of an underage kid who carries a drink he should not have. The gargoyle is a dark shadow, a cold mist off a Scottish loch. When he is gone, the heat rises again, shrouding the virgin in the snarl of flailing limbs. I am patient; I wait for him to struggle free, to come out.

The virgin flinches at the first hand that touches him. His avoidance is graceful, like a vine twisting its way up a trellis pole. He is light, agile, seemingly oblivious. Yet concentrated in his body is complete self-awareness, wielded like a weapon, powerful and pulsing, as if he is standing outside of himself, next to me on the dais, and also watching himself dance.

Next to him wrestle two short boys of identical build who are identically dressed in baggy Structure X pants and oversize white T-shirts, cut narrow beneath their tight latissimi dorsi. Chains glint at their necks. They maul each other. Their hair is cut short and clean. Their foreheads glisten.

Watching them, the virgin surrenders to the hands that want him. Someone approaches from behind and grinds his groin against the virgin's ass. His hands flutter along the virgin's shoulder, under his whirling glow-stick arms, to his chest. In front of the virgin, a worn 50-year-old in the clothes of someone half his age twists to his knees. (He will regret it tomorrow.) He presses his face against the boy's crotch, miming fellatio to the techno beat. His eyes are half-closed in a pose of ecstasy.

It is a joy to be wanted, the virgin thinks. It is the very first time. He has never before been wanted physically, intensely—never like this. The floor beneath him explodes with light. Other men sense that he is available and close in.

I feel no jealousy. I get off on the older men wanting him, just as he gets off on being wanted. I have no fear of losing him to the trolls because on some deep, mystical level I have always known he is like me, a comrade-in-arms, a brother, a warrior, of the same generation and tribe, a squire, a page, a knight-in-training. He is me a short two years ago.

I trail him to the basement below the dance floor. It is a dungeon; the walls are painted black. Teeth and eyes have purple magic in the ultraviolet light. The men's room reeks of ass. In one stall, a four-legged beast, trapped, heaves and groans in its cage. A frantic boy has dropped his pants and totters about the room, bound at the ankles, laughing, offering himself to whomever will take him. The gargoyles come for him, cover him, and carry him out.

Boys come in, boys go out. Money passes, then one of the old dragons from the bar is on his knees. He has become a groom, a valet, a faithful servant, servicing the boy-knight who took the money. Friends block the gargoyles' further entry. The dragon grips the boy's pale ass until it bruises, taking the whole cock in as if he were a starving serf scavenging bread cast off from a carriage into the road—the leavings of young kings.

The virgin is wide-eyed at the urinal; he cannot pee, he cannot look away. The dragon gets lower, opens wider. His mouth is a cave into which the boy's nuts disappear. The dragon rolls them around like a set of dice, strokes the hard hidden shaft all the way to the ass, slicks his finger, and presses. The boy gives off an obligatory moan, and no one can tell if it's real. The court jester, a short, ugly Jewish boy in Buddy Holly glasses, cracks jokes about the old man's health, his heart rate, and the likelihood that anyone would be willing to give him CPR.

I ambush the virgin outside the men's room door. Thrust him against the wall, kiss him hard. His chest strains up against me; his heart seems to come out and flog me; he defends himself as best he can. Then, at the moment I was going to release him, he nearly pokes my eye out, grabbing the back of my head, and thrusting his tongue into the open wound in my face that is my mouth. I bite gently. I drop slowly. I am in the barnyard of his armpit, nipping the cherry-pit nipple through the shirt. He groans. The groan is quite real. His sweat is the froth from a cauldron. His hips are handles.

Then the DJ's voice summons us to battle. He announces the contests, the challenges, the jousts, the will of some unseen king.

The virgin considers the invitation. By that time, he has been in the club an hour or more. He knows what he wants; he has sloughed off the old men like a dead skin. There is a moment of brief fear as he wavers; it hasn't occurred to me that he might turn me down.

He does not turn me down. He has seen something in me. Some intimation of the destiny I felt earlier. He trusts something in me, wants something in me. His eyes do not leave me. They have not strayed over my shoulder to someone prettier. They have fixed on me, they have appointed me a worthy opponent. They have booked me for the night. It is a matter of ripeness. It is an appointment arranged by the gods.

The music is louder and faster; the lights are brighter and more urgent. On one side of us, the short, muscled, white T-shirt boys are sucking face. The pretty pouting disdainful boy has found a better match; he is dancing, he is complete. His eyes flicker over me, stopping proudly to display the partner he has found so that he can show me that he has settled for nothing but the best. I forgive his arrogance, for it is erotic and necessary; it is no longer against me, as when he had nobody but still rejected me; it is with me in solidarity; it says, *We all find what we need.* He pays tribute, nodding at the virgin, who is at my side and very hot.

The exchange of glances is a gauntlet thrown down. The virgin peels off his own shirt. His wrists become bound over his head, until it seems he is suspended by his arms, or a set of thumbscrews. He matches the pouting boy pec for pec, nipple for nipple, six-pack for six-pack. His ribs are a basket, his belly a loaf of fresh bread into which I drive my thumbs to release the steam. My touch dissolves him in laughter, and he leans against me, momentarily legless. His cock stabs me.

Then he loops the shirt around my neck, as if it were a noose or a garland, and leaves it there. He runs his hands over his own body, touches his shoulder, his nipple, passes over the rippled belly, plays at the band of his boxers. His eyes are on me, watching me watch him, as if he is taking instruction. There are a hundred hands now. His chest heaves, and his breath also seems to be a hand kneading and plumping him, filling the flesh. The sweat that runs from the V of his neck between the pecs and into the belly is also a hand. The lights play all over him. And then my hand is there too, unbidden, on the collarbone, cupping the shoulder as if it were a breast, inexorably dropping, dropping, dropping. To the waistband, a line of hair, a dew of sweat. Shaping him, transforming him, effecting a change.

There is no laughter this time. He presses against me, he trembles, he does not own his hips. My hands work around his back, under his boxers, on the two cheeks that move with the music. They bunch, escape me, and then come back. My eyes meet his eyes, and his do not drop. They enter me, wound me, dodge, feint, then strike again, eye to eye, blow for blow, strength matched to strength. And at our side the white T-shirts cling to one another, and the proud boy undulates like a long slow river, and the heat rises, and voices crow, and the pulse pounds my heart into something new and impervious, impregnable and hard, a shield, a mighty weapon.

All dancers are warriors. Gay warriors. Battle-tested, synchronized, born to watch one another's backs. To stand tall, to hurl lances, to slay beasts, to sing poetry that makes the sky weep. We are indestructible. The world quakes at our coming. The virgin will soon be in our ranks.

It is easy to believe. The dance pit is a jousting ring. The warriors are deep in the fray—young, strong, pretty, proud; bellies that are a tangle of writhing snakes, hair dyed to the color of electricity, hands and wrists armored in a chain mail of silver thumb rings and hammered bracelets; defined, hard, in mutual contest, straining one against the other, heaving against one another and yet on the same side, the same team, all at battle peak.

When last call sounds, would that there were some challenge for the virgin to accept with his brothers, some gauntlet to take up, some grail to find. But there is none. The enemy is flitting and elusive, so we fight among ourselves, practicing our martial arts, because we are dimly aware, even here, even under the protective pulse of this safe haven, this bounded arena, that we must toughen for the long haul, questing, alone, out in the hostile world.

Afterward, we spill out of the club and ransack the streets. There is a party. The boy comes willingly, without fear, without coercion, hungry and cocksure. His pride is his greatest weapon. He thinks he knows all there is to know. He thinks he is already one of us—that his training is done.

This time, we have left the timid behind. There are only warriors left at this round table, none but the young and proud with stiff cocks and raging blood. The virgin's eyes consume the sumptuous feast. Clothes are shed, strewn to the side like armor. We resort to purer Grecian contests, the greater tests of manhood; the barest, rawest, most basic contests of man on man with neither accoutrement nor shield, only the natural armor of our own hearts.

I lie back and instruct him to sit on my face. He crouches. I slide my finger into his ass and spread it. I touch, taste, lick. Eat him out ferociously, lapping like a dog, biting, thrusting, sucking, teasing

with the tip of my tongue until his stink is spread all over my cheeks.
When I'm done, he vows, "I can't do that to you."
I pet his shoulder as if I understand. His arms are rubbery.
"I could never do that," he insists.
I make him take it back. I instruct him that he should never shrink from a challenge. I remind him how sacred are a warrior's vows. I give him the battle skills that he needs. And the minor props he should carry: lube, latex, and a sense of abandon, a sense that finally he is among his own people. And in a moment, I am proud: His face is deep in my buttocks, and he performs like a champion.
I am on all fours, still teaching, always teaching. The virgin abandons my ass and steps around in front of me. He kneels solemnly. My mouth closes over his mushroom tip. His hands close around the back of my head. Behind me, another warrior has taken the virgin's place. His hand finds and plumbs my ass, testing my depth, my resilience. A breath relaxes me; both cocks enter me, one on each end. I am infinitely capacious; I believe I could take in a world of cocks and each one would make me stronger.
"Fuck that ass. Fuck that ass," the boy says without jealousy to the warrior behind me. The boy's hard stare enters me as the warrior's cock enters me from behind. The boy bends, his belly wrinkles, my head bobs, his lips brush my ear. Something runs down my neck, from my ear down the knobs of my spine over the bubble ass, runs a message down to the cock that enters there, that frays my ass lips and jostles my kidneys.
Warrior, the messenger says, *we have battles ahead.*
Hackles raised, goose bumps pricked, the boy is harder, is arched, is straining, is willing himself not to be defeated. My hand closes under his package. His sack is like a leather pouch in which a shaman keeps his secrets. My finger finds his ass again, returning thrust for thrust. The virgin's nut draws up as he approaches his climax. The virgin pulls his cock free from where it's buried to the hilt in my mouth. He issues a cry of triumph.
"How much do you want it?" he asks. "Tell me how much you want it."
Spit or swallow is a metaphor for life. You can treat everything as bitter, but then you'll go hungry. You've got to force yourself to like

hot jizz, force yourself to put your tongue in places your old self would not have dreamed. You force yourself until the gesture is no longer forced, but part of you. It becomes an appetite, and then you are strong. And so the virgin becomes a warrior; thus so he is dubbed a knight, blooded, daubed with the thick chrism that comes from cock.

My orgasm obliterates the world. There is nothing but a bare moor left, no watch kept in the castle's dark tower. The fires have burned low; breezes rush around in the corners, stirring and collecting shadow, and running home again.

I wake much later in a pile of bare limbs. I am the first to stand among the bodies of my naked comrades. The dream is intact; the warriors are fallen. I kiss the virgin, who is now a knight. I take a shaky step, alone, into a sharp, new morning. I will never be defeated.

Riding With Walter
by Greg Wharton

Walter is standing on the seat, his head proudly hanging out the window, his tail wagging with happiness. This is his favorite thing, cruising in my truck with me, teary-eyed in the wind, his muzzle drooling over everything it comes in contact with.

"Where to, huh? What do you say we hit the Dunes today? Go for a little road trip? Huh, buddy? Got anything better to do?"

I have to get out of the city. Last night is a blur. One fucking blur. I don't know what got in to me, what I was thinking. Oh, but I do know. That ass. A perfect ass.

It's not like I haven't looked before. Eddie and I spend a lot of time together. He's my sister's husband. So I've looked, checked out the package every so often. He's very handsome, sexy. I just never thought too much about it. He's married: family. Besides, he always wears big baggy pants.

I pull into traffic heading west to 94 that will take me out of the city and to the Indiana Dunes. My hair feels grainy, as I rub my fingers through it. I didn't bathe when I got up, just brushed my teeth, grabbed my cutoffs, my keys, and Walter. Eddie was long gone.

I bring my hand to my face and feel a stirring in my cock as I breathe deep. His smell. All over my hands. His scent so strong on my fingertips: come, sweat, his ass. Like caramel, sweet caramel. I breathe deep, swooning at the smell of his ass on my fingers…

Shit! I swerve back into my lane before nearly hitting the car next to me! God, that was close. Walter gives me a look like he knows what I was thinking about, then goes back to hanging out the window, drool and all.

"You were no help at all you know," I snap at Walter as if last night were his fault.

Last night, shit, last night…I could hardly blame Walter, though; ignoring me and sleeping next to Eddie on the bed, like it was natural he was naked in my bed. Like Eddie belonged there.

• • •

I knew it was him from the stomps on the steps. His footsteps were unmistakable, always hitting the same creaks loudly every time he visited. The same sounds that no one else seemed to make when they climbed the stairs to my second-floor flat. But he did. Every time.

I opened the door before he knocked, happy to see him.

"What's up, Eddie?" My smile quickly dropped, once I saw his sad face and puffy red eyes.

"She left, John. She left me. Well, not for good, I don't think. Just for tonight she went to your folks. She's pissed, real pissed. I think I pushed her too far this time."

He cried on my shoulder, and I, uncomfortably, did my best to comfort him through four rounds of Coronas, a pack of Camels, and three hours of reruns on Nick at Nite. He genuinely didn't understand why my sister was pissed off. He wanted kids now, and she didn't. Christ, she had just been made a partner at her firm. She didn't have time. And I don't think she was ready. But Eddie was old-fashioned Latino: from a large family and ready for his wife to pop out some kids.

I finally tired and told him to stay with me instead of driving home. I made up the couch, tucked him in like a 5-year-old, and went to bed more than a little tipsy.

I'm not sure what time it was when I had to pee. I tiptoed through the living room and made it to the bathroom without a sound. On my way back through, I looked over at my guest. The streetlights were casting light through the room and caught Eddie asleep on his stomach—his sheet kicked aside and his perfect brown butt cheeks in full view.

My God, they were perfect! Chiseled mounds of dimpled bubble butt just staring at me. I froze. He looked so angelic. I could almost imagine the billowy white angel wings sprouting from his shoulder blades. A beautiful brown angel asleep on my couch.

Without thinking, my hand went to my cock and stroked through my briefs. He looked so good. So good! I reached inside and wrapped my hand around my now-growing hard-on, wondering what his cock looked like, when I saw his ass move. Not just move; flex. His ass cheeks were flexing. My mind was slow to realize what my eyes were seeing. I then looked at his face and saw him watching me. Watching me watching him and jerking off!

Oh, shit! But he was smiling. A smile unlike any I'd ever seen from Eddie. This one was wicked. Absolutely wicked.

He didn't say anything, just slowly stretched his body out full, then readjusted himself, lifting his ass into the air and reaching under to obviously stroke. His ass cheeks bobbed in the air as he jerked, calling my name, taunting me.

I didn't think, I just moved. Not to the bedroom as you would assume, but to the couch and straight to his ass—his big beautiful ass that he was obviously offering me. I wasn't thinking of Eddie and my sister anymore. My sister didn't exist. Just Eddie. And Eddie's large muscled ass dancing just inches from my face. And what I intended to do to it.

Before my face even found its target, I heard him moan. Long and deep, as if he was in ecstasy. My cock jerked in its confinement. Then my lips grazed his ass, first up one smooth cheek, then the other, until my nose, full of his heavy scent, guided my mouth to the puckered hole. I gave it a first-date kiss, gentle and soft at first, then more needy, finally exploring with my tongue, hungrily and deep, as if I hadn't eaten in days and he was a meal.

• • •

With one hand on the steering wheel, I unbutton my cutoffs and free my hard cock. I begin stroking hard, trying my best to keep my eyes focused on the road, my precome dripping in anticipation over my fist. I lick my lips, the taste of him still there or possibly just imagined at this point. *Oh, Eddie!* I pull harder and harder, stretching my cock's skin for all its worth, my foot pressing against the gas pedal, trying to outrun my desire and last night. To outrun my thoughts of Eddie.

• • •

I came the first time without even touching myself, both my hands under his body, between his legs, jerking on his thick brown cock, my tongue fucking his asshole deeply. When he came, he cried out my name loudly, repeatedly, his ass constricting over and over around my tongue, his cock furiously pumping in my fists. And I came. And came.

• • •

What am I gonna do? I think, as my orgasm builds up in my balls. *What can I do? Nothing.* We'll both pretend it didn't happen. He didn't let me eat his ass out. He didn't let me jerk him off. I didn't lick the come from his body, didn't kiss his sweet mouth.

"What am I gonna do, Walter?"

We'll pretend that he didn't get hard and come again, this time inside my mouth. And he didn't stick his large fingers up my ass and fuck me while I shot all over his chest and neck. We didn't fall asleep spooned together on my bed, like we were in love. We'll pretend it didn't happen. Maybe we'll just pretend it didn't happen.

When I shoot, my come splatters all over the wheel and the dashboard. The speedometer reads 85 as I cross the Indiana state line. We're almost to the dunes, the beach, and a swim. I relax my foot to a steady 65, and rub my come into my cutoffs and skin as best as I can.

I'm still hard, so I leave my cock uncovered. I'm still hard and thinking of Eddie. I'm thinking about Eddie and my sister. I'm thinking of Eddie and his sweet ass...his sweet, delicious ass. I suck my fingers, pretending they're his. And I'm thinking about what I'm gonna do about the mess I've gotten myself into when I pull into the lot at the beach and park.

But I'm already thinking of when I can taste him again. *I need to taste him again.* I bring my sticky fingers to my lips.

Walter hasn't moved from his favorite spot standing on the seat, his head proudly hanging out the window, his tail wagging with happiness, teary-eyed from the wind, his muzzle drooling all over the side of my truck.

Wherever

by Simon Sheppard

This all started a few years back.

I travel a lot. A lot. I was in India, of all places. On the outskirts of Delhi, there's a place called Humayun's Tomb—kind of a precursor to the Taj Mahal—a big Muslim mausoleum with an immense domed interior. It's imposing, maybe even a bit creepy. It's also not a big tourist destination, being kind of in the middle of nowhere, and one spring afternoon I found myself all alone in this huge old place. I looked up, surrounded by the past, the presence of death, of history and...well, I just got horny, intensely horny. I looked out through a doorway and across the garden—nobody coming.

I unzipped my pants and pulled out my cock, which was already half-hard. Now, I'm sure if some mullah somewhere is reading this story, he's getting righteously pissed off, so let me say right here that no sacrilege was intended. And even if it were, hey, I'm an equal-opportunity offender; when I was going to Berkeley, I had sex in a church pew, though it *was* a Unitarian Church, so maybe that doesn't count.

Anyway, I stood there and beat off in the immensity of the place. No sound but the cawing of ravens in the warm distance. It didn't take me long. Staring up into the architectural void, my muscles tightened, hips thrust forward, and I had one of the most intense orgasms of my life, my jizz spewing across the geometries of the inlaid floor, shattering the order of a perfectly arranged universe. I licked off my hand, stuffed my dick back in my pants, and took a few snapshots.

The next time I did something like that, it was somewhere very far from Delhi in the spring. I was in St. Louis in the middle of a pelting rainstorm, driving a friend's old Ford Festiva cross-country—don't ask—when the car broke down in the caffeinated middle of the night on a deserted street right near the Gateway Arch. It was pissing down rain, blurring the sharp steel profile of the floodlit parabola. I'd never been to St. Louis before—in fact, had never been to Missouri—and I had no idea of what I was going to do, not at 3 A.M. And I was decisively horny. At first I sat there, the still-alive radio blaring out some banal '80s oldie, my hand working my dick through my jeans. Then I figured, *What the hell,* and pulled out my cock. Staring up at Saarinen's great meaningless curve, I wondered if I was somehow queer for arches and domes, a parabola fetishist. Whatever. I got out of the car, my hard, slightly curved, and—if I do say so myself—impressive dick throbbing.

I stood facing the Festiva, so if any other damp, unfortunate soul happened by, he'd probably mistake me for a drunk taking a piss. I stared upward to the crest of the immense arch. Cold rain soaking most all of me, I clamped down hard on my dick, squeezing and pulling at it, forcing it farther and farther away from St. Louis and closer and closer toward the point of no return. My eyes lost focus, my mouth filled with rain, and my sperm, one more liquid amidst the storm, flew in mini-arcs onto the white Festiva, where it was washed presumably into the gutter, maybe to eventually join the timeless flow of the mighty Mississippi. Or else headed, who knows, to some purification plant, perhaps winding up in the drinking glass of some adamant Republican.

My parabola-equals-lust theory was put to the test some six months later in Paris, when I'd finally dried out from that night in St. Louis. I got up just before dawn and made my way to the Place du Trocadéro, just across the Seine from one of the greatest phallic erections of modern man, the Eiffel Tower. I was gratified to note that my dick responded equally well to another sort of architecture. There wasn't a gendarme in sight. With the help of my camera's auto timer, I was able to document myself shooting my nut in front of Monsieur Eiffel's masterwork.

Now there was no stopping me. I managed to engage in sneaky self-abuse wherever I went. The Colossi of Memnon in Egypt's Valley of the Kings. The dungeon of a Crusader's castle. Chichén Itzá. In San Francisco, on the way back from a trip to the Golden Gate Bridge, I beat off in the near-empty last car of a subway train, though the thrill was squelched when I realized that two other guys in the car were doing exactly the same thing.

And I documented each shot of come with a self-timed photo, which I then posted up on a Web site that began getting an inordinate number of hits. Somebody even started a jealous rumor that the shots were Photoshopped fakes. They're not, of course. I just happen to have a job that takes me all over the world. And a hyperactive libido.

I was spending a week in New York. To celebrate the freedom of the flesh, I thought a trip to Lady Liberty was in order. I got up bright and early and headed down to the tip of Manhattan, catching the very first boat to Liberty Island. When the ferry docked, I sprinted to the statue's entrance, despite the admonitions of the U.S. Park Police, and was the first visitor to arrive at the gate. A backpack check—no bomb—was followed by an elevator ride partway up, then the endless, nauseatingly spiraling stairs that led to the crown of the Lady With the Torch. I'd been in training, so I fairly flew up the stairs, upward through the narrowing torso, all the way to the top. I'd left all the other tourists far behind me, their fading footsteps almost inaudible. I had a few precious minutes all to myself. After barely glancing through the surprisingly small windows toward the skyline of Manhattan, I found a place to set up my camera, pushed the self-timer button, spit in my hand, and, calf muscles screaming, got to work. I stroked my anxious hard-on for all its pleasure-soaked nerves were worth, but I didn't, damn it, have time to unleash my huddled spermatozoa yearning to breathe free. Tourists' multilingual voices were coming steadily closer. And closer still. The camera clicked, and I managed to put away my dick just moments before two fairly homely German guys in their 20s struggled up the final flight of stairs. I'd worn a loose jacket to cover the evidence, and so, as the small space in the crown quickly grew more crowded, I headed back down. Mission accomplished.

I was in the statue's museum, next to a mock-up of the Lady's gigantic sandal-clad foot, when it happened. Three uniformed officers of the U.S. Park Police came up to me, and asked me to "come this way, please, Sir."

OK, how the hell was I to know that the statue's insides are always under constant video surveillance? Listen, it's not like I'm bent on bombing the Statue of Liberty into copper smithereens. It's not even like they said it was—that I had committed an obscene act. I mean, I'm an artist, and jacking off is part of my art—a vital part—and what the fuck's an "obscene act" anyway?

I guess they expected me to plead guilty and skulk off, but listen, it's been centuries since the Puritans landed here, bringing their damn puritanical ways with them, and enough is enough. So I told them I wanted a lawyer, which is why you're here, and now there's just one thing I want to know.

Do you think you can get me off?

Seeing Red
by Bob Vickery

I never know when it's going to happen—the next attack, that is.

Today, it's on the bus on the way to the dentist. As with all the other times, everything starts out completely normal: I'm just sitting there, staring out the window, my mind idle. The bus pulls over to the next stop; people push on board, nothing special. And then I see him.

He boards the bus like the dawn exploding, his hair as fiery and bright and red as the sun when it first clears the horizon. I'm blinded; it takes a few seconds before I can even begin to see beyond his blazing hair. When my vision clears, I take in the tight body on display beneath the jeans and Muscle System T-shirt (that's the gayest gym in town—he must be queer), then the masculine, not-quite-handsome face (the chin too strong, the nose too prominent, the brown eyes, though bright and expressive, set a little too close together). He pushes through the crowd, his eyes idly scanning the bus. For one brief moment, his gaze locks with mine, then he looks away. As inevitable as a law of nature, I feel my brain whir and click, my heart start pounding, and my chest tighten. *No,* I think fiercely, *I will not let this happen!* I aim my gaze down at my shoes, breathing hard, fighting for control. But damn if my head doesn't lift of its own accord, and soon I have my eyes trained full on the guy again, burning holes in him. Of course, he's completely oblivious to me.

Shit, shit, shit! I fish my cell phone out of my jacket pocket and punch in my dentist's number. When I get the receptionist on the line, I tell her that I'm sorry but I'm going to have to cancel the appointment. She cops an attitude, but eventually we reschedule and I hang up. He's taken a seat across the aisle from me and two rows up. I can only see the back of his neck and a quarter profile of his face, but beneath the fiery hair his skin is the pale, fair skin of a redhead, splattered with freckles. I wedge myself between the window and my seat, drinking him in. I feel like I'm falling into a pit. *You can still put a stop to this,* I tell myself. But I know the symptoms well enough to realize I'm going downhill in a car without any brakes, and all I can do now is sit back and experience the ride. I've never been able to resist a redhead.

Several blocks later the bus stops, and a handful of people get off, including the man. I get off too and stand there at the stop, watching him walk down the street, taking in the wide shoulders and tight haunches, the sexy little pivot his butt makes with each step. There's a sudden break in the clouds, and the sun pours down onto the street, igniting his hair into pure fire. I close my eyes and take a deep breath. When he's half a block away, I start following him. After a couple of blocks, he enters a storefront business with the words ANDRINI'S WINDOWS painted in gold and blue over the front window. Next to the two-story office is an asphalt lot with a fleet of trucks, surrounded by a cyclone fence. I cross the street and loiter in the entrance of a Chinese bakery, my eyes trained on the building. A few minutes later I see a truck pull out of the lot and disappear down the street, the redhead behind the wheel.

I know what I have to do.

• • •

I know what I have to do. I hail a cab because I don't want to lose time waiting for a bus. Once I get to my apartment, I make a beeline to my back porch where I keep my tools. I pull a hammer out of one of the tool-chest drawers and return to the living room. A wide, tall window overlooks the street. I walk over to it, raise my arm, and shatter the pane with the hammer. There's a brief music of tinkling glass as shards burst out and rain down on the sidewalk below. I stand at the window, staring out the jagged hole I made. A breeze blows through my hair. After a couple of beats, I retrieve the Yellow Pages, look up a number, and dial it.

"Andrini's Windows," a woman's voice answers.

"Hi. I've got something of an emergency here. Someone just threw a rock through my front living room window, and I need to get it replaced."

"I'm afraid we can't get anybody out there until tomorrow, sir."

Shit. "Look," I say, forcing my voice to sound calm and reasonable. "This really is an emergency. I live on the second floor, and anybody can climb in. I really need to have the glass replaced tonight. I'll be willing to pay extra, cover any overtime that's involved."

There's a long silence. I hear the rustling of papers. "All right," the receptionist says. "I'll see what I can do. But you'll have to wait until the end of the day, when all the other orders are finished."

"Thank you," I say, relief flooding over me. I pause. "Look," I say. "Just so that I'll recognize him, what does your guy look like?"

"He'll identify himself at the door, sir."

"Yeah, yeah, I know," I say. "But could you just give me a physical description? I just want to make sure I'm letting the right person into my apartment."

There's a brief pause. "It'll most likely be Harvey," she says. "He's mid 20s, tall, red hair…"

"Thanks," I say and hang up. *Harvey…*

• • •

When the doorbell finally rings, my heart begins hammering hard enough to hurt. I squat, put my head between my knees, and breathe deeply. The doorbell rings again. I straighten up, walk to the door, and push the intercom button.

"Who is it?" I ask.

"Andrini's Windows," a voice—Harvey's voice—answers in a rough baritone.

I buzz him in. *Get cool, Josh,* I tell myself. After a minute I hear Harvey's footsteps as he walks down the hall to my door. There's a knock on the door.

I throw the door open. Harvey stands framed in the doorway, just as I remember him, his face impassive, his brown eyes regarding me calmly. Same jeans, same Muscle System T-shirt, only it's plastered to his chest with sweat. Harvey must have had a busy day. The hall light is dim, and Harvey's red hair gleams dully.

"Come in, come in," I say. I step aside, and Harvey walks into my living room.

"Dispatch told me you got a broken window," he says, his eyes sweeping the room. They rest on the jagged hole of the front window. He looks at me. "Damn! How did that happen?"

"It was the weirdest thing," I say. "I was just sitting here watching TV, when someone threw a rock through the window." I shake my head. "Probably some street punk."

Harvey walks up to the window and sticks his head out, cautiously avoiding the shards. He pulls back in and looks at me quizzically. "There are glass splinters on the sidewalk down below," he says. "It looks more like the window was broken from the inside."

"Oh, yeah, that," I say. "Well, you see, I swept the broken glass up in here and just dumped it out the window."

Harvey gives me a sharp look but doesn't say anything. He unclips a tape measure from his tool belt and quickly takes the window's dimensions. He's got his back to me, and as he lifts his head, I stare at the tangle of orange hair he presents to me. I imagine running my fingers through it, tugging it, curling my hands into fists with fiery strands of hair sprouting between my knuckles. Harvey turns to me, and I quickly compose my face. "This is a standard window size," he says. "I think I have a pane in the truck that will fit."

"Terrific," I say.

Harvey leaves to get the glass from his truck, which is parked out in front of my apartment. I stand by the window and watch him pull the pane out from the truck's back. In the sunlight, his red hair gleams. *Maybe I could drug him,* I think. *I could offer him a beer doped up with something, and then, when he's out cold, strip him naked and tie him to my bedposts.* But that thought is too crazy even for me, and I push it back down its dark little hole. Harvey comes back with the pane of glass and carefully leans it against the wall. He takes a knife and begins digging out the last remnants of glass from the slots in the frame. The window faces west, and the late-afternoon sun pours down upon him. Harvey is soon drenched in sweat; it trickles down his face and stains his armpits and back. His shirt flutters from a slight breeze that blows in. The sunlight picks up individual strands of hair and makes them gleam like copper wire.

"Would you like a beer?" I ask.

Harvey turns his head and glances at me over his shoulder. He hesitates for the briefest moment. "Yeah," he says. "Sure."

I get two Coronas from the refrigerator, walk back to the living room, and hand one to Harvey. "Cheers," I say.

"Cheers," Harvey says. He tilts his head back and takes a deep swig. I watch his Adam's apple rise and fall in his muscular throat as he gulps the beer down. He wipes his hand across his mouth, puts the bottle on the floor, and resumes working.

By the time Harvey's done with the window, we've graduated to smoking doobies. The Doors have been replaced in my CD player by Janis Joplin's *Pearl* album. Harvey takes a toke and passes me the joint. "Man," he laughs, smoke bursting out of his mouth. "Don't you ever listen to anything later than the fuckin' '60s?" He's lounging back on my couch now, his legs spread wide apart, his tools left in a pile by the new window. His eyes are just beginning to glaze over, and he's wearing the loopy grin of your typical stoner.

"No," I say. "I'm stuck in a fuckin' time warp."

We sit there in silence for a few beats, Janis wailing away with "Piece of My Heart." I stare at the bulge in Harvey's crotch and then raise my eyes to his face. Harvey's eyes are trained on me. We still don't say anything for a while. "Can I suck your cock?" I finally ask.

Harvey's grin widens. "I thought you'd never ask." He starts to unbuckle his belt.

"No, wait," I say. "Let me." I cross the room and drop to my knees in front of him. I start at his feet, unlacing his work boots and sliding them off, along with his socks. Then I unbuckle his belt, forcing my hands not to tremble, and unzip his fly. I glance up at Harvey's face, and he returns my look, his face impassive. I hook my fingers under his belt loops, Harvey raises his hips, and I pull his jeans down and off. Harvey is wearing cotton briefs, and his hard dick strains against them, a drop of pre-jizz darkening the white cloth. "Jesus," I murmur. My blood is singing in my ears in the high whine of a ripsaw. I take a deep breath, slip my hand under the elastic band, and slowly slide Harvey's briefs down.

A line of pubic hair clears the waistband: tightly curled, carrot-orange, jungle-dense. I keep pulling the shorts, and the base of Harvey's dick appears, wonderfully thick. As the shorts continue to descend, I can see more of Harvey's fat, pink shaft, trace the blue veins that snake their way up the pale column. Harvey's boner pushes up against the elastic band, revealing itself inch by inch. When the cloth finally clears the swollen, flaring head, his dick snaps up and slaps against his belly. I yank the shorts all the way down over his feet and toss them aside.

Harvey sits there on my couch, his legs spread far apart, his feet planted firmly on the floor. I drink him in with my eyes: the fat, pink dick resting against the pale skin of his belly, the balls hanging low in their fleshy sac, and that glorious explosion of orange pubic hair. I slide my hands under Harvey's T-shirt, stroking and pulling at the hard flesh of his torso, tweaking the nubs of his nipples, as I bury my face in his balls and breathe deeply. Their ripe, musky scent fills my nostrils. "Damn..." I mutter. I open my mouth and suck Harvey's ball sac inside, bathing his nuts with my tongue. Harvey nudges my face with his hard dick. I slide my tongue up the long, thick shaft, and when I get to Harvey's dick head, I roll my tongue around it, nipping it gently, feeling the give and take of the rubbery, red fist of flesh between my teeth and tongue. I slide my mouth down the full length of Harvey's dick, twisting my head, until my throat is crammed full and my nose is pressed hard against his orange pubes. He gasps, and for the briefest moment, we hold that pose, my mouth full of cock, Harvey's balls pressing against my chin, his nipples firmly squeezed between my thumbs and forefingers. Then Harvey pumps his hips, breaking the spell, and begins the serious business of fucking my mouth with slow, deep thrusts.

I proceed to make love to Harvey's dick, opening my throat to it, taking whatever he gives. Harvey's thrusts get faster, pick up a staccato beat, and I wrap my hand around his shaft so that my fist follows my mouth up and down. I break away for a second and let my eyes sweep up Harvey's muscular torso to his face. Harvey's eyes are bright and fierce and they burn into mine. "You're a good little cocksucker, aren't you?" he growls. "You really know how to work a man's dick."

"Pull off your shirt," I say. "I want to see you naked."

Harvey peels off the sweat-dampened T-shirt and tosses it on the floor. Unlike his pale hips, Harvey's torso is lightly tanned and splattered with darker freckles, as if someone had dipped a brush into a can of brown paint and shaken it over him. His nipples are wide and the color of old pennies. I reach down for a half-finished Corona that stands on the floor by the couch, and tilt it over Harvey's body, watching the beer foam up and stream down his torso, spilling over the pubes and around his dick. I drag my tongue once again over Harvey's cock and balls, tasting the sour pungency of the beer mingled with the taste of Harvey's sweaty flesh.

Harvey pulls me up and plants his mouth on mine. We play dueling tongues for a while as I wrap my hands around Harvey's dick and beat him off. Harvey reaches down and squeezes my crotch. "Get naked," he orders.

I lead him back to my bedroom, dropping my clothes on the floor behind me. By the time we fall onto the bed together, we're both naked. I climb on top of Harvey's body, kissing him again as I feel the full length of his bare flesh against mine. Harvey wraps his hand around both our dicks and squeezes them tight together. I look down at the two cocks pressed together, encircled by Harvey's fist, and I kiss Harvey again as he beats us off. He slowly drags his tongue down my neck, around my left nipple and then my right, gently nipping them, working them to hardness. I look down at the tousle of fiery hair inches from my face, feeling Harvey's tongue descend my torso, swirl around my navel, and engulf my cock. "Turn around," I pant. "I want to suck your cock while you do that to me."

Harvey grins and pivots his body around, and then we're both fucking face and eating dick. I reach up and run my hands over Harvey's ass, the cheeks firm and muscular, smooth as sun-warmed stone under my fingertips.

After we sixty-nine for a few minutes, Harvey turns his head toward me. "I want to plow your ass right now," he growls. "Any problems with that?"

"No," I say. "None at all." I open the drawer of the bedside table and pull out lube and rubbers. In a matter of seconds, Harvey is sheathed and lubed, and my legs are wrapped around his torso. Harvey's dick head pokes against my asshole, and I breathe out, relaxing my muscles, accepting Harvey's fat red dick as it slowly works its way inside me.

"Sweet Jesus," I groan.

"You like that, baby?" Harvey grunts, his eyes bright and savage. "Does it feel good having my dick full up your ass?" He doesn't wait for an answer but starts thrusting in and out, churning his hips, his torso squirming against mine. Harvey's face is inches above mine, and his mouth is pulled back into a fierce grin. I reach up, running my fingers through his blazing hair, feeling how wiry it is, like bristles of a brush. I pull Harvey down and kiss him hard, biting his lips. Harvey shoves his dick deep up my ass, slapping his balls hard against me. I meet him stroke for stroke, thrusting my hips up every time his dick plunges deep inside me, squeezing my ass muscles hard against the shaft of flesh. Harvey's face is dripping with sweat now—it splashes down onto my face, stinging my eyes, filling my open mouth with its salty tang. His body slaps against mine with wet, smacking sounds. He wraps his hand around my hard dick and beats me off, timing his strokes with each thrust of his dick. We fuck like a well-oiled machine, thrust meeting counterthrust, eyes locked together, breaths in sync. Harvey gives a small whimper. He thrusts again, and the whimper gets louder, longer, his lips pulled back into a snarl. I reach down and cup Harvey's balls in my hand, tugging on them. They're pulled up tight, and I know it won't be long before he squirts his load. Harvey pulls his dick almost completely out of my ass, its head just barely penetrating me, and then he slides it full in with a slow, hard thrust. I squeeze tight, and Harvey's whimper turns into a long, dragged-out groan. I feel his body spasm against me, and I kiss him as the orgasm sweeps over him. Harvey thrashes in my arms, his dick pumping a steady load of jism into the condom up my ass, one pulse after another. Finally, Harvey collapses on top of me, spent, his face buried against my neck.

A minute later, I sit on Harvey's chest and jerk off as he tweaks my nipples. When the orgasm finally comes, my dick squirts my load high, above Harvey's face and into the coppery tangle of his hair.

I drag my tongue over the red strands, cleaning them, eating my sperm. I stay there like that for a while, my face buried in Harvey's hair. *So fuckin' beautiful,* I think. Twenty minutes later he's dressed and out the door.

Red Hot Valentine

by Dale Chase

I'm not partial to redheads. They're generally too all-American, too wholesome, and that's not what I'm after. So it surprises me when I notice this guy. I remind myself I don't like his type, but find I'm not listening.

His hair is a riot of red curls, but it works, has a certain likable chaos, and I wonder if maybe he plans it, stands in front of a mirror, gels it into place, then messes it up, doing an eggbeater thing with his fingers. I can see him at it. Naked, of course.

I've never had a redhead. Too pale, too pink. Too Midwestern. But he's gorgeous, irresistible. He's with a date and so am I; it's Valentine's Day. (Maybe that's why I'm so drawn to his fiery countenance, his redness. Come to think of it, he does look kind of like Cupid all grown up; I know I'd have no objection to him shooting me with his arrow.) We're both having dinner, and he's at the next table, facing me and looking over his date's shoulder—as am I. We're both carrying on conversations with our dates, and I wonder if his dick is getting hard. Mine sure is.

He's dressed casually in a white shirt and slacks. His date is bleached blond, dark at the roots—and elsewhere, I suppose. This encourages me since I'm brown-haired with brown eyes. I think of the contrast as I eat my dinner, my olive skin against his pink. I become animated with Rick, my date, because I want to show myself off to the redhead. I make Rick laugh. I look into his eyes—we're headed for bed after dinner—lean forward and tell him what I'm going to do to him, then let my gaze move past, carry the energy one table down. And then the redhead's date gets up and goes to the john, and I'm left with a clear view. I notice there's a little blue logo on his shirt, and I want to read it. The shirt fits him rather well, and I can see well-defined pecs under the fabric. Every time Rick looks down at his meal, I glance past him; one time the redhead, with great care so I'll take note, slides his hand across the table, off the edge, and down to his crotch. I look at it, then back up to his face, pass a few seconds of up-and-down gawking, then go back to Rick, who's saying, "Hey, you listening?"

"Sure," I lie, but I still don't pay attention because the redhead gets up just as his date returns. He doesn't look at me; he just heads for the john, and I interrupt Rick. "Gotta pee," I say, hoping he won't notice the bulge in my pants.

The redhead is at a urinal when I come in. I glance at his dick, which is long, pink. I head for a stall, and when the restroom is empty he joins me. I'm stroking my cock when he opens the door. He's left his fly open; his dick is on the rise. He takes hold, brings it to mine, and rubs the heads together. We play a bit, and precome is soon liberally smeared. Then his hand slips onto my cock, my hand onto his cock, and we pull at one another while I gaze into eyes that are a vibrant blue. He's not freckled like most redheads, and I wonder if he's been kept indoors, cultivated into this magnificent specimen, grown up now, turned out into the world, fresh and eager. Cupid at 23.

It registers in the back of my mind that we're on the clock, but I know I'll think of some excuse if Rick gets pissed, because I need time with this guy. I stop stroking him and get his shorts down, get a look at his red pubes. I chuckle because they seem almost absurd, yet I kneel, get my nose into them and breathe in his scent. I lick the long pink cock, working my way to the tip, then slide it into my mouth. I look up as I begin to suck and see a grin on the redhead's face, beautiful white teeth, pink tongue skating across his lower lip.

He's a mouthful. I take all I can, but he's an absolute pole. I get a hand into his silky bush, pet him as I feed. Behind us, others come and go, toilets flush, water runs. A guy enters the next stall and takes a shit as I suck cock. Surely he sees four legs in our stall, two on knees. He spends a long time in his stall, and I wonder if he's imagining us in our stall—what we're doing, if he'd like a go. Will he wait till we emerge, meanwhile playing his own mind games? Maybe return to his table primed for fucking?

The redhead grabs the sides of my head and holds me still while he begins to thrust. I cradle him with my tongue, and soon we've got a good mouth-fuck going while I work my meat, thinking about getting into him, getting on him, riding the shit out of his sweet ass while he spews come all over the floor. Then he pulls out, waving his wet dick at me, and he starts rubbing it against my cheeks and my forehead, poking the head at my eyes. He's getting really worked up, and I know what he needs, but he seems to want to draw things out, torture himself a bit. He starts slapping his cock against me, hips working as if he's fucking rather than flailing. He's breathing hard, and I wonder if this is a regular thing for him, holding back when most of us would take that hot poker and put it where it needs to go.

Suddenly, he grips my shoulders, pulling me up, apparently having gotten to where he needs to be. I stand up, and he rasps, "Fuck me," and hands me a condom. I drop my pants, suit up, and lube myself with spit; only when I'm ready does he turn and spread his cheeks. And there it is, the pinkest pucker I've ever seen, a rosy little hole that's winking at me, begging. I push in a finger, then two, and he lets out a soft groan, and the guy in the next stall does too. I almost laugh, but I give the redhead a good little reaming while my dick drools in wait. And then I withdraw, get into position, and his eager ass wiggles in anticipation. I watch the dance for a second, then shove in, everything at once, maximum dick. He lets out a grunt, then a series of loud exhales as I start to fuck him.

His ass is hot, and I think about that as I ride him, that redness of his, like he's fiery inside. Maybe that's what the red hair means. He squeezes his muscle as I go in, clamping on to me, and it sends a wave up my dick and back into my ass, which fires me all the more. I start to pound him as a result, fleshy slaps echoing through the room, and I don't care who hears us. I'm totally gone, and the guy in the next stall must be too, because I hear the unmistakable sound of stroking dick, not to mention little groans of ecstasy that are beyond the expected sounds from a man in his position. And then he lets go, and I almost laugh, hearing his noisy climax while my own has yet to arrive. Then he's quiet, listening, I suppose, or mopping up before rejoining the family. I can just hear his companion asking, "What took you so long, dear?"

I hear his zipper; the toilet flushes, he exits. There's the sound of him washing hands, then the swing of the outer door. I want to say something about it to the redhead but don't. Ours is to be a pure relationship: cock and ass. He's got his hands on the tile, his big cock unattended, and I like that. It's all about my dick plowing his ass. I start slamming into him, and I keep on reaming him until the ache starts in my balls, my spine. Everything in me tenses, drawing up, every ounce of energy centered in my crotch, and I can't help but utter a raspy "Oh, shit" as I come. A monumental pulsing begins, and I unleash long streams of jism. It takes what seems like minutes to unload, and afterward my cock is still viable, as if this particular ass can take me above and beyond my limits. I'm gasping for breath, sweat is running down my face and my back, and I'm so blissed out that I'm almost delirious.

The redhead pulls away, turns, rolls the rubber off my cock and discards it, then strokes my meat, cups my balls. "Turn around," he whispers. He takes another condom from his pocket and pulls it onto his rigid prick. "My turn," he says when he's ready.

We change places, and my hands are suddenly on the tile. I think of Rick as the redhead's cock head finds my hole. I see him fidgeting at the table, meal gone, and I hope to hell he doesn't get impatient enough to come looking for me. But then I've got a dick going up my chute, and I don't care about anything or anyone except getting fucked, that singular pleasure of a cock going up my rectum. And the redhead has a memorable one, far longer than Rick's, and as it pushes deep into my bowels, I grind back onto it to let him know I want it up there all the way, that I can take the longest of hoses.

And then he's doing it, fucking me full-out, making me wince as he blazes new territory. My dick is hard again, and I get a hand on it because he's pounding me so hard the juice is stirring.

His stroke is incredibly long. He uses every inch of that salami, pulling nearly out, then ramming back in, so it's kind of a slow-motion fuck, which is almost funny because up front I'm jerking frantically as a climax teases. I want so badly to go over while he's doing me—there is nothing better than coming with a dick up your ass—and then, as if nature has answered my call, I start squirting juice, powerful shots of cream splattering the tile. The redhead offers a low chuckle as he watches, and then he sucks in a long breath and holds it, and I know he's coming. When he exhales, it's in breathy grunts in time to his squirts. Again our fuck-slap echoes through the room.

I've still got a hand on my dick, even though I'm empty. I hold on as he unloads inside me, pumping steadily in his ultra-long strokes. He keeps on even when his breathing has returned to normal, slowing gradually. When he finally pulls out, I turn and watch him strip away the rubber. His prong is flushed red, come smeared over the head. I reach down, run a finger through it, play around the slippery crown, hating the fact that there are people waiting for us. I think about what his date is in for, feel a jealous pang, and it drives me back down to my knees. I get my face back into those wild red pubes, lick his spent prick, then go under to his balls where I suck one, then the other. I start thinking maybe he's done, but when I get a finger around back into his hole and start to prod, his prong comes alive. He starts riding my hand and I add a second finger, reaming him while up front I'm slurping nuts and jerking dick. He starts moaning, and I'm pumping like crazy, then he lets out an "Oh, shit," and cream oozes from his cock. His ass muscle clamps on to my fingers, and he works me as I work him, squeezing out the last of it. But, of course, that's not the last of it, at least not for me. When I stand up, he goes down, sucks my prick into his mouth, and we're off again, him doing to me what I did to him, fingers up my ass and me going at it back and front. I have a vague recollection of being on the clock, but a moment later I'm coming again, and time seems to stand still. As I empty I find myself wishing again this didn't have to end.

The redhead finally stands, gives me a smile, and pulls up his shorts, and I do the same. I think about asking for his number but don't. Something tells me it wouldn't fly. He leaves the stall first, washes his hands, and exits. I stand there still reeling, wishing I didn't have to come down. After a few deep breaths, my thoughts are focused ahead. I exit the stall, wash up, and rejoin Rick.

"Where were you?" he asks.

"Sorry. I ran into someone from work. Couldn't get unstuck. You know how it is."

"Let's go."

My dinner is cold. The redhead is eating ice cream and talking to his date, more into it than before. When we stand, I steal a glance, as does he. *I'd do you again in a minute,* his face says. My dick twitches. I'd do him right there on the table in front of his date and Rick and the whole damned restaurant. The moment is exhilarating yet painful. Rick takes my arm and we leave. He's all over me in the car because he's ready for some major fucking, and I'll certainly oblige because it is Valentine's Day, after all, and I like Rick, I honestly do. But he's not what the redhead was. As I drive, I think about those red pubes, and later, as I pump my cock into Rick, I picture pristine pink instead of tawny gold, and I think about that long ropy dick that is probably at that very moment up a willing ass, doing Cupid proud.

The Auction

by Derek Adams

I've got a problem. The trouble is, I just can't seem to resist the lure of bidding at an auction. Take me to a warehouse full of brand-new merchandise, and I'm a model of restraint. Take me to an auction, however, and you'll need two strong men to keep me from bidding on something I don't really need.

This wouldn't be a problem if I had lots of money—then I could call myself a collector. Unfortunately, I'm just a regular guy who works in a printing plant and lives in a small apartment. It's gotten so bad that my friends are starting to think I might be going over the edge because of all the shit I haul home. One quick look around my place makes it pretty clear that I don't pay a hell of a lot of attention to my friends.

On the night in question, I was on my way to the bus stop, when I happened to notice an auction in progress at Foster Galleries. Naturally, I had to go in and check it out. I signed up for a bidding card, then made my way over to a vacant seat in the front row.

I gotta admit, I couldn't tell you a damned thing about the big oil painting that was up for bid when I sat down, but I could go on all day about the guy who was holding it. At first, all I could see was a pair of muscular legs encased in faded denim and a couple of big hands holding onto an ornate gold frame. Then he shifted his stance, and a four-inch swath of bare belly came into view, ridged with muscle and split down the center by a lush trail of fur. The long silk glowed a reddish brown in the stage lights. Stray wisps curled over his wide leather belt.

The bidding went on for quite a while, giving me plenty of time to take in all the details. With every breath the dude took, his chiseled gut would swell slightly; then, as he exhaled, his abs would flex into ridges. My gaze slipped below that delectable band of pale flesh to a substantial bulge straining against the frayed buttonholes of his fly. No doubt that trickle of fuzz on his belly widened as it flowed down to his crotch where it formed a dense, silky bush that curled around the base of what I imagined to be a fat, veiny cock.

When the bidding finally ended, the guy lowered the picture, and I got my first glimpse of him from the waist up. The view was a pleasant one. His hair was brown and shaggy, his cheeks were pink, and his luxuriant mustache drooped down to the strong line of his jaw. His cheeks and chiseled chin, although freshly shaved, were already covered by a heavy shadow. The guy's wide-set eyes were chocolate-brown pools framed by luxuriantly long lashes. I would've been content to look a lot longer, but he tugged his sweatshirt down over his belt, then turned and hauled the picture off the stage.

The next time my Adonis appeared, he was carrying a delicate vase that was dwarfed by his big hands. The sleeves of his faded sweatshirt had been hacked off at the shoulders, baring his impressive arms. His forearms were thatched with silky hair from elbow to wrist. Thick veins snaked across the curve of his swollen biceps, throbbing with his pulse. He blushed fetchingly when someone in the audience—not me, I swear it!—let out a loud wolf whistle that could've been meant only for him.

Just when I thought it couldn't get any better, the auctioneer asked the guy to hold the vase up to the light. This move afforded me my first glimpse of the damp chestnut fur that curled in the shadowed hollows of his armpits and trailed across the pale skin of his inner arm. I sat there, my cock throbbing against the inside of my thigh, wondering if I'd be able to jump up on stage and suck the sweat out of those curls before I got rushed by management and thrown out on my ass!

When my sexy pal rolled a heavy oak cabinet out onto the stage, I saw right away that it would be perfect for housing my stereo components. My hand shot up in the air and stayed there till I was the proud owner of the damned thing. I watched a few last items go up for bid, then made my way over to the office and waited in a long line to pay up. By the time I finally had my sales receipt in hand, the crowd had dispersed, and the auctioneer was turning off the lights. I clambered up onstage to get a closer look at my new purchase. Damn! It needed refinishing, not to mention it was heavy as a mother.

"Nice piece of oak," a sexy baritone voice observed. I looked up. It was the dude I'd been fantasizing about all evening. He was standing behind the cabinet, arms folded across his broad chest, smiling at me. Unlike the furniture, the closer I got to the guy, the better he looked!

"Thanks," I replied. "I was figuring it'd be just perfect for my stereo. Only thing is, I'm not quite sure how I'm going to get it over to my place. Maybe the auction house will store it till I can borrow a truck from one of my buddies."

"I got a truck," the guy said. "You going far?"

"I live on Capitol Hill," I replied quickly, thinking this whole scenario was too good to be true—not to mention too good to pass up. "You're sure it's no trouble?"

"I got nothing else to do." The guy grinned, displaying a double row of perfect white teeth. "I'll go and get my truck and bring it around back."

"Great—hey, what's your name?"

"Dave."

"Pleased to meet you, Dave. I'm Rick." I stuck out my hand, and he enveloped it with his big paw. A bolt of heat shot through me, direct from his palm to my balls.

We wrestled the cabinet into the back of his truck, then drove to my place and hauled it up to the fourth floor. I looked around my small apartment, wondering just where the hell I was going to put my newest prize.

"You've got some great stuff," Dave said.

"I'm glad you like it. Most of my buddies think I'm out of my mind." I shrugged. "I can't seem to help it."

"I'm really into antiques myself. Matter of fact, I plan to open my own shop one of these days. I'm already saving money for it." As he walked slowly around the room, checking things out, I took the opportunity to check *him* out. He was hot from every angle—great face, great ass, great basket. If I didn't get a grip, I'd be jumping the dude—or drooling on his shoes!

"Mind if I sit down?" Dave asked, flopping down onto a vintage overstuffed sofa without waiting for a reply.

"Make yourself comfortable," I muttered, my attention suddenly distracted by the way his faded jeans molded themselves to the muscles in his thighs as he settled back into the cushions. I also couldn't help noticing that the bulge at his crotch became more clearly defined as he spread his legs wide, gradually resolving itself into a long, thick cylinder that stretched south from the oversize mound of his balls.

"Is it me, or is it hot in here?" he asked.

"Our elderly landlady is very cold-natured," I told him. I suppose I could've opened a window to cool things off a little bit, but of course I didn't. I mean, come on, man. I'm not stupid! Instead, I started unbuttoning my shirt, intent on warming things up even more.

Dave whistled appreciatively as I tossed my shirt over the back of a chair. Earlier in the week, I'd struck a pose that had looked pretty hot when I caught a glimpse of myself in the bathroom mirror: thumbs in the waistband of my jeans, pecs flexed. Now Dave followed my lead. He stood up and pulled his sweatshirt over his head, baring his furry, muscular torso. I licked my lips. He tossed the sweatshirt aside, and we stood there for a few moments, silently admiring one another's assets. Dave rocked back on his heels and stuffed his hands in his pockets. "Totally buff, man!"

"Thanks," I replied, my cheeks growing hot as I listened to his words of praise. "I work at it."

"No doubt." As Dave eyed my chiseled torso, the tip of his tongue snaked lazily across his upper lip. "I wish I had your abs, man." He stroked his furry gut, sending my blood pressure soaring into the danger zone. "Fortunately, my arms are pretty tight." Dave flexed, damn near knocking me off my feet.

"Looking good," I gulped, eyeing his broad hairy chest hungrily. The chestnut growth was so thick in the valley between his pecs that you could barely see skin. I reached out and splayed my hand against his hard belly. Long silky hairs curled around my fingers, damn near sending me into sensory overload. Dave growled sexily.

"You like it?" he asked. I nodded enthusiastically. He gripped my wrist and pulled my hand up over his torso. My fingers disappeared into the dense mat in the center of his chest.

"Fucking hot," I moaned, stroking his hairy chest.

Dave stepped forward, closing the gap between us. We stood toe to toe for a couple of heartbeats; then he leaned forward. The hairs on his chest touched my skin, tickling me, making my cock throb. I leaned against him, my hands on his waist, my fingertips brushing across the triangle of hair at the base of his spine. His lips brushed mine, then his tongue flickered teasingly across my mouth.

I caressed his forearms, the muscled bulk of his biceps, his hard chest. My fingertips grazed his nipples. When I pinched the swollen flesh, his eyes flew open and his hands tightened around my waist. I pressed against him. His hard cock throbbed against my thigh.

Dave stepped back from me and began unbuckling his belt. I stripped, then leaned back against the oak cabinet that now dominated the living room and watched him. He stepped out of his jeans and kicked them aside. The man had great legs. An impressive expanse of sculpted muscle and gleaming fur stretched from the tops of his white crew socks to his briefs, where the thin cotton fabric was rapidly losing the battle to keep his boy toys under wraps. I gazed at him hungrily, my cock pointing at the ceiling, my balls drawn up in a tight knot.

"Nice," Dave muttered huskily as he reached around behind me and squeezed my ass cheeks. His fingertips grazed my asshole. "Very nice."

I dropped to my knees and worked Dave's briefs down over his narrow hips. His hard-on clipped me on the jaw as it rose high in the air. I licked my lips hungrily as I caught sight of his cock for the first time. It was long and thick, jutting out of his bush, the come slit gaping like a tiny mouth. A drop of clear juice quivered on the tip, then drooled down and dribbled onto my chest. I smeared the hot goo across my nipples and groaned with pleasure.

Dave pulled me to my feet, grinning lewdly as he wrapped his fingers around his cock shaft and brought it down against the broad back of my meat. Hot juice splattered from my knob to my bush. I shivered with lust, eager to have him, to feel his cock crammed into me up to the hilt. I longed to feel his power as he fucked the jism right out of me.

"Wanna fuck?" he asked, hands already on me, turning me around, sure of my response. I braced my hands on the oak cabinet, watching over my shoulder as Dave retrieved a rubber from the pocket of his jeans and rolled the latex down his thick rod. Once safely sheathed, he mounted me, his chest against my back, his hard-on pumping in my crack. I felt the heat of his knob, then a rapidly increasing pressure as he pushed it in. I thrust my ass back, groaning as he plowed deep into me.

After a few blissful minutes of feeling Dave's cock as it pistoned in and out of my chute, I grabbed his narrow hips and stopped him in mid pump. I wriggled my butt and dislodged his hard-on, then twisted around in his arms till we were belly to belly, cock to cock. "Now then, fuck me while I watch."

Dave picked me up and set me on top of the oak cabinet. I gripped the edges and threw my legs up, resting my ankles on Dave's broad shoulders. He pressed his knob against my hole, but didn't penetrate. I savored his heat as his knob throbbed against my ass lips. When I could wait no longer, I closed my fist around his dangling balls and began pulling him forward. He slid into me, stretching my man-hole wide. I let out a long sigh as I watched the last thick inch disappear.

Dave climbed up on the cabinet with me, knees tight against my ass, hands planted on either side of my head. I bucked and heaved under his weight, fucking myself on his big, hard cock. The feel of Dave's fur against my chest and the backs of my thighs was incredibly sexy.

Dave fucked like a man possessed. His nuts bounced against my ass at first, then drew up tight against his hard-on. His breath started getting ragged and rough. I clasped my hands around his neck and whispered in his ear, encouraging him to fuck even harder.

"I'm gonna blow, man," he cried out, his hips slamming against my ass, making the old cabinet creak and groan. I started jerking my own cock, priming myself to blow right along with him. His prick flexed inside of me, and then I felt his jism ballooning the tip of the rubber buried up my ass. Dave shuddered and bucked, sweat pouring off him, his hot breath blasting against my neck. I cried out and let loose, spraying both our chests and bellies with my load. My orgasm was so intense I saw stars. Afterward, I lay under him, my cock pinned between us, his cock still deep inside my body.

After a second rambunctious, bone-jolting fuck that damn near reduced the old cabinet I'd bought to sawdust, Dave helped me move it back against the wall. Before he left, we made a date for a repeat performance the next night. You see, there's this auction, and Dave will be working. Oh, don't get me wrong. I won't be going to the auction. Dave and I are meeting afterward at a little bar down the street from the gallery. Safer that way. Believe me, the next time I hear a man shouting out "Going, going, gone," it won't be the auctioneer!

Sight Unseen
by Les Richards

Dawn filters through Venetian blinds and softens the contours of Gary's face below me. Even through dimness I see ecstasy there. He could be a teen instead of mid 20s. My boner's all the way inside him, my heart beating solid thumps of happiness—such bliss being part of this guy. To feel my cock rubbing inside his love channel. Smell his sexy-guy sweat. He's softly moaning, breath more like gasps than breathing. I lean down, cover his lips with mine.

After two years, it seems each day is more revealing, more erotic. Black hair falling across his forehead, green eyes I can gaze into without making him self-conscious. His body responds to my thrusts, humping against me. He reaches around and cups my ass cheeks, pulling me even farther into him. His dick is a rod against my belly.

"All your come," he whispers lovingly into my ear. "All your come inside me!"

Breath roars along my throat. Repeating his name. Our mouths join again, tongues together. My nads jerk into me, and I shoot up into his ass. Again and again. My come actually becoming part of him. It's the benefit of the monogamy thing and tests. Gary full of me and my love.

• • •

Later, in the kitchen, I watch him prepare eggs, toast, and coffee. We've been inspecting houses, two or three finally to choose from. He carefully measures tablespoons of coffee into the coffeemaker without spilling grounds on the counter. I smile at his dexterity, a smile he is oblivious to. I wonder how he'll cope with learning the map of a new place where we'll live. But I'll be with him. He turns my way. He always seems to know where I am in a room. I can tell by his pleasant smirk that he's remembering earlier this morning. Then he begins cracking eggs into a bowl for the omelet.

"I told Rog to stop by." He's using a whisk to whip eggs. "Put another plate on the table."

I know where I want to shove the plate. Roger's getting to me. He's too eager to be around Gary. Gary has a sense about most people's feelings; he says that voices are almost as revealing as sight. So I figure he knows Roger wants him.

I answer the doorbell, and Roger smiles at me, passing me and going on into the kitchen. He pauses behind Gary at the stove, whispers something into his ear, brushes a hand across his butt, and the two of them laugh. Roger tilts his head, with its slicked-back brown hair. His dark eyes stare blatantly at me. As if I'm intruding. He's as hot-looking as any model my agency places in magazines.

"This is some guy here!" He lays an almost proprietary hand on Gary's shoulder. "Wait'll he sees which one of us is best-looking. The sexiest!"

Maybe Gary'll see each of us for who we are, I think. If anything, he should see the love that must shine through my face. I wonder if there's love somewhere behind the lust in Roger's eyes. Wonder how Gary'll decipher which it is.

They chatter about celebrities, gossip they've heard. I eat my omelet, butter toast, wonder just how far Roger thinks he can take this. He gives me a good indication when he says, "Gary'll be at the studio all day. I want a long session." He looks from Gary to me, his face smug. "I'm almost there. Finished."

I tell myself I started it all. I wanted a portrait of Gary. We'd heard about Roger at somebody's house, and Gary telephoned him. He showed up at our apartment the next day. Tall, muscled legs below shorts, good shoulders, and a face you wanted to look at again. I noticed interest flicker through Gary's expression when he heard Roger's voice for the first time. Deep, with an occasional insinuation you couldn't mistake. There wasn't insinuation in the way he watched Gary. It was straight-out intention. He'd stood still while

Gary's fingers traced his throat, jaw, cheekbones, his brow, gently touched his lips.

I was such a secure fool then.

"I'll pick him up at 5," I say now, not lifting my gaze from the plate in front of me. "It'll give us more time at the gym."

"I'll drive him back myself," Roger says.

"But I haven't seen what you've done."

Gary covers my hand with his. "Won't be long. He says you'll really like it!"

I push back my chair, pull Gary close to me. Feel his heat radiating against me. Don't care shit if Roger's watching. "You'll be looking at yourself in a mirror soon." I kiss his lips softly. See Roger stiffen in the corner of my vision.

Roger frowns. "He's not enthusiastic about it."

I turn to Gary. "What've you been saying?" *Does he confide in Roger and not me?*

Gary's expression remains impassive.

"Eye surgery's always improving," I urge. "Dr. Carson sounds like he's expecting great things."

"Don't you get it?" Roger's voice is insistent. "He's doing it for you!"

Gary turns away. Roger stares at me, places a hand on my guy's shoulder. And I walk out to my car. Can't believe the three of us are in some sort of triangle. But Gary had turned away from me. I almost make a U-turn to drive home and tell him to forget the surgery. *Christ! I can't begin to compete with Roger in the looks department.* I just want Gary to be able to gaze around himself, appreciate the sun and sky, trees and mountain ridges, see the faces of people who come to the club to hear him play piano and occasionally sing standards in his sensual way.

• • •

I spend the morning approving ad layouts for a couple of our largest clients. I try to study them and find I'm wondering what's going on with Gary and Roger. I only half-listen to a friend during lunch, order a second martini, am conscious of his dubious stare. I leave the office earlier than usual, decide to stop by Roger's studio, drive Gary to the gym. I can't wait for the feel of him next to me. I realize it's the only reassurance I'll settle for.

Roger's studio is in a one-story house surrounded by trees. I park in the drive and climb shallow steps to the front door. It's ajar, and I step into a cool hall. See Roger in cargoes, bare and tanned above his belt. And just then Gary passes the door to what I see is a bedroom. He is naked except for a towel around his waist.

Roger stares at me. I stand there, pulse throbbing inside my ears. Full of anger, hurt, even fear. Gary steps into the hall. His face turns toward me. "Someone's here, Rog?" His hand secures the towel around his hips. Roger can't seem to push words through his mouth. It's like he's reading a threat in my gaze before I turn to Gary.

"I came to drive you home," I say, forgetting the gym.

"Hey! I'm just outta the shower." His voice and his face register pleasant surprise. Until he suddenly seems to see within his mind's eye what I've walked into. "I was just…getting dressed."

I don't say it's evident. I don't say anything. Roger comes to life and invites me into the studio. "Long as you're here, you might as well take a look. Gare wanted to surprise you."

Gare! Gare is already doing a frigging good job of surprising me.

I stand in the doorway to the studio, and Roger pulls aside a canvas sheet draped across a large painting. I catch my breath. Warm flesh colors capture Gary's body, the glow of his skin. He's peering across a shoulder, his spine curving to ass cheeks I know so well and the fulfillment for me they conceal. It's almost as though he's turned to smile at me. The slender legs are the ones he wraps around me when our passion is white-hot.

The house is silent around us. Gary walks into the room, wearing a shirt and khakis now, a hand outstretched.

"Rog says it only needs a few touches. I wanted it framed before you saw it."

He slides an arm around my shoulders. I can't respond. I must feel like stone beneath his warmth.

• • •

He lets me help prepare supper. I wonder if he wants me close because day after tomorrow he'll be checking into the hospital for maybe a week's stay. Or is it some sort of attempt to soothe me after walking into whatever it was I walked into this afternoon? It's a long evening. He's brushing his teeth when I crawl into bed, turn my face toward the windows. I hear him move into the bedroom, feel the bed sink beneath him. And his arms wrap around me. Unthinking, hungry for him, I turn and pull him to me. We kiss, our tongues filling mouths. I'm sucking his nipples, he's caressing my ass. We slide along the sheets until our lips are around each other's cocks and we are sucking, loving the familiar taste. I'll never get enough of teasing his slit through his foreskin. And later, when Gary's ass is slowly riding my cock, moving up and down on its hardness, I smile a smile he can't see, but I know he senses it.

"Guess I acted stupid this afternoon," I whisper. Sometimes, when he's riding me slowly like this, we talk. Intimate things. "I'm sorry I ruined your surprise."

He stops his languorous movement. My stiff cock is engulfed by heat inside his ass. He looks down at me as if he can see my face in the moonlight. "You think Rog's been fucking me?"

Something stark about his features in the dim light. I can't bear to see him unhappy. "Forget it, babe," I say.

"You think I'd be barebacking you if I was doing it with Rog?"

I jet a gushing, uncontrollable stream inside him. And simultaneously, a look of surprise on his face, he splashes all over me. My belly, my neck. And I am holding him close, breathing in his scent as we fall asleep. I'm thinking that I haven't answered his question.

• • •

He isn't in the apartment this morning. An overnight bag is missing, some of his clothes. He must've padded around on bare feet while I was sound asleep. And he probably called a cab. Unless he telephoned Roger. I won't let myself believe it and drive to his brother's house.

"He doesn't want to see you," Angus says. "What the shit's going on with you two?"

"I was rotten to him yesterday."

Angus frowns. "That's hard to believe." He tries his best to understand his younger gay brother's life. "Listen, I'd let him alone tonight. He's going to the club to play. It'll take his mind off the hospital and things." His smile is consoling. "Don't worry. I'll drive him."

• • •

I can't stay away from the club. Stand at the bar, a good distance from the piano where Gary is playing and singing an old standard, "You've Changed." The place is quiet, everyone engrossed with Gary. Straight couples mostly at the tables, but there are always some gays whenever Gary appears. I wonder if he is singing to me, even though he doesn't know I'm listening, watching him. A pain somewhere behind my heart. Long to drive him home later, like I usually do. Make slow, intense love to him. Melded together. Not just physically, my bare cock inside him. But soulfully. Like we are used to. Like I might never again do with him.

Roger is seated at a table next to the piano. He's a clean silhouette against a soft spot bathing Gary. I grip my glass, wondering why it doesn't crack and slice my fingers. I move forward, but a big hand is holding me back. "No," Angus says softly, suddenly there. "Go home. I'll take care of him. Get him to the hospital tomorrow."

I can't sleep tonight. Know I should be with Gary during these long hours before morning.

• • •

Angus—nobody—can talk me out of being in the hospital waiting room this morning. I should have been with Gary last night. I long to tell him how wrong I was to suspect him of anything with Roger. He had posed nude and was getting dressed when I drove up to the house. And I stabbed him to the heart with my suspicions. Sure, it had seemed—

"You look like hell." Roger's standing in the waiting room doorway. "He won't see anybody. But Angus is with him."

I stare at the floor. I won't blame Gary if he never looks my way again. *Christ!* Within a few days he might see this miserable bastard. Me!—who should be sharing the suspense with him, comforting him, before they take him upstairs to surgery.

Roger and I sit there, not speaking. Much later, he brings me a container of coffee and drops into a chair opposite me. "I'm in love with him." He says it matter-of-factly, but a tremor edges his words.

"He loves you?"

Roger doesn't answer.

I want to slam my fist into his white teeth. Throw coffee across his face. Do something violent. Protest this impossible idea. "So you've been fucking him. Getting inspiration for the portrait!"

He shakes his head. "I've never touched him." He gives me a wistful smile. "Except to position him the way I want him standing."

I remember what Gary said about not barebacking if he'd fucked around with Roger. But did it make any difference now?

• • •

No one but Angus has seen Gary for more than a week. Days spin endlessly. Nights are lonely. I curl up on my guy's side of the bed, as if I can catch something of his fragrance, just a whiff. Wake up with a start when I dream we are belly to belly, cocks touching. His lips against my lips, tongues dueling. I try telephoning his room, but he isn't answering. Angus catches me on my cell phone and says the surgeon will be removing bandages tomorrow afternoon.

Roger's in the waiting room when Angus comes in and says the bandages are off and the operation has been successful. I feel this bright elation. Gary will be seeing things around him for the first time since he was 11—a new life beginning for him.

He's sitting up in bed, and I realize he's *watching* Roger and me walk into the room. *Watching us!* I'm smiling like a kid who's just been given a catcher's glove for his birthday. And at the same time I'm unable to fathom what I'm facing.

Roger leans down and wraps arms around Gary's shoulders. Gary stares past him at me. I see a new comprehension across his face. It jars me. Because he is seeing the guy he's shared his life and body with for the past two years. He pulls loose from Roger's embrace and gazes up at me. "Just like I pictured." He's grinning. I know that pleased grin so well. He turns to me, nodding at Roger. "Isn't he the coolest-looking guy?" Roger glances across his shoulder at me. It's like his eyes are pleading for me to forgive him.

Gary kisses his cheek. Leans back against stacked pillows. "I'll see you later," he says to Roger and then rolls his head to face me. Roger smiles his way out of the room. I almost turn to follow him, but Gary has caught my hand. His fingers, his hand, strong. His eyes green and clear, as though he's always seen things as distinctly as now.

"A rugged man," he says. His gaze moves over me. "I could always tell. Craggy. Not pretty."

He's trying to be kind about things. I wonder if he feels betrayed. He pulls me closer until I'm sitting on the side of the bed. His fingers move along my throat, across my Adam's apple. Trace my jaw, prominent nose, cheekbones, brows. His gaze moves along my chest, lingers below my belt, along my legs. I see his eyes darken, as if there is some crucial thing he must tell me.

"Don't ever leave me." That's all he says.

I sit transfixed, not believing; but some sort of happiness—call it joy—is making me shiver. He pulls me into his arms. Our mouths, our tongues, our breaths locked together.

• • •

A Saturday morning, days later in bed, he lies wrapped in my arms. He keeps marveling how sunlight illuminates our room. His cock is hard in my hand. He leans down to lick away precome from mine. He's examined my body from forehead to feet since the day I drove him home from the hospital. Watched how my nipples harden, remarked on the difference between scrotum skin and cock skin. Admired the flat belly I work to keep that way. Licked and sniffed armpits. Raised brows at my firm ass. Now I maneuver down to his ass cheeks, spread them, and tongue his pucker, wetting him for what I know he wants. What I want.

While he is slowly riding my cock, he looks down at me. Returns my smile. It's something I'll get used to, Gary being able to read my expressions.

"He was getting to me," he says. "I mean, he kept saying these flattering things. I came close to ruining all this. I could tell by your voice you suspected." He begins to hasten his ride. "I kept hoping you'd—" He catches his breath.

His cream sprays my chest, drips from my chin. And I moan and shoot deep into him. Realize I'd taken him for granted while he was a prisoner in the dark. He was human. Responding. But now he is here in the light with me.

Critic's Choice
by Karl Taggart

I didn't tell him I was a writer until after I'd fucked him, and even then wasn't totally honest about it. He was a well-known literary critic; I was a pornographer. Match made in hell.

At first I didn't realize who he was. He'd turned from the bar to survey the room and caught my eye. Slim, elegant, dressed in dark slacks and a white turtleneck. Graying hair, high forehead, cerebral look. He was incredibly handsome. He had an aristocratic face, the kind you'd expect to see in some English country manor or maybe the House of Lords: high cheekbones, sharp chin, everything sculpted, perfect, but with the hint of softness that age brings. Not always unwelcome, I'd found, especially in guys like him. I knew instantly what he wanted and moved in. He bought me a drink and got his hand onto my crotch, groping until I was hard, tracing the length of my cock, rubbing it along my thigh.

We took a cab to his condo in that burgeoning area of San Francisco called South Beach. It was there that I found out who he was. *Holy shit,* I thought. He'd said his name was Jason, but a glance at his bookshelf told me he was Jason Falk. Recognition hit full force. My cock went limp—along with the rest of me.

He offered a drink, and I took it, downing it quickly while he undid my jeans and got his mouth on me. As he licked and pulled, I savored the feel but found there was something between us—that reputation of his: literary predator. He had destroyed more than one up-and-coming writer.

I'd had no idea he was gay. I knew him only by his penetrating essays and scathing reviews, watching as he deconstructed everyone and everything he encountered. Sexual orientation seemed a minor point—even now, but here he was sucking dick like the rest of us. Suddenly human.

Who he was soon mattered little. When he had me hard, he rose and stripped. He had to be a good 45, but it was a well-maintained middle age. Only the slightest thickening at the waist, a smattering of gray in his pubes. His chest was smooth, nipples dark. Not a particularly muscular build, but trim. His foreskin was ample, cock head concealed, his balls riding low in the sac. The sight of him made my cock twitch.

"Fuck me," he said when he stood naked. No kissing, no prelims, just an overpowering need. He led me to his bedroom, pointed to a bowl of condoms and jar of lube, then crawled onto the bed, got on all fours, stuck his rump up. He reached back and pulled open his cheeks. His hole pulsed at me.

His hips were narrow, the kind I liked; his crack, nearly hairless. I stripped, then ran a gob of grease into him, and he moaned, squirmed, started riding my fingers. When I pulled out, he began chanting "fuck me"—so I did. I shoved my prick into him and just kept going, thrusting full-out from the very first. He started a kind of keening sound, and I could tell he was absolutely gone, that life for him was a dick up the ass—fuck literature.

I made things last. Every time I felt close, I eased up, which caused him to squirm and moan and beg. It was apparent that he liked to be ridden hard. When I'd pick up the pace, he'd squeeze his muscle with approval, let out a groan.

Twice I added lube, enjoying the sight of his gaping hole. He got a hand on his dick now and then but didn't do any stroking. Everything was about me doing him—him taking all I could give and still wanting more. When I finally let go, I made it known, pounding him until his butt cheeks were red and liquefied lube ran down onto his balls. I let out a verbal stream as well—him still doing his fuck-me chant; me doing a fuck-you rant back at him, louder with each squirt—until I could have been screaming at that point, for all I knew.

When I pulled out, he rolled onto his back and pulled his legs high, the ultimate presentation: stiff cock dripping precome, asshole dripping as well. He was breathing hard, and I knew he was ready for the grand finale. I shoved two fingers into him and, with my other hand, grabbed his dick and started pumping, and it was at this point that I again thought about who he was. The world saw him as inviolate—the almighty critic, judge, jury and executioner—but I knew the reality. He let out a cry as he came, eyes closed, head pushed back into the pillow. His substantial cock shot big gobs of jizz up onto his chest as his entire body shuddered through the climax. Afterward he lay inert, silent. I simply watched.

"Karl, wasn't it?" he said finally, eyes still closed.

"Yes."

"What do you do for a living, Karl?"

"Why do you ask?"

"I like to know something about the men who fuck me."

"I'm a writer."

The pause was significant, and I wondered if he thought I'd orchestrated this to get into his good graces, manuscript concealed somewhere in the heap of clothes on the floor.

"Indeed," he said. "What do you write?"

I've never been ashamed of what I do—am quite proud, actually. But at that moment, with that man, it wasn't the disclosure I wanted to make. "Novels, short stories."

"And are you published?"

"Yes. The stories, not the novels."

"Any I might have seen?"

"I doubt it. Small magazines."

"But you persevere."

"Yes, I persevere."

"Good."

Suddenly, I couldn't resist telling him, "I didn't know who you were at first."

"And you do now?"

"I caught a look at your books when we came in."

"Ah, the essays, yes. Bit of a giveaway. Not a problem, is it, fucking the critic? Every writer's dream, I'd imagine."

He rolled over onto his side, propped up on one elbow, and studied me, hand tracing my nipples, stomach, then getting down to my cock. "Magnificent," he said as he petted it. When I began to harden, he crawled down and got me into his mouth again, sucking fiercely, as if we'd just begun. He got a hand on my balls and worked everything until his face was flushed, sweat across his forehead. He pulled back and said, "I need so much more. Can you stay?" He licked the tip of my dick for emphasis.

"Sure," I told him, and I pushed his head down onto my cock, made him suck it until I was ready. Then I rolled him onto his back, got his legs up, and made him wait while I pulled on another rubber, lubed my dick. The sight of him like that intoxicated me, and I knew I'd stay as long as he wanted, maybe longer. The best thing about a writer's life is that there are no hours. The only thing I get up for is a good lay.

"Fuck me," Jason murmured, more to himself, I thought, than me. I'd enjoyed a few pig bottoms, but this guy's energy was a different kind of relentless. I got the idea this was all part of who he was, that maybe after destroying people on paper he needed to do penance in bed—get reamed over and over after he'd undoubtedly spent the day doing the equivalent to someone's life work. I found myself aroused by the opportunity to issue punishment. After all, how many writers get to fuck a critic? I let my dick hover at his hole, poking around like some anteater looking for a meal. "Fuck me," Jason said, louder this time. He held onto his cock, which remained soft, and kept his legs high. I could tell he loved the position: abject, submissive, stark contrast to the man on paper. Literary top, sexual bottom. I smiled as this ran through my mind and, in acknowledgment, pushed my cock into him.

We kept it up for hours, drinking and fucking until dawn came, then fell into a heavy sleep. When I awoke, I had no idea of the time and was alone in bed. I got up, washed my face, wrapped a towel around my waist, and went to find Jason.

He was at his desk, clad in a green silk robe. He typed steadily, even when I came up behind him. "Have a good sleep?" he asked, fingers still hitting the keys. I knew how that was, how you can get words lined up in your head and carry on a conversation while still typing, nothing able to derail you.

"What are you writing?" I asked.

"A review of the new Fleming book. I started it yesterday, then went out instead and met you. I must get back to it."

"Is the book any good?" I'd read all of Tony Fleming's novels and thought them wonderful, looked forward to the new one.

Jason sighed, stopped typing, and sat back. "He's done better."

"You liked his other work?"

"Not particularly, but at least it was coherent. This new one is an exhibitionistic jumble, the kind of peacock display that gives literature a bad name."

I put my hands on his shoulders, dug my fingers in. He squirmed with discomfort. "You must let me finish," he said, and put his hands back on the keyboard. I let him type a couple lines, but the thought of what he was doing stirred me. My cock was filling, and as he pounded the keys I slid my hands down inside his robe and pulled it open.

"Karl—" he started to protest.

"That's enough criticism for a while."

"But I have to—"

I pulled the chair out from under him, which sent him to the floor, where I held him down, stripped away the robe, rolled him onto his stomach, and stuck a finger up his ass. "You don't have to do a goddamned thing," I growled. As I lubed him with spit, I thought about fucking him until he expired, obliterating that anger he vented on us, venom fueled by his own inadequacy, because critics were usually failed writers who'd turned.

"Karl, please," he said, as if there was a struggle taking place, when in reality he lay waiting, pucker twitching in anticipation of his punishment. I pulled open his cheeks, stared at the eager hole, and he said it again: "Please." But this time the plea was there; he wanted his penance. He had to be taken.

"You want me to fuck you," I said, and he uttered a long, high-pitched moan and stuck his ass up at me. When I made no move, he pulled open his cheeks, working his muscle so his hole opened and closed like a fish's mouth. Still I waited, and he worked his own finger over to his rim, played around, then went in. "You need a dick up there, don't you, Jason? You need fucking in the worst way."

"Please," he rasped as he fingered himself.

"What do you want?" I teased, sitting back on my haunches. "You have to tell me."

"Stick your cock in me. Fuck me."

"How much fucking do you need, Jason?"

"Lots," he said with a whimper. "I need cock. I have to have it. There is never enough."

I lubed my swollen meat and got up behind him, prodded his hole, and he cried out, "Christ almighty, do it!"

I hesitated, savoring the final moment, the ultimate control. My dick was poised at his rim. I wanted so badly to do it, to drive up into him until he choked, gag him with my cock, but I held back. "Do it," he begged. "Fuck me."

I was dripping precome, inflamed by the sight of him, his unholy need mixed in with my own. I wrapped a hand around myself and started to stroke, pumping steadily while he begged. He writhed on the floor, got a hand around to his crack, a finger to his hole, and, as he pushed into himself, I came, squirting gobs of cream onto his sorry ass.

Traveling Tailor

by Sean Wolfe

"Goddamn it!"

Adam slammed his fist down on his desk and kicked the heavy wooden leg. Of all the times for shitty luck to show its face.

He hadn't split the seam in his pants since he was a fat, awkward kid. It had been a common occurrence back then, and the other kids had been merciless in their teasing. To this day he could remember running home crying and slamming the door behind him to shut out their laughter.

But that was 20 years ago, and now as he was approaching 30, things had all turned around. Later this afternoon, Adam Gomez was going to pitch the ad campaign that everyone knew would make him the youngest partner in Dallas's largest advertising agency—not to mention the only Latino partner. Smith, Davidson, & Young would soon become Smith, Davidson, Young, & Gomez.

This meeting was the last step before making it official. This afternoon's presentation would surely clench the Bruce Callahan account that had eluded the agency for more than 10 years, and it was just two hours away. Adam was dressed in his finest suit—then, as he sat down at his desk just a few moments ago, he heard the undeniable rip of his inseam. When he moved his leg to look down in disgust at the tear, it spread even farther, stretching from mid thigh to just below his knee.

He cursed himself for all the hours he'd spent at the gym over the last three or four years. No longer the fat kid in town, he was now just over six feet of solid, lean but bulging muscle—muscle that ripped his pant leg. He'd grown into a striking young man. His black hair, deep brown eyes, smooth copper skin and bright white smile were complemented by the strong jawline and cheekbones that had appeared when he lost his weight. Add that to his charm, talent, and strong ambition, and there was absolutely nothing working against him anymore—except for the goddamned tear in his pant leg.

"Karen," he shouted into his intercom to his secretary, "I need you in here now."

"I'm sorry, Mr. Gomez," came a tiny, scared voice. "Karen isn't here. She took some papers across the street for Mr. Davidson."

Adam switched the intercom button off and swore under his breath. Davidson had his own secretary, so why the hell was he always pulling Karen away to run his errands? Sweat began to bead his brow as he fumed.

It was then that he remembered the tailor shop that occupied the small space on the first floor of his office building, right before the elevators. He'd passed it every day for years, smiling politely at the elderly woman who was always busy behind the counter. Traveling Tailor, the shop was called, because it catered to downtown offices and traveled to its customers who didn't have time to come to them.

He rummaged through his desk drawer for the building directory and frantically flipped the pages until he spotted the simple black and white ad. He dialed the number quickly, then took a deep breath in order to compose himself before speaking.

"Traveling Tailor," came a sweet elderly woman's voice over the line. It was thick with an accent Adam struggled to place. Russian maybe, or German. He wasn't sure.

"Hi. This is Adam Gomez, with Smith, Davidson & Young. We're in your same building, up on the 58th floor."

"Yes, Mr. Gomez, how can I help you?"

"Well, I have somewhat of an emergency," Adam stammered. "Actually it's a really big emergency. I just ripped my pant leg, and I have a very important meeting in a couple of hours. I really need your help."

"Yes, sir. I am in the middle of another emergency right now. Ms. Cartwright on the 32nd floor has pulled her hem." Adam thought he heard a tone of sarcasm in her voice.

"But this is really important," he said, biting his bottom lip. "My meeting is in an hour," he lied and sat forward in his chair.

"Ms. Cartwright's meeting is in 20 minutes."

Adam swatted at the air around the phone and gave the old woman the middle finger.

"But I'm almost finished here. I can maybe come up there in about half an hour."

"That would be fine," Adam said between clenched teeth. He knew this was his only chance at fixing the huge rip in his pants. "Thank you."

"My pleasure, sir," the old woman said. "I'll be up as soon as I can."

Adam hung up the phone and counted to 10. It wouldn't do any good to brood or get angry. He had to keep his cool. He had to be ready for the most important pitch of his career.

Adam picked up the only file on the desk in front of him. While scanning the file's contents, he continued practicing the right combination of inflection and gestures that would close the biggest account in his company's history. The Callahan account was worth more than $60 million, and Adam wanted to be sure that his presentation would be perfect.

He was shocked when Karen buzzed him only 15 minutes later.

"Adam, Mr. Callahan is on Line 2 for you. And the traveling tailor is here for you," she said with a puzzled tone.

"Great!" Adam said as he picked up the cordless phone and hit the button for Line 2. "Send her in."

"Bruce, how are you?" he asked as the door to his office opened, and he stood up to walk around to the front of his desk.

A young blond boy of about 19 walked in carrying a small case and closed the door behind him. He was wearing a letter jacket from Texas A&M University and looked like he must play for one of the school's athletic teams. His hair was slightly ruffled, and his cheeks had a blush to them that hinted of robust young sexuality.

Adam leaned against the front of his desk and spread his legs so that the young man could see the huge tear. The boy knelt down in front of Adam and pulled on the torn pant leg to see what he had to work with.

"I spoke with a woman," Adam whispered as he covered the mouthpiece of the phone. Bruce Callahan was in the middle of a long exhortation regarding the upcoming meeting.

"Yeah," the boy replied quietly, "Gramma said it was an emergency, so she sent me up. Don't worry, I know what I'm doing."

Adam nodded and went back to his conversation.

"I know, Bruce, but don't worry about a thing. I'm all set here," he said, and looked down at the kid again.

The boy's face was inches from his crotch, and Adam felt his cock stir inside his pants as the kid's hot breath hit his bare leg through the ripped seam. The tailor's hands brushed his thigh a couple of times, and Adam panicked as he noticed the long line of his hardening cock spread across the front of his slacks. *Damn, I should've worn briefs instead of boxers today,* he thought.

"Yes, we're fully expecting they will be upset," Adam spoke into the receiver.

The blond kid reached inside the gaping hole in the leg of Adam's pants and caressed Adam's smooth, muscular thigh.

Was that an intentional squeeze? Adam blushed as his cock started to throb. The kid looked up and smiled, and his bright blue eyes sparkled as he licked his lips.

Adam swallowed hard and tried to keep his calm. "You know how much we appreciate this Bruce," he stuttered out as the kid's hands found their way to his belt and began to unbuckle it. "Don't worry about a thing."

The front of Adam's pants unbuttoned quickly, and Adam felt the young tailor press his face against the bulging crotch as his arms wrapped around Adam's legs. Precome was already leaking out of the head of his cock when the blond boy slid the waist of the pants down Adam's long legs.

"Me too." Adam breathed heavily and closed his eyes. The college student had reached inside Adam's boxers and pulled out his throbbing uncut cock.

"Bruce, I've got to run," Adam said quickly. The boy wrapped his fist around Adam's long, fat pole and slowly slid the foreskin back and forth along the length. "Something unexpected has just come up. I'll call you back."

Adam reached around to hang up the phone just as the hot, wet mouth covered his cock head. The kid's tongue tickled his knob for a moment, then he sucked greedily on the thick shaft.

"Shit, kid, that feels good."

The tailor swallowed half of Adam's dick and looked up and winked. Adam slid his long cock all the way inside the boy's throat a couple of times.

"You're good," Adam said as he pulled completely out of the young man's hot mouth.

"Thanks," the college student/tailor said, and stood up to face Adam. "I'm Rick," he said, and leaned in to kiss Adam on the lips.

"Adam," Adam stammered out between deep kisses. He tasted himself on Rick's tongue.

"So, Adam," Rick said as he pulled away and began to undress himself, "I hear you have somewhat of an emergency."

"Um...yeah..." Adam replied absently, dumbfounded as the kid boldly stripped right there in his office.

"Well, now so do I," Rick said as he dropped his jacket and pulled off his T-shirt, revealing his well-muscled chest and hard, flat stomach.

"Really? And what exactly is your emergency?"

"This," Rick replied breathlessly as he unbuttoned his jeans and quickly pushed them to his ankles. He wore no underwear, and his hard cock sprung up, pointing directly at Adam. The trail of blond hair that started at Rick's navel and spread down into his pubic bush took Adam's breath away.

"That does look like it needs some immediate attention," Adam said, breathing heavily as he stroked his cock.

"It most certainly does," Rick replied, stroking himself as well. "If we're gonna get these slacks of yours fixed before your meeting, you'd better stop talking and start fucking me."

"Well, let's get to it," Adam growled, loosening his tie and pulling off his shirt, then sliding his boxers down and kicking them off.

Rick turned his back to Adam and leaned forward. His ass was extremely well-muscled and had a light coating of baby-fine blond hair. Adam squeezed the cheeks in both hands, then pressed his cock against the crack between them.

"That's it, Adam," Rick moaned, spreading his cheeks wider. "Fuck me."

Normally Adam would start by licking the ass he was about to fuck, getting it relaxed and wet, but Rick was obviously in no mood for foreplay. That suited Adam just fine, since he was pressed for time anyway. Retrieving a condom and some lube from his briefcase, he pulled on the rubber and juiced up his cock and then Rick's hungry ass. He spread some lube around the tiny puckered hole and moaned loudly as he rubbed his giant cock up and down the length of Rick's ass crack.

Rick reached behind him with one hand and moved Adam's throbbing dick right to his twitching hole. Then he took a deep breath and slowly slid backward onto the fat cock, until it was buried deep inside him.

"Damn, you're huge," he whispered, short of breath.

"You asked for it," Adam grunted, and began sliding in and out of one of the hottest, tightest asses he'd fucked in years.

Rick's ass muscles squeezed the big dick, and Adam felt his foreskin moving across his long, thick shaft inside the rubber as he fucked the kid. He reached around and pinched Rick's nipples and ran his hand along the college kid's washboard stomach. They found a rhythm very quickly, and fucked as if they'd been partners for years.

Adam could usually go for quite a while, he knew it was going to be different with Rick. The kid was damn talented, working and squeezing Adam's hot cock with his muscles as Adam's dick burrowed deep into his ass.

When Rick reached down and stroked his own cock, his ass tightened even more strongly around Adam's fiery cock, and Adam felt the come churn in his balls as it prepared to shoot out his shaft.

"Fuck, Adam, I'm gonna shoot," Rick almost yelled. Before he even finished the sentence, Adam saw the kid's load spewing across the floor. Several jets flew out, and with each one, the ass muscles enveloping Adam's cock grew tighter and hotter.

"Me too." Adam breathed deep and pumped faster and deeper.

Rick pulled himself off Adam's cock and fell to the floor, facing the huge brown dick as Adam ripped off the rubber. He closed his eyes just as the first shot squirted out, and kept his head tilted back as Adam's load sprayed across his face, landing on his forehead and his cheeks.

"Man, you have a great cock," Rick said, leaning backwards and resting on his hands.

"And you have a great ass."

Just then the intercom buzzed, and Karen's voice broke through.

"Adam, there's a Mrs. Schneider on Line 1 for you. Something about a traveling tailor?"

"Tell her I'll be just one minute, please."

"Yes, sir."

Rick was already getting up and starting to dress.

Adam picked his pants up from the floor and handed them to the tailor. He would definitely have to give this kid a big tip, he noted to himself as he stood naked in the middle of the office, glistening with sweat, trying to catch his breath.

"I'll have these fixed for you in no time," Rick said. He kissed Adam on the lips and pushed him down into the big leather chair. "Gramma's on Line 1," he smiled. "She doesn't like to be kept waiting."

"This is Adam Gomez," Adam said calmly into the phone as his heavy uncut dick lay limp between his legs. "Yes, he's here. He's getting me all fixed up right now."

Working Up a Sweat
by Thom Wolf

I knew it was going to be a good night.

As I walked through the doors to the club, an old Kylie Minogue track was brewing up a storm on the dance floor. Fucking excellent, pure glad-to-be-alive pop. The dance floor was already packed. The club was sweating. Dry ice blasted over the crowd. I breathed in deeply—the best fucking smell in the world. I was high. Ready for anything.

I was looking pretty good too. I was wearing my favorite trousers—black, tight across the butt and thighs, and a cool new top—white, tight, and sleeveless. My limbs were tanned and firm, and I was showing off my latest tattoo: a black tribal band around my right bicep. I didn't walk around the club, I *prowled.*

I was feeling pleasantly drunk. I'd had a couple of very strong vodka martinis at home while I was getting dressed, and I had been to three other bars before hitting the club. I don't do drugs these days, apart from the occasional spliff. Hard drugs don't agree with me; they make me do very silly things. Things (or men) I'd rather forget about.

I went straight up to the balcony so I could have a good look at the club before I went into action. I bought a drink at the upstairs bar: vodka martini again, only this time it was a ready-to-drink bottle. Not as nice nor as strong as my own cocktails, but good enough to have the desired effects.

The balcony was just as packed as the rest of the club. The full length of the rail was thronged with men, most of them half-naked—posing, dancing, cruising. I shoved my way in next to a couple of young bunnies dressed in tight disco-wedgie hot pants and not much else. Cute, but a bit too cute for me.

I leaned over the rail and gazed out over the floor beneath me. There had to be about 500 people gyrating against each other down there. With keen eyes I scanned the crowd and searched for a face—the right face. I knew what I was looking for. He had to be tall and strong and over 25. Handsome but not pretty. A little bit mean, a little bit dangerous. I wouldn't make do with anything less than what I was used to.

After five minutes I finally found him.

He was dancing at the edge of the floor. Alone. He was wearing blue jeans and a black shirt that was stretched tight across his broad chest. His hair was bleached blond, almost white, and cut very short. His face was angular, square-cut. I couldn't put an exact age on him from this distance, but he was somewhere in his 30s.

I watched him pull a bottle of poppers out of his pocket. He unscrewed the cap and raised the bottle, inhaling through both nostrils. A sudden blast of dry ice enveloped him.

It was time to go down for a closer look.

I finished my drink and dumped the empty bottle at the bar before heading downstairs to the dance floor. It took me a couple of minutes to find him again. The place was so busy that it was a real struggle to fight my way through the sweaty crowd. A couple of guys made a grab for me as I hurried past them. I shot them both a glance that said, *Get out of my way,* and pushed onward in search of my potential sex partner. Luckily for me, he hadn't moved.

He was still there at the edge of the floor, dancing alone.

I stood back for a moment before making a move, just to be certain that I did want to make the effort with this one.

It didn't take long to make that decision. This guy was fucking gorgeous.

I guessed his age to somewhere around 35. Up close he was a big bastard with an immense set of shoulders, but his broad chest tapered down over his stomach to a very compact waist. His face was moody, almost hard-looking, but there was no denying that he was a handsome fucker.

Any lingering qualms evaporated.

I was going to have him.

He didn't even see me coming. One moment he was all on his own, dancing away quite happily to a Tina Cousins remix, and the next I was right there with him. I slipped through the throng of sweaty arms and torsos to take up my place in front of him. I raised my arms above my head and gave myself over to the music.

He couldn't take his eyes off me. He was hooked. I ground my hips and my torso, swaying nearer and nearer to him until we were less than a foot apart. My eyes held contact with his steely blue gaze. I licked a film of sweat off my top lip. He smiled. His mouth was long and wide. There was a sexy little gap between his two front teeth.

I spun around and moved my tight ass back and forth in front of his crotch. My butt grazed against his bulge. He was hard.

I turned back around and arched my back to the powerful track, thrusting my hips even nearer to him. Rubbing my hard bulge against his own.

He dug the poppers out of his jeans and unscrewed the top, offering the bottle to me. I took it from him and held it up to my nose, inhaling the contents slowly through each nostril. The chemical fumes had an instant effect. I felt the music more deeply, and my desire to fuck this guy increased a hundredfold. I gave him back the bottle and he sniffed from it again before stuffing it back into his jeans.

We moved closer, both of us seduced by the music and each other. He leaned in toward my ear.

"Who are you?" he shouted over the noise of the dance floor.

"I'm the guy you're having sex with tonight," I shouted back.

He laughed. "I'm Jack."

"Thom."

I slid my hands around his waist. It was tight and trim. I swayed my body against him, rubbing my hips against his. Our cocks brushed, kept apart by just a few layers of clothing. We were both rock-hard.

I felt his huge hand in the small of my back, and he drew me tight against his wide chest. I leant into his embrace and found his lips. We kissed passionately. Our lips yielded to the pressure. His tongue slipped into my mouth. I pressed against it with my own, forcing it between his teeth and into his mouth. I tasted the smoke and booze on his breath and throbbed even harder.

His hands slid down my back and over the curve of my ass. He held it in both hands, lifting me even closer. I could feel his raw strength. I grabbed hold of his ass. It was tight and firm, just the way I like 'em. I shoved a hand down the back of his jeans. He murmured something into my mouth. He wasn't wearing any underwear. His butt was hot and sweaty. I felt his cock swell against my hips as I kneaded the taut muscle.

My fingers slipped into the tight crack. The cleft was wet. I had a sudden urge to tear his jeans down around his calves and get my face stuck right into the crack, to lick out all of that fresh, funky sweat. But I resisted. I didn't wanted to get thrown out just as the two of us were starting to get going.

My fingers quickly located his hole. It was smooth and wet, and when I pressed the tip of my finger against it, it opened effortlessly. I pressed in right up to the knuckle. Jack started kissing me with even greater passion. His ass lips fluttered around my finger.

I slipped my free hand round to the front of his jeans to get a feel of what he had down there. Wow. I wasn't disappointed. He had a good, solid piece of throbbing meat. I squeezed the thick shaft and traced the outline, trying to get an indication of size. There was a good eight inches there—at least.

That was enough fooling around. It was time to get serious with this guy.

I slowly removed my finger from his ass and withdrew it from the rear of his jeans. I raised it to my nose and inhaled his scent. It was soft and savory and very fucking horny. The smell heightened my arousal.

"Come on," I said, taking his hand in mine. I led him off the dance floor.

Though this club wasn't my regular haunt, I knew it well enough. I knew all the dark spots, all the lovers' corners and hiding places. On the ground floor there was a good spot by the fire exit. It was hidden away around a corner, out of sight of the main club. It was a popular location for casual sex. There were already two guys there getting a blow job from a third when I led Jack into the corner. I ignored the other men. For the moment, I had enough to be getting on with.

I shoved Jack up against the brick wall. Though he was bigger than me, surprise gave me the upper hand. He tried to kiss me again, but I avoided his lips and dropped down to my knees in front of him. My hands worked quickly. In no time at all, I had his belt unbuckled and had ripped open the fly of his jeans. His cock leaped to freedom.

My God. My eyes widened. After so many years and so many forgettable cocks, it's always nice to be surprised. This was a beauty. I had been right in my estimation; the shaft was about eight inches long. But it was the sheer girth of his piece that really impressed me. It was like a can of beer. My fingers could not close around it. He had a foreskin too, which is an all-too-rare delight, and a cute Prince Albert crowning his piss slit. His balls were big and low-hanging in their smooth sack. I realized that Jack was completely shaved: pubes, balls, ass crack—the lot.

I wrapped my hand round the shaft as best I could and started to jerk him off slowly. I was never quite sure how to handle pierced guys, so I started to lick his head and piss slit, taking extra care around the steel sleeper. There was no way I would ever get his shaft into my mouth, so I would just have to make do with polishing off his head for him.

There was already a good stream of precome drooling out of his slit, and the flow increased considerably when I tightened my grip on the shaft and jerked him harder. It tasted strong and salty, as strong as some other guys' full load. I gently poked his piercing with my tongue. That caused him to sigh.

"Does it hurt?" I asked.

"I'd tell you if it did," he replied.

I guess he knew what he was talking about, so I nipped the sleeper between my teeth and tugged at it gently. The big man groaned.

Jack reached down, stuck his hands under my arms, and yanked me to my feet. He had the advantage of strength; there was no use fighting him, so I just let him do what he wanted. He spun me around and shoved my face against the cold brick wall. I realized that a crowd of five or six guys had gathered to watch us.

His hands slid round my waist. He unfastened my trousers and dragged them all the way down to my ankles. I wasn't wearing underwear either. My ass was bare for anyone to see.

"Nice ass," Jack growled, giving it a hard slap. "Bend over and give us all a look at it."

The crowd around us had moved in closer. Their faces were pretty indistinguishable to my sex-crazed brain.

I spread my legs as far as my tight trousers would allow and bent over, sticking out my ass. Though my pubes are trimmed into a tidy bush, my ass is as smooth and shaven as Jack's. I spread my crack with both hands and pouted my ass lips for the benefit of my audience.

"Nice," Jack said shoving a finger straight into me. He curved his finger rounded the bend and found my prostate. My cock leaped as he stroked it. A big gob of precome oozed over my cock head. I moved my ass, forcing it back onto his hand. He knew what I was hungry for.

He pulled out his finger.

"You got a rubber?"

"In my pocket," I said, my face still pressed up against the cold brick wall.

Jack searched through the pockets of my trousers and quickly found what he was looking for. I never leave the house without at least three condoms and a couple of sachets of lube.

He tore open the lube and smeared it all around my expectant hole. My asshole grabbed at his fingers as he greased it up. He stuffed some of it inside me, making sure that I was well-lubricated. I guess he knew from experience that guys needed a lot of lube to get his big prick into them.

He gave me his bottle of poppers. "Here. You'll probably need these."

I didn't argue. I unscrewed the top while he sheathed himself up. Then his big blunt tip slipped into the crack of my ass and pushed against my hole. This was it. I steadied my legs and took a big sniff from the little brown bottle. Jack pressed forward. My asshole stretched, it burned. Thank God for amyl. The big crown popped the resistance of my sphincter, and he was in me. He pushed all the way in until his smooth balls pressed against the cheeks of my ass.

I had both hands pressed against the wall to steady myself.

The guys who were watching us moved in even closer.

Jack began to fuck me with long, hard strokes. After another sniff of amyl, I was suddenly fuck-crazed. I wanted it as hard and as fast as he could give it. This was the real thing. In those moments it meant more to me than anything else in life.

He grabbed my hips and dragged my ass back onto his cock while he fucked it mercilessly. The rhythm was frantic. His hips slapped loudly against my wet buttocks. I tightened my hole, gripping him as though my life depended on it.

Through half-lidded eyes I saw that a couple of the other guys had started to jerk off. Jack seemed to notice this at the same time. Without losing a beat, he pulled me away from the wall and spun me around in their direction.

The two guys didn't have to be told what to do. They stepped forward and held their cocks out toward me. I took one in my mouth and the other in my right hand. The guy in my mouth was young, early 20s, the skin on his cock was naturally very smooth with an almost sweet flavor. The other man was older, mid 40s, and his dick was thick and hairy. After sucking off the kid for a few moments, I alternated between the two of them, deep-throating them in turn.

Watching me suck cock really got Jack going. He was fucking my ass like a madman. My insides seemed to shift around him.

Something wet hit me across the back of my neck. Someone out of sight had just shot his load over me. The hot liquid trickled over my skin.

Jack's hips bucked. His cock swelled, and I knew from the irregularity of his strokes that he was coming. I swallowed the older guy's cock while Jack emptied his nuts into me. He pulled out when he was finished.

My ass suddenly felt deserted. Somebody else was quick to take Jack's place. I didn't see his face or know who he was, but another cock slipped into my fuck-hungry ass. This guy was not as big as Jack, but that didn't matter. It was a cock, and that was all I wanted. He immediately picked up a fast rhythm.

Jack was standing beside me now, watching. He pulled the spunk-heavy condom off his cock and tossed it down on the floor at my feet.

The older guy suddenly swelled inside my mouth. He quickly whipped his cock out of me. I finished him off with a few short handstrokes. His cock jerked, and the first spurt landed right across my left cheeks. He blasted one white ropy strand after another, splattering my face with his load. He wiped his cock across my face, smearing his load all over me before stepping aside.

I still had a tight grip on the younger man's cock. I pulled him forward and slipped his dick into the far recesses of my throat. He jerked his hips, fucking my face. I grabbed hold of his lean thighs to steady myself as I took a hard pounding from in front and behind. My own dick was slapping hard against my belly, as my body rocked between these two men.

There was more wetness as one of the other guys out there shot his load all over my back and into my hair.

The two men inside seemed ready to come together. They both pulled out. The man who was fucking me ripped off his condom and blasted his load all over the sweaty cheeks of my ass. I could feel the warm wet trickle all the way down the back of my thighs. The younger man erupted in my face, covering me in even more strong-smelling spunk.

Jack grabbed hold of me and helped me to stand up.

"It's your turn now," he said, holding me against his broad chest.

He grabbed my cock and slipped his fist quickly up and down the shaft, palming the head. It was fucking exquisite. I erupted in his hand. My load bubbled over the top of my head and dribbled down the back of Jack's hand and onto the floor. It was almost too much pleasure to bare.

I didn't even get to see who the other man was who had fucked me. When I opened my eyes he was gone. A couple of new men had started fucking in the corner, and they were now the focus of everyone's attention.

I ran my hand through my hair. It was soaked with sweat and come.

"I think I need to clean myself up," I said, pulling up my trousers.

Jack smiled and kissed me on the mouth. "Go to the bathroom and sort yourself out. And then meet me at the bar," he said. "I want to buy you a drink after all that."

I didn't usually socialize with men after I had finished fucking them. I told him so.

"But this is different," Jack said.

"How?"

"Because we haven't finished fucking yet!"

Partners in Crime

by Trevor J. Callahan Jr.

I've always had a thing for uniforms—that's what brought Dave and me together. In fact, that's how this whole thing started.

We were lounging together, our uniforms tossed aside, my ass a little sore and his cock completely spent. By this time we'd done it all—cops, firemen, delivery guys, Boy Scouts, soldiers, surgeons, servants, stable boys, even medieval knights—and frankly, we were getting a little bored.

"That was fun, but it would be nice to get some fresh ass and cock in our little games," Dave said. "No offense," he added quickly, but none was taken. I knew what he meant. Sure, it was fun playing with each other, but we needed a way to find some other playmates and spice things up. And then it hit me.

"Why don't we just go out in our uniforms and round up a couple of good-looking guys to play with?" I said.

"That's easier said than done," Dave quipped. "And where would we go to find these guys, huh?"

The biggest grin spread across my face. "Rest Area 18," I said.

Rest Area 18 was a notorious cruising ground—someone was always giving someone else head in the bathroom. "Listen," I continued. "We could show up, wait for a couple of good-looking guys to go in, and then just saunter in there and have some fun."

Dave was mulling over the idea in his head, but I could tell it turned him on. "I don't know," he said. "What if no one shows up?"

"They will," I said, still grinning. "I'll make sure of it. What do you say?"

Dave's grin matched mine. "I say let's do it, 'partner.'"

• • •

The next Sunday morning we donned our uniforms (matching, of course) and drove down to Rest Area 18. We went in to make sure the joint was empty, and then we staked out a good spot in the woods—close enough to see who went in the bathroom, but not so close that we could be seen. We figured that on Sunday morning most folks would be in church, and the only guys stopping by would be looking for some action—which we were planning on providing.

"Explain this all to me again," Dave said.

"It's simple," I said. "I posted a note in an online chat room for guys into uniforms and role-playing. I explained what we wanted to do, and I told them to show up if they wanted to play along and join in."

"And you did this when?"

I shrugged. "Last night."

"So if no one shows up—"

"They will," I replied. "Give them time. They'll be here, ready to play along completely. You'll see."

For about a half-hour no one stopped by. Finally, our patience was rewarded. A small Dodge pulled up, and out strode this cute Latino guy. He looked to be in his late 20s, with curly black hair, a pretty hot body, a very nice butt, and a small dark mustache. He looked around before going straight into the john; when he didn't come out after a few minutes, we knew we had one. Excited, we waited for someone else to show up.

Finally, about 20 anxious minutes later, a small Ford pickup pulled up. "Hel-lo," Dave said as this tight little blond boy got out. We guessed he was some frat boy from the local college; he was about 5 foot 7, with a lean frame and another sweet ass. He looked very nervous, waiting outside the men's room for about five minutes before finally heading inside.

Dave and I waited a few more minutes to give the guys time to get going, then we headed toward the door. We put our ears to it, and we were pretty sure we could make out some light moaning. Grinning, we burst in.

"Nobody move!" Dave shouted as we made our way back to the

last stall. "Police!" We moved quickly, and, sure enough, we caught them in the act. Blondie stood there, a more than shell-shocked look on his face, his pants around his ankles, his dick already dripping, while the Latino guy was on his knees in front of him, his own hard cock in his hands. Both of them looked like deer caught in headlights.

"Well, what have we got here?" Dave said. I could tell he was loving every minute of this. The blond guy started to stuff his stiff prick back into his pants, but I wasn't having any of that. "He said not to move, asshole!" I warned blondie, and sure enough, he put his hands in the air, leaving that sweet young prick hanging out for all to see.

"Look at this, Malloy," Dave said, using the fake name I had picked for myself earlier. "Looks like we found us a couple of faggots, huh?"

"I'd say you're right, Morelli," I agreed, using his fake name. "Got us a couple of cocksuckers."

The Latino guy just eyed us warily, though he didn't lose any of his hard-on; boy, did he have ample cock! The blond guy looked ready to freak out at any moment, but his dick was still hard as a rock too.

"Get out here, boys, and keep your hands up in the air where I can see them," Dave barked to the two guys. Shuffling their feet, the two guys slowly walked out of the stall. "Turn around," Dave growled, and they did. "Spread 'em!" The blond was in front of Dave, the Latino stud in front of me. We patted them down, and it took all of my will not to grab that guy's hot dark cock. But we acted totally professional, playing our parts to the hilt.

"Officer," the Latino guy said, "let's be reasonable. Can't I just—"

"You sayin' I'm not reasonable, boy?" I yelled, pretending to be pissed off. I grabbed him by the collar of his denim jacket and pushed him up against the wall. "You don't want to see me get unreasonable, do you, homo?"

The guy shook his head. "No, sir."

"Good," I said, letting him go and spinning him around.

Dave already had blondie facing forward. "Shall I call it in, Morelli?" I said to Dave. Before he could respond, the blond boy jumped in.

"Please, sir," he said to Dave. "I ain't no faggot, I swear. Please."

"You ain't no faggot?" Dave sneered. "What were you just doing here a minute ago, boy?"

"I was just horny, that's all. My girlfriend's away. I've never done anything like this before, I swear."

"You trying to tell me you've never sucked dick before, boy?" Dave asked incredulously. The blond boy nodded. Damn! Acting like a virgin cocksucker—could this guy play along or what?

"Well, what do you know about that, Malloy?" Dave said to me. "We got ourselves a cherry faggot here."

"Oh, come on, Morelli," I said. "Let's give these guys a break."

"Yeah, give us a break," the Latino guy said. I silenced him with a look.

I could see the blond boy begging with his eyes. "I don't know," Dave said. Finally, he seemed to consent. Thank God! My cock was getting ready to bust through my pants! "I tell you what, boys," he said. "We'll let you go, all right."

"Thank you," the blond boy whimpered. He looked almost ready to cry.

"After you suck our dicks," Dave added.

"What?" the blond boy asked. The Latino guy grinned. He'd been waiting to get to this part.

"You heard me," Dave said. He put his hand on the blond boy's shoulder and pushed him to his knees. "I want you to suck my dick, faggot. I want you to suck my dick and swallow my load."

"But I've never done that before," he whimpered.

Dave shrugged. "It's either that, or we go to the station," he said. Dave let his words sink in. "So, what's it gonna be, fag?"

The blond boy shrugged, and finally he nodded.

"Good choice," Dave said, unbuckling his belt and whipping out his whopping hard cock.

The Latino guy kneeled down in front of me and waited for me to get my own seven-inch poker out. Released from my pants, my cock seemed to swell even bigger as the Latino guy sized it up for a moment. "That's a pretty big dick, Officer," he said.

"Just suck it, queer," I said, and he slid my dick easily all the way down his throat.

Man, did it feel good to have his hot lips and tongue all over my throbbing cock! "Yeah, that's it, faggot. Suck my hot cock, you cocksucker," I moaned.

Dave's boy, still playing his part, was a little more reluctant. Finally, Dave grabbed hold of his head. "Get ready, fag," he said. The blond boy opened wide, and Dave shoved half of his fat dick right down the guy's throat.

The blond boy got accustomed to Dave's cock quickly, and in a few minutes he'd built up a good rhythm going up and down Dave's dick.

"This guy's a born cocksucker," Dave growled. He grabbed a good handful of blond hair and started ramming his dick into the guy's mouth. "How you doing, Malloy?" he asked.

"Just fine," I gasped. I didn't need to shove my cock into the Latino guy's mouth; he was eagerly swallowing every inch I had.

For about five minutes Dave and I shouted encouragement to the two studs sucking on our pricks. Pretty soon I could feel that familiar tingle. "Shit, man, I'm gonna fucking come!" I said. "Swallow it, faggot! Take every drop of that load, boy!" I shouted as I shot streak after streak of jizz down that Latino guy's throat. The guy not only swallowed my load, but kept right on sucking my prick until he got every last drop of come out of me.

Dave was twitching, and I could tell he was getting ready to blow too.

"Ughhh!" he said as his cock began to spew out his load. The blond boy was surprised by this; he swallowed the first couple of squirts, but then he managed to pull away, only to get the rest of Dave's load all over his pretty blond frat boy face. "Yeah, faggot!" Dave moaned as he dribbled the last bit of come from his cock.

Both our guys now had raging hard-ons, and frankly, there was nothing I would have loved more than returning the favor of the hot blow job I had just received. But Dave and I returned to our serious-minded police roles. We put our own cocks away, pulled the two guys up off the floor, and let them try to put their stiff pricks back into their pants. "Now get out of here!" Dave yelled at them. The blond boy looked at him for a minute, come still streaking down his face. "Can't I wash my face off?" he said. "Go!" Dave yelled, and without hesitation, the blond boy dashed out of the bathroom and into the daylight.

The Latino guy was a little slower about it. "You know, Officer," he said, "I might be back here next Sunday at the same time, if you're interested."

"Get moving," I told him, but he could tell by my grin that I just might be back next Sunday after all. I watched his sweet ass as he walked out of the bathroom and headed for his car.

Dave and I turned to each other and just laughed. "All right!" he said. "That rocked!"

"Man, those guys were really into it! That blond boy really acted cherry!"

"Yeah, well," Dave said, "I don't think he was acting too hard."

"No way!"

Dave grinned. "I could just tell. I think he saw your message and thought this might be a good way to find out what sucking cock was all about."

"You have all the luck," I said to Dave. "So now what? Shall we wait in the bushes again? See if anyone else shows up?"

Dave shook his head. "Nah. Let's go home and get out of these uniforms."

And that's just what we did.

Technically Speaking

by Dominic Santi

Jeremy and I are not really brothers. OK, so the law says we're related now. Fuck that. I was in love with him long before his dad got into my mom's pants. I mean, what's not to love? He's a hunk, with a strong, smooth, distance-runner's body. He has short blond curls and a laugh that makes my balls tighten. And his thick, cut cock fits perfectly in my hand when I throw him on his back and fuck him into next week. We looked enough alike that our college friends called us "The Twins." But back then, we weren't related in anybody's book. We screwed our brains out freshman year. Who'd have guessed my roommate's divorced father would fall for my widowed mom on Parent's Weekend? I mean, shit like that only happens on TV, you know?

But Mom and "Dad" got married the next summer. Jeremy and I still needed to live at home rent free, while we worked three months of city road-crew jobs to pay our fall tuition. But what had seemed a recipe for disaster worked out pretty well when we discovered the only spare bedroom in the new house had just enough space for bunk beds. Things got even better when we figured out how to oil the bed frame so it wouldn't squeak.

Much better. Jeremy would brace his feet on the lower bunk, grab hold of the heavy steel top rail, and squat back to fuck his permanently horny hole over my full-to-bursting dick. Damn, his ass was hot. And it was always hungry. Every morning, his firm, tanned body sucked the come from my nuts before I was even all the way awake. I wasn't taking any chances with interruptions, either. I'd taken to locking the door when we went to bed at night, using the excuse that since it was too hot to sleep in clothes, we needed our privacy.

• • •

"You got a load for me, dude?"

I forced one eye open, staring out at the gray predawn light. I do not understand how anybody can be that cheerful in the morning, even when he knows he's going to get fucked.

"The alarm hasn't gone off yet, asshole." I pulled the sheet over my head and snuggled back down into the covers.

"Damn right, I'm an asshole." I heard a soft thump as Jeremy's bare feet hit the floor. "And my ass is all yours. Wanna lick it? Give it a big ol' tongue-fuck good-morning kiss?"

Like I could resist an offer like that. I groaned and peeked out—and came eye to eye with the winking shadow of the beautiful sphincter I knew and loved so well. Jeremy was bent almost in half, holding his firm white ass globes wide open, and thrusting his butt into my bunk.

"I'm waiting, hot stuff."

Without saying a word, I rolled to my side, leaned forward, and swiped my tongue up Jeremy's crack. He jerked, bumping his shoulder on the bed frame. Then he moaned and pushed his ass back at me.

"Do it again, Kyle. That felt good."

"Tasted good too," I said, inhaling deeply as his ass lips fluttered against my tongue. My dick strained up into the covers, morning-hard. Jeremy's musky odor was strong from sleep, and I indulged myself, licking until his skin was wet with my saliva and my cheeks were imprinted with the scent of his ass. His skin was sensitive, still lightly abraded from yesterday's marathon rim session with my unshaven face. When he was really wiggling, I pointed my tongue and tickled his sphincter.

"Fuck!"

He stifled his yelp fast, but I still tipped back, my ears cocked, listening for footsteps in the hall. There was nothing but the ticking of the clock and our heavy breathing, and the calls of a couple of idiot birds outside the window. I leaned forward again and licked a slow circle around his asshole.

"Keep it down," I growled.

"I really want to be fucked," he whispered, wiggling against me. "I mean it, Kyle. I really want your dick in me, dude."

"You're not going to get it if you wake up the whole house." My arm was going to sleep, and my back was getting stiff. "Move." With one final swipe, I followed Jeremy's ass out of the bed and stood up.

I stretched high, reaching up over my head, one arm at a time, while I arched my back and felt my cock swaying hard and full in front of me. The air was the perfect temperature for being naked. The sky had lightened almost imperceptibly, enough that I could make out the smooth cut of the washboard abs above Jeremy's upthrust, glistening cock. He walked over and wrapped his arms around me and squeezed.

"Jeez, I love you, Kyle."

I hugged him back, moaning as our cocks slid together. We both had raging morning boners. But to be honest, I was sort of glad he couldn't see my face right then. I was still getting used to him saying the *L* word. I liked it—a lot. And I was pretty sure I felt that way about him. But the whole idea scared the crap out of me. It was going to take a while for me to get the words out.

Jeremy had said he was willing to be patient. So I distracted myself, sucking his tongue into my mouth and rubbing our lips and tits and cocks together, running my hands over his back and arms to get the feel of him, and trembling when he did the same to me.

"I want you to eat my ass," he whispered, seducing my mouth until I thought I was going to faint. "I want your tongue to tickle my hole and your lips to press against mine, like this." He kissed me soft and wet and slow, gently at first, then harder, his cock sliding hot and silky over mine. "Then I want you to slide your tongue up my ass, just…like…this."

I shuddered against him as his tongue swept deep into my mouth.

"And when you're in me, I want you to pull me open with your fingers and lick so far inside me you can hardly breathe." I gasped as his finger firmly pulled my lower jaw down so that I was open to his tongue's assault. "I want you to suck my ass lips and slobber me full of spit and fuck me with your tongue until the only thing in the world I feel is the heat of your mouth on my hole." He ground his cock against mine. "In and out, lover, in and out..."

"Fuck, man," I whispered, panting against him, sucking softly on his lower lip as my cock slid on the precome drooling down his shaft. "But, dude, I'll chafe you again." I reached down to run my hands over the smooth, rounded curves of his ass. "If I rim you today, the whole inside of your crack is going to be sore. Again."

"I know that, dude." His grin moved over my lips. "I like it."

He thrust his hips against me, then reached down and grabbed our cocks in his fist, stroking them up and down in a slow, sure rhythm—one that was going to make me come in about two seconds flat. I shoved him away. "Turn around, fucker."

He grabbed the railing, then he lifted first one foot, then the other, onto the bottom mattress, spreading his legs wide as he pulled himself up and arched his ass out to me. "Come and get it."

I dropped to my knees in back of him, cupping his ass cheeks in my palms and slowly pulling the rounded globes apart. It was light enough now to see the dusky rose of his beautifully wrinkled pucker, and the fainter pink of his abraded ass skin. I leaned forward, nuzzling softly, burying myself again in the heavenly scent of Jeremy's ass. He stiffened and moaned. I did too, feeling the precome run down my shaft as I kissed deep into his crack.

"Tender?" I whispered.

"Fuck, yeah," he gasped. "Do it some more, dude!"

I did. Only this time I licked first, so his skin would be even more sensitized. And when his ass was wet with spit again, I once more rubbed my morning stubble gently over the sensitive skin surrounding his hole. Jeremy went nuts, clenching and shaking above me. I pulled his cheeks further apart, kissing his sphincter and letting everything I felt for him flow over my lips and into his delicately quivering anus. I licked and poked and swiped, fast and slow, up and down, back and forth, and in circles. I started and stopped until he was panting against me, arching back and shaking as his anal gate finally, slowly yielded. And when I felt the last remnants of resistance give way, I pressed my tongue past the smooth-walled ring guarding his hole and sank into the heat of Jeremy's ass.

"Kyle!" He breathed my name and his whole body stilled. I tongued him long and slow, nuzzling him as I came up for air, then sliding back in again, each swipe a little more easy as his ass ring opened to me. Burying my face deep, I reached between his legs and cupped his balls, squeezing them gently, rolling them around in my fingers as I slowly and rhythmically tongue-fucked him. Then I slid my palm up the underside of his rock-hard dick.

"Oh, God!" he whispered, barely breathing as I tongued his hole and jacked his precome-slicked cock.

"You taste good," I said, wrapping my hand around him and stroking up. I pushed my tongue back deep inside him and sucked his ass lips. He shuddered, and I felt the juice ooze out of his own wildly throbbing dick. In the distance I heard a shower starting down the hall. My hand stilled.

Jeremy stiffened slightly. I knew he'd heard it too. But all he did was press back against me.

"I meant what I said, Kyle. Fuck 'em if they don't like it."

He shook as I twisted my hand up and over the head of his dick. I'd decided I didn't care what anybody else thought of us, either. I sucked hard on his ass lips, jerking him off as I worked my way around his quivering pucker. Then I pushed my entire tongue inside him.

"Oh, fuck, man," he panted. "Do it now!"

I stood, my arms shaking as I kissed the back of his neck. My tongue was almost numb, and thick with the taste and smell of his ass. Jeremy cried out when I slid two fingers up him, then three.

"You're so nice and loose, babe." I reached into the nightstand drawer and pulled out a strip of condoms and the pump bottle of lube. Squirting a huge glob into my hand, I touched my fingertips to him. He jumped, first at the cold, then leaned forward on a moan as I stuffed the cool gel up his hole and a fourth finger slid easily into him.

"Just right," I whispered, gloving on a rubber and slathering myself full of lube. I moved in back of him, holding his hips as he positioned himself so that his ass lips rested against the tip of my cock. Then I waited, motionless, letting the pleasure wash through me in waves as Jeremy's asshole slowly and exquisitely kissed its way down my shaft.

As his heat enclosed me, I fought to keep from coming. I kept my hands on his hips, resting, using the connection only for balance. Jeremy fucked himself over my cock, jerking me off with his asshole until the jizz bubbled up out of my balls and all I could do was stand there, gasping and shaking, while I spurted hot come up his chute and Jeremy fucked me all the way through a mind-blinding orgasm. When I thought I couldn't stand it another second, he thrust back hard against me, grinding against my pelvis, his ass muscles clenching and spasming over my hypersensitive dick and the smell of his come gooping out onto the mattress filling my nostrils. He fell back against me, and I grabbed him hard around the waist, taking his weight and holding him close while he lowered his shaking legs to the floor and slowly let go of the railing. Strands of come dripped from his cock, as I pulled free and helped him ease into my bed. I threw the rubber and spooned up in back of him, pulling the covers over us.

"Fifteen minutes before the alarm goes off, lover boy, and Dad's in the bathroom. Let's get some sleep."

I think Jeremy was snoring before I'd finished speaking. I held him close and drifted off, thinking, *I could get used to this: love. I really could.* The next thing I knew, the alarm was ringing. And fuck, I had to piss. But I let Jeremy go first.

Street Smarts

by Pierce Lloyd

I found myself driving through an unfamiliar neighborhood as rain spattered my windshield. I had just finished an evening seminar titled "The Sky's The Limit: Changing Your Career Path, Changing Your Destiny." I do corporate training seminars, teaching mostly middle-aged men how to get ahead in business. It's a good gig to have at 26, and I was lucky to have found a lucrative niche in the corporate world.

Driving back from the seminar in the growing darkness, I feared I would get lost, which was ironic, because I had once lived just a few miles from where I now was. We moved a lot when I was growing up, and I spent the eighth through eleventh grades at a school on the other side of town. Unfortunately, my bad sense of direction, coupled with the fact that I had never owned a car in high school, now left me wandering in an unsavory neighborhood. So I pulled over to get my bearings...and realized I was already lost.

I decided to continue along my current route, figuring I would only get more confused if I turned down a side street. After a while, I spotted a bookstore that was still open. *Better ask directions,* I thought. *Only straight men are afraid to ask directions.*

It was a porn shop, of course; no other type of bookstore would be open in this neighborhood this late at night. As I parked, a couple of street youths—hustlers—whistled at me from the other side of the parking lot.

"Wanna play?" one of them called out.

Ignoring them, I entered the store, which had an extensive gay section. The hefty and friendly overnight clerk gave me detailed directions as to how to get back to my hotel. I wrote them down, not quite understanding, and thanked him.

After a few minor purchases, I was on my way back to the car. The hustlers looked bored, and I wondered how much business they got on a night like this. I scanned them, feeling a little guilty, until I saw a guy whom I found attractive. He had a small goatee and looked young. He had a very narrow waist and slight biceps. He wore wide-leg jeans and a baseball cap.

He noticed me checking him out and called out to me, "Like what you see?" He raised an eyebrow, and I couldn't help but feel sorry for him. I mean, I thought my job was tough.

"You know your way around this area?" I said.

"Well enough."

"I just need help getting back to my hotel. I can't find my way back."

"I can show you—" he said. "I can show you around. I can show you a good time. I can show you whatever you want for a hundred bucks."

"A hundred bucks is a little steep for me," I said, "especially since I just need a tour guide. Tell you what: I'll give you $50, and I'll buy you dinner. And don't tell me that's not the best you're gonna do tonight."

He grunted. "Sit-down dinner?"

"Sure. Sit-down dinner."

"Fine," he said, ambling up to my car.

"Whoa," I said. "Before you get in my car, I need to know that you're safe. Open up that backpack."

He grumbled, but complied. Inside his backpack he had an extra pair of clothes, some condoms, lube, and a worn copy of *The Catcher in the Rye.*

"Satisfied?" he said.

"Sure. Good book?" I asked.

"Got it from a trick," he said. "S'OK so far."

We got into the car.

"Got a name?" I asked my new guide.

"Chas," he said, enunciating the *ch* sound so it wouldn't sound like "jazz."

"Short for Charles?"

"Yeah, but I don't like Charles, and I don't like Charlie. So it's Chas."

"It has a nice ring to it."

Chas gave me directions, and we drove in silence for a while, until he spoke again.

"You know, you look kinda familiar. Have I been with you before?"

I assured him that he hadn't.

"Oh. Maybe I'm wrong."

Another bout of silence, then: "How about a hand job?"

"Do you want to give or receive?" I queried him, mostly jokingly. Mostly, because I have to admit that sex had crossed my mind. I'm not a saint. I had no explicit intention of getting into his pants when I asked him to get into my car, but at the same time, I had picked him because he was cute.

"I don't know. Either," he said. I guess it was a question he didn't get very often.

"No thanks. I'm fine for now."

"Whatever. You sure I don't know you?"

I looked at him. Nope, no recollection. Then I look more closely and realized that he was familiar to me. His face, his sneer…I'd seen him before.

And then I remembered him. I had gone to high school with him. It was a big school, and we hadn't really known each other. He was Charlie then: a jock without a personality.

"I think we went to high school together. Charlie?"

"It's Chas now. Where did you go to school? What's your name?"

I told him.

"Yeah, maybe…did I used to make fun of you?"

When Chas was still Charlie, his locker had been across the hall from mine. He was two years younger than me, but it didn't matter; he was still higher on the social pecking order. As I recalled, he and his friends had made fun of me once or twice.

"You used to call me a fag," I told him.

"I think you're right. I'm sorry if I did. I didn't mean anything by it."

"I know you didn't." I understood. When we're adolescents, we all do things that don't make sense, that we feel we have to do. I'm sure I had whole months in high school that I wasn't proud of.

We drove for a while. I got bored.

"Take off your pants," I told him. He looked at me warily.

"Look, you offered. And I'll pay you, and still buy you dinner."

"Yeah, yeah, OK," Chas said, sliding his jeans down quickly. His T-shirt was long enough to cover his genitals. His legs were pale and thin, but his thighs and calves had the tautness of a guy who spends a lot of time on his feet.

I reached over and lifted his shirt. His penis was flaccid, just a few inches long in this state. It was topped by a smattering of neatly trimmed brown pubic hair.

I rested a finger on his shaft, gently, and caressed him. He began to stir, slightly at first, then more and more as I teasingly kept touching him.

Driving became difficult as I rubbed Chas's cock more vigorously. Neither of us said a word, but soon he was sporting a raging erection. As his penis throbbed, I inched my fingers down to his ass, where I found the tender lips of his hole. I pushed one finger inside curiously, and Chas slid his hips forward to accommodate me. Soon I had plunged my index finger deep inside him, and he grunted at the sensation. I inserted another finger. His breathing grew heavier as my hand dry-fucked his warm hole.

As we neared the hotel, I stopped and put both hands on the steering wheel.

"Who's the fag now?" I asked. It came out a little nastier than I had intended.

Chas snorted and said, "Shut up." Sensing that I was done with my game, he pulled his pants back up, although his hard-on was still pretty evident through his jeans.

Dinner at the hotel restaurant started with the two of us silent. As Chas ate, however, he became talkative, and I soon learned more about him. He had gotten into drugs in high school and avoided college. After a while, his parents ordered him to leave their house, which he did. He started turning tricks shortly thereafter.

Now, he claimed, he had been sober for two months. He lived in an apartment with four other guys.

"It's kinda crowded, so we sleep in shifts. It's all right for me, I guess, 'cause I work nights," he said.

When dinner was over, we both looked around kind of hesitantly.

"Hey, bud, I owe you some money," I said. "Let's not settle our debts here. Why don't you come on up? You can freshen up, maybe use the shower if you want."

Chas and I retired to my room, where he accepted my offer of a hot shower. When he came out, wrapped in a hotel towel and looking just a bit more appealing now that he was fresh scrubbed, I handed him a $50 bill.

"Here ya go," I said.

"Thanks." He put the money in his shoe.

"Listen..." I began, "you can crash here if you want to. I mean, it's a terrible night out. You might as well get some sleep."

"Serious?"

"Sure." I added, "Watch some cable if you want. I'm going to take a shower."

When I finished, I half-expected him to have run out with my luggage. He hadn't, though. Instead, he was curled up under the covers, asleep.

I put on a pair of boxers and slipped into bed. Chas awoke and whirled around. I saw that he was sleeping in the nude.

"A little edgy?" I smiled.

"A little."

Once I was settled in, he sidled up next to me and put an arm around me.

"Hey, it's OK," I said. "We don't have to—"

He shushed me.

"Will you hold me? It's been a long time since I've fallen asleep with somebody holding me." So we spooned, his back to my chest, and in that position we drifted off to sleep.

I woke a few hours later, my arm slightly numb and my cock stiff from a piss hard-on. I gently extracted myself from the bed and crept to the bathroom. When I returned, still half-hard, I tried to approximate the position I had been in before.

Chas stirred. "You have a hard-on?" he asked, sliding his hand up my leg to my penis, which responded by becoming fully erect again. He spun around in bed, and I felt his erection rub my own. "Me too." He smiled.

I smiled too, saying nothing, and felt my boxers sliding down my legs. Chas disappeared beneath the covers, and I felt his lips embrace my cock.

Nothing had ever felt like this before. I vacillated between moaning and making mental notes on how to improve my cocksucking skills. Suddenly, Chas stopped sucking me; moments later, his lips were on my ass.

I had never been rimmed before, and didn't know that it could feel like this. I bit into the blanket in front of me as Chas's lips formed a seal around my asshole and his tongue worked its way up into my crevice.

What am I doing? The thought entered my head and was then quickly forgotten. Chas emerged from under the blankets and kissed me, giggling, as I realized he was letting me taste my ass on his lips. I could feel his cock, hard and urgent against my abdomen. I put my arms around him and pulled him to me.

Soon I eased a curious finger down his back and into his fuzzy butt crack, where I began to play with his asshole. I pressed, and found his ass once again yielding.

"Aw yeah, that's it..." Chas said in a throaty voice.

"You don't have to talk dirty for me, Chas," I said. He smiled.

"So noted. Awww yeah..." he moaned as I continued fingering his ass.

After a few minutes of hot and heavy making out and finger-fucking, Chas spun around toward me. He didn't have to tell me what to do next.

"You want it in you, don't you?" I asked. As a response, he slid his crack up and down against my cock. Reaching into his bag, which was on the floor next to the bed, Chas retrieved a condom and some lube and handed them back to me.

I'm not terribly well-hung, but the head of my cock is fairly thick. I eased it into his opening, and then tried to nudge it carefully past his limber sphincter. He still let out a gasp, but was soon welcoming my whole shaft into his butt.

"Yeah, that's it," he sighed.

A minute later, I was fucking him. It took me a moment to get in stride, as I contemplated for a second the absurdity of the situation.

Here I was with a former classmate turned prostitute, and I was having the time of my life. It was unquestionably the most erotic sex I had ever had, partly because I could now clearly remember lusting after Chas when I had known him as Charlie.

To hell with memories. Living in the moment was just as much fun, and the way Chas's ass gripped my cock was definitely better than any memory. I plunged in as deep as I could, over and over. I reached around his tight abs and grasped his hard cock, stroking it with my clenched fist.

"Oh, babe, I'm too sensitive," he gasped. "Gotta slow down."

I tried, honestly I did, to temper the pace with which I manhandled his meat. But his engorged prick must have been pretty damn near close to exploding already, because within seconds he was spasming in my hand.

"Unnngghhhh..." he moaned, as I felt spurt after spurt of semen flood past my fingertips. Within seconds, the sheet beneath us was covered with a warm, milky puddle.

Chas seemed exhausted for half a second, then devoted all of his energies to making me come. He arched his back and tightened his butt's hold on my cock as I tried to pound into him as forcefully as I could. I wanted to hold out, but I was no match for his increased friction, and I soon blew my load within him.

We collapsed, spent, and kissed briefly before drifting off to sleep.

When I awoke, groggy, Chas was not in bed next to me. I worried that perhaps he had gotten up and slipped off with my wallet and watch...but then he emerged from the bathroom, freshly showered again.

He looked sheepish.

"Good morning," he said.

"Morning," I replied.

He sat on the bed and dressed, then stood up.

"I want to give you this," he said, handing me the money I had given him the previous night. "I...it's stupid, but I make it a rule not to take money from friends."

I looked at him. "You're right," I said after a moment. "We are friends."

He smiled, about to say something.

"However," I said, pressing the money back into his palm, "this is cash I agreed to pay you to help me with directions. Whatever happened after that, well, if you don't want to charge me...that's your loss." I winked.

He blushed. "Thanks, I guess." He continued, "I gotta head out...I'm supposed to meet a friend."

I nodded. "Is this the part where I ask you if this is really what you want to do with your life?"

"I think this is that part, yeah," he said with a smirk. "And the answer is no. But right now I gotta do what it takes to survive."

I nodded again. "I want you to contact me," I said as I gave him my card, "for more than one reason. Of course, I'd like to see you again. But more importantly, I'm an expert at helping people find better jobs. That's what I do for a living."

"Really?" he asked. "No kidding?"

"Funny how things work out, isn't it?" I said.

"Yeah," he said, still smirking. "Funny."

Almost Better Than Sex

by Simon Sheppard

I'd just been stood up by another liar from AOL.

Well, maybe *liar* is too strong a word...

I'd just been stood up by another tweaked-out, game-playing asshole shitbag from AOL. It was 1 A.M., and I was horny, itching to go out and pound some butt. So when the guy who said he'd phone me after I signed off *didn't* phone me—when the number *he'd* given *me* turned out to be a recorded message about transit information—I was pissed off. Pissed off with a hard-on. The first few months I'd been online, I'd taken this sort of thing personally—or at least as evidence of the general decline of truth and morality in late capitalist culture. Now I realized it was just the ways things were. But it was damned annoying nonetheless.

I signed back on. At 1 A.M. on a weeknight, the online community, such as it is, consists largely of the sexually desperate, the chemically stimulated, and guppies in pajamas brushing their teeth in anticipation of another day of designing software—the better to keep their Grand Cherokees purring on down the freeway. It's the time of night when hope springs eternal, only to bang its head against the virtual wall. I'd already opened Netscape and moseyed on over to my favorite porn Web site, anticipating a quick, half-hearted wank into a paper towel, to be followed by a deep and dreamless sleep.

I was, though, also still parked in one of the M4M chat rooms, hoping my affair with some porn star's GIFs would be interrupted by the chime of an Instant Message. It was: "Hello, sir."

My cruising profile instructs boys to call me "sir." OK, like any minor perversion, it probably seems silly to guys who aren't into it, but I like it. And boys do too.

His screen name was unfamiliar and utterly cryptic. I opened the Get Profile window, typed his name in, and clicked. His profile was nondescript as well.

"Sir?"

"I'm here, boy," I typed. "Age?" I wasn't about to get busted for inadvertently chatting with jailbait.

"Eighteen," he returned.

Well, *close* to jailbait.

"And what are you into?"

The answer came up in the little window: "Following orders."

My dick, which had been half-deflated from frustration, sprang smartly to attention. "You looking to play now?" I typed out.

"Yes."

"You looking to go out or stay in?"

"I'm in Hoboken."

New Jersey was a mere 3,000 miles away.

"I want you to tell me," he continued, "what to do, and I'll do it and send pictures of it to you while we chat."

I didn't have one of those CUseeMe setups that makes it possible to send blurry, jerky video from one computer to another, so his idea suited me just fine. "Yes," I typed, somewhat dubious. "OK."

"You've got mail," his next message read.

The E-mail consisted of a photo divided into four smaller pictures. The first two shots were of his dick: in one pic, half-hard; in the other, fully erect and tied up with a piece of cord around the base. It was a nice dick. Now, I know that just what constitutes a "nice dick" is pretty much indefinable, but let's face it, we all know one when we see one. He'd clipped his body hair really short and shaved around his cock and balls. Not my favorite look, but on him it looked good.

The lower left photo featured a neatly laid-out array of sex toys: three dildos of varying size, two flesh-colored, one bright red; a cock ring; a bunch of clothespins; several cords; and most suggestive of all, a disposable diaper. And the bottom right picture was even more well-arranged—nine small numbered panels, each containing a different style of underwear: briefs, boxers, jockstraps, a dance belt. I had to hand it to the kid: He was organized.

"So tell me what you want me to do."

I spit in my hand and started stroking. I was more than ready to be a nasty motherfucker, but if there's one thing I've learned about sex, it's that pacing is important. I decided to start slow. "Put on number 6," I commanded.

"Yes, sir." There was a longish pause.

You've got mail, my computer notified me.

I opened the message he'd sent and downloaded the file: a nice-looking torso wearing translucent white briefs that just barely hid a prominent erection.

"Nice," I typed. "Now wet them down." I figured the picture with briefs could have been anyone and come from anywhere. But if he sent me a picture on command, he was on the level.

"With piss, sir?" he asked.

"Yes." While I waited, I spit on my hand again and massaged my hard-on.

You've got mail.

He'd wet his briefs, all right. A damp stain, spreading from his cock head, rendered the cloth transparent. This was getting good. I thought so, and my dick thought so too.

"Take off the briefs and show me your dick, boy."

In a minute, a picture of his hard-on, lazing stiffly against his thigh, appeared on my screen. Not a huge dick, which was fine with me. Just handsome and juicy-looking and ready to be shoved around.

"Take a cord and tie up your dick and balls."

In less than a minute I could see that he had. He'd done a so-so job of dick bondage; I could have done better, made it prettier, but his shaft was bulging now, and his hairless ball sac was nicely stretched out.

"Show me your hole."

You've got mail. A shot from behind, his fingertips spreading his hole wide. It was one of those Biology 101 shots, the kind where you can see past the sphincter to the red wetness inside. Way back in my youth, when I first saw split-beaver shots in straight porn magazines, I thought they were gross. Now, staring up into a boy's vulnerable insides, I almost came.

"Put a dildo in there."

"Which one, sir?"

"Start with the small one, the red one."

The pacing of all this was immaculate. A command, a minute of jacking-off while I waited to be obeyed, then the results appearing on my screen.

New picture: his ass from behind again. His butt was hairy, but he'd shaved around the crack, and in the middle of the naked flesh, he was pressing the dildo into himself. The base was red jelly against his smooth young flesh—like a really perverted Gummi Bear. I had to take my hand off my dick; coming now was unthinkable. Not when I had more to command him to do, limits to push.

The doorbell rang. It was 2 in the fucking morning. *Who the fuck could it be, a neighborhood drunk?* I wondered. Fuck it, whoever it was would just have to go away. I just hoped it wasn't an emergency. Whatever. I wasn't going to call a halt to this, not even if the house was burning down.

"You still playing with the dildo?" I asked the boy.

"Yes, sir. Is that OK?"

"Take it out and suck it clean. Let me see it in your mouth."

He typed back, "I can't show you my face."

"Just your mouth. Now."

"Yes, sir."

A profile from chin to nostrils appeared on my screen. Nice mouth, face just a bit fleshy, apparently. Pretty lips, wrapped around a dirty dildo. I didn't have to touch myself to stay hard. I'd found myself a kinky boy. Or, rather, he'd found me.

"Now show me your pussy again," I told him.

Seconds later the boy's shaved ass reappeared on the screen, a little the worse for wear. His hole was stretched wide open and wasn't altogether clean. *This is incredible,* I thought. *I should write a story about it.*

I gave my dick a tug, squeezed at the tip till I sent myself to the brink of orgasm, then backed off.

"Are enjoying this, you sick pig?"

"Yes, Daddy."

"Good boy. Now I want you to..." I typed, and the computer crashed.

Damn, damn, damn! My Mac had frozen, and I had to do a hard restart, wait for the extensions to load, launch AOL, sign on...talk about coitus interruptus!

Finally back online, I brought up an INSTANT MESSAGE window, typed out "Sorry, crashed," and clicked on SEND.

An AOL window brought the bad news: "Member is not currently online."

Fuck! He probably figured I'd flaked, and gone off to clean up and jack off. Oh, well. At least he wasn't playing online with somebody else. He might be a perverted, exhibitionistic pussyboy, but at least he wasn't a slut.

My computer chimed at me. An INSTANT MESSAGE window appeared. "Sorry, sir, I got bumped." Par for the online course, but now we were back in business.

I was in the mood to have him hurt a bit for me.

"Those clothespins?" I asked.

"Yes, Daddy?"

"I want you to use them."

"Yes, Daddy."

"Put one on each tit and show me."

His chest was well-built, not quite lean, with close-trimmed hair. Perfect. A clothespin was fastened to each nipple, jutting outward. I was imagining what he was feeling, all the way across the country, as the wooden clothespins chomped down into his tender flesh, initial discomfort changing to more focused pain, then intense, searing sensation, then something else.

"Now your dick. Put clothespins on your dick. Start with your ball sac."

"Yes, sir."

There was a longer pause than usual. I guess he was adjusting the clothespins over the stretched flesh of his sac. Then a message, not a pic: "Daddy?"

"Yes?"

"Where on my dick?"

I told him to put a clothespin where the base of his dick met his sac, then start fastening more up the underside of his cock, stretching out the delicate flesh, clamping the pins down. I loved this; it was delicious.

Eventually, the next GIF came—a nice angle: him lying back, shot from below. At the top of the frame, the clothespins were still on his tits. Below closer up, on his dick and balls, he'd clamped three clothespins on the sac, four more running up the shaft. What a fine lad.

"It hurts, Daddy."

"I know. Have you done this before?"

"No," he said. I almost came.

I looked at the little clock on the upper right of the screen. It was getting late. But I was unwilling to give this up. Somewhere across the continent, in frozen moments of time, a boy was somehow giving himself to me. One of the things I usually like about amateur porn is the giveaway detail: the glimpse of work stacked up on a computer table; an unfortunate choice of carpets or drapes; even in some precious instances a bookshelf, the exhibitionist's choice of reading matter open to analysis. This boy's photos, though, were tightly cropped. There was no world outside the frame, nothing but the electronic sheen of flesh—although turned bluish by my monitor, delectable nonetheless. Naked flesh offered up to me.

"Daddy? Sir?" he said, bringing me out of my thoughts.

"Yes?"

"Are you still there?"

"Sorry, yes."

"What do you want me to do next?"

"Show me your face."

A pause, a hesitation. Then a polite refusal. And I realized he'd made the right choice, even if for the wrong reasons. Maybe all he wanted was the safety of anonymity, but that anonymity was a gift for me. As long as he remained faceless, featureless, he could be damn near anyone, and that meant he could be everyone, everyone I'd ever desired or come on to or fucked. He was, in some utterly cyber-erotic fashion, the embodiment of desire, only he surely didn't know that, and if I'd told him, he might have laughed at my pretentiousness and offered to stick the dildo back up his ass.

"Stick a dildo back up your ass."

"Which dildo?"

"The big one."

The next picture that appeared on my screen showed his shaved asshole stretched around a larger, flesh-colored toy. His dick, still covered by clothespins, stood straight up. Nice.

"Nice," I let him know.

"Now what?"

Now what, indeed. If this were the real world, we might have come by now. We'd be wiping up, making small talk...about computers probably. If he was like too many young guys, he might be heading out to the back porch for a cigarette. Instead, we each were in ultimate control of our own lusts. There would be no surprise touch of his hand on my dick, a touch that would send me spiraling over the brink of orgasm. There would be no postcoital moment when our eyes accidentally meet. Here in electronic space, despite his apparent surrender of control, despite my losing my head over him—or rather over the pixels that defined his presence—we each had only to flick a button for the whole thing to end.

And it was getting very, very late.

I thought about it, then typed out, "I want you to come."

"But, sir, can't we do this longer?"

"Come."

"Please?"

"Now. And show me."

I planned to make myself spurt the moment I saw the pic of jizz on his belly. I stroked gently, delaying the release. And then the bedroom door opened. My boyfriend, his voice as bleary as his eyes, stuck his head through the living room door. "You still up?" he asked.

"Yeah. I'll come to bed soon."

He glanced down at my hand...my dick. "Slut." He smiled and tottered off to the bathroom for a pee.

When he was safely back in bed, I checked my mailbox, opened the E-mail titled "Last One," clicked DOWNLOAD NOW, grabbed the paper towel I'd left beside the mousepad, and watched as his picture opened. He'd taken the clothespins off his dick but added two to his balls—a fan of five. His hand was still on his dick, obscuring most of the shaft, leaving the head visible. And just slightly out of focus, come was splashed across his torso, all the way up to one of his clothespinned nipples. I imagined the ocean smell, the way his juice was viscously dripping down over his bare flesh. And I shot off, hard and long, into Bounty, the quicker picker-upper.

"Thanks," I typed out, adding a little smiley-face: :-)

"No, thank *you,* sir."

"What's your name?"

"Jason," he typed. Maybe it was, and maybe it wasn't.

"I'm Simon. I'll add you to my Buddy List."

"And you're on mine," he said.

"Gotta get to bed," I told him. "Thanks again."

"No problem. My pleasure. Bye."

"Bye." And I signed off, the computer saying *Goodbye* to me as well.

I finished wiping off my dick and used my right hand, the clean one, to click the mouse to shut down.

The base-level directory on my hard disk was still corrupted. I would be short of sleep the next day. Somewhere on the East Coast, a boy was wiping up and cleaning off his toys, and I would never see his face. The hard disk purred to a stop. The computer went silent. The screen went dark.

I threw the power switch on the surge protector and headed off to a deep and dreamless sleep.

Groovy Gang Bang

by Lance Rush

The invitation read: "Break out your faded jeans, tie-dyed tees, and bandannas. Step into those old desert boots or sandals, and prepare for a walk on the wild side."

The guy throwing this soiree was one of my more creative friends from work. Once I arrived, I felt stranded in the scenery of an old episode of *Rowan and Martin's Laugh-In*—psychedelic pinks, electric blues, lava lamps, Peter Max posters, Beatles' music cut with Motown, the stink of patchouli incense—and everyone walked around saying "Groovy!" Hot guys were sweating to the oldies or sitting on the floor in the lotus position, smoking funny cigarettes.

Well into the night, the crowd became a meat market, and the meat being marketed was even more evident in retro-tight jeans. A scruffy, goateed, longhaired hippie shot me the spacey eye as he rubbed a long Levi's-shrouded schlong. Then I locked eyes with a big muscular dude in hurt-me-tight hip-huggers.The next time he sauntered by, he purposely rubbed against my ass. I turned. He grinned and said, "Pretty trippy party, isn't it?"

"Yeah. I guess it is," I said, noticing that several men were heading into separate rooms.

"Hey. My name's Peter," the stocky stud said, boldly stroking his thick, foreboding-looking namesake.

"I'm sure it is," I said. "I'm Kevin."

Unlike most guys from the '60s, there wasn't a scrawny bone in Peter's body. I dug his deep-brown hooded eyes and crooked dick of a nose. I figured it had been banged around in a street fight, a scrimmage, or something equally hot and disfiguring. His neck was thick as a halfback's, as was his chest, and his legs were fucking enormous.

If I could've chosen any stud in the place, it would've been him, or maybe that longhaired, apparently long-donged hippie dude who resembled a lean Hell's Angel. When he noticed Peter and me talking, he gave me the evil eye, as if I was about to cheat on him. Actually, I was, because just then Big Peter leaned in, fellatio-close, and said, "Let's go upstairs. I hear the water bed's *very* groovy."

He gestured to the bulge in those hip-huggers, then made his cock jump. The decision was made—upstairs it was!

I got a heaping eyeful of his plump, rounded ass as he climbed the stairs. His hugely inflated thighs excited me. He walked with the jock-strutting confidence of a man used to people moving the hell out of his way.

Past the winding stairs, down the paisley hallway, we made it into a lavender psychedelic room. Inside, a king-size water bed with a large mirror looming overhead awaited us. The room smelled like fresh man-sex.

Peter shot me a hot sexy stare as he ran his hand along his barrel chest. I wondered what vanity stimulant he was on that made him keep touching himself. He pinched the plump nipples under his tee and massaged the coarse nature trail running down his belly. He was really into the whole self-appreciation trip, so I decided I'd appreciate him too. I gripped his arms, traced the hard contours of his chest, and bit down on one nipple to see how he'd react.

He *reacted* by slamming his bulk into me and holding my head to his barrel chest. I could almost smell his beef marinating under those jeans. He pushed me downward, and my cheek lay against the thin warm shield of denim. I let my tongue roam the growing shape of his swelling cock. I dove between his strapping legs and rattled along the balls simmering under sweaty denim. Peter groaned, then suddenly bucked his hips impatiently.

"Go on, man. Whip it out!" he taunted. "Tonight's theme is 'Free Love,'" he reminded me.

Taking his cue, I unzipped him. Reaching deep inside those hip-huggers, I wrestled his fleshy pole through the narrow opening. Oh, shit! That fucker sprang forth—big, thick, and buoyant with a large club-like head.

He made it bounce at my lips, and I darted my tongue along the dense bulbous crest. Oh! The thick salty wedge hit my tongue with a *whomp!* He pushed, forcing my throat to flex, and I attacked with a greedy slurp. Mmm! But sucking Peter's monstrous dick was like trying to suck my own fist! Slobber slid down his nuts as he ground that fat cockmeat against my lips. I could feel its impressive throb, feel how the veins pulsated as I gobbled all I possibly could.

Then, all of the sudden another voice piped into the room: "So you like big men, huh?"

I turned, and standing at the door was that lean, tall, blond hippie dude from downstairs! He stood watching us, long legs spread, belt buckle dangling as he rubbed down his long lean thigh.

"Is he any good?" he inquired with a rough edge.

"Fucking fantastic!" Peter replied. "Far-fuckin'-out! You wanna watch or play?" Peter asked. Then he turned to me. "Oh, by the way, this is my lover David."

During that impromptu intro, Peter never stopped thrusting his fat cock down my throat.

David sauntered over and stood beside us. His growing meat resembled a freaking hammer in his jeans. I shoved my hand down his pants. Past his scratchy ride of cock hair throbbed his long, veiny dagger of a dick, hardening as my fingers prowled. I jerked the shaft slowly through his pants, all the while still sucking Peter's rod.

David unbuttoned his shirt. He had a defined and wiry build. His hard pecs pitched with willful breathing. Releasing Peter for a moment, I leaned up and munched on David's tit. It grew full and hot, as my tongue encircled it. He yanked down his baggy jeans, and with a pop, his long stretch of uncut meat stabbed the air. I raked its slimy hood, and a musk of sex emanated from its folds. I stepped back to witness both cocks. David's was longer, Peter's was thicker, and both those fuckers were throbbing.

"Go ahead and blow him!" Peter said. "I don't mind. I'm sure David won't. Go on, take care of my man." Peter personally slid a rubber down his lover's long, rigid dick.

It pulsated mightily. I pumped the bottom half. Come-heavy balls swung back and forth as I grabbed his pitching ass. Taking his whopper into my lips, I sucked it slow and evenly. It seemed no matter what I did, David's long, vein-riddled cock kept lengthening down my gullet.

"Yeah! Suck my big crooked dick, man!" David said. "Suck the fucking crook out of it!"

"Take all 11 inches down, if you can," Peter said.

David dick-fed me inch by inch as I clutched his slowly pumping ass, which was firm and warm and starting to sweat. Peter reached down and slowly stroked my hard dick, which by then was rearing up like a fucking cobra! He got a rubber from the candy dish and quickly rolled it onto my cock. David kept pushing his long pipe through the snatch of my lips, and soon he commenced face-fucking me with vengeance. For all my fevered slurping, I couldn't deep-throat the fucker. The one time I tried, that bastard held me to a gag!

"Stop showing off! No need to choke him!" Peter admonished, licking my balls between strokes, and slapping his damp, fat monster cock to my thigh.

"Man! This guy is great! Look at him almost get it down," David groaned, as he pumped my throat with inspired vigor. Then he tumbled on top of me. We both landed on the buoyant bed, his body smothering me as I sucked.

Flowing to the liquid motion of the mattress, David straddled my face and commenced to hump. Below me, Big Peter was licking, lacquering, swinging on my schlong. Somehow between sucks we formed a daisy chain, and together we writhed, groaned, and floated with amazing fluidity. Oh! This trip was growing groovier!

Peter's broad thighs formed gigantic tanned mountains, and his chunky cock was the summit. I scaled the fat shaft, up its widened base, prowling every vein all the way to the crest, and then I gobbled. The more I sucked, the thicker his fucktool grew. The more David sucked me, the harder I felt the push of come rising up my balls. Together we were a writhing bundle of hard throttling cocks, clapping balls, and gyrating asses.

Then, all at once, our suction ceased. Shaking his fat, hot, seductive cock my way, Peter announced, "Time for you get fucked, Kevin."

"Yeah. Look at his freakin' dick, man. He's hot for it!" David said.

Big Peter rose, jeans still plastered around his mighty calves as he snatched a handful of rubbers. Peering at my butt like an ass-hungry carnivore, he wrestled a blue ribbed one down his big fat vertical dick. From the speakers came the sounds of "Devil with A Blue Dress On" just as Peter tapped that wide blue-hued wedge in his fist.

Lanky David stood by in a haze, slowly stroking his schlong.

"Now, spread that ass for me. Mmm. It's nice," Peter said. Then, in a smooth tackling motion, he pulled my legs behind my head. All at once, he stunned me as his tongue cut a path through my hairless crack. Oh! I trembled as he ferociously attacked my bud, holding me to a shiver. He had me pinned down, and the cock of his tongue was bound and determined to rim deeper.

"Yes. Oh, yes. That's it! Lick it, man! Oh, that feels fantastic!" I howled.

"Go for it, Pete" David coached. "Lick that hot butt hole! Oh, yeah. Tear it up!"

My inflamed dick stabbed the air. Glancing up, Peter asked, "Is it good? Like it? You want more, or are you ready for my fuck?"

"Yeah. Oh shit, yeah, dude! Go ahead. Fuck me with that thing!"

I lay back on the water bed, rippling, flowing, ready to have the stuffing fucked out of me. Peter pushed my legs to the side. He aimed that enlarged pipe to my chute, and that fiercely bloated head and long thick steely shaft burst through. Oh! My butt hole registered every inch of his lunge as my eyes widened with shock

"Shit, man!" I gasped. "You got a fucking thick cock!"

Peter squeezed my cheeks tight around his pole as it surged thicker and stiffer up my ass. His rhythm slowly built. Pulling back and lunging, his fat cock blasted up my gut—forcefully!

David jumped in, swinging his dangling prick in my face, aiming it to my lips. Soon, David was driving that fucking pipe down my gulping throat.

Peter's drilling dick began to wallop my ass so hard, I could feel my fucking colon throb! Shit! With those two big cocks rammed in my two horny holes, my boiling load was imminent.

But as I took one by ass, one by mouth, and our party was rocking like that freaking bed, I had one breathless request: "O-O-OK, Peter. I, wanna, fuck, you, now," I huffed.

"Far-out! He pitches too!" David said, slapping his schlong to my face.

As the song "Respect" wailed "Sock it to me, sock it to me, sock it to me," Peter began rapidly socking it to me. His brutishly fat dick continued to torpedo up my chute. I figured he hadn't heard me. With one sharp thud, he stuffed me with so much cock that I bellowed "Enough!"

Then suddenly, with a tug, he pulled his inflamed dick from my deepest bowel. I felt relieved. Peter looked at David, who shrugged. Both decided I was worthy of fucking that brawny piece of ass.

"Go on. Have at it," David said. "Fuck my man's hot ass."

Shit! I'd never seen a more sumptuously rounded butt. Spreading a dollop of lube along its perfect seam, I couldn't believe I'd soon be sinking inside the pucker of an ass so fine. Peter got on his hands and knees, his outrageously buffed sinews flexed everywhere I looked. My cock head pierced his small pink slit, pushing through the tightest tunnel. But once inside, his bunghole accommodated my swollen cock with ease. Those awesome thighs tightened, and his asshole snatched me. Oh! His constricting grip left me groaning.

"Go ahead, man. Give it to him," David urged, as Peter slowly wound his ass around.

With that invitation, I commenced fucking Peter with quick stabbing lunges. The bed swayed and ebbed around us. Peter's accepting walls absorbed my thrusts. His ass was incredible. So deep and pliant, it settled into my fluid friction. David jerked off wildly as I kept pounding my hot cock up his lover's tight man-cunt. Peter fell forward, slamming his monster appendage into the undulating mattress. I went deeper, lurching my dick full-speed, as Peter writhed and bellowed, "Aw! *Damn!* Now you're fuckin', man! Do it. Plow it. Ride me! More! I can take it!"

"Nothing beats a hunky whore, huh?!" David gloated. That's when he laid his sweating skull to my back and squeezed my nipples hard, and I knew that long-dicked motherfucker was going to have at it.

"You still got a rubber on that thing?" I asked, still plowing inside Peter's hot ass.

"I got *two* on, 'cause when I fuck a man, I get wild."

That was all he said. Next came the head of David's long hippie dick ripping through me! Oh! The steely hard probe of his shaft followed. As he sunk all 11 horny inches through my ass, I groaned in anguish, then lost control.

"Oh! Aw! Shit! Take it easy back there!"

With the steady puncture of his spike ramming my asshole, I was losing my way with Peter. Through deep restless breaths, I tried to relax my violated sphincter. But David pulled back and threw me a violent fuck!

"Far-out!" both bellowed, as David plunged that long, hard dick inside my anus, then pulled it *far out!* It was hard to move with that dong battling up my ass. Then Peter rose to his hands and knees, giving me better access. I jabbed him deeper as David held my cheeks higher, and that dick hit it so hard, I thought we'd kill the fucking bed!

"Fuck him! Blast that dick up his tight ass." David demanded of me as he blasted his dick up mine. Below, Peter was beginning squirm. I grabbed his fat prick and commenced to jerking that big hot fucker until it squirted like a Super Soaker!

"That's right. Fuck him! Beat him off! He loves it!" David insisted as his lover's jizz slopped my fist.

That was it. With one last melding thrust, I jammed deep, pulled out, ripped off the safe, and jism sprinted from my dick, spraying Peter's rollicking cheeks. Then David yanked his schlong from my battered chute and scalded my rump in hot ropes of ball lava.

"Shit! You guys are too much! Fuckin' far-out!" I panted.

It had been one strenuous party in that psychedelic room, and that night we all managed to get our groove on. Far-out!

Whatever Happened to…?
by M. Christian

Betty used to be someone.

If she had an audience—pretty rare these days—she'd say, "I used to be Bouncin' Betty," and then she'd wait for remembrance to sweep across their faces (or, more likely, face). If none came, she would prompt, "*The* Bouncin' Betty, Dame of the Chateau, Queen of Halloween. Had my own disc: *Betty Got Back*. They played it looped at Folsom and Gay Day." Then she'd pull out her scrapbook. "This is a picture of me with Pussy; we played together the whole day. She said I was the best she'd ever seen. This is me at the Empress Ball. Here I am at Wigstock. I took first prize two years running; my trophy's over there on the mantle." On and on.

"Used to love to hit the ladies' johns around the city, especially on Folsom, Halloween, or Pride. Loved it! The *Weekly* even did a spot on me. Hang on, it's around here somewhere.... Ha! Here it is: 'King of the Queens.' Don't care for the title much, but I like the article. It even talks about the time I flashed the Republican Women's Auxiliary. Remember that? Well, darlin', they had this big hullaballo about bullshit family values, so I got all Betty'd up and walked right into their meeting, asking if I could use their damned ladies' room. Well, they got all offended and said it was 'for ladies only,' so I lifted my skirt and showed them my Special Surprise. I'd shaved my—well, you know, *organ*—and then had an artiste friend paint on a pussy: slit, clit, and all. So I tucked and flashed them. You should've seen their faces. Hit the fucking floor—excuse the unladylike word. But they did! They were so flabbergasted, they even let me use their ladies' room. Took a mean ol' nasty dump in there too.

Stunk up the place something awful." On and on.

Most people were polite. But eventually their eyes would glaze over, and they'd start to sneak covert, then not so covert, glances at their watches. Others heeded the rumors and avoided her parlor altogether.

Sitting in her Victorian front room, Betty smoothed her white panty hose, straightened her little-girl pink pinafore, rubbed a smudge off her (now) spotless white patent leathers, fluffed her ruffles, and ran hesitant, slightly shaking fingers, through her cascades of golden wig curls. Catching sight of the wrinkled face hiding beneath her rouged and painted face in her antique dressing mirror, she thought with a sigh, *The only thing worse than an ex-drag queen is an* old *ex-drag queen.*

"Here comes Mommy!"

Dressed especially for Betty (perfect glossy stilettos, antique-style white garters and hose, straight white A-line skirt, cat's-eye glasses and a high, but not too high, beehive wig), Joan came in, catching Betty leafing through her scrapbook and lingering misty-eyed over wrinkled flyers and faded clippings—as if her constant rereading of them had worn away the ink. Tapping Betty on the shoulder, she said, "Time to put those things away, dear," with venom laced into the sugar words.

When Betty didn't close her fragile scrapbook quickly enough, Joan reached down, yanked up Betty's pink pinafore, and attached two nasty plastic clothespins to her tiny nipples.

• • •

Hissing against the sudden pain, Betty did as she was told, moving carefully against the tugging ache from her nipples and pushing back against the cloth back of her wheelchair. Involuntarily, her legs kicked out and knocked—but not over—the table. Realizing what she'd done, she snapped her eyes open and quickly scanned to make sure the breakfast things hadn't spilled onto her precious scrapbook. Luckily, the only spill was the coffee, and it had just made a muddy pool on its saucer.

"Next time," Joan said, kneeling and bouncing the clothespins up and down, "maybe you'll pay attention when I'm talking to you."

"Yes, Mommy."

Joan had never gotten to be someone.

Oh, sure, she had a great figure, perfectly made for pumps, sequins, feathers, and the proper but not extreme use of a girdle. But Joan had...other talents. Ones that didn't jibe with the femme mystique she could wear so well. At first, when she and Betty were an infant "item" in the drag scene, her talents were the cause of snickers and gossip: Betty tagging along on the arm of the big girl with the scary reputation and inclinations. They didn't snigger long, though. Not when talk of Joan's talents went from giggly rumors to awed worship. For a brief while (though Betty would never admit it) Joan's infamy had eclipsed Betty's glamorous fame. Joan had been speeding down the highway toward the Big Time and maybe a shot at crossover. "RuPaul with a whip," is what some called her.

She'd been—*was*—that good.

Speeding down the highway: Too accurate, that. Speeding, taillights out of nowhere, a faint alcohol daze, spinning, flying glass, spasming metal, the smell of gas and blood, the howl of sirens. And the deep, painful moans of Betty.

Betty lived: a life in her chair.

With the caring boredom of someone who's done it too many times, Joan snapped on a glove. After parting Betty's thighs with a flashing sweep she materialized a straight-razor with a mother-of-pearl handle and slashed away Betty's panty hose, exposing her fat cock and darkly furred balls.

Running her hand up and around Betty's ass and crotch, Joan checked her for rashes, all the while squeezing the twin clothespins on the old diva's nipples. "Has Mommy's Little Girl been good?" she said, acid playing through her words, lacing them with frustrated menace—a perfect acting job.

"I guess so, Mommy," Betty said in vulnerable tones, hanging her head in shame. Her voice was real.

"What do you mean, 'I guess so?'" Betty said, with theatrical anger, flipping at the clothespins and smiling with real satisfaction as Betty hissed in a breath against the jerking pain. "Don't you know if you've been good or not?"

"I-I played with myself." Betty said, head down lower if possible—chin to breastbone—a pink flush dying her cheeks a candy color.

"And what does that make you?"

"N-Naughty."

"And what happens to naughty little girls?"

Joan squirmed: humiliation, the pain from the clothespins, the acidic scorn... "They get punished." Her voice was small and tight, squeezed out from where she was slouching, hiding.

"That's right. *Punished.* Do you like to get punished, Betty?"

Betty's squirms got more animated, more convulsive. Despite the pins on her aching nipples, she reached up and tried to pull her pink pinafore down. "No," she said, shivering as the action put more strain on the clothespins.

"No one does, Betty. No one does. But you've been bad, haven't you? You've been a naughty little girl. You played with yourself against my orders!" Joan's shrill scream smashed around the dusty, claustrophobic room.

Shocked, Betty let go of her dress and the tension from the clothespins snapped it back up, showing her thickening cock. Humiliated, Betty blushed multiple shades of red and wrestled the dress down again, hissing like a tiny snake as the pins, again, bent back on her nipples. "I'm...(sniffle, sniffle)...sorry."

"Not good enough," Joan said, getting up and walking out the door. She returned a few minutes later carrying a large domed silver serving tray. Seeing it, Betty whimpered pathetically.

"In this house," Joan said, sitting next to Betty's wheelchair, "we have rules. They may be harsh, they may be unfair, but they're the rules nonetheless. *My* rules. You agree?"

Scared eyes the size of hard-boiled eggs, Betty squeaked, "N-No."

"You don't agree with me?" Joan roared, a drag queen express-train bearing down on little Betty tied to the tracks. "Of all the impudent, disrespectful—"

"No," Betty managed to fight out of herself, "I-I mean I don't want to—"

"But this is punishment, Betty. No one wants to be punished. But you played with yourself. You know the punishment for that."

A fatalistic veil fell over Betty. She took in a rasping breath, held it for a minute, let it out in a oscillating whistle. She steeled herself, gathered herself, readied herself for an invisible crowd, an audience, a performance. "I know the punishment," she said.

"Then why do you keep doing it?" Joan asked, taking the dome off the tray.

"No," squeaked little frilly Betty.

"Oh, yes," Joan said, eyes lit with dancing maniac fires. "Very definitely yes."

Betty tried (sort of) to struggle as Joan pulled her dress up again. She stopped completely, though, and bent back in a stiff curve against the pain when Joan slapped the clothespins. As Betty made a harmonica sound through clenched teeth, Joan got out a soft wooden paddle and carefully, precisely, placed it under Betty's cock and balls—wedging it under Betty's thighs.

Betty started to whimper, but Joan ignored her as she dabbled her balls with first alcohol and then Betadine.

Next were two Velcro restraints. One went neatly around each of Betty's thin arms, holding her securely to her chair.

"Maybe next time you won't be so tempted..."

Betty nodded *yes* very hard, all but smacking her breastbone with her chin: an extremely enthusiastic *yes!*

Joan could have been a star. She could've been a *real* star. Anyone who'd ever seen her thought the same thing: She was so talented, so precise that she could've gone pro, become a legend. She had a feel for it, and—God—to see her face as she got out her needles, you knew she had a *taste* for it. She loved it.

Carefully, she put on her gloves. Moving like a geisha, she uncapped a 20-gauge and got down to where she could really see Betty's cock and balls. "Breathe," she whispered, pushing Betty's thighs apart as far as she could, stretching her scrotum until the dark red skin turned a pale pink.

Betty breathed in twice, three times. Then Joan put the needle through.

Coughing out a deep primordial tone that belonged more to a sweat lodge than a Grand Dame of the Empress Ball, Betty squished her eyes shut.

"Very nice, baby," Joan said, picking up another needle. "Very,

very nice, my sweet little girl."

"Thank you, Mommy," Betty panted, preparing herself for the next.

Joan slid in the next needle: just the right amount of pressure to pierce Betty's scrotum and slide it into the wooden paddle. Joan's fingers, as always, *danced*. She had a way with sharps: They were her instrument of choice. Hands flashing like a magician, she made the amphlets appear, then, popping off their clear plastic caps, *disappear* into Betty's scrotum.

Joan could have been a star: She was *that* damned good.

For Betty, it really was magic. Black, white, gray... *magic.* The way Joan made the needles appear—materializing out of nowhere—and then vanish with a rolling wave of pain, like the thunderclap following a flash of lightning: pure magic. One needle quick, one needle slow, one needle quick, one needle quick—varying the delivery, the details, to keep Betty from falling back into an expected routine. She was on pins and needles, literally, waiting for when/where/how the next needle-tip would come—right side, right side, left side, right side. Her expectations and fear made the pain that much sharper, that much more brittle and jagged. Betty tasted it like blood (and had to run a quick tongue around the inside of her mouth to see if she'd bitten herself; she hadn't): a sharp, metallic kind of broken expectation. It went from fear and dipped into almost terror. She didn't know where the next needle was going to land, what the next kind of pain would be.

All the time, Joan was talking: "You're a slutty girl, aren't you? You can't hide it from Mommy, you know. Mommies can tell. I can tell. Your panties are wet, aren't they? Dripping wet. And this, your clit, is nice and big and hard, isn't it? Wet panties. Hard clit. You're a slut. You're thinking of getting fucked, right now. You're sitting there while I punish you for rubbing your puss and you're thinking of getting fucked. That's now much of a slut you are. I'm sitting her jamming fucking needles into your cunt and you're thinking of getting fucked. That's a slut, girl. That's a righteous slut, to take pins in your puss and still want to fuck. Look at this clit! That's the biggest clit I've ever seen, and Mommy's seen some fat fucking clits in her day, girl! This is a fucking huge clit..." *Whack!* Joan backhanded

Betty's cock hard enough to hurt, but not hard enough to tear the amphlets—a true artist. "This is a monster slutty clit. You're dripping, aren't you, girl? Yeah, I can tell. I can tell that you're just aching to get fucked, all wet and open and ready. Yeah. I can tell..."

Eight needles. Betty's cock wasn't going anyplace, even though it was trying. Painfully hard, it strained and pulled against the pinning needles. But Joan's placement was so perfect, it could just reach its height before feeling the painful tugs of the amphlets. No tearing, not a lot of blood, just a ring of deep ache around Betty's cock and balls. Joan definitely had true talent. Star, *legend,* potential.

"Bet you taste good, girl. Bet you taste real good. Bet you'd like your Mommy more than anything to taste your sweet puss. Bet you ache for it, more than the fucking pins. Yeah, I know you do. I can smell it on you like cheap fucking perfume. Toilet water. You must have really laid on the "Come Suck Me" stuff this morning, slut, 'cause it sure as shit stinks on you something awful. You reek of it, bitch. My fucking head is just full of the smell of you wanting my mouth on your clit. But if you want it so bad, you have to ask for it."

"Please..."

"Beg for it."

"Pretty please..."

"Whimper. Come on, you've done it before. Do it again."

"With sugar on it..."

"Such a fucking slut," Joan said, reaching around and behind her to the pile of supplies on the silver tray. In a flash—more magic—she had something in her mouth. In another flash—still more magic—she had her mouth over Betty's cock. She was very, very good with more than sleight of hand, because Betty never saw, or felt, the Gold Circle slide over her throbbing dick. All she felt was her Bitch Mommy, Joan, drop her wide-open mouth onto her straining-and-screaming with pain cock.

Joan's mouth was a hot wet blanket. The best kind of mouth. True talent. Good in a dress? A guy in hose. Good voice? Gravel pouring out of a dump truck. Good dancer? Sore toes from the Empress Ball to the bus stop. Joan's skill was in her needles, her canes, crops, whips, clamps, ropes, and her mouth. Especially her cocksucking mouth.

She could have been a star. Well, she was—for Betty.

Two of the needles pulled free—they vanished before they could poke anything—and the six others strained and all but tore Betty's screaming scrotum as she came, jetting so hard and hot and heavy that her come felt like hot lead squirting into Joan's mouth.

Betty heaved and panted for what must have been a minute but felt like hours, until her dick lost its erect weight in Joan's mouth. With her audience done, Joan put away her pigeons (she took the clothespins off with a deep rumbling moan from Betty); she tucked away her top hat (she quickly pulled the needles, swabbed the points with alcohol and Betadine); and she put away the rest of her magic tricks as well (she removed the restraints and gave Betty a quick sponge with a warm rag and a sweet kiss on her dewed forehead).

Getting up to make them both a snack, Joan felt Betty's thin hand catch the hem of her only slightly ruffled dress. "Don't go yet," Betty said in a tired but happy voice.

Joan smiled, a crease on her face, and crouched next to Betty's chair. "What," she said with a small laugh, "and give up show business?"

Sweet

by R.J. March

"My wife was going to throw this shirt out," he said. "I caught her using it as a dustrag once. It's my favorite. She just doesn't get it." He pulled off his trousers. "Yeah, it's got some holes in it, but it still works. It's not too worn out. I can still wear it, right?"

He was tall, sold pharmaceuticals. Shawn knew this because, just when he'd been parking his Montero in the lot outside, he saw the man retrieve a gym bag out of a car trunk packed with cases of pharmaceutical samples. Shawn watched the man pull warm-up pants up his long legs, covering his boxers, which were distracting in their simplicity, riding low, barely covering his hipbones. He had Kennedy looks.

He wasn't talking to Shawn, but to the man on the other side of him, the semipro wrestler Shawn recognized from an article in the local paper. Shawn stared into his gym bag, its contents not nearly as interesting as the tall one's upcurled toes. He grabbed his shorts and undid the fastenings of his jeans and stood a while in his briefs, not totally convinced that the semipro wrestler wasn't lingering to watch the pharm rep take off his Brooks Brothers oxford to put on the favorite shirt, the one wrested from the mean old wife. Shawn got into his shorts and tried to pick a CD to listen to, going through a very comprehensive collection of circuit party discs: *White, Black, Blue,* etc. The pharm rep elbowed his way out of his crispy white tee, laying bare the beautiful geography of his torso, hairless save for a few errant curlies around his butterscotch nipples. Shawn did his best not to give pause, but was unable to stop the arrest of his movements in the sight of such…such fucking sweetness.

Shawn had been a member of this gym for over five years, and crushes came and went. He had to admire his own tenacity, if nothing else. The membership did not always provide for much eye candy, but he didn't see the sense in switching gyms, because it really was about fitness, wasn't it? He began to think of the whole experience as a kind of living magazine to be perused—the muscle growth was an added bonus for your subscription! He came to the gym to flip some pages and do some bench presses. He wasn't much of a reader these days. He just liked to look at the pretty pictures.

The semipro did some lazy stretches—always suspect in a locker-room setting, Shawn noted—and the pharm rep glanced down at Shawn's end of the bench. He had just pulled The Shirt down over his beautiful head and said, "Now, isn't this perfect?"

Shawn gave a little snort, unable to help himself, and tried to keep his eyes off the dimple that sat smugly and rightfully under the pharm rep's fat lower lip. He glanced cursorily at the rep's shoulders, at the alleged holes there. "That is..."—he struggled to find the right word—"ah...perfect," he said, feeling as though he'd aced something.

"Damn straight," the rep said, slapping his own chest hard to emphasize his point. "It's a guy thing," he said proudly.

"Perfect," Shawn said to himself later, walking past the rep doing chin-ups, his shirt rising and baring the man's beautiful married gut. "I hate this fucking place."

• • •

Shawn showered afterward, embarrassingly alone. The general notion at this gym was that only the "fags" showered here—everyone else took his dirty, sweaty body home to clean up. Shawn scrubbed himself with a plastic loofah but was unable to rid himself of the horniness that clung to him as a result of his workout. His cock kept bobbing upward, threatening fullness, an awkward hard-on no towel could cover. He turned down the hot water until he was shivering and goose-fleshed, but there was no dousing the fire down below. He kept his back to the shower room entrance and waited until the locker room sounded empty. He turned off the water and grabbed for his towel, wrapping it around his waist and binding his rigid prick up against his belly. He looked as though he was trying to hide a bottle of wine.

He opened the shower curtain, and there was Dean the Queen. Who else would be sitting right in front of the showers, tying and retying the laces of his sneakers? Dean looked infinitely disappointed to see Shawn, although it was plain that he did not miss Shawn's gut-bound hard-on.

"You sure know how to make cleanup fun," he quipped. "And you're all alone!"

"Yup," Shawn muttered, making his way to his locker. Keeping his towel on, he prudishly stepped into his underwear and, back turned, got himself into his jeans. He heard Dean the Queen sigh, and turned to see him picking up his gloves and belt and heading out to the gym floor.

In his car, Shawn readjusted his erection and played with the radio. His SHeDAISY disc was in his bag in the backseat. The effort to retrieve it was enough of a pain in the ass to make him settle on the disc already in the CD player: *The Best of the Ohio Players.*

"Fi-yah!" he sang along with them. "Fi-yah!"

• • •

Shawn saw the pharm rep again, this time out at a bar called the Spruce. He was by himself and so was Shawn. Their eyes met in the mirror behind the bar, and Shawn saw him trying to register the familiarity. He leaned forward, looking down at Shawn, and said, "Long time no see." Shawn smiled and said, "Yeah." Pharm nodded, smiling too, and Shawn felt as though he was missing something, some piece of information that was vital to this small exchange. It felt coded, indecipherable, until the pharm rep moved down a couple of stools, getting himself beside Shawn. He ordered shots for the two of them, then, grinning into Shawn's face with breath boozy, said with hushed gruffness, "You thought I forgot you, didn't you? Yeah, I'm sorry I didn't call like I said I would, but you know how it goes."

Shawn gave a vague shrug that seemed somewhat meaningful to the pharm rep.

"I even remember your name," Pharm Rep said, pointing. "Billy. No, um..."

"It's Shawn."

Pharm Rep's face dulled; he looked momentarily stupid. *Funny what bourbon does to a man's features,* Shawn thought. The man's wedding ring reflected a glint of bar light, catching Shawn's eye. The man started twisting it then, the ring, while watching Shawn's face. "I remember you," he said.

"I bet you don't," Shawn said, playing along. Whatever the game was, Shawn was all for it, remembering the man's bare torso, his long, thick-muscled legs, his beautiful proportions.

The man grinned hard, leaning toward Shawn. "Up on the hill," he whispered, nodding.

"Yeah?" Shawn said.

Pharm Rep stopped grinning. "You're the one who don't remember," he said.

"Sure, I do, sure," Shawn said. "You sell drugs."

The rep had to figure out whether or not Shawn was being funny, which explained the delayed laugh. "Yeah, right!"

"But your name," Shawn said, shaking his head. "I just can'..."

The rep lifted his glass, looking over the rim of it at Shawn. "Look, I can't remember what name I gave you, either." He paused, taking a drink. "It's Paul." He set his glass down hard. "Damn glad to know you, Shawn," he said brightly, holding out his hand for Shawn to shake.

"Yeah," Shawn said, taking the offered hand in his. It was big and warm, with slender fingers, and gripped Shawn's tightly.

"What was that I just ordered for us, them shots?"

Shawn had to think about it. "Um..." He shrugged his shoulders. "Couldn't tell you," he said.

Paul grinned lewdly, leaning in toward Shawn for a moment before straightening up and giving the bar a look over. "I fucking know everyone here," he said, his mouth rigid. "Ever feel like you're living in a fucking fishbowl?"

Shawn shook his head. He wasn't a native, but he'd learned that most of the men and women in town had come here when they were underaged. Many had gone away for college but later moved back and lived not far from their parents. There was something about this town—some charm, some hold—but Shawn was blind to whatever it was; he'd be out of here as soon as the next best thing came along.

"We should get the fuck outta here—know what I mean?"

Shawn nodded, knowing.

• • •

"The old lady, she's not bad—don't get me wrong. She's fine, she's real fine," the rep was saying, his hands going though his curly dirty-blond hair. His eyes were green, his face long. He lumbered ahead of Shawn like a basketball player bereft of his ball and heading for the showers—not an altogether bad combination. "Chemistry!" he shouted suddenly. "What happened to the fucking chemistry?"

They sat in Shawn's Montero, parked behind a cement building that might have been a garage, might have been an office building. The windows were down, welcoming the first real warm night of the season. The radio was on low, playing songs Shawn knew by heart—songs by Shelby Lynne and Aimee Mann. He watched as Paul undid the fastenings of his pants, pushing them down his thighs—which were also known by Shawn by heart. Paul's cock stood through the gaping fly of his boxers, a stony monument. He put his thumb and forefinger to his mouth and then to the end of his tall prick.

"She's all right," Paul said, closing his eyes for a second, maybe imagining her, Shawn was thinking. Then Paul undid the first few bottom buttons of his shirt, baring his stomach, its tautness obvious. Shawn swallowed, looking out the windows of the SUV.

"Are you sure it's cool to be here?" he asked.

"It was cool enough last time," Paul said, smirking.

"Last time?" Shawn said. "There isn't a last time, except for maybe this time."

Paul froze, his hand arrested mid stroke. He made an "oops" face. "You know, I was wondering what happened to your Jetta," he said.

"So you're saying I have a queer twin running around town?"

"No," Paul said, resuming his jacking off. "You don't look like him at all, now that I think about it. He had red hair and was, like, 6 foot 3. I could have looked him in the eye if I'd wanted to."

He leaned over then and kissed Shawn, and Shawn tasted the bourbon and a mint Paul had managed to suck on without Shawn's knowing. Paul's free hand kneaded the front of Shawn's jeans.

"I know you from somewhere, though," Paul said, his mouth still on Shawn's, tongue swirling and confusing the words.

"The gym," Shawn garbled back.

"Shweet," Paul said, nodding, finding the fly of Shawn's jeans and tugging on the obstinate zipper. After much digging he found Shawn's solid prick, fat and half-curled, nestled in moist pubes. He hauled it out and went down on it, lapping the tapered end. Shawn placed one hand on the back of Paul's head and the other on the headrest behind him. His cock buzzed into the hot mouth, guided by Paul's tight grip, making it pulse and throb. He forced Paul all the way down, eliminating Paul's fist, wanting to feel the man's lips against his pubes and balls. Paul came up spitting hairs, saliva shining on his smiling lips.

"Easy, pal," he said, tugging on his own prick, leaning back to look Shawn over. "I remember you now," he said.

"Yeah, right," Shawn said, jerking his cock. He watched the split head of Paul's cock drool a bubble or two of precome. "I still don't think this is such a great place."

"Don't worry about it," Paul replied. "I own this building. Nobody's gonna come back here unless I ask 'em to."

In the back of the Montero, seats down, there was room to roll around, room to grapple and undress. The sun was going down fast, and in the dusky light, Shawn licked remembered nipples, narrow hips, and tightened ball sac, fingering the man's knotted butt hole—tight at first, then giving, opening like some secret door. Paul moaned and used his hips to feed Shawn more of his dick, riding the mouth, forcing his prick deeper into Shawn's opened throat, muttering out loud about Shawn's cocksucking skills. "You're fucking awesome, man, fucking awesome." He slid his pole in and out, his hands on either side of Shawn's hips, dropping his head to lick Shawn's slick shaft and shrunk-up balls.

"You like to fuck?" Shawn heard. He tried to say yes.

"Cool," Paul said, leaning back, squatting on Shawn's face, filling his mouth with cock, his balls filling Shawn's nostrils with their rich aroma. "Finger-fuck me, dude."

Shawn's finger was already planted, so he added a second. He uncorked his mouth from Paul's long prong and went to work on his dangling balls instead, liking the way they stopped his throat and nose simultaneously, the bag suede-like and luxurious and breath-taking. He probed around Paul's insides, making the man squirm and giggle, his dick bopping on Shawn's forehead and leaving little sticky kisses.

Paul shifted and pivoted, straddling Shawn's hips. He held on to Shawn's prick firmly and pushed it up into his asshole, then squatted a little and took more. He had no trouble with Shawn's length or thickness; he was a regular pro, Shawn was thinking, watching Paul dip his ass, filling himself with Shawn's cock. He sat himself down, resting his butt cheeks on Shawn's hipbones. There wasn't enough dick to fill him, it seemed; he wanted more and more. He fingered Shawn's little nipples, twisting and pulling them until Shawn yelped. He bounced against Shawn's pelvis and leaned back, moving his feet up toward Shawn's armpits, getting more feisty, giving himself a nasty fuck on Shawn's back-bent prick.

"Oh, man," he said, sweating, winking at Shawn. "You sure know how to fuck."

"No," Shawn said, "*you* know how to fuck."

"You don't like?" Paul asked, slowing down—but not much.

"Oh, I like, I like."

Paul pushed his fanny forward. "Aw, you feel that?" he asked.

Shawn felt something, the beginnings of something. It roiled around his groin and tickled his nuts up tight and swirled up his shaft and circled the knob of his cock. Paul continued his fanny slams and Shawn's breathing stopped. He opened his mouth, wanting to say something meaningful, but only nasty words came to mind, nothing more noble than "Ride me, you fucking cock jockey!"

Shawn watched Paul's face freeze, his prick waving stiffly, un-touched up until then. Paul managed to continue in tripod position, fisting his shaft roughly—his breathing hoarse, his language coarse—as he banged himself on Shawn's exploding prick, sucking up every last drop and spraying Shawn and the felt ceiling above them with a copious load that would have done a porn star proud. Shawn had never seen so much jizz come out of one man at one time. He took a deep breath and licked the corner of his mouth. He put his hands over his head, stretching, liking the way his cock felt up inside Paul. He closed his eyes for a second, and Paul leaned forward finally, putting his face on Shawn's come-dotted shoulder.

"I messed you up," he said quietly.

Shawn smiled. "Oh, boy, I'll say you did."

• • •

Shawn holds up The Shirt. "I swear to God, Paul, I'm throwing this away."

Paul glances up from the television, squinting at the tattered T-shirt Shawn is dangling by a ragged sleeve. "Aw, hon," he says. "It's not that bad."

"You can't wear this at the gym—your nipples show." He sees Paul grin and play distractedly with the absent wedding ring on his finger. Shawn bunches up the shirt and holds it under his nose, breathing in the smell of his lover, thinking—and not for the first time—*Sweet.*

The Well of Az-zahr

by Barry Alexander

I waited in the desert hills until the sun was almost down before I drove my goats home. Though night had swallowed the valleys, heat still radiated from rock and parched earth as I picked my way down the trail. The first stars hung over the village, and lamps glowed in the windows along the deserted street. The scent of roast kid and hot bread drifting from the houses made my stomach growl. My own supper of goat cheese and stone bread waited. Though I knew everyone was inside, I pulled the folds of my kaf closer around my face, feeling safer with that concealment, even in the dusky shadows of evening.

The men of Qafar always let me use the well after their flocks were watered, and for that I was grateful, but I knew better than to presume on that favor. Years of taunts and flung stones had taught me to avoid the villagers and to keep my face covered, even though the men of Qafar did not veil.

I did not blame them for their insults. How could I? I did not know my offense, but a god had struck me at birth. The god's slap covered my cheek, the imprint of his fingers clear in the dark red bruise that covered my face. My parents were so horrified, they left me on the village rubbish heap. I did not blame them, either. Who would want a child so ugly he was slapped by a god?

Since his goats would not care what I looked like, a goatherd picked me up and raised me on watered goat's milk. When I displeased him, which was often, he slapped me. But he fed me and clothed me when no one else would look at me, and when he died childless, his goats became mine. They became my friends, even leaving their grazing to gather around me and listen as I played my pipes or sang for them.

The goats surrounded the trough, bleating and butting their heads against me, eager for a drink after a long day in the rocky desert hills. Grass was scarce this far into the month of Haddar, and we had scavenged far. I knew better than to let my goats browse the common pasture with the villagers' sheep.

I bowed my head and thanked Az-zahr for the gift of water, as I did every day. The Well of Az-zahr was very old and very deep, but in the time of my 18th Haddar, it was starting to dry. The villagers had begun charging passing caravans for its use. I was grateful they did not charge me.

I set aside a cup of the muddy water to clear, then drew bucket after bucket to fill the trough. My arms ached by the time the goats were satisfied.

I heard a sound and looked out to the vast desert where night hovered on great blue-black wings above the last glow of the sun. A man walked out of the desert. His body was whip-lean, and his stride was long as he came to the well. Like the Kuaret, the wanderers of the desert wastes, the stranger was enveloped in night-blue fabric. But there was no ornament about him, and he was alone and on foot. I wondered how he had come to be lost from his caravan and his mount. I pulled my kaf closer about my face as he approached.

His face was swathed in several folds of the same blue fabric. His dark blue eyes gleamed in the pale evening light. Somehow, those eyes made me think of pools of water, wider and deeper than any I had ever known. I realized I was staring and quickly looked down. The man's eyes crinkled, as if he'd just smiled, and strange stars danced in the rippling pools of his eyes.

"You are up late, boy," he said in a voice as deep and quiet as his eyes. "I have walked a long way. I thirst."

I hurried to offer him the cup I had set aside. The man took the cup. His slim, brown fingers brushed my hand, and I felt a strange quivering deep inside. I had never seen such fine hands, uncallused and so clean. If his hands were so smooth, I wondered how smooth the rest of his body must be. What would it be like to touch such fine skin, to feel those slender fingers touching me? And I blushed at the boldness of my thoughts.

Then the man did something no Kuaret man would ever do—he unfastened his kaf and gave me his face. Kuaret men merely lifted the veil to drink. Only those closest to them were allowed to see a warrior's visage.

I had never seen a man like him before. His skin was smooth and clean-shaven, high of cheek and firm-jawed. Once, after a caravan had passed, I found a small stone carving. A villager had taken it from me, of course, but I had never forgotten the face on it, the most beautiful I had ever seen—wolf-gentle, hawk-fierce. And now, that same face looked at me with grave amusement, as if used to such reactions.

As the man raised the water to his full lips, I remembered the mud that had settled to the bottom. I was ashamed I only had dirty water to offer. "I'm sorry the water isn't clear. The well is going dry."

"All water is good when you thirst." He drank deeply and handed the cup back. Our fingers touched again and I trembled. "I owe you a gift. In the morning, take the trail between the Painted Cliffs. But you must tell no one what you find."

It would not have been polite to call the man a liar, so I promised to follow the trail. I told him he could find lodging at the elder's house and pointed the way. When I turned back, he was gone. He moved as silently as the night. I could not even hear his footsteps.

• • •

It was a long walk to the Painted Cliffs. I knew the trail led only to a dry as bone canyon, but I had promised. As I neared the pass, the goats began to bleat and then began to run. I followed them as they ran down a twisting trail I had never noticed before. Then the trail opened, and I stopped in amazement. A wide green valley stretched before me, greener and lusher than anything I had ever seen. Even more wondrous was the stream of water sparkling in the sunlight.

The lush grass tickled my bare legs as I ran after the goats. I waded into the stream and sighed with pleasure at the cool caress of water.

I pulled my safan over my head and tossed it onto the bank. It felt strange being naked in the bright sunlight. It was oddly arousing. I knew I was alone, but I felt like someone was watching. The sensation was not exactly unpleasant, but it was disturbing, nevertheless. The water felt like cold silk on my bare skin.

I tossed my head cloth on the grass as well, and shook my hair free. Water swirled around my thighs, tickling the bottom of my balls and pushing cool fingers between the rounds of my ass.

I cupped a handful of the clear water and trickled it over my chest. I laughed at its cool kiss. I ducked under the water and came up sputtering. I leaped and splashed as gleefully as a young child.

Nose-deep in the lush grass, the goats were too content to notice my antics.

It was a new delight to feel sun on my skin and grass tickling my feet. Even more wonderful was the feel of my manhood swinging full and heavy between my legs. There seemed no need to cover myself here. Naked, I explored the valley.

Birds sang in the branches of the fruit trees beside the stream. Bees bumbled drunkenly among the overripe dates fermenting on the ground. White butterflies danced over a field of scarlet poppies. I could not remember a more wonderful day. I feasted on plump dates and ripe pomegranates. When I could hold no more, I sat in the lush grass and played my pipes, trying to capture the music of water and bird and bee.

The goats were so full of sweet grass, they gathered in the shade and listened to my music. I grew sleepy and stretched out on the cool grass, languidly stroking my half-hard shaft. It felt so warm and smooth under my fingers. I loved touching myself, but sometimes I ached to touch someone else, the way I once watched two men touching and holding each other as they lay together in a hidden hollow. They had seemed to find so much joy in exploring each other's bodies, the soft gasps of pleasure, the hurried groping. But I knew no one would ever touch me like that, not with my face.

But when I was alone, I could pretend that I was beautiful. That the fingers sliding up and down my cock were not my own. That the hand that caressed my chest belonged to another. I traced the edges of my lips with my thumb and wondered what it would be like to kiss someone. Sometimes I saw couples kissing in the shadows. Their soft gasps and frenzied touching excited me, but I always left quickly. Watching them made me feel alone as I never did when I was in the hills with the goats.

Lulled by the music of water and the song of insects, my eyes grew heavy.

I woke when a shadow blocked the sun, but I felt too good to open my eyes. And for a moment, I thought I still dreamed. Warm fingers drew spirals and arabesques over my chest. I groaned when the fingers touched my nipples. They squeezed gently, and a line of fire trailed straight to my cock. I became aware of someone's soft breathing and the clean, spicy scent of a man. I wanted it to be a dream. I was afraid to wake and have that touch disappear. I knew it had to be a joke, someone from the village wanting to see me aroused so they could laugh at me and torment me. Maybe if I kept my eyes closed they would go away, or better still keep doing what they were doing.

But I couldn't resist opening my eyes. And when I did so I looked into the dark blue eyes of the stranger.

Ashamed to have him see my face, I grabbed for the kaf to conceal my shame. But his hand closed on mine. "No, you have no need to hide yourself from me."

I trembled as a wave of desire tore through me. The dark clear eyes seemed to gaze straight through me to all the hidden secret places deep inside.

"Do you not yet know me? The voice was so soft, and deeply it rumbled through my naked body. Then the hand gently touched the mark on my cheek. The warm brown fingers covering the dark imprint. "It is my mark you bear, Tiral. I claimed you at your birth."

And then I knew him, knew this handsome stranger with the glorious eyes and the voice as sweet and strong as the song of the desert—Az-zahr, the owner of the well—and it would seem the owner of Tiral.

"Why?" I couldn't help asking. "Why would you want me?"

"I knew what you would become—this fine straight body, your gentle heart, the music in your soul—and I wanted no other man to touch you. You are mine. I have waited a long time for you, and you will not deny me."

I had no wish to deny him anything.

He bent over me and his lips touched mine. His lips were warm and hard as they pressed against mine. I opened my mouth and shuddered as his tongue laved mine with wetness. Every touch, every stroke sent ripples of pleasure through my body. I couldn't get enough of him. His tongue was sweeter and more luscious than any fruit. I felt like crying when he finally broke the kiss.

With a graceful move, he flung off his kaf and the deep blue robes of the Kuaret and stood proudly naked before me. Muscles rippled under his sleek skin. He looked as lithe and powerful as a desert lion. His hair was long and sand-colored and blew in the wind that came sweeping in from the desert. And his face—wolf-proud, hawk-fierce.

My eyes lowered to the thick shaft swaying between his thighs, and I gulped. It was so big. His sac was covered with coils of hair like fine gold wires. His lean flanks were etched with golden hair. His staff was straight and thick, a mighty scepter with a crown like a ripe pomegranate. I wanted to taste his fruit, to glide my tongue over the glistening globe. My mouth watered. And I realized I was staring and quickly looked away. I could not meet his eyes.

He put his hand under my chin and made me look at him. He smiled, and I felt my heart tremble. "Look, touch, do as you will. If you are hungry, eat. If you are thirsty, drink."

His skin was the finest thing I'd ever touched. He smelled so wonderful. I kissed the base of his throat and trailed my tongue along his shoulder and down his chest. His scent was stronger here, and I followed it to its source. Tufts of fine gold hair filled the deep hollow under his arm. I took a deep breath, and my cock dripped my juices onto his belly. Tentatively, I stuck my tongue out and tasted—warm, salty, a little pungent. I loved the taste of him. He lifted his arm and folded it behind his head so I could explore the moist hollow. I flattened my tongue and washed him. The fine hairs tickled my lips, and I sucked on them, drinking the moisture. His hand stroked down my spine and cupped the small mound of my ass, and I sighed and pressed tighter against him. His cock was hard and hot, sometimes twitching against my thigh as I nuzzled into the warm hollow under his arm. He guided my head back to his chest, and I tongued his flat nipples and caught the tip of one between my teeth.

It hardened beneath my lips, and I suckled the tender point as greedily as a newborn child. But I still thirsted.

I looked down at the massive column of flesh rising from the god's groin like a pillar of living rock rising from the belly of the desert. I was so thirsty and here was the source. Moisture dripped from the open slit—the clean, rich scent filled my nostrils.

"You have thirsted long. Here is the font. Drink deeply."

I trembled as I knelt in worship. I had to taste. I leaned forward letting my lips brush the glistening crown. My tongue sought the opening. I licked. The taste overwhelmed me—like cool water after a burning day in the hills, like rare and precious drops of rain, but better, much better—sweet and musky and all male. I pushed my tongue into the warm and quivering slit, and more of his juices drizzled on my tongue, sweet as honey.

His strong hands held my head in place as he used my mouth as a sheath for his weapon, plunging inside me again and again. I sucked as hard as I could. He stiffened, and his muscles convulsed as he spewed deep inside my throat. I pulled back so I could taste him. He was better than anything I had ever tasted. I did not think I could ever get enough of him. He flooded my mouth. I could not hold it all. It dripped down my chin and trickled over my chest. I did not think he was ever going to stop, and I swallowed and swallowed more of his precious juices.

Even as my thirst was quenched, my hunger for him grew. I wanted all of him. I wanted him deep inside me, where I would never forget his presence. His shaft did not soften. It stood proudly erect, a spire of flesh pointing to the sky.

He pushed against my shoulder, and I lay back. I looked up at him as he towered over me. His body was perfect, every muscle sharply chiseled. I could have looked at him forever, but my body ached with need. I moaned and drew my legs up, lewdly exposing myself to him. His eyes darkened with desire, and for a moment, I was afraid at the intensity in them. Then he smiled as he dropped down to cover my body with his, and I was proud that his desire matched my own.

His cock pushed against my portal, slow and sure like a conqueror entering the city he has taken, demanding entrance. I had no wish to deny it; I was his. There was pain as he entered me. I expected it. His was no mortal shaft. I welcomed him in the only way I knew how. I pushed back against him, asking for more of the giant ram that battered at my closed portal. It could not be denied. I opened for him, my hole blooming like a flower after rain.

He entered me slowly, triumphantly. I strained to take all of him. When I finally felt his balls against me, I sighed in contentment. The pain was forgotten as he moved within me. Each stroke of his body was increasingly sweet. I wrapped my legs around his thrusting hips, striving for more of the wondrous feelings. My cock danced between us, painting his abdomen with my fluids. He pumped harder, rocking my body with the force of his thrusts. His mouth plundered mine, driving his tongue deep into my throat. I couldn't hold back. My body arched as fire tore through me. I thought I was going to die from joy. I had no idea it could be like that. His seed spurted inside me, hot and so abundant, and I did not think I could contain it all.

At last he finished. He lowered himself to my trembling body and kissed the tears from my eyes. I did not want to move. Pierced by his shaft, suspended between earth and sky, pleasure and pain, I felt truly loved. He filled the emptiness inside me, giving me life the way water makes the desert bloom.

He took me again and again, filling my body with his seed and driving me to ever higher peaks of ecstasy. My body was an instrument for his pleasure. Nothing else existed. He was tireless, riding me to an agonizing surfeit of pleasure. When I thought I could bear no more, he took me again, gently this time. His slightest touch sent rivers of desire through my body. The pleasure was so great this time that my body could not contain it. It surged through my body, sweeping me along in a rush of fire and night. I cried out in ecstasy, then the darkness claimed me

When I awoke, he was gone. Rain is rare in the desert. And always welcome. Men die of thirst between rains and already I longed for the taste of him. Once I had tasted him, I knew no other could ever quench my desire. I knew I had given him pleasure. I could only hope that he would return.

Weeks passed, and still there was no rain. Yet every day I found abundant water in the secret valley. My goats and I drank our fill of the cold, clean water. My goats grew strong and sleek and gave more milk than ever. I felt sorry for the villagers' sheep. They grew thinner every day with the endless search for grass. I tried to tell the villagers about the valley, but my words turned to gibberish, and the men laughed and taunted me. It seemed the god had bound me to silence.

Men began looking at me suspiciously when I sold my milk at market. They muttered about pacts with demons and made the sign against evil when I passed. I began to stay later in the hills to avoid them. Then one moonlit evening they were waiting for me.

I did not like the look on the faces of the men standing beside my goat pens. I hesitated, and some of the men moved to block my path. Then they were all shouting and calling me vile names. I ran when they picked up rocks. I dodged most of the stones. But I was tiring, and they were getting closer.

Every breath sliced through my body like a blade. Stones thudded against my skin. I wrapped arms around my head to protect it and ran with my head down. I could feel them gaining and forced my legs to run faster.

I ran headfirst into someone. Hands reached for my shoulders, but I twisted away, falling as my legs gave out. I huddled into a ball and waited for the stones.

They didn't come. I heard the men whooping for air, but the curses had stopped and so had the stones. I could hear the light, regular breathing of someone who stood close to me.

Fearfully, I raised my face. Between me and the angry villagers stood a tall blue-robed figure—Az-zahr. The villagers did not know him, but they were afraid, though he was one and they were many.

"You will not touch him," he said in such a cold, quiet voice that I wondered the men did not shiver at the bite of it.

"You have forgotten everything your fathers taught you about guest rights. It is the well of Az-zahr, not the well of Qafar—a gift in ages past so that thirsty men might drink. It has never belonged to you."

He took my hand and pulled me to my feet. I felt the same erotic charge that I had felt earlier. My erection sprang to life beneath my robes. Az-zahr looked down and smiled, acknowledging the tribute of my body with a squeeze of his hand. I was not ashamed, though I knew everyone in the village could see my erection pushing against my robes. No one said a word. One by one, the men dropped their stones.

"Your well has been drying for a long time, but it is not yet as dry as your hearts."

With graceful movements of his hands, he flung off his kaf and the deep blue robes of the Kuaret. The villagers and I saw a tall, slim man clothed in strange, tight-fitting garments that molded his body like skin.

"Az-zahr," I said, overwhelmed again by his sheer beauty.

The god turned and blinded me with his smile. "You at least have not forgotten," he said, and his voice was like a caress. And I thought of all those places I had dared to touch this god, and my whole body burned with desire.

Then the warmth vanished as he spoke to the people of Qafar. "The well was a gift," he said. "The water was given freely to all, but I see how you repay gifts. I take back what was given."

The wind rose, sweeping in from the desert and swirling around Az-zahr. The people wrapped their headcloths around their faces, but they could still feel sand sting on their hands and feet. Their sand-stung eyes watered beneath the shrouding folds of cloth; they could see nothing. Bowed beneath the force of the wind, their ears heard nothing but the roar and whine of wind as it swept about them.

I watched in awe as a whirlwind of sand and dust swept around the village. But not a strand of Az-zahr's golden hair moved and not a single grain of sand touched me.

The men shouted and cried in fear as the wind threatened to sweep them away. I was glad to see them afraid. But as I looked at the people of Qafar, the men who had stoned me, the boys who had taunted me, the women who had cursed me, and the children who hid behind their mothers, I knew that all would die without the well. I looked at the faces of fear and anger and resentment, and I knew what I had to do.

"Az-zahr, please, spare them.

"Enough," Az-zahr said in a quiet voice that carried over the wild song of the wind. Silence flowed out of him and the wind stilled. Cautiously, the people unwrapped their faces and shook the sand from their clothes. Slowly, they began to edge away.

"As you wish. But why would you do such a thing for them?"

"I cannot stay in this place," I said slowly, realizing that for the first time. "I would take nothing from this place to remember it. But I think that if I didn't ask you to spare them, I would always have those faces following me."

Az-zahr laughed. "I think you will have no trouble forgetting. Come."

He reached out for his robe and the soft blue fabric swirled around us, wrapping us both in a veil of darkness. My senses spun as the wind swept us away, but I was not afraid. Az-zahr's arms surrounded me, and his lips took my breath away.

Gravity

by Greg Wharton

It started with a kiss: one tender, soft kiss. We were parked out by the Henderson's old place—you know, by that house out on County Road AA that has the front-yard billboard big enough for the cars traveling south on the interstate to see: ASK JESUS TO MAKE HELEN WELL. Only nobody knows who Helen is, or was.

Coal and I had just got off work. We'd closed down the Dixie Queen together. It was summer, hot, boring. Just out of school, nothing going on, nothing much to look forward to but a cold beer. We drove past my house, and I grabbed a couple six-packs from the fridge and motored down to AA, where we could watch the lights of the interstate as cars drove past on their way somewhere else.

There was a bit of breeze while we were just shooting the shit together in his beat-up Camaro. Coal and I always had got along well in school, but we'd never talked much, other than locker-room lies. Then this old sappy song came on the radio—*"God, I miss the girl"*—and he was babbling like a baby. Crying and saying how he didn't understand how Deb could've hurt him like she did. Deb was his girlfriend.

"Shit, Coal. I'm sorry, man. Don't cry, shit."

And I took him in my arms. It was OK; he was hurting. I took him in my arms and squeezed. He let me. I squeezed his strong body to mine, hoping I could make him stop hurting. Before I knew what I was doing, my hands took his sweet face and pulled it to mine. I kissed a tear that was slowly weeping down his cheek, then his eye. I gently ran my tongue over his lips, then between to his bright white teeth. I was surprised at my sudden aroused state.

It was like my chest was supporting a great weight, like the witches in old New England who'd been tortured by being laid down and having stone after stone placed on top of them. Only this felt good—real good, and I was hard. I was touching Coal, and I was hard.

He looked into my eyes. We kissed: one tender, soft kiss. My life was suddenly very different.

• • •

"Gravity, motherfucker! Gravity!" he yells as he bounces up from the bed on his strong legs and taps his palms on the ceiling. "Gravity."

We are so looped—a double feature at the Zucker Drive-in, two tabs of blotter acid each, and a bottle of spiced rum–looped. Coal said at the drive-in that he wanted to fuck me in a hotel—and I wanted him to, so we drove to Tipp City, and while he hid in the car and giggled an idiot, I got us a room.

"Come on, Vic. Come on! Gravity!"

I'm watching him from the other bed as he does his trampoline jumps, his fat cock bouncing up and slapping his brown tanned belly with every descent, large heavy balls making thumping noises against his thighs. My vision is blurred; his leaps, whether slowed down or sped up, I can't tell. He's just a white blur of light and motion with a hard-on.

A hard-on I want to eat. I want to eat him. I picture it on a bed of lettuce with a slice of Wonder Bread and a couple fluorescent pickles.

It has been a week since the kiss. He had kissed me back, but then said he had to get home and drove like a bastard out of hell to get me back by my place, dropping me off and speeding away without a word about what had happened. I ran in the house, into the bathroom, and jerked off, coming on the mirror above the sink in an explosion with just five quick jerks of my fist.

Nothing more was said until earlier today at work when he showed me the acid and asked if I wanted to see the monster pictures at the Zucker.

"Gravity!" And he's suddenly flying across the room at me, using his full weight to knock me off the bed with a loud thump. His hand grips my cock through my boxers and starts pumping, keeping time with his other hand wrapped around his own.

I'm laughing, uncontrolled and hard—the effect of the drug or the rum or him. My head bends to the plate of cock, but first I flick away the pickles. I lick the bead of come off his piss slit, then wedge the head into my mouth. Not knowing what to do with the slice of Wonder Bread and lettuce, I fling them across the room, sending trails of color with them. His cock's head seems to be larger than my mouth, but somehow I manage to make it fit.

The stinky brown shag carpet burns as we twist and bend over and around each other, but I don't care. I am too enthralled with the taste of his body, the pinpricks of sensation my skin is experiencing, his deep musky scent, like the locker room at our old school, but better. I have already come once, in his mouth. But he hasn't stopped stroking me with his lips. I have my middle finger up his ass, and he is fucking hard into my throat, his knees on either side of my head, balls flapping heavily against my eyes with each thrust. His ass swallows my finger, then two. I think of my arm up inside him, and then he's pulsating, his cock expanding, contracting, pumping, emptying. My mind flashes greens, then blues, then bright white-silver. I think, *Gravity, Coal, gravity*. His fat cock finally shoots, and I know I love him. He pushes farther into me, down my throat. His come tastes like the pepperoni sausage we put on the mini-pizzas at the Queen, and I pull his thick red cock out with my hand and squeeze, and it sprays my mouth and lips and tongue as I mouth, *"I love you, I love you,"* and his ass squeezes my fingers tight, and he screams "Vic, oh, Vic, oh!"

• • •

For two weeks we meet every day as best friends. As lovers. We explore each other's bodies; we talk, get high. I can't believe it, but I feel as if somebody really, finally, knows me. Nobody at work suspects the truth that two of Piqua's recently graduated have joined the ranks of faggot brotherhood. That the king jock from Piqua High, Coal, goes down on cock: mine.

We meet before work, after work, and on nights when we close the Queen alone, we suck and fondle and paw between customers. I let him fuck me. The first time, when he shot deep inside me, I heard him say it. He said, "I love you, Vic." Soft and sweet as anyone could possibly say it. He didn't know it, but I cried as his cock plowed hard into my ass again, exploding within minutes of the first.

He said that he wanted to go away; get out of southern Ohio. Maybe Chicago. That we were good together. Who cared about what people would think? He didn't. I didn't anymore.

And then it ends. No kiss. No tender soft kiss, just cold, flat words through the phone wires. He calls me on the phone and severs my life force, just as if he would've taken his favorite hunting knife and slit deep into my throat.

"Why not, man? What happened? What the fuck happened?"

"It's just over, Vic. Forget it!"

"Forget it? Coal, shit. I love you! I thought—"

"Shut up. You do not! Stop sounding like a fag, Vic! It's over!"

It's over, just like that. After he hangs up, I pull my cock out and roughly, angrily grind as I think about what he just said. I wrap the phone cord tightly around my balls until they look like they will burst; I start to cry. He said Deb was pregnant and wouldn't have an abortion. Somehow his dad had found out, and now Coal is getting married. Married! I feel like my life has just ended. I want to feel his soft lips on mine again.

• • •

I imagine his blade forcing its way into my throat and the pain it causes. I see Deb's face smiling as he kills me, my blood flowing freely, draining.

I come all over my sneakers just as the alarm sounds, not even realizing what the alarm means. I rub the spunk from my hands on my jeans and wander out the front door staring at the sky's dark green color. My dick is hanging out, and I don't care. I walk out to the cornfield in a daze.

I am peeing on the old weathered scarecrow my dad and I put up when I was 9 when I first hear it. Thunder? The wind whips the stream of pee on me, and I fall down, yanking my jeans off, not concerned with anyone seeing—I just want to be free of them. I pull off my T-shirt and rub my hands over my chest and belly, yanking on my nipples as if I could pull them off. Nobody's around. There's never anyone around. I hate it here! I hate…

It sounds like a train is headed right at me, and a smile forms on my tear-stained face. It's a fucking tornado! Huge and black, covering the entire horizon. Electricity sparkles around me, and my body hair stands at attention. I watch it pick up Aunt Felice's house and devour it, then the barn across the field. I am awestruck, and my cock juts out strong and stiff. Running isn't even an option I consider. I raise my arms to the sky and think of what has happened the past couple weeks with Coal. I picture his bright teeth when he smiled at me. *My Coal. My love. Over.* I have nothing; feel nothing. I ask Jesus to make me well. Fuck Helen. I am lifted from the ground violently; arms spread skyward like a rocket launching, my eardrums bursting from the overwhelming roar, and I am flying into my new destiny.

Gravity, motherfucker, gravity.

Contributor Biographies

Derek Adams is the author of a popular series of erotic novels featuring intrepid detective Miles Diamond. He has also penned over 100 short stories, which he insists are ongoing chapters in his autobiography. Mr. Adams currently lives near Seattle and keeps in shape by working out whenever he can find a man willing to do a few push-ups with him.

Barry Alexander's erotic fiction has appeared in magazines such as *In Touch, Indulge, Men, Freshmen, Honcho,* and *Playguy* as well as the short story collection *All the Right Places.* Alexander has stories in several anthologies including *Friction 1, 2,* and *3, Heat Wave, Boys on the Prowl, Feeling Frisky, Skin Flicks 1* and *2, Casting Couch Confessions, Rent Boys, Freshmen Club,* and *Divine Meat.* Alexander lives in Iowa with one dog and a cat with a porcelain fetish.

A native Californian, **Bearmuffin** lives in San Diego with two leatherbears in a stimulating ménage à trois. He has written gay erotica for *Honcho, Torso, Manscape,* and *Hot Shots.*

Trevor Callahan Jr.'s fiction has appeared in numerous magazines and anthologies. He lives and writes in southern New England.

Dale Chase has had over 50 stories published in *Men, Freshmen, In Touch,* and *Indulge*. His work has appeared in several anthologies, including *Friction 2, 3,* and *4, Twink,* and *Bearotica.* One story has been acquired by independent filmmaker Edgar Bravo and will soon reach the big screen. Chase lives near San Francisco.

M. Christian is the author of the critically acclaimed and best-selling book of erotic stories, *Dirty Words.* He is the editor of *The Burning Pen: Sex Writers on Sex Writing; Guilty Pleasures: True Stories of Erotic Indulgences; Midsummer Night's Dreams: One Story, Many Tales;* and *Eros Ex Machina: Eroticizing the Mechanical.* He is co-editor with Simon Sheppard of *Rough Stuff: Tales of Gay Men, Sex, and Power.* His short fiction has appeared in more than 100 anthologies and periodicals. He lives in San Francisco.

JackFritscher.com, like fellow-author Anne Rice, has two careers: literary and erotic. The Web sites JackFritscher.com, PalmDrive-Publishing.com, and PalmDrive Video.com integrate into GLBT culture his 14 books, 400 short stories, thousands of photographs, and 140 video features. His four novels include *Some Dance to Remember,* a 15-character epic of San Francisco's Golden Age 1970–1982 (Alyson Publications). His bio-memoir of his life with his notorious lover, photographer Robert Mapplethorpe, is *Mapplethorpe: Assault with a Deadly Camera.* He may be contacted at Jack@JackFritscher.com

Aaron Hawkings travels the world as a novelist, dabbling in gay porn as a side dish. He seeks out new and enticing experiences to write about.

Greg Herren is the author of the novel *Murder in the Rue Dauphine* and the forthcoming *Bourbon Street Blues.* He is currently editor of *Lambda Book Report* and assistant editor of *The James White Review.* He is also editing the anthologies *Full Body Contact* and *Gay Gothic.* His work has appeared in *Rebel Yell 2, Friction 4,* and *Men for All Seasons,* and the publications *Harrington Gay Men's Fiction Quarterly, Gay and Lesbian Review, A&U, XY, Men, Unzipped, Instinct, Genre,* and *Where New Orleans.*

Kevin Johnson is 26 years old, British, and just moved to the States last year with his boyfriend of six years. He has a degree in English and used to work for an airline, flying around the world with his boyfriend to seduce as many boys as possible. He now works for a gay magazine in New York City alongside Chelsea boys all day long.

Pierce Lloyd lives in Southern California, where he has too little time and too much fun. He began writing erotica in college because it beat studying for tests.

Phillip Mackenzie Jr. is a freelance writer and entertainment consultant who lives in Los Angeles.

R. J. March is the author of *Looking for Trouble: The Erotic Fiction of R. J. March.* His work has appeared in numerous magazines and anthologies, and is also featured on the Web site Nightcharm.com. He is currently at work on another collection of erotica, due to be published in 2002. He lives in Pennsylvania.

Grant Mather lives in Canada, where he is a computer nerd who also writes a gay porn tale or two, including one about his first-time experience in a bathhouse!

Alan Mills has been published in three previous editions of *Friction,* as well as *Casting Couch Confessions, Quickies 2, Divine Meat, Skinflicks,* and *What The Fuck.* Alan was once the editor of *In Touch, Indulge,* and *Blackmale,* and his work has been featured in those magazines as well. He currently lives in West Hollywood, California, and works in the film industry. He is actively looking for more material to write erotica about.

Mac O'Neill is also the author of *Boys' Town.* He lives in Florida, and is working on a new novel. His short stories and interviews have appeared in *Blueboy, In Touch, Mandate, Brush Creek Media,* and *Advocate Men.*

Scott Pomfret is an attorney and writer in Boston. His work has previously appeared in *Friction 4* and *Indulge* as well as numerous literary journals and gay publications.

Les Richards is a pseudonym for a mystery writer who lives on the edge of a Maryland woods with his cat, Jim. His mystery novels have been published in the United States and Europe. His short stories have won two government grants. His erotic stories have appeared in *In Touch, Indulge,* and *Friction 4.* His ambition: to write the great American gay mystery novel.

A New York–based writer, critic, poet-playwright, **Lance Rush** has been published in *Empire Magazine, In the Family,* and *New York Daily News.* His erotica has graced the steamy pages of *Coming Out, FQ, Honcho, Inches, Mandate, Torso,* and several of the better anthologies. "The Long Blue Moan," his long-awaited novel, will be published in Spring 2002 (under the name, L.M. Ross).

Dominic Santi, a former technical writer turned rogue, is co-editor with Debra Hyde of the sex and politics anthology, *Strange Bedfellows.* Santi's dirty stories appear in *Friction 2, 3,* and *4, Best Gay Erotica 2000, Best Bisexual Erotica 1* and *2, Best Transgendered Erotica, Tough Guys,* and dozens of other smutty anthologies and magazines.

Simon Sheppard is the author of *Hotter Than Hell and Other Stories* and co-editor with M. Christian of *Rough Stuff: Tales of Gay Men, Sex, and Power.* His short fiction has appeared in several editions of *Friction* and *Best American Erotica* along with numerous other anthologies and magazines. His nonfiction column, Sex Talk, appears in gay papers nationwide. He lives in San Francisco.

Mel Smith is a single mom now working as a locker-room attendant at a high school. She had been in the fire service for four years and law enforcement for 13. In her spare time she lives her dream of writing. Only one of her stories has actually been published, but three more are due for publication: two in *In Touch* and one in the anthology *Best Gay Erotica* (Cleis Press).

Jay Starre lives in Vancouver, British Columbia, where he sits at his desk pounding out gay erotic tales. His stories have been published in magazines such as *Honcho, Blueboy, International Leatherman, Torso,* and *In Touch,* and in the anthologies *Hard Drive, Rent Boys, Friction 4,* and *Skin Flicks 2.*

Karl Taggart, a new arrival on the erotica scene, recently had several stories published in *Men.* He's the office manager for a suburban San Francisco insurance company. His coworkers have no idea a porn writer lurks in their midst.

Bob Vickery (www.bobvickery.com) is a regular contributor to various Web sites and magazines, particularly *Men* and *Freshmen.* He has three anthologies of stories: *Cock Tales, Skin Deep,* and the forthcoming *Cocksure.* He has stories in numerous anthologies, including *Friction 1, 2, 3,* and *4, Best Gay Erotica 1999 and 2001, Best American Erotica 1997 and 2000, Quickies 1 and 2, Best Bisexual Erotica 1 and 2,* and *Queer Dharma.* In his spare time he bakes muffins for a Zen Buddhist monastery in Northern California.

David Wayne resides in upstate New York, where he is completing his Ph.D. dissertation in, of all things, physics. Countless hours of his formative years were expended poring over the good bits of his mother's accumulation of Harlequin Romances. He started writing erotica for himself at the tender age of 13. "For the Asking" is his first story intended for public consumption.

Greg Wharton is the founder and publisher of Suspect Thoughts Press and editor of the Web 'zine *Suspect Thoughts: A Journal of Subversive Writing* (www.suspectthoughts.com). He is the erotica editor for *Velvet Mafia* at www.velvetmafia.com and editor of the Suspect Thoughts Press anthology *Of the Flesh: Dangerous New Fiction.* His short fiction, reviews, and creative nonfiction have been widely published online and in print. He is hard at work on a novel and a collection of short fiction.

Thom Wolf is the author of *Words Made Flesh.* He lives and works in the United Kingdom. He has been writing erotica since he was 18. His work has appeared in *In Touch, Indulge, Men,* and *Overload,* and the anthologies *Friction 3, Twink,* and *Bearotica.* He likes yoga, music, and sex, of course, and is a rabid Kylie Minogue fan. He is now working on a new novel.

Sean Wolfe lives in Denver with his partner of 11 years. In the past two years he has been published in *Men, Freshmen, Playguy,* and *Inches* magazines. His work has also appeared in *Friction 3* and *4.* He is not, however, a sex maniac. He just completed his first nonerotic gay novel and is hard at work on his second. He facilitates a weekly gay men's writers group and works at Category Six Books, Denver's only bookstore dedicated to gay men.

Publication Information

Books

Buttmen ("Riding With Walter") was edited by Alan Bell and published by West Beach Books.

Dirty Words ("Whatever Happened to…?") was written by M. Christian and published by Alyson Books, www.alyson.com.

Hard Drive ("Almost Better Than Sex," "Pig") was edited by Miguel Angel and published by Alyson Books, www.alyson.com.

Magazines

Beau ("Fantasy Cavern") can be contacted at (800) 964-6247.

Black Sheets ("Exhibit 114a") can be contacted at (800) 818-8823.

Coming Out ("Virgin in the Bathhouse") can be contacted at (800) 964-6247.

Freshmen ("Courtside"; "Patience is a Virtue"; "Red Hot Valentine"; "Str8 Guyz"; "Street Smarts"; "Traveling Tailor") can be contacted at (800) 757-7069.

Inches ("Long Road Home") can be contacted at (888) 664-7827.

Indulge ("Chain Male"; "The Sordid Life"; "Working Up a Sweat") can be contacted at (800) 637-0101.

In Touch ("Body Parts"; "Nasty"; "Sight Unseen"; "The Well of Az-zahr") can be contacted at (800) 637-0101.

Mandate ("Groovy Gang Bang"; "Kinky Wet Khakis") can be contacted at (212) 966-8400.

Men ("The Auction"; "Critic's Choice"; "For the Asking"; "Full Nelson"; "A Night at the El Gallo"; "On a Night Like This"; "Partners in Crime"; "Seeing Red"; "Sliding Home"; "Sweet"; "Who Walks in Moonlight") can be contacted at (800) 757-7069.

Torso ("Ripped Rasslers") can be contacted at (888) 664-7827.

Online

ExquisiteCorpse.com ("Gravity") is online at www.exquisitecorpse.com.

Good Vibrations ("Gay Pride Day in East Jesus, Minnesota"; "Wherever") is online at www.goodvibes.com.

JackFritscher.com ("From Nada to Mañana") is online at www.jackfritscher.com.

Nightcharm.com ("Heads and Tails"; "Technically Speaking") is online at www.nightcharm.com.